THE ANTIPOPE

Robert Rankin

CORGI BOOKS

THE ANTIPOPE
A CORGI BOOK : 9780552138413

Originally published in Great Britain by Pan Books Ltd

PRINTING HISTORY
Pan Press edition published 1981
Corgi edition published 1991

31

Set in 10/11½pt Planton by
County Typesetters, Margate, Kent.

Corgi Books are published by Transworld Publishers,
61–63 Uxbridge Road, London W5 5SA,
a division of The Random House Group Ltd.

Addresses for Random House Group Ltd companies
outside the UK can be found at: www.randomhouse.co.uk

**Penguin Random House is committed to a sustainable future for
our business, our readers and our planet. This book is made from
Forest Stewardship Council® certified paper.**

Printed and bound in Great Britain by Clays Ltd, Elcograf S.p.A.

Magus to the Hermetic Order of the Golden Sprout, 12th Dan Master of Dimac, poet, adventurer, swordsman and concert pianist; big game hunter, Best dressed Man of 1933; mountaineer, lone yachtsman, Shakespearian actor and topless go-go dancer; Robert Rankin's hobbies include passive smoking, communicating with the dead and lying about his achievements. He lives in Sussex with his wife and family.

Robert Rankin is the author of *The Fandom of the Operator*, *Web Site Story*, *Waiting for Godalming*, *Sex and Drugs and Sausage Rolls*, *Snuff Fiction*, *Apocalypso*, *The Dance of the Voodoo Handbag*, *Sprout Mask Replica*, *Nostradamus Ate My Hamster*, *A Dog Called Demolition*, *The Garden of Unearthly Delights*, *The Most Amazing Man Who Ever Lived*, *The Greatest Show Off Earth*, *Raiders of the Lost Car Park*, *The Book of Ultimate Truths*, the *Armageddon* quartet (three books), and the *Brentford* trilogy (five books) which are all published by Corgi books.

For more information on Robert Rankin and his books, see his website at:
www.lostcarpark.com/sproutlore

For my son Robert

Prologue

A long finger of early spring sunshine poked down between the flatblocks and reached through the dusty panes of the Flying Swan's saloon bar window, glistening off a pint beer glass and into the eye of Neville, the part-time barman.

Neville held the glass at arms' length and examined it with his good eye. It was very clean, small rainbows ran about its rim. It was a good shape too, gently rising to fill the hand with an engagingly feminine bulge. Very nice. There was a lot of joy to be had in the contemplation of a pint glass; in terms of plain reality of course, there was a deal more to be had in the draining of one.

The battered Guinness clock above the bar struck a silent 11 o'clock. Once its chimes had cut like a butcher's knife through the merry converse of the Swan's patrons. But it had been silent now these three long years, since Jim Pooley had muted it with a well-aimed pint pot. These days its lame thuds went unheeded and Neville was forced to more radical methods for clearing the bar come closing. Even the most drunken of revellers could understand a blow to the skull from the knobkerry he kept below the bar counter.

At the last thud of the Guinness clock Neville replaced the dazzling glass. Lifting the hinged bar top, he sidled towards the saloon-bar door. The Brentford sun glinted upon his Bryl-creemed scalp as he stood nobly framed in that famous portal, softly sniffing the air. Buses came and went in the morning haze, bound for exotic destinations west of London. An unfragrant miasma drifted from the Star of Bombay Curry Garden, sparrows along the

7

telephone lines sang the songs their parents had taught them. The day seemed dreamy and calm.

Neville twitched his sensitive nostrils. He had a sudden strange premonition that today was not going to be like any other.

He was dead right.

1

Jim Pooley, that despoiler of pub clocks, sat in the Memorial Library, pawing over ancient tomes in a never-ending search for the cosmic truths which might lead a man along the narrow winding pathway towards self-fulfilment and ultimate enlightenment. 'Looking up form and keeping out of the rain' was what the Head Librarian called it. 'Mr Pooley,' she said, in those hushed yet urgent tones affected by those of her station. 'Mr Pooley, why don't you take your paper around to the bookie's and there study in an atmosphere which must surely be more conducive to your purposes?'

Pooley, eyes fixed upon his paper as if in a trance, mouthed, 'You have a wonderful body on you there, Mrs Naylor.'

Mrs Naylor, who lip-read every word as she had done upon a thousand other such occasions, reddened slightly but maintained her dignity. 'Why can't you look at the books once in a while just to keep up appearances?'

'I have books of my own,' said Jim silently, 'but I come here to absorb the atmosphere of this noble edifice and to feast my eyes upon your supple limbs.'

'You haven't even a ticket, Mr Pooley.'

'Give us a French kiss,' said Jim loudly.

Mrs Naylor fled back to her desk and Pooley was left to his own devices. His eyes swept over the endless columns of racehorses. Somewhere he knew, amid this vast assortment, existed six horses which would win today at good odds, and if placed in a 'Yankee' accumulator would gross £250,000 at the very least. Such knowledge, of course, is generalized, and it is the subtle particularities of

9

knowing which horses to choose that make the thing difficult.

Pooley licked the end of his Biro, especially blessed by Father Moity for the purpose. He held it up to the shaft of sunlight which had suddenly and unexpectedly appeared through an upper window. Nearly spent, more than half of its black life-fluid ebbed away, and upon what? Upon ill-considered betting slips, that was upon what. Pooley sighed, his concentration gone. The delicate balance had been upset, and all through Mrs Naylor's chatter.

Oh well, thought Pooley, the sun is now over the yardarm. He rose from his seat, evoking a screech from the rubber-soled chair legs which cut Mrs Naylor like a rapier's edge. He strode purposefully towards the door, and on reaching it turned upon his heel. 'I shall be around then this evening directly your husband has departed for his night shift,' he announced.

Mrs Naylor fainted.

As Neville stood in the door of the Flying Swan musing upon the day's peculiarity, a beggar of dreadful aspect and sorry footwear shuffled towards him from the direction of Sprite Street and the Dock. He noted quite without thinking that an air of darkness and foreboding accompanied this lone wanderer.

'Ugh,' said Neville. He felt twin shudders originate within his monogrammed carpet slippers, wriggle up the hairs of his legs and meet in the small of his back, where as one united shudder they continued upwards, finally (although all this took but a second or two) travelling out of the top of his head leaving several strands of Brylcreem defying gravity. Neville felt a sudden need to cross himself, and performed that function with somewhat startled embarrassment.

He returned to the bar to await the arrival of the solitary traveller. Time passed however, and no such shadow darkened the Swan's doorway. Neville sloped over to the door and gazed cautiously up the street. Of ill-omened tramps the street was empty.

Neville scratched his magnificent nostrils with a nicotined finger and shrugged grandiloquently. 'Now there's a thing,' he said to himself.

'Could I have a glass of water please?' said a voice at his elbow.

Neville controlled his bladder only by the merest of lucky chances. 'Lord save me,' he gasped, turning in shock to the quizzical face of the materialized tramp.

'Sorry, did I startle you?' asked the creature with what seemed to be genuine concern. 'It's a bad habit of mine, I really must control it.'

By this time Neville was back behind the bar, the top bolted shut and his shaking hands about glass and whisky optic. 'What do you want?'

'A glass of water, if I may.'

'This isn't a municipal bloody drinking fountain,' said Neville gruffly. 'This is an alehouse.'

'My apologies,' said the tramp. 'We have I think got off to a rather poor start. Perhaps I might have a pint of something.'

Neville downed his large whisky with a practised flick of the wrist and indicated the row of enamel silver-tipped beer pumps. 'State your preference,' he said and here a note of pride entered his voice. 'We have a selection of eight ales on pump. A selection which exceeds Jack Lane's by four and the New Inn by three. I think you will find it a hard business to out-rival the Swan in this respect.'

The tramp seemed fascinated by this intelligence. 'Eight, eh?' He walked slowly the length of the bar past the eight gleaming enamel sentinels. His right forefinger ran along the brass rim of the bar top and to Neville's horror deftly removed the polish, leaving in its place a trail like that of a slug. Halting at the end he became suddenly aware of Neville's eyes and that the barman was involuntarily clenching and unclenching his fists.

'Sorry,' he said, raising his finger and examining it with distaste, 'again I have blotted my copybook.'

Neville was about to reach for his knobkerry when the friendly and reassuringly familiar figure of Jim Pooley appeared through the bar door whistling a tuneless lament and tapping his right knee with his racing paper. Jim mounted his very favourite bar stool with time-worn ease and addressed Neville with a cheery 'Mine will be a pint of Large please, Neville, and good morning.'

The part-time barman dragged his gaze from the unsightly tramp and drew Jim Pooley a fine glass of the true water.

'Ah,' said Jim, having drained half in a single draught, 'the first one is always the finest.' Pushing the exact amount across the bar top for fear that prices might have risen overnight, he sought anew the inspiration, his by divine right, that had so recently been denied him in the Memorial Library.

'I feel a winner coming on,' he said softly. This was occasionally a means of getting a free top-up at this hour of the day.

Neville made no reply.

'I think this might well be the big one,' continued Jim. Neville maintained a stony silence. He did not appear to be breathing.

'I wouldn't be at all surprised if . . .' At this point Jim Pooley looked up from his paper and caught sight of the part-time barman's ghastly aspect. 'Whatever's up, Neville?'

Neville clutched at his breath. 'Did you see him leave?' he stuttered.

'Who leave? I didn't see anybody.'

'He . . .' Neville peered over the bar top at the brass rim. It shone as unsullied and pristine as it had done when he had polished it not fifteen minutes previous.

12

'A tramp.'

'What tramp?'

Neville decanted himself another large scotch and threw it down his throat.

'Well I never noticed any tramp,' said Jim Pooley, 'although, and you'll think this ridiculous when I tell you.'

'What?' said Neville shakily.

'Well, when I came in here just now I felt the strangest of compunctions, I felt as if I wanted to cross myself.'

Neville did not reply.

A scratch of the bell, a screech of brakes, a rattle of front wheel against kerb and a hearty 'Hi-O-Silver' and John Omally had arrived at the Flying Swan. 'You stay here and enjoy the sun, I'll be out later,' he told his bike, and with a jovial 'God save all here and mine's a pint of Large please, Neville' he entered the bar.

Neville watched his approach closely, and noted to his satisfaction that Omally showed no inclination whatever towards crossing himself. Neville pulled the Irishman a pint and smiled contentedly to himself as Omally pushed the exact amount of change across the counter.

'How's yourself then, Jim?' said Omally.

'I feel a winner coming on,' Pooley confided loudly.

'Now is that a fact, then it's lucky you are to be sure.' Omally accepted his pint and drained half in three gulps.

'You are late today,' said Pooley by way of conversation.

'I had a bit of bike trouble over on the allotment, Marchant and I were not seeing eye to eye.'

Pooley nodded. 'Your bike Marchant would be all the better for the occasional squirt of Three-in-One and possibly a visit to a specialist once in a while.'

'Certainly the old lad is not what he was. I had to threaten him with premature burial before I could get it out that he needed new front brake blocks and a patch on his back tyre.'

'Bikes are not what they were,' said Jim. He finished his pint. 'This one's done for,' he said sadly.

'Seems so,' said John Omally.

'Whose shout is it?' said Jim.

'Whose was it last time?' said John.

Jim Pooley scratched his head. 'There you have me,' said himself.

'I think you were both buying your own,' said Neville, who had heard such discussions as these go on for upwards of an hour before one of these stalwarts cracked under the pressure.

'Lend me a pound John,' said Jim Pooley.

'Away into the night boy,' the other replied.

'We'll call it ten bob then.'

'We'll call it a good try and forget about it.'

Jim Pooley grudgingly patted his pockets, to the amazement of all present including himself he withdrew a pound note. Neville pulled Jim Pooley another pint and taking the pound note with both hands he carried it reverently to the till where he laid it as a corpse to rest. Jim Pooley counted and recounted his change. The terrible knowledge that Jim had the price of two more pints within his very pockets made Omally more companionable than ever.

'So how's tricks, then, Jim?' asked the Irishman, although his eyes were unable to tear themselves away from Pooley's waistcoat pocket.

'I have been experiencing a slight cash flow problem,' said Pooley. 'In fact, I am on my way now to pay several important and pressing debts which if payment was deferred by even minutes might spell doom to certain widely known political figures.'

'Ah, you were always a man of strong social conscience, Jim.'

Pooley nodded sagely. 'You yourself are a man of extraordinary perception at times, John.'

'I know how to call a spade,' said John Omally.

'That you do.'

Whilst this fascinating conversation was in progress Neville, who had now become convinced that the ill-favoured tramp had never left the Flying Swan but was hiding somewhere within awaiting closing time to rifle the till, was bobbing to and fro about the bar squinting into dark and obscure corners and straining his eyes about the upper portions of the room. He suddenly became aware that he was being observed.

'I'll just go and check the pumps,' he muttered, and vanished down the cellar steps.

Pooley and Omally drank a moment in silence. 'He has been having visions,' said Jim.

'Has he?' said John. 'An uncle of mine used to have visions. Said that a gigantic pig called Black Tony used to creep up on him and jog his arm when he was filling in his betting slips – blamed that pig for many a poor day's sport, did my uncle.'

'It's tramps with Neville,' Jim confided.

'What, nudging his arm and that?'

'No, just appearing like.'

'Oh.'

The two prepared to drink again in silence but found their glasses empty. With perplexity they faced each other.

'It's time I was away about my business,' said Jim, rising to his feet.

'Will you not be staying to have one more before you go?' John asked. Neville, rising like a titan from the cellar depths, caught this remark; being a publican, he was inured against most forms of sudden shock.

'Same again lads?' he asked.

'Two of similar,' said John.

Jim eyed him with open suspicion.

'Ten and six,' said Neville pulling two more pints.

15

'Jim,' said John.

'John?' said Jim.

'I don't quite know how to put this, Jim.'

Jim raised his right hand as in benediction; Neville thought for one ghastly moment that he was going to cross himself. 'John,' said Jim, 'John, I know what you are going to say, you are going to say that you wish to buy me a drink, that in fact it would be an honour for you to buy me a drink and that such would give you a pleasure that like good friendship is a jewel without price. You are going to say all this to me, John, because you have said it all before, then when you have made these eloquent and endearing remarks you will begin to bewail your lot, to curse the fates that treat you in so shabby a manner, that harass and misuse you, that push you to the very limits of your endurance, and which by their metaphysical and devious means deprive you of your hard and honestly earned pennies, and having done so you will confess supreme embarrassment, implore the very ground to swallow you up and possibly shed the occasional deeply felt tear, then and only then you will beg, impeach, implore and with supreme dignity of stature approach me for the loan of the very ten shillings and sixpence most recently mentioned by our esteemed bar lord here.

'I am conscious that this request for funds will be made in the most polite and eloquent fashion and that the wretchedness you will feel when it will be a profound and poignant thing to behold and so considering all this and considering that Neville is not a man well known for offering credit and that you are my noblest friend and that to attempt to drink and run as it were would bring down a social stigma upon both our heads I will gladly pay for this round.'

Omally stood, head bowed, during this touching oration. No more words were spoken and Neville received the ten and sixpence in a duly respectful manner. The two drained

16

their glasses and Jim excused himself quietly and vanished off into the direction of the bookie shop.

Neville pushed Jim's glass into the washer and spoke softly to the pensive Omally. 'You have a good friend there in that Jim Pooley,' he said.

John nodded. 'God moves in mysterious circles,' he said.

'How so?'

'Well' – and here John Omally drained his pint glass to the bottom – 'I was touched to my very soul by Jim's remarks over the purchase of these drinks but strange as the man is he mistook the remark that I made to him completely.'

'Oh?' said Neville.

'Yes,' said John. 'I had no intention of borrowing the price of a drink whatever.'

'What then?' said Neville.

'I merely thought to mention to him in as discreet a manner as possible that his flies were undone, but I shan't bother now.'

John Omally offered Neville all his best for the time of day and left the bar.

2

Archroy had rented the section of allotment land nearest to the viaduct ever since it had been bequeathed to him five years before by a half-forgotten uncle. Each night during the season he would come from his shift at the wiper works and sit in the doorway of his hut smoking his pipe and musing about the doings of the day. Omally owned two adjacent strips, having won one of them from Peg's husband at the paper shop, and old Pete had a further one.

Over in the corner was the untouched plot that had once belonged to Raymond, who in a previous episode had been snatched away into outer space by the invisible star creatures from Alpha Centauri. You could see a lot of life on an allotment.

This particular warm spring evening Archroy lazed upon an orange box smoking the blend of his taste and thinking that the world would be a better place if there was a bounty put upon the heads of gypsy car-dealers. Not that he had anything against them in general, but in particular he was very resentful. Archroy was not only the tenant of an allotment, he was also a man of marriage. Archroy's marriage was a nebulous affair, he working day shifts and his wife working nights. Their paths rarely crossed. Omally thought this was the ideal state of wedded bliss and prayed for a woman who might wed him then take a job overseas.

Archroy accepted the acclaim of his fellows for choosing so wisely, but privately he was ill at ease. Certainly he saw little of his wife, but of her workings and machinations the catalogue was endless. Archroy kept coming home to find new furniture and carpets; one day he stuck his head up in the roof and discovered that his loft had been insulated. Strangely, Archroy was never asked by his wife to contribute to any of these extravagant ventures. Possibly because he rarely saw the woman, but mainly he suspected, because an alien hand was at work in his stuccoed semi-detached. He suspected that his wife had a lover, in fact not one lover but many. Archroy had an inkling that his wife was putting it about a bit.

He had found five minutes one evening just as they were changing shifts to interview his suspect spouse. Archroy had noticed that his old Morris Minor, which his wife described as 'an eyesore', was no longer upon its blocks in the garage but seemed to have cried 'horse and hattock' and been carried away by the fairies.

18

'Woman,' he addressed his wife, for he had quite forgotten her name, 'woman, where is my car?'

'Gone,' said she, straightening her headscarf in the mock rococo hall mirror. 'I have sold your car and if you will pardon me saying so I have made a handsome profit.'

Archroy stiffened in his shirtsleeves. 'But I was working on that car, it needed but an engine and a few wheels and I would have had it working!'

'A truck came and took it away,' said his wife.

Archroy pulled at his hair. 'Where's my car gone to, who took it?'

'It was a gypsy,' said his wife.

'A gypsy, you part with my priceless car to a damned gyppo?'

'I got a good price.'

Archroy blew tobacco smoke down his nose and made himself cough.

'It's on the mantelpiece in a brown envelope,' said his wife, smearing gaudy red lipstick about her upper lip.

Archroy tore into the front room and tore open the envelope. Pouring the contents into his hand he found five brown beans. 'What? What?' Archroy began to foam at the mouth. 'Beans?'

'He assured me that they were magic beans,' his wife said, slamming the door behind her.

Thus it was that Archroy sat this particular evening in the doorway of his allotment shed, bewailing his lot and cursing not only car dealers but untrue wives and all those born of romany extraction. 'Magic beans,' he grimaced as he turned the offenders over in his palm. 'Magic bloody beans, I'll bet he gave her more than just magic bloody beans.'

The 6.20 steamed over the viaduct and told Archroy that now would be as good a time as ever to repair to the Swan to see what the lads were up to. He was about to pocket his magic beans and rise from his orange-box when a stark black shadow fell upon him and sent an involuntary shudder up the wee lad's back.

'Might I have a look at those beans you have there mister?' The voice came from a disreputable tramp of dreadful aspect and sorry footwear. 'Sorry, did I startle you?' asked the creature with what seemed to be a voice of genuine concern. 'It's a bad habit of mine, I really must control it.'

'What do you want here?' snarled Archroy, outraged at this trespass upon his thoughts and land.

'About the beans?' the tramp said.

Archroy pocketed his beans. 'Clear off!' he said, climbing to his feet. The tramp raised his right hand and made a strange gesture. Archroy slumped back on to his orange-box, suddenly weak at the knees.

'Those beans,' said the tramp. Archroy felt about in his pocket and handed the tramp the five magic beans.

'Ah.' The tramp held one between thumb and forefinger. 'As I thought, most interesting. You say that your wife received them in payment for your old Morris Minor?'

Archroy didn't remember saying anything of the kind but he nodded bleakly.

'They are beans of great singularity,' said the tramp. 'I have seen beans and I have seen beans.' He returned the articles to Archroy's still-extended hand. 'These are beans indeed!'

'But, magic?' said Archroy.

The tramp stroked the stubble of his chin with an ill-washed knuckle. 'Ah,' he said, 'magic is it? Well that is a question. Let us say that they have certain *outré* qualities.'

'Oh,' said Archroy. He felt a little better about the beans now, the loss of his trusty Morris Minor seemed less important than possessing something with *outré* qualities, whatever *outré* might mean. 'What are you doing on my allotment?' Archroy asked in a polite tone.

The tramp described a runic symbol in the dust at Archroy's feet with the toecap of his sorry right shoe. 'You might say that I am here to meet someone,' he said, 'and there again you might not, if you were to say here is a man upon a mission you would be correct, but also at the same time you would be mistaken. There is much about my presence here that is anomalous, much that is straightforward, much that . . .'

'I must be on my way now,' said Archroy, attempting to rise and feeling at his knees. They offered him no support. 'I am incapacitated,' he announced.

'. . . Much that will be known, much that will remain unexplained,' continued the tramp.

Archroy wondered if he had eaten something untoward, toadstools in his hotpot, or slug pellets in his thermos flask. He had read of strange distillations from the Amazon which administered upon the head of a pin could paralyse a bull elephant. There were also forms of nerve gas that might find their way into the sucking section of a fellow's briar.

The tramp meanwhile had ceased speaking. Now he stared about the allotment in an interested fashion. 'And you say that Omally won one of those plots from Peg's husband at the paper shop?'

Archroy was certain he had not. 'The one over in the corner with the chimney,' he said. 'That one there is the property of old Pete, it has been in his family for three generations and he has made an arrangement with the council to be buried there upon his demise, Blot the Schoolkeeper runs the one to the west backing on to the girls' school, it is better not to ask what goes on in his shed.'

Archroy rose to point out the plot but to his amazement discovered that the old tramp had gone. 'Well I never,' said Archroy, crossing himself, 'well I never did.'

3

No-one could ever accuse Peg's husband from the paper shop of being dull. His wife, when enquired of by customers as to her husband's latest venture, would cup her hands upon her outlandish hips and say, 'There's never a dull moment is there?' This rhetorical question left most in doubt as to a reply, so the kindly soul would add, 'You've got to laugh haven't you?' which occasionally got a response, or 'It's a great old life if you don't weaken', which didn't.

Her husband, however, shunned such platitudes and preferred, during moments of acute brain activity, to deal exclusively in the proverb. On the occasion of his bike going missing for the thirteenth time from its appointed rack at the Rubber Factory he was heard to mutter, 'Time is a great healer.' And during that particularly hot summer when someone set fire to his runner beans, 'Every cloud has a silver lining.'

Norman's proverbs never quite matched up to the situation to which they were applied, yet seemed in some bizarre way to aid him to the solution of extremely obtuse problems. This lent him the air of a mystic, which made him regularly sought after by drunks in need of advice. His 'ventures', as they were termed, were never devoid of interest. 'Wading to France', for example, which began, as so many tales have a tendency to do, one lunchtime in the saloon bar of the Flying Swan.

'There is much talk lately of these Channel swimmers,' John Omally had said by way of conversation as he perused his copy of the *Brentford Mercury*. 'They do say that the dear fellows lose the better part of three stone

22

from the swimming.' There was an informed nodding as Omally continued, 'There's a king's ransom to be had in that game if a fellow has the way of it.'

Norman, who had been listening and was currently between ventures, felt a sudden surge of regret that he had never learned to swim. 'It never rains but it pours,' he said, which gave most to suspect that he was having an idea.

'You don't swim at all do you, Norman?' asked the astute Omally, sensing money in the air.

'Sadly no,' said Norman, 'but I wade.' With these portentous words he left the saloon bar.

Little was heard of Norman for some weeks and his wife answered Omally's repeated enquiries with the encouraging 'You certainly see some sights' and 'It takes all sorts to make a world doesn't it?'

The Irishman was pretty much at his wits' end when his eye caught a tiny paragraph on an inside page of the *Brentford Mercury*: 'Local Man to Wade Channel.' Omally read the short paragraph once, then again slowly; then, thinking that he must have misread it, he gave the thing a careful word-for-word scrutiny.

Norman Hartnell, local Rubberware Foreman (not to be confused with the other Norman Hartnell) stated yesterday in an exclusive interview with the *Mercury* that it was his intention within the forseeable future to have constructed certain marine apparatus which will make it possible for him to become the first man to wade to France from England. Mr Hartnell (not to be confused with the other Norman Hartnell) told the *Mercury* in this exclusive interview when asked his reason for this attempt that 'Kind words butter no parsnips.' Mr Hartnell is 43.

'What other Norman Hartnell?' queried John Omally, whose only claim to fashion consciousness was tucking his shirt in all the way round even when wearing a jacket. There was still no word from Norman, and Omally even took to phoning the offices of the *Brentford Mercury* daily for news. He was not a man to be cheated of his pennies, and the more time passed the more he became convinced that whatever plans were hatching in Norman's obtuse cranium, he, Omally, was due at least part of any income deriving from their fruition. 'It was me reading about the Channel swimming that started it all, was it not?' he asked. Those present at the bar nodded gravely.

'You have a moral right,' said Neville.

'You should get a contract drawn up,' said Jim Pooley.

'He owes you,' said Archroy.

That Saturday the *Brentford Mercury*, which had for some days been refusing to accept John Omally's reverse-charge calls, announced in large and impressive type: BRENTFORD CHANNEL WADER NAMES THE DAY. Omally read this startling headline over the shoulder of the paper's owner and gasped in disbelief. 'He's naming the day and he still hasn't brought me in on it.'

'Pardon?' said the stranger.

'Fares please,' said the bus conductor.

Omally, who had in his palm a number of pennies exactly equal either to his bus fare or to the price of a copy of the *Brentford Mercury*, shouted, 'Stop that dog,' and leapt off the bus at the next set of traffic lights.

On the well-worn bench afront the Memorial Library he studied the newspaper. There were the headlines, below them a photograph of Norman smiling hideously with the caption: 'All roads lead to Rome, says plucky Brentonian.'

Omally read paragraph after paragraph, desperately trying to pluck out something substantial enough to merit legal action. Yes, the plucky Brentonian had been working for some months now upon certain marine apparatus

24

suitable to his requirements. He had made several unsuccessful tests with these (Omally raised his eyebrows at this intelligence). He had gauged his exact course through careful study of coastal topography and undersea mappings loaned to him by the Royal Maritime Museum. He had allowed for spring tides, onshore drift, wind variations and even shoals of fish that might be encountered en route. He was certain of success. He had been given the go-ahead by the Royal Navy, who had agreed to escort him with helicopter and motor torpedo boat and keep in contact with him by certain sophisticated pieces of top-secret equipment which Norman had kindly agreed to test for them during the walk over.

It was believed that this crossing would herald a new era in international travel. A veritable golden age was about to dawn, and without a doubt the patent holder of this aquatic legware was sitting on (or more rightly in) a proverbial goldmine, not to mention a piece of history. Omally groaned. 'Proverbial goldmine, he'll love that.' The more he read, the less he liked what he read and the less he liked it the more cheated he felt and the more furious he became. The cross-Channel walk was scheduled for the following Saturday; it was to be covered by both channels and shown live on *World of Sport*. Norman was to appear that very evening on the Russell Harty Show.

Omally tore the newspaper to ribbons and flung the pieces to the four winds.

It is not a long walk from the library to Peg's paper shop, one simply turns right down Braemar Road, right at the bottom past the football ground, left into Mafeking Avenue and left again up Albany Road into Ealing Road. John Omally covered this distance in a time that would have made Roger Bannister hang up his spikes in defeat. Panting, he stood in the doorway attempting to compose himself.

Two pensioners came out of the shop. 'Proverbial

goldmine,' said one. 'Place in history,' said the other.

Omally made an attempt to enter, but found to his amazement that the usually empty and dust-hung place of business bore a sprightly and jubilant appearance, and was going great guns in the customer stakes. Bunting hung about the door and 'Good Luck Norman', emblazoned upon lengths of coloured toilet-roll, festooned the front window – which suddenly bereft of its timeless Woodbine display now blazed with photographs of Royal Navy cruisers and postcards of Captain Webb. 'Souvenir Channel Trews on Sale Now' said a card. 'Bottled Channel Water' said another. Below this was a display of seashells and a number of jam jars apparently filled with seawater 'Bottled by the Wader Himself' and priced at a quid a time.

Omally made another attempt to enter but again found his way barred, this time by a number of schoolgirls wearing 'Norman Wades OK' t-shirts.

'What is the meaning of all this?' muttered the Irishman as he edged his way forward. Over the heads of the crowd he could see that Peg had taken on two extra salesgirls. Peg's gargantuan frame, sporting a 'Norman Wades OK' t-shirt the size of a bell tent, could be made out swinging bundles of the *Brentford Mercury* on to the counter and dispensing souvenir windmills and flags to all comers. The cash register was ringing like a fire alarm. Of Norman, however, there was no sign. Omally edged his way nearer to the counter and made some attempt to draw Peg's attention.

'The Norman action dolls are four pounds, love,' he heard her say. 'Yes, that's right, three for a tenner.'

Omally clutched at the counter for support. 'Peg,' he stammered, 'Peg I say.' Peg finally caught sight of the swaying Irishman. 'Hold on John love, and I'll be with you,' she said. 'Yes love, the Bottled Channel Water can be made available for bulk export purchase.'

The proverbial light at the end of the dark corridor, to which no doubt Norman had previously alluded in some moment of irrelevance, was beginning to appear before Omally's bloodshot eyes. 'Could I have a word with Norman, please Peg?' he asked.

'He's at present in conference with members of the press prior to an enforced period of lamaic meditation necessary for him to attune himself to the correct cosmic state of awareness required for his walk,' said the suddenly lucid Peg.

Omally nodded thoughtfully. 'No doubt then he will neither reveal himself nor the now legendary legwear prior to the great event.'

'It's unlikely, love,' said Peg, then, 'Excuse me a moment. Yes, I can do you a gross of the "Wade Against the Nazis" beany hats at cost if you are willing to do a deal on the film rights.'

Omally slid quietly away from the shop and along the road to the Flying Swan. He ignored the 'Wade for Britain' banner which hung above the bar, and also the Disabled War Wounded Waders Fund tin that Pooley rattled beneath his nose. He ordered a pint of Large. 'I have been cheated of my place in history,' he told Neville.

'Do you want a regular Large or Wader's Jubilee Ale?' asked the part-time barman. 'Only the brewery seem to have overestimated demand and I've got rather a lot going begging as it were.' One look at Omally's fearful countenance set Neville straight. He drew Omally a pint of the usual and drew the Irishman's attention to a figure in a white coat who was tampering with the antique jukebox. 'The brewery sent him down too, said we needed a few topical tunes to set the scene as it were, said that with all the extra trade the pub would be attracting some attempt on our part to join in the festivities would be appreciated.'

Omally cocked a quizzical eyebrow at the aged machine.

'You mean that it actually works. I thought it was broken beyond repair.'

'I suspect that it will not take him long to discover that it is only lacking a fuse in its plug.'

Omally's face took on a strangely guilty expression.

'I have seen the selection he proposes to substitute,' said Neville gravely. 'And I fear that it is even grimmer than the one you have for so long protected our ears against.'

'It has a nautical feel to it, I suspect.'

'There is more than a hint of the shanty.'

'HMS Pinafore?'

'And that.'

'I suppose,' said Omally, hardly wishing to continue the conversation, or possibly even to draw breath, 'that there would not be a number or two upon the jukebox by the Norman Hartnell Singers or Norm and the Waders?'

'You are certainly given to moments of rare psychic presentiment,' said the part-time barman.

At this point there occurred an event of surpassing unreality, still talked of at the Flying Swan. John Omally, resident drinker at that establishment for fifteen long years, rose from his stool and left undrunk an entire pint of the brewery's finest, bought and paid for by himself. Not a mere drip in the bottom you understand, nor an unfortunate, cigar-filled, post darts-match casualty, but an entire complete, untouched, pristine one-pint glass of that wholesome and lifegiving beverage, so beloved of the inebriate throughout five counties.

Some say that during the following month John Omally joined an order of Trappist monks, others that he swore temporary allegiance to the Foreign Legion. Others still hint that the Irishman had learned through the agency of previous generations a form of suspended animation, much favoured by the ancients for purposes of imposed hibernation in times of famine. Whatever the case may be, Mr Omally vanished from Brentford, leaving a vacuum that nobody could fill. His loss was a sorry thing to behold within the portals of the Flying Swan, time seemed to stand still within those walls. Pooley took on the look of a gargoyle standing alone at the bar, drinking in silence, his only movements those born of necessity.

But what of Norman Hartnell (not to be confused with the other Norman Hartnell)? Certainly Norman's ventures had, as has been noted, tended to verge upon the weird. This one in particular had transcended bounds of normality. When Peg made grandiose statements about her husband's press conferences and tendencies towards lamaic meditation it may be said without fear of contradiction that the fat woman was shooting a line through her metaphorical titfer. Norman, who by nature was a harmless, if verbally extravagant, eccentric, had finally played directly into the hands of that volatile and conniving fat woman. She had watched him night after night experiment with inflatable rubber footwear, bouyant undergarments and stilted appliances. She had watched him vanish beneath the murky waters of the Grand Union Canal time after time, only to re-emerge with still more enthusiasm for the project. Only on his last semi-fatal attempt had she realized the futility of his quest; if any money was to be made out of it, then she'd have to do it.

Since she was somewhat more than twice her husband's weight it had been a simple matter one dark night to subdue him and instal him in the coal cellar, where, other than for continual cramps and the worrisome attention of curious rodents, he was ideally situated for lamaic meditation should he so wish.

The long-standing and quite fornicatious relationship that she was having with the editor of the *Brentford Mercury* was enough to seal poor Norman's fate. When the police, having received many phone calls from simple souls during the week enquiring after their daily papers and packets of Woodbines, broke into Peg's paper shop they found the bound and gagged figure of the erstwhile Channel Wader. Blinking in the sunlight, he had seemed quite unable to answer the inquisitions by various television companies, newspaper combines and foreign press agencies, each of whom had paid large cash sums for exclusive rights to the Channel Wade. Many questions were asked, but few answered.

Peg had upped and awayed it with her pressman stud, never to be heard of again. Norman simply shrugged his shoulders and remarked, 'A rolling stone gathers no moss yet many hands make light work.' These proverbial cosmic truths meant little to the scores of creditors who daily beseiged his paper shop, but as Norman had no legal responsibility, his wife having signed all the contracts, little could be done.

A few pennies were made by others than Peg and her paramour; Jim Pooley had successfully rattled his tin under enough noses to buy Omally several pints of consolation upon his return.

Neville had a hard job of it to sell the Wader's Jubilee Ale, which was only purchased by those of perverse humour and loud voice. It was only a chance event, that of a night of heavy rain, which saved the day, washing as it did the Jubilee labels from the bottles to reveal that they contained nothing more than standard brown ale.

Norman seemed strangely unmoved by the whole business, considering that his wife had left him penniless. Perhaps the fact that his wife had also left him wifeless had something to do with it. Possibly he still secretly harboured the wish to wade to France, but principle alone would have forbidden him to relay this information to another soul. Still, as Jim Pooley said, 'Time and tide wait for Norman.'

4

If there were one ideal spot in Brentford for the poet to stand whilst seeking inspiration, or for the artist to set up his three-legged easel, then it would certainly not be the Canal Bridge on the Hounslow Road, which marks the lower left-hand point of the mysterious Brentford Triangle. Even potential suicides shun the place, feeling that an unsuccessful attempt might result in all sorts of nasty poisonings and unsavoury disease.

Leo Felix, Brentonian and Rastafarian, runs a used car business from the canal's western shore. Here the cream of the snips come to stand wing to wing, gleaming with touch-up spray and plastic filler, their mileometers professionally readjusted and their 'only one owner's inevitably proving to be either members of the clergy or little old ladies.

Norman had never owned a motor car, although there had been times when he had considered building one or even constructing a more efficient substitute for the internal combustion engine possibly fueled upon beer-bottle tops or defunct filtertips. His wife had viewed these flights of fancy with her traditional cynicism, guffawing hideously and slapping her preposterous thighs with hands like one-pound packets of pork sausages.

Norman squinted thoughtfully down into the murky waters, finding in the rainbow swirls a dark beauty; he was well rid of that one, and that was a fact. He was at least his own master now, and with his wife gone he had left his job at the Rubber Factory to work full time in the paper shop. It's not a bad old life if you don't weaken, he thought to himself. A trouble shared is a trouble halved.

'And it is a long straight road that has no turning,' said a voice at Norman's elbow.

Norman nodded. 'The thought had recently crossed my mind,' he said dreamily. Suddenly he turned to stare full into the face of a shabby-looking tramp of dreadful aspect and sorry footwear.

'Sorry, did I startle you?' asked the creature with what seemed to be a voice of genuine concern. 'It's a bad habit of mine and I really must control it.'

'Oh no,' said Norman, 'it is just that on a Wednesday afternoon which is my early closing day I often come down here for an hour or two of quiet solitude and rarely expect to see another soul.'

The tramp smiled respectfully. 'There are times when a man must be alone,' he said.

'Exactly,' said Norman. The two gazed reflectively into the filthy waters for a moment or two. Norman's thoughts were soft, wavering things, whose limits were easily containable within the acceptable norms of local behaviour.

The tramp's, however, hovered in a spectrum that encompassed such dark and unfathomable colours that even to briefly contemplate their grim hues would be to trespass upon territories so ghastly and macabre that the very prospect would spell doom in any one of a dozen popular dialects.

'Can I treat you to a cup of tea along at the Plume?' the tramp asked.

Norman felt no affinity towards the tramp, but he felt strangely compelled to nod at this unexpected invitation. The two left the canal bridge and strolled up the Brentford High Street towards the Plume Café. This establishment, which stands at a point not twenty yards from the junction of Ealing Road and the High Street, can be said at times to play host to as many Brentonians as the Flying Swan itself. Those times being, of course, those when the Swan is closed.

The Plume is presided over by an enormous blonde of

32

eg-like proportions known to all Brentford as Lily Marlene. Why Lily Marlene is uncertain, since the sign above the door says 'Proprietor Mrs Veronica Smith'. Lily presides over all with the air of a brothel madam, her expansive bosoms moving in and out of the shadows behind the counter like twin dirigibles. Whatever happened to Mrs Veronica Smith no-one has ever dared ask.

Norman swung open the shattered glass door and entered the Plume Café followed by a sinister tramp. In the gloom behind the counter, unseen by human eye, Lily Marlene made a shadowy sign of the cross.

'What will it be?' Norman asked the tramp, who had seated himself beside the window and showed no inclination whatever to do any buying.

'I shall have one of Lily's surprising coffees I think,' the creature replied.

Norman strode to the counter. 'Two coffees please, Lil,' he requested of the hovering bosoms, which withdrew into the darkness of their hangar and returned in the company of a pair of arms. These generous appendages bore at their fingers' end a brace of coffees in the traditional glass cups. Norman paid up and carried the steaming cups back to the table.

'Cheers,' said the tramp, holding his cup up to the light and peering into its bottom.

'What are you looking for?' queried Norman.

'Aha,' the tramp said, tapping his nose significantly. 'Now you are asking me a question.'

'I am,' said Norman.

'And I shall answer you,' said the tramp, 'with a short tale which although brief is informative and morally satisfying.'

Norman said, 'Many a mickle makes a muckle,' and it was clear that his thoughts were elsewhere.

'A friend of mine used to drink coffee, I say used to, for all I know he still does, but as I have heard neither hide nor hair of him for five years I must remain uncertain upon this point.'

Norman yawned. 'Sorry,' he said, 'I had a rough night.'

The tramp continued unabashed. 'This friend of mine used to drink coffee in a glass cup not dissimilar to this and one day as he finished a cup do you know what he found had been slipped into it?'

'The King's Shilling,' said Norman. 'I've heard this story.'

'The King's Shilling,' said the tramp, who was plainly ignoring Norman's remarks, 'He tipped it into his hand and said the fatal "Look at this lads", and within a trice the pressmen were upon him.'

'I've had some dealings with the press myself,' said Norman.

'The pressmen were upon him and he was dragged away screaming to a waiting bungboat and thence to who knows where.'

The tramp made this last statement with such an air of sombre authenticity that his voice echoed as if coming from some dark and evil dungeon. Norman, who was lining up another sarcastic comment, held his counsel.

'You said just now that you had heard the story,' said the tramp in a leaden tone.

'Did I?' said Norman, perspiring freely about the brow. 'I don't think I did.'

'You did.'

'Oh.'

'Then let me put you straight on this, Norman.' Norman did not recall telling the tramp his name, and this added to his growing unease. 'Let it be known to you that this story, which although brief was in its way informative and morally satisfying, was a true and authentic tale involving a personal acquaintance of mine and let no other man, be he living, dead or whatever say otherwise!'

Norman fingered his collar, which had grown suddenly

34

tight. 'I wouldn't,' he said in a voice of tortured conviction. 'Not me.'

'Good,' said the tramp. Leaning forward across the table he stared hard into Norman's eyes much in the manner of a cobra mesmerizing a rabbit. Norman prepared his nostrils to receive the ghastly reek of dereliction and wretchedness generally associated with the ill-washed brotherhood of the highway. Strangely no such stench assailed his delicate nasal apparatus, rather a soft yet strangely haunting odour, one that Norman could not quite put a name or place to. The scent touched a nerve of recollection somewhere in his past, and he felt a cold shudder creeping up his backbone.

Norman became transfixed. The tramp's eyes, two red dots, seemed to swell and expand, filling all the Plume Café, engulfing even Lily's giant breasts. Two huge red suns glittering and glowing, gleaming with strange and hideous fires. Awesome and horrendous, they devoured Norman, scorching him and shrivelling him to a blackened crisp. He could feel his clothes crackling in the heat, the skin blistering from his hands and the nails peeling back to reveal blackening stumps of bone. The glass melted from his wristwatch and Mickey's face puckered and vanished in the all-consuming furnace. Norman knew that he was dead, that his wife had slipped from his grasp and that he was far, far away watching this destruction of his human form from some place of safety. Yet he was also there, there in that blazing skeleton, there inside the warped and shrinking skull watching and watching.

'Are you going to drink these coffees or shall I pour them down the sink?' said Lily Marlene.

Norman shook himself awake with a start. The tramp had gone and the two coffees were cold and undrunk. He looked at his watch; Mickey's head nodded to and fro as it always had. It was nearing five-thirty p.m. An hour had passed since he had entered the Plume.

35

'Where did the tramp go?' asked Norman.

'I don't know anything about any tramp,' said Lily. 'All I know is you buy two cups of coffee then fall asleep and let them go cold. Reckon if you want to sleep it off you can do it as well in your own bed as here, so bugger off home, will you Norman?'

Norman rose shakily from his seat. 'I think I shall go round to the Flying Swan instead,' he said. 'For still waters run deep, you know.'

'And it never rains but it bloody buckets down,' Lily called facetiously after the receding figure.

Neville the part-time barman drew the bolts upon the saloon bar door and swung it open. Nervously he stuck his head out and sniffed the early evening air; it smelt pretty much as it always did. He sniffed it a few more times for good measure. Neville believed strongly that a lot more went on in the air than was generally understood by man. 'Dogs have the way of it,' he had often said. 'Dogs and a few gifted men.' 'It is more than just pee on a post,' he had told Omally. 'Dogs sense with their noses rather than simply smell with them.'

This line of conversation was a bit out of Omally's range, but he thought he recalled a joke about a dog with no nose. 'A dog is a wise animal, that much I know,' said the Irishman. 'Back in the old country few men would venture out of doors of a night without a dog at their heels. The faithful fellow would sit at his master's elbow the evening, and if in the course of conversation the master felt the need for a bit of support he would nudge his dog and the animal, who would have been following every word, would assist him.'

It was always remarkable to Neville that at times when Omally was stuck for something to say he would simply resort to the first thing that came into his head no matter how thoroughly absurd it might be. 'You are saying that the dog would advise his master, then?' said the long-suffering part-time barman.

'Heavens no,' said Omally. 'The dear creature would simply go for the other fellow's throat thus cutting short any chance of his master losing the argument.'

As Neville stood in the pub doorway, sniffing the air and thinking to discern the possibility of snow, his eyes were treated to a spectacle which spelt dread.

Norman was stumbling towards the Flying Swan crossing himself wildly and reciting the rosary.

'Oh no,' groaned the part-time barman. He dropped the notice that he had painted that very afternoon, fled behind the counter and lunged at the whisky optic. Norman entered the Flying Swan at a trot and tripped immediately upon a newly painted notice which read NO TRAMPS. Picking this up in the trembling fingers he too said, 'Oh no!'

Neville anticipated the shopman's request and thrust another glass beneath the optic. 'Evening Norman,' he said in a restrained voice, 'how are things with you?'

'Did you paint this sign, Neville!' Norman demanded. Neville nodded. 'Give me a . . .' Neville pushed the glass across the counter. 'Oh yes, that's the one.'

Norman drained the glass with one gulp. Pausing to feel the life-giving liquid flowing down and about his insides Norman said slowly, 'You know, don't you?'

'Know?' said Neville with some degree of hesitation.

'About the tramp, you've seen him too, haven't you?' Neville nodded again. 'Thank God,' Norman said, 'I thought I was going mad.'

The part-time barman drew off two more scotches and the two men drank in silence, one either side of the bar. 'I was up on the canal bridge,' said Norman and began to relate his story. Neville listened carefully as the tale unfolded, only nodding thoughtfully here and there and making the occasional remark such as 'The King's

Shilling, eh?' and 'Strange and pungent odour eh?' by way of punctuation.

Norman paused to take another gulp of whisky. Neville was taking careful stock of how many were being drunk and would shortly call the shopkeeper to account. 'And the next thing, you looked up and he was gone,' prompted the part-time barman.

Norman nodded. 'Gone without a by your leave or kiss my ankle. I wonder who on earth he might be?'

'Who who might be?' The voice belonged to James Pooley, whose carefully calculated betting system had until five minutes previous been putting the wind up the local bookie.

'How did the afternoon go for you, Jim?' asked Neville. Pooley shook his head dismally. 'I was doing another six-horse special and was up to £150,000 by the fifth and what do you know?'

Neville said, 'Your sixth horse chose to go the pretty way round?'

'Tis true,' said the blighted Knight of the Turf.

Neville pulled a pint of Large and Jim pushed the exact amount in odd pennies and halfpennies across the bar top. Neville scooped this up and tossed it without counting into the till. This was an error on his part, for the exact amount this time included three metal tokens from the New Inn's fruit machine and an old washer Jim had been trying to pass for the last six months.

Jim watched his money vanish into the till with some degree of surprise – things must be pretty bad with Neville, he thought. Suddenly he caught sight of the NO TRAMPS sign lying upon the bar top. 'Don't tell me,' he said, 'Your tramp has returned.'

Neville threw an alarmed and involuntary glance from the sign to the open door. 'He has not,' said the barman, 'but Norman has also had an encounter with the wretch.'

'And Archroy,' said Jim.

'What?' said Neville and Norman together.

'On his allotment last night, quizzed him over some lucky beans his evil wife took in exchange for his Morris Minor.'

'Ah,' said Norman, 'I saw that same Morris Minor on Leo's forecort this very afternoon.'

'All roads lead to Rome,' said Jim, which Norman found most infuriating.

'About the tramp,' said Neville, 'what did Archroy say about him?'

'Seemed he was interested in Omally's allotment patch.'

'There is certainly something more than odd about this tramp,' said Norman. 'I wonder if anybody else has seen him?'

Pooley stroked his chin. If there was one thing he liked, it was a really good mystery. Not of the Agatha Christie variety you understand, Jim's love was for the cosmic mystery. Many of the more famous ones he had solved with very little difficulty. Regarding the tramp, he had already come to a conclusion. 'He is a wandering Jew,' he said.

'Are you serious?' said Norman.

'Certainly,' said Pooley. 'And Omally who is by his birth a Catholic will back me up on this – the Wandering Jew was said to have spat upon Our Lord at the time of the Passion and been cursed to wander the planet for ever awaiting Christ's return, at which time he would be given a chance to apologize.'

'And you think that this Jew is currently doing his wandering through Brentford?'

'Why not? In two thousand years he must have covered most of the globe; he's bound to turn up here sooner or later.'

'Why doesn't he come forward to authenticate the Turin shroud then?' said Neville.

The other two turned cynical eyes on him. 'Would you?'

39

'Do you realize then,' said Neville, who was suddenly warming to the idea, 'that if he is the Wandering Jew, well we have met a man who once stared upon Jesus.'

There was a reverent silence, each man momentarily alone with his thoughts. Norman and Neville both recalled how they had felt the need to cross themselves; this seemed to reinforce their conviction that Jim Pooley might have struck the nail firmly upon the proverbial head. It was a staggering proposition. Norman was the first to find his voice. 'No,' he said shortly, 'those eyes never looked upon Christ, although they may certainly have looked upon . . .'

'God save all here,' said John Omally, striding into the Swan. Somehow the talkers at the bar had formed themselves into what appeared to be a conspiratorial huddle. 'Hello,' said John, 'plotting the downfall of the English is it I hope?'

'We were discussing the Wandering Jew,' said Pooley.

'Gracious,' said John 'and were you now, certainly there'd be a penny or two to be made in the meeting up with that fellow.' The shifting eyes put Omally upon the alert. 'He's not been in and I've bloody well missed him?'

'Not exactly,' said Neville.

'Not exactly is it, well let me tell you my dear fellow that if you see him lurking hereabouts you tell him that John Vincent Omally of Moby Dick Terrace would like a word in his kosher shell-like.'

Neville pulled Omally a pint of Large and accepted the exact coinage from the Irishman; upon cashing up the sum he discovered Jim's washer. Jim, observing this, excused himself and went to the toilet. Shrugging hopelessly the part-time barman took up his No Tramps sign and crossed the bar. Before the open door he hesitated. His mind was performing rapid calculations.

If this tramp was the Wandering Jew maybe he could be persuaded to . . . well some business proposition, he

40

would most certainly have seen a few rare old sights, a walking history book, why a man with a literary leaning, himself for instance, could come to some arrangement. This Jew might have personal reminiscences of, well, Shakespeare, Napoleon, Beethoven, he might have strolled around the Great Exhibition of 1851, rubbed shoulders with Queen Victoria, met Attila the Hun (not at the Great Exhibition, of course). The list was endless, there would surely be a great many pennies to be had, as Omally said. Neville fingered the painted sign. The tramp certainly carried with him an aura of great evil. Maybe if he was the Jew he would kill anyone who suspected him, he had nothing to lose. Christ's second coming might be centuries off, what were a few corpses along the way. Maybe he didn't want redemption anyway, maybe . . . But it was all too much, Neville gritted his teeth and hung the sign up at the saloon bar door. Jew or no Jew, he wanted no part whatever of the mystery tramp.

Alone in the privacy of the gents, Jim Pooley's head harboured similar thoughts to those of Neville's; Jim however had not had personal contact with the tramp and could feel only a good healthy yearning to make a few pennies out of what was after all *his* theory. It would be necessary, however, to divert Omally's thoughts from this; in fact it would be best for one and all if the Irishman never got to hear about the tramp at all. After all Omally was a little greedy when it came to the making of pennies and he might not share whatever knowledge came his way. Pooley would make a few discreet enquiries round and about; others must have seen the tramp. He could quiz Archroy more thoroughly, he'd be there now on his allotment.

Pooley left the gents and rejoined Norman at the bar. 'Where is John Omally?' he asked, eyeing the Irishman's empty glass.

'I was telling him about the tramp,' said Norman, 'and he left in a hurry to speak to Archroy.'

'Damn,' said Jim Pooley, 'I mean, oh really, well I think I'll take a stroll down that way myself and sniff the air.'

'There's a great deal more to sniffing the air than one might realize,' said Neville, informatively.

But Jim Pooley had left the bar and naught was to be seen of his passing but foam sliding down a hastily emptied pint glass and a pub door that swung silently to and fro upon its hinge. A pub door that now lacked a NO TRAMPS sign.

'If our man the Jew is wandering hereabouts,' said Jim to himself upon spying it, 'there is no point in discouraging the arrival of the goose that may just be about to lay the proverbial golden egg.'

Norman would have cried if he'd heard that one.

Archroy stood alone upon his allotment patch, pipe jammed firmly between his teeth and grey swirls of smoke escaping the bowl at regulated intervals. His thumbs were clasped into his waistcoat pockets and there was a purposeful set to his features. Archroy was lost in thought. The sun sinking behind the chemical factory painted his features with a ruddy hue, the naturally anaemic Archroy appearing for once to look in the peak of health. Sighing heavily he withdrew from his pockets the five magic beans. Turning them again and again in his hand he wondered at their appearance.

They certainly were, how had the tramp put it, beans of great singularity. Of their shape, it could be said that they were irregular. Certainly but for their hue and texture they presented few similarities. There was a tropical look to them; they seemed also if held in certain lights to show some slight signs of luminescence.

Yes they were singular beans indeed, but magic? The tramp had hinted that the term was somewhat open-ended to say the least. Beanstalk material perhaps? That was too obvious, thought Archroy, some other magic quality then?

Could these beans cure leprosy, impassion virgins, bestow immortality? Could beans such as these unburden a man of a suspect spouse?

Archroy held up the largest of the beans and squinted at it in perplexity. Surely it was slightly larger, slightly better formed than it had been upon his last inspection. He knelt down and placed the beans in a row upon the top of his tobacco tin. 'Well I never did,' said Archroy, 'now there is a thing.'

Suddenly Archroy remembered a science fiction film he had seen on the television at the New Inn. These seed pods came down from outer space and grew into people, then while you were asleep they took over your mind. He had never understood what had happened to the real people when their duplicates took over. Still, it had been a good film and it made him feel rather uneasy. He examined each bean in turn. None resembled him in the least, except for one that had a bit on it that looked a little like the lobe of his right ear. 'Good Lord,' said Archroy, 'say it isn't true.'

'It's not true,' said John Omally, who was developing a useful knack of sneaking up on folk.

'John,' said Archroy, who had seen Omally coming, 'how much would you give me for five magic beans?'

Omally took up one of the suspect items and turned it on his palm. 'Have you as yet discovered in what way their magic properties manifest themselves?'

'Sadly no,' said Archroy, 'I fear that I may not have the time to develop the proposition to any satisfactory extent, being an individual sorely put upon by the fates to the degree that I have hardly a minute to myself nowadays.'

'That is a great shame,' said John, who knew a rat when somebody thrust one up his nose for a sniff. 'Their value I feel would be greatly enhanced if their use could be determined. In their present state I doubt that they are worth more than the price of a pint.'

Archroy sniffed disdainfully, his trusty Morris Minor exchanged for the price of a pint, the injustice of it. 'I have a feeling that large things may be expected of these beans, great oaks from little acorns as it were.'

'There is little of the acorn in these beans,' said Omally. 'More of the mango, I think, or possibly the Amazonian sprout.'

'Exotic fruit and veg are always at a premium,' said Archroy. 'Especially when home grown, on an allotment such as this perhaps.'

Omally nodded thoughtfully. 'I will tell you what I will do Archroy,' said he. 'We will go down to my plot, select a likely spot and there under your supervision we shall plant one of these magic beans, we will nurture it with loving care, water it when we think fit and generally pamper its growth until we see what develops. We will both take this moment a solemn vow that neither of us will uproot it or tamper with it in any way and that whatever should appear will be split fifty-fifty should it prove profitable.'

Archroy said, 'I feel that you will have the better half of the deal, Omally, although I am sure that this is unintentional upon your part and that you act purely out of a spirit of friendship and cameraderie.'

'The beans are certainly worthless at this moment,' said Omally ingeniously. 'And the responsibility of what grows upon an allotment is solely that of the tenant. What for instance if your beans prove to be the seeds of some forbidden and illegal drug or some poison cactus, will you take half the responsibility then?'

Archroy thought for a moment. 'Let us not talk of such depressing things, rather let us enter into this venture with the spirit of enterprise and the hope of fine things to come.'

Omally shook his companion by the hand and the two swore a great covenant that fell only slightly short of blood brotherhood. Without further ado they strode to Omally's plot, selected a space which they marked with a bean pole, and planted the magic bean.

'We shall water it tomorrow night,' said Omally, 'then together watch its progress. This project must be maintained in total secrecy,' he added, tapping his nose significantly. 'Come now, let us adjourn to my rooms and drink a toast to our success, there is something I should like to discuss with you in private.'

Jim Pooley watched the two botanical conspirators vanish into the distance from his nest in the long grass. Emerging stiffly, stretching his legs and twisting his neck, he drew himself erect. With many furtive sideways glances, stealthily he stole over to Omally's plot and dug up the magic bean, which he wiped clean of dirt and secreted in his coat pocket. With devious care he selected a seed potato from the sack at Omally's shed door and planted this in the place of the bean, erasing all traces of his treachery with a practised hand.

Then with a melodramatic chuckle and light feet Jim Pooley departed the St Mary's Allotment.

5

Professor Slocombe lived in a large rambling Georgian house on Brentford's Butts Estate. The house had been the property of the Slocombes through numerous generations and the professor's ancestry could be traced back to Brentford's earliest inhabitants. Therefore the Professor, whose string of doctorates, master's degrees and obscure testimonials ran in letters after his name like some Einsteinian calculation, had a deep and profound love for the place. He had produced privately a vast tome entitled:

THE COMPLETE AND ABSOLUTE HISTORY OF BRENTFORD
Being a study of the various unusual and extradictionary circumstances that have prevailed throughout History and which have in their way contributed to the unique visual and asthetic aspects inherent in both landscape and people of this locality. Giving also especial reference to religious dogma, racial type, ethnic groupings and vegetation indigenous to the area.

The Professor was constantly revising this mighty volume. His researches had of late taken him into uncharted regions of the occult and the esoteric. Most of the Professor's time was spent in his study, his private library rivalling that of the Bodleian. Showcases packed with strange objects lined the walls, working models of da Vinciesque flying machines, stuffed beasts of mythical origin, brass astrolabes, charts of the heavens, rows of apothecary jars, pickled homunculi and dried mandragora lined each available inch of shelf space and spilled off into every corner, nook and cranny. The whole effect was one to summon up visions of medieval alchemists bent over their seething cauldrons in each of the philosopher's stone. The professor himself was white-haired and decrepit, walking only with the aid of an ivory-topped cane. His eyes, however, glittered with a fierce and vibrant energy.

Fulfilling as he did the role of ornamental hermit, the Professor made one daily appearance upon the streets of Brentford. This ritual was accompanied by much ceremony and involved him making a slow perambulation about Brentford's boundaries. Clad on even the warmest of days in a striking black coat with astrakhan collar, his white hair streaming behind him, this venerable gentleman trod his weary morning path, never a pace out of step with that of the day previous.

Jim Pooley said that should this phenomenon cease, like the ravens leaving the Tower of London, it would spell doom and no good whatever to this sceptred isle. Jim was a regular visitor to the Professor, acting as he did as self-appointed gardener, and held the aged person in great reverence.

He had once taught the Professor to play darts, reasoning that excellence in this particular form of pub sport was entirely the product of skill and much practice, both of which Jim had to a high degree. He had explained the rules and handed the Professor a set of darts. The old man had taken one or two wild throws at the board with little success. Then, pausing for a moment, he took several snippings from the flights with a pair of nail scissors, licked the points and proceeded to beat Jim Pooley, one of the Swan's most eminent dart players, to the tune of £10. Pooley assumed that he had either become subject to some subtle form of hypnosis or that the Professor was a master of telekinesis. What ever the case the Professor earned Jim's undying admiration. He did not even resent the loss of the £10, because he was never a man to undervalue education.

This particular warm spring evening the Professor sat at his desk examining a crumbling copy of the *Necronomicon* through an oversized magnifying glass. A soft breeze rustled amongst the honeysuckle which encircled the open French windows and from not far off the Memorial Library clock struck eight o'clock.

The Professor made several jottings in a school exercise book and without looking up said, 'Are you going to skulk about out there all evening, Jim Pooley, or will you join me for a small sherry?'

'I will join you for a sherry,' said Jim, who showed no surprise whatever at the Professor's uncanny perception, 'but as to a small one, that is a matter I suggest we discuss.'

The Professor rang a tiny Indian brass bell that lay half hidden among the crowded papers upon his desk. There

47

was a knock and the study door swung open to reveal an elderly retainer, if anything even more white-haired and ancient than the Professor himself.

'Would it be the sherry, sir?' said the ancient, proffering a silver tray upon which rested a filled crystal decanter and two minuscule glasses.

'It would indeed, Gammon, leave it there if you would.' The Professor indicated a delicately carved Siamese table beside the white marble fireplace. The elderly retainer did as he was bid and silently departed.

The Professor decanted two glasses of sherry and handed one to Jim. 'So,' said he, 'and to what do I owe this pleasure then, Jim?'

'It is this way,' Pooley began. 'It is well known hereabouts and in particular to myself that you are a man of extensive knowledge, widely travelled and well versed in certain matters that remain to the man in the street inexplicable conundra.'

The Professor raised an eyebrow. 'Indeed?' said he.

'Well,' Jim continued, 'I have recently had come into my possession an object which causes me some degree of perplexity.'

The Professor said 'Indeed' once more.

'Yes,' said Jim. 'How I came by it is irrelevant but I think that you as a learned and scholarly man might find it of some interest.'

The Professor nodded thoughtfully and replaced his glass upon the tray. 'Well now, Jim,' he said. 'Firstly, I must say that I am always pleased to see you, your visits are rarely devoid of interest, your conversation is generally stimulating and it is often a challenge to match wits with you over some of your more extravagant theories. Secondly, I must say now that whatever it is you have with you is no doubt something of great singularity but that should it be anything short of the philosopher's stone or one of the hydra's teeth I do not wish to purchase it.'

Pooley's face took on a wounded expression.

'So, if we understand each other completely I will gladly examine the object which you have in your possession and give you whatever information I can regarding it should the thing prove to be genuine.'

Pooley nodded and withdrew from his pocket the magic bean, which had been carefully wrapped in his despicable handkerchief.

'Only the object,' said the Professor, eyeing Pooley's hankie with disgust, 'I have no wish to contract some deadly virus from that hideous rag.'

Pooley unwrapped the bean and handed it to the Professor. Jim noticed that it seemed slightly larger than upon previous inspection and he also noticed the unusual expression that had crossed the Professor's face. The usually benign countenance had become distorted, the colour, what little there was of it, had drained from his face, and a blue tinge had crept across his lips. This grotesque manifestation lasted only for a moment or two before the Professor regained his composure.

'Put it over there on to that marble base,' he said with a quavering voice. Pooley, shaken by the Professor's terrifying reaction, obeyed without hesitation.

'Put that glass dome over it,' the Professor said. Pooley did so.

'Are you all right, Professor?' he asked in a voice of some concern. 'Can I get you a glass of water or anything?'

'No,' said the Professor, 'no, no, I'll be all right, it's just that, well,' he looked Pooley squarely in the eye, 'where did you get that thing?'

'I found it,' said Pooley who had no intention of giving very much away.

'Where though, where did you find it?'

Pooley stroked his chin. Clearly the bean had well rattled the old gentleman, clearly it was more than just any old bean, it was indeed a bean of great singularity, therefore possibly a bean of great value. He would not mention that Archroy had four more of them. 'It is valuable then?' he asked nonchalantly.

'Where did you find it?' the Professor repeated in a voice of grave concern.

'I dug it up,' said Jim.

The Professor gripped Pooley's lapels in his sinewy fingers and made some attempt to shake him vigorously. The effort, however, exhausted him and he sank back into the armchair. 'Jim,' he said in a tone of such sincerity that Pooley realized that something was about to happen which would not be to his advantage. 'Jim you have there' – he indicated the bean beneath the glass dome – 'something, if I am not mistaken, and I sadly fear that I am not, something so heinous that it is best not spoken of. I only hope that you have not had it in your possession long enough to become contaminated by it.'

'Contaminated!' Pooley yanked his handkerchief out of his pocket and hurled it into the fire which blazed away in the hearth no matter what the season. 'What is it?' said Pooley, a worried sweat breaking out on his brow. 'Is it poison then?'

'Worse than that, I fear.'

Worse than poison? Pooley's mind turned several somersaults. What could be worse than poison in a bean?

'Help me up if you please.' Pooley aided the Professor to one of the massive bookcases flanking the study door. 'That green volume with the gold lettering, hand me that down if you will.' Pooley obliged and the Professor placed the great book upon his desk and leafed slowly through the pages.

'My glass, if you would.' Pooley handed him the magnifier and peered over the ancient's shoulder. To his dismay the book was written in Latin. There was, however, on a facing page covered by a slip of tissue paper an illustration in fading colours of a bean apparently identical to that which now rested beneath the dome. The Professor ran his glass to and fro across the page, raising his eye occasionally to take in both bean and illustration. Then, sitting back in his chair with a sigh, he said, 'You've certainly pulled off the big one this time, Jim.'

Pooley, uncertain whether or not this was meant as a compliment, remained silent.

'Phaseolus Satanicus,' the Professor said, 'Phaseolus being in general the genus of the ever popular and edible bean, Satanicus being quite another matter. Now this book' – he tapped at the vellum page with his exquisite fingertip – 'this book is the work of one James Murrell, known as the Hadleigh Seer, who enumerated and copied the masterworks, astrological charts and almanacs of previous and largely forgotten mages and minor wizards. Little remains of his work, but I have through means that I care not to divulge come into the possession of this one volume. It is a book entirely dedicated to the detailed study of what you might term magical herbs, spices, seeds and beans. It lists the pharmaceutical, thaumaturgical and metaphysical uses of these and includes within its skin bindings certain notes upon plants and seedlings which the ancients referred to as sacred. Either because of their mindbending qualities when distilled or because they possessed certain characteristics which were outside the scope of normal explanation.'

'So there are magical properties adherent to this particular bean then?' said Pooley.

'I should not care to call them magical,' said the Professor, 'but let me tell you that this bean of yours pays allegiance to the powers of darkness to a point that it is better not thought of, let alone mentioned in the public bar of the Flying Swan.'

'I prefer to patronize the saloon bar actually,' said Pooley, 'but pray continue, I find your monologue fascinating.'

'I shall read to you directly from the book,' said the Professor, 'then when I have finished we shall see if you still find my monologue fascinating.'

Pooley poured himself yet another sherry and wondered whether he might interest the Professor in a home-brew lager kit.

'"Phaseolus Satanicus",' the Professor read once more. 'This first passage is a loose translation from the Greek. "And when the casket was opened and when the evil one set his burning hoof upon the plains of earth, then did Pandora weep those five bitter tears. And where those tears fell on the fields of men there did they take root and flourish withal. And Ephimetheus seeing the ill work that his wife had performed snatched forth those five dark saplings and cast them into the places of absolute night from whence should man go onward to seek them then surely he should never more return."'

'That's all very well,' said Jim Pooley.

'The next quotation comes from Jean-François Champollion, 1790–1832, the man who originally deciphered the Egyptian hieroglyphic system. "Anubis stared upon the manchild that had come before him and questioned him over his possessions and the pharoah did answer saying I bear seventeen oxon, fifteen caskets of gold and precious stones. Carvings and set tableaus of rich embellishment and the five that dwell within the sacred house where none may tread. And Anubis took fright, even he that stands guardian over the realms of the beyond was afeared and he turned back the manchild that stood before the sacred river saying never shall you cross until your weight is above the holy balance. Which never can it be for the five set the scales heavily against you."'

Pooley reached for the sherry decanter but found to his dismay that it was empty. 'This five whatever they are sound somewhat sinister,' said he, 'but the threat seems also a trifle nebulous.'

The Professor looked up from his antique tome. 'This book was handwritten some three centuries ago,' said he, 'not by some casual dilettante of the occult but by a mage of the first order. I have given you two quotations which he sought out, neither of which seem to impress you very much. Now I shall read to you what James Murrel wrote in his own hand regarding the five beans which had at the time of his writing come by means unfathomable into his possession. "I am plagued this evening as I write with thoughts of the five I have here before me. Their echoes are strong and their power terrific. My ears take in strange cries that come not from an earthly throat and visions dance before my eyes whose very nature and habit appal me and fill my soul with dark horror. I know now what these may be and what, if they were to receive the touch of the dark one, they might become. It is my intention to destroy them by fire and by water and by the power of the mother church. Would that I had never set eyes upon them for no more will sleep come unto me a blessed healer."' The Professor slammed shut the book. 'The illustration of the bean is still clear in Murrel's hand, there can be no mistake.'

Pooley was silent. The Professor's voice had induced in him a state of semi-hypnosis. What it all meant was still unclear but that there was a distinctly unsavoury taint to the beans was certain.

'Where are the other four?' said the Professor.

'Archroy has them,' said Pooley promptly.

'I do not fully understand the implications myself,' said the Professor. 'These beans, it would seem, are objects of grim omen – their appearance at various intervals in history always precede times of great ill, plague, war, famine and the like. On each occasion a dark figure to whom in some inexplicable way these five beans appear to owe some allegiance is always mentioned – what his ultimate purpose may be I shudder to think.' The Professor crossed himself.

Upon the verandah, shielded by the trelliswork of honeysuckle, a tramp of hideous aspect and sorry footwear watched the Professor with eyes that glowed faintly in the late twilight. He ran a nicotine-stained finger across a cultivated rose and watched in silence as the petals withered beneath his touch. Mouthing something in a long-dead tongue he slipped away down the garden path and melted into the gathering darkness.

Jim Pooley sat upon his favourite seat before the Memorial Library, deep in thought. It was nearing midnight and growing decidedly cold. Above him a proud full moon swam amongst shredded clouds and the stars came and went, wormholes in the wooden floor of heaven. Jim turned up the collar of his tweed jacket and sat, shoulders hunched and hands lost in his bottomless trouser pockets.

All this bean business had become a little too much for him. After all, he'd only gone around to the Professor to get the damn thing identified. This was Brentford in the twentieth century, not some superstitious medieval village in the grip of witch mania. Pandora's Box indeed! Jim searched about for his tobacco tin, and the clock struck twelve. The search proved fruitless and Pooley recalled placing the tin upon the Professor's mantelpiece while he was asking the old man for a refill of the sherry decanter.

Jim sighed dismally. It had not been a very successful night, all things considered. His tobacco growing dry on the fireplace whilst his bean lay valueless in its glass prison. Pooley thought back over all that the Professor had said. Could the old boy be pulling a fast one? Jim had left the bean there after all, and no money had changed hands. Possibly the Professor had instantly recognized the bean as an object of great value and dragged up all this Phaseolus Satanicus stuff simply to put the wind up him. Jim scratched the stubble upon his chin.

No, that couldn't be it, the Professor had been

genuinely shocked when he saw the bean and it was most certainly the same as the illustration in the ancient book. No-one could make up stories like that on the spur of the moment could they? And he had known of the existence of the four others. All this intense thinking coupled with the intake of two pints of fine sherry was beginning to give Jim a headache. Better to forget the bean then, let the Professor do what he pleased with it.

Pooley rose and stretched his arms. Another thought suddenly crossed his mind. 'If these beans are dangerous,' the thought said, 'then it would be best to inform Archroy of this fact as the four he carries with him may possibly do him harm.'

Jim sat down again upon the bench.

'But if you tell him,' said another thought, 'then he will ask how you know all this and you will have to confess to the abduction of the bean from Omally's allotment.'

This thought did not please Pooley whatsoever.

'But he is your friend,' said the first thought in an angelic voice, 'and you would feel very guilty should any ill befall him that you are empowered to prevent.' Pooley nodded and rose once more to his feet.

'Better not to get involved,' said the second thought. 'Who is to say that the Professor's suppositions are correct?' Pooley bit his lip. It was all a terrible dilemma. He let the angelic thought have the final word upon the matter.

'If the Professor had told you that the bean was that of a plant which bears gold doubloons upon its boughs each spring you would have believed him. You went there to take advantage of his boundless knowledge, did you not?' Pooley nodded meekly. 'So if the Professor says that the beans are evil and must be destroyed you would do well to follow his advice.' Pooley seemed satisfied by this and took some steps into the direction of home. Then as if jerked to a standstill by a rope he stopped.

'But then I must somehow get those four other beans from Archroy,' he said. 'And in some way that I will not implicate myself in any duplicity.' Jim Pooley wished with all his might that he had never set eyes upon any beans whatever, be they baked, curried, buttered, soya or magic to the slightest degree.

A new thought came to Pooley, one whose voice he did not recognize but one which was so sound in logic that Pooley felt very grateful that it had chosen his head to come into. 'Why don't you go around to Archroy's now, while he is away on the night shift, gain entrance to his house and remove the four magic beans?' The angelic thought had some doubts about this but was finally cowed into submission.

'I do this deed for Archroy,' said Jim Pooley. 'A noble venture for which I expect to receive no thanks, as by its very nature the perpetrator of the deed must remain anonymous.'

Jim girded up his loins and strode purposefully into the direction of Archroy's house. It was seldom indeed that a noble thought entered his head and the entry of this one filled Jim with reckless confidence. He would climb on to Archroy's garage and pull down the aluminium ladder, then go round and try all the upper windows, one of which must surely have been left open. Once inside, if the beans were there, he would most certainly find them.

Having checked that there were no late night revellers returning to their haunts, or policemen out upon their lonely beats, Pooley slid away down the side alley beside Archroy's garage. His stealth and silence were there sadly impaired however, by a noisy collision with Omally's bicycle Marchant which was resting against the garage wall lost in the shadows. Jim and Marchant crashed noisily to the ground, Marchant ringing his bell in protest at his rude awakening and Jim swearing great oaths upon every form of two-wheeled conveyance known to mankind.

With much shooshing and hand flapping, Jim rose to his feet, flat cap cocked over one eye and trouser turnup firmly in the grip of Marchant's back brake. Amid more cursing and the distinctive sound of tearing tweed, Jim fought his way free of the bicycle's evil grasp and limped on up the alley.

He stopped suddenly in his tracks and gazed up in amazement, for there propped up against the side wall and leading directly to an open upstairs window was Archroy's extendable aluminium ladder. 'Luck indeed,' said Jim Pooley, gripping it delightedly and testing its footings for safety.

He was all of five rungs up when a small clear voice in his head said, 'Pooley, why do you think that there would be a ladder resting so conveniently against Archroy's wall and leading directly to an open upstairs window?'

Pooley arrested his ascent and thought for a moment or two. Perhaps Archroy was cleaning his windows and forgot to remove the ladder? The small voice said, 'Come now, Pooley.'

'I'll just shin up and have a quick shufty in through the window,' Pooley told the voice. He accomplished the ascent with admirable dexterity, considering that the effects of the Professor's sherry seemed to be increasing by the minute. The full moon shone down through the bedroom window, flooding the room with its septic light. Pooley's head rose cautiously above the window sill and came to rest, his nose hooked over it in the manner of the legendary Chad. As his eyes took in the situation the words that escaped his lips in an amazed whisper were generally of a sort totally unprintable.

There upon continental quilt, bouncing and gyrating in a frenzy of sexual abandonment, was Archroy's wife. Locked in passionate congress with this insatiable female was none other than John Vincent Omally, bachelor of this parish.

'Bastard,' mouthed Jim Pooley, which was at least in the Oxford Dictionary. 'The conniving treacherous . . .' his mind sought about for an adjective suitable to the expression of his displeasure. It was during the search that Pooley's eyes alighted upon the very objects which had led him to the unexpected viewing of this lewd and certainly x-certificate performance.

There they lay, glowing with a faint luminescence, upon the dressing-table inches away from the window. Pooley spied them with great satisfaction, feeling that his noble quest had been justly rewarded by instantaneous success achieved with only the minimum of physical exertion and with next to no danger to life or limb. This feeling of well-being was, however, almost immediately succeeded by one of disgust. For although the beans lay in attitudes suggestive of lifelessness, it was obvious to Jim from where he clung to his airy perch that they were very much on the alert. They were quite definitely watching and apparently thoroughly enjoying the erotic spectacle. They exuded such a sense of dark evil and inhuman nastiness that Jim was hard put to it to subdue the disgust which rose within him like an out-of-season vindaloo.

Taking a deep yet silent breath, he thrust his hand through the window and snatched up the sinister beans from their grandstand seats on the dressing-table. Omally's bum, glowing ivory in the moonlight, rose and fell undeterred. Pooley thrust the beans into his coat pocket and made haste down the ladder.

Here he transferred the beans into a drawstring bag sanctified by the Professor for the purpose. 'Another job jobbed,' said Pooley with some relief. The operations had been a remarkable success, handled with alacrity, diligence, dexterity and skill. High upon Olympus hosts of ancient Pooleys opened a bottle of champagne and toasted their descendant.

Pooley strode down the alley with a jaunty spring to his

step. He had not gone but three yards, however, when the vengeful left pedal of Marchant caught him by the sound trouser-cuff and upended him into the muddy gloom.

'You swine,' growled Pooley, lashing out with his boots in as many directions as possible.

'Who's there?' said a voice from an upper window.

Jim edged along the side wall of the house, gained the street and took to his heels. In the darkened alleyway Omally's bike chuckled mechanically to its iron self and rang its bell in delight. On High Olympus the Pooleys sought other amusements.

6

Captain Carson stood upon the porch of the Seamen's Mission taking in the fresh morning air. The Mission was situated on the Butts Estate not a stone's throw from Professor Slocombe's house. It was a fine Victorian building, built in an era when craftsmen took a pride in their work and knew nothing of time and a half and guaranteed Sunday working. Now the once-proud structure had fallen into bitter disrepair; its chimney pots leaned at crazy angles, its roof lacked many essential tiles, paint peeled from the carved gables. That which the tireless assault of wind and weather had not achieved without, had been amply accomplished within by woodworm and a multifarious variety of fungi, dry rot and deathwatch beetle.

The Captain stood framed in the doorway, master of his land-bound ship. Thirty years he had been at the helm. The Mission, bequeathed to the borough by a long dead Victorian benefactor and maintained by a substantial foundation, was the Captain's pride. A fine figure of a man, still erect and dignified although now the graveyard side of seventy, the Captain took a pull upon his cherrywood pipe and let escape a blue swirl of seaman's smoke. His white hair and tabby beard, the faded blue of his rollneck sweater, the bellbottom trousers and yachting sandals all bespoke in him a man who lived and breathed for nothing but the salt winds of the briny deep and the roar of the shorebound breakers.

Sad to say the Captain had never seen the sea. He had taken the job at the Mission at a time when jobs were few and far between and one took what one could. The only stipulation given had been that the applicant must be a man of nautical bent with a love of the sea who would maintain the Mission to the highest ideals and qualities of his Majesty's Fleet.

Togging up at a theatrical outfitter's with his last few pennies Horatio B. Carson applied for the post. His characterization must have been as convincing as that of Charles Laughton in *Mutiny on the Bounty*, because 'Captain' Carson was immediately accepted for the job.

His duties were not arduous. Few if any sailors had ever honoured the Mission with their visits. However, a proliferation of down and outs, ne'er-do-wells, roguish knights of the road, shoelace pedlars and grimy individuals smelling strongly of meths and cheap sherry had soon appeared upon the doorstep. The Captain welcomed each in turn, extending to them the utmost courtesy, carrying their sorry bundles and opening doors before them.

'Here is your room, sir,' he would say, drawing their attention to the luxuriance of the pillows and the fine quality of the bedcovers. 'Our last lodger had to leave in something of a hurry,' he would explain. 'He, like your good self, was a seafaring man and the doctors at the isolation hospital said that there would have been some hope of saving his life had they been able to identify the crippling and particularly virulent form of disease to which he so sadly succumbed. I haven't had a chance to fumigate the room yet, but I am sure that your travels must by now have made you immune to most sicknesses, even of the horrendously disfiguring and painful variety which so sorrowfully took him from us.'

At this point the Captain would remove his hat, place it over his heart and look skyward. The tramp to which he was addressing this tragic monologue would follow the direction of his eyes then make his exit, often at astonishing speed, with talk of 'pressing engagements' and 'business elsewhere'.

In the thirty long years of the Captain's residence, no visitor, no matter how apparent his need or dire his circumstance, be his tale one to raise a tear in a glass eyeball, no visitor had ever spent a single night within the Seamen's Mission.

On this particular morning as the Captain stood upon the porch his thoughts dwelt mainly upon money, the strange ways of fate and the scourge of homosexuality. He knew that he could not expect many more years within the Mission and that his days were most definitely numbered. The job supplied no pension, and with the swelling list of forged signatures speaking of the enormous physical effort required of one man to maintain the Mission there had been talk of employing a younger person. The yearly meeting between himself and the Foundation's trustees had been but a week before and he, the Captain, had handed over his tailored accounts and spoken modestly of his good works. But a new face had appeared upon the Committee this year, a young and eager face. During the previous twelve months one of the Trustees had died and the lot had fallen to his nephew to succeed him.

Young Brian Crowley had no love for elderly sea captains. His distaste for such patriarchs was only exceeded by his out-and-out hatred for tramps, loafers, down-and-outs, gypsies, foreigners and women. The limp-wristed Brian cared little for anybody other than an Italian waiter who worked at the Adelaide Tea Rooms. He had promised to set Mario up in his own restaurant, the dago waiter being a veritable 'wizard-de-cuisine' and exceptionally well hung into the bargain.

The fates, which had conspired to arrange the sad demise of his dear uncle and Brian's succession to the Foundation committee, had also decreed that this year the Council would raise their annual offer for the purchase of the Mission to a more than adequate sum.

The Captain sucked again upon his pipe. He could read faces well enough, and young Brian's had been an open book. It might well be the time to shape up and ship out. His nest-egg was by now pretty substantial, enough for a small cottage somewhere, possibly by the sea. It might be nice to actually see the waves breaking on a beach. 'I wonder if they make a lot of noise?' he said to himself.

Suddenly far up the road a flicker of movement caught his eye. He watched with passing interest as a ragged figure turned the corner beside the Memorial Library and shambled towards him with an odd yet purposeful gait.

It was the figure of a tramp. The Captain raised his nautical glass to view the apparition. A swift glance was enough. 'Ugh!' said the Captain.

The tramp plodded nearer and nearer, and the Captain rummaged about in his vast mental storehouse for a tale of woe suitable to the occasion. Strangely none seemed readily available. The tramp trod closer, his big floppy boots stomping down into the ground. The Captain began to whistle an uneasy version of the famous shanty 'Orange Claw Hammer'.

The tramp was crossing the road towards the Mission. He stopped. The Captain ceased his whistling. The birds were silent and the Captain could no longer smell the fragrant scent of honeysuckle. He felt cold, and even though the early summer sun breathed down upon him a shiver arose at the base of his spine. The Captain held his breath. Of a sudden the wretch turned upon his heel and stalked away down a side turning. As if at a signal the birds burst forth again into a cascade of song and the Captain regained the use of his nostrils. He let free a sigh of utmost relief and reached into his sleeve for his matches.

'Could I trouble you for a glass of water, please?' said a voice at his elbow.

The Captain turned in horror, spilling his matches to the ground. Beside him stood a tramp of hideous aspect. 'Sorry, did I startle you?' said the creature with what seemed to be a voice of genuine concern. 'It is a bad habit of mine, I really most control it.'

'Damn you, sir,' swore the Captain, 'creepin' up on a fella.'

'My apologies,' said the tramp, removing the battered relic which served him as hat, and bowing to the ground. 'But if you would be so kind, a glass of water would serve well at this time.'

The Captain muttered a terse 'Come in then' and led his unspeakable visitor into the Mission. 'You caught me at a bad moment,' he said.

The tramp found no cause to reply.

'I was just having a moment or two's fresh air before I continue my search.' The Captain drew the tramp a glass of water. The tramp received it with a great show of gratitude. 'My thanks,' said he.

'Yes,' the Captain continued, 'my search.'

The tramp seemed uninterested in the Captain's search but he nodded politely.

'Yes, carelessly I have upset my case of deadly scorpions; I fear that they have gone to earth in the sleeping quarters.'

'Scorpions indeed?' said the tramp. 'I have some

experience in such matters, I will help you search.'

The Captain eyed his visitor with suspicion. 'That will not be necessary, I should not like there to be an unfortunate accident, these fellows are wantonly vicious in their attitude towards any but myself.'

'If you are on such good terms, possibly you should just put out some milk and give them a call,' said the tramp helpfully.

The Captain sucked strongly upon his pipe. 'I fear that that would prove futile,' he said. 'Devious fellows scorpions, and mine I believe to be deaf.'

'Devious indeed,' said the tramp. 'Have you seen this trick?' He held the glass of water out at arm's length and stared into it with a fixed and steady gaze. The Captain watched in puzzlement, his eyes flickering between the glass and the tramp's glaring red pupils, which now began to glitter with a strange and sinister light.

Bubbles began to appear in the glass; one by one they popped to the surface, growing in force one upon another they burst upwards; steam began to rise.

The Captain said, 'It's boiling, be damned!'

The tramp handed the churning glass to the Captain, who gingerly received it. 'I should like a room for the night,' said the tramp.

'The water is cold,' said the Captain, dumbfounded.

'A trick, no more. About the room?'

'The scorpions!'

The tramp said, 'I don't think we need worry about the scorpions. I have here in my pocket a trained cobra that will easily seek out any scorpions lounging about.'

'Hold there,' said the Captain. 'That surely will not be necessary. I think that the warm sun may well have drawn any errant insects beyond the bounds of the Mission.'

'That is good to hear,' said the tramp. 'Now, about the room?'

'This room is vacant.' The Captain swung open a door

to reveal a neatly dressed cubicle. 'It is sad that it carries such a dreadful reputation.'

'Indeed?' The tramp prodded the bed and turned back the woollen coverlet.

'Yes, no soul has ever stayed a full night in it, none reveal what horrors take hold of them, but of those who attempted to remain, one committed suicide and three more are even now residents at St Bernard's Asylum, hopeless lunatics.'

'Indeed?' The tramp sat down upon the bed and bounced soundlessly upon the steady springs.

'Gibbering they were,' said the Captain. 'I have sailed the seven seas and seen sights that would blast the sanity from a lesser man but I can tell you I was shaken when I saw the looks upon the faces of those unlucky fellows.'

The tramp shook his head slowly. 'My word,' was all he would say. The Captain had an uneasy feeling that Brian Crowley had a hand in this. 'The hospitality of the Mission is well known,' said the tramp. 'Only last week I bumped into Alfredo Beranti and Roger Kilharric both joyfully extolling the virtues of your beneficient establishment.'

The Captain scratched at his head. The names seemed strangely familiar. 'And Dennis Cunningham,' the tramp continued, 'forever praising the haute-cuisine.' The Captain became suddenly weak about the knees. He knew those names well enough, they were three of the cast of imaginary tramps with which he peopled the pages of his yearly accounts.

'And Old Wainwright McCarthy,' the tramp said, 'and . . .'

'No, no,' screamed the Captain in an unnatural voice, 'enough, enough!'

'What time is dinner to be served?'

'Dinner?'

'Knobby Giltrap spoke highly of the shepherd's pie.'

'Six o'clock,' said the Captain.

'A little early, perhaps?'

'Seven then,' said the Captain, 'or eight if you please.'

'Seven will be fine,' smiled the tramp. 'Now I think I shall take a brief nap. Pray awaken me at six thirty.'

With that the Captain was ushered from the cubicle and out into the corridor, where he stood in the semi-darkness chewing upon the stem of his pipe, his breath coming and going in rapid grunts.

'And don't over-season my veg,' came a voice through the panelled cubicle door.

The tramp sat back in the Captain's chair and eased open the lower buttons of his waistcoat. 'Very palatable,' said he.

The Captain had watched with set features whilst the tramp devoured two bowls of soup, all the shepherd's pie, a plate of potatoes, two double helpings of peas, a bowl of custard and a large slice of chocolate gâteau.

'Is there anything to follow?' asked the tramp politely.

'To follow?'

'Well, brandy, a cigar, or even a fill for my pipe?'

The Captain rose to his feet pulling away the napkin from his roll neck. 'Now see here!' he roared.

'Gaffer Tim Garney was telling me of your generosity with the navy plug?'

The Captain flung the tramp his tobacco pouch. 'Shag,' said he, slumping into a chair.

'Shag then, my thanks again.' The framp took to filling his pipe, his glittering eyes wandering towards the Captain's brandy bottle.

'I expect you'll be wanting to make an early start tomorrow?' said the Captain.

The tramp said, 'Excuse me?'

'Well,' the Captain replied, 'I know you fellows, can't keep you cooped up under a roof for very long. Life of freedom eh, knights of the road, the sky above, the earth below?'

The tramp scratched his head, raising small clouds of blue dust. 'There I am afraid you are mistaken. Please do not construe from my appearance that I incline towards the life of the casual wanderer. On the contrary, my every movement is guided towards inevitable consequence. I follow my kharma as all must.'

'Indeed?' said the Captain. 'Well, far be it from me to hinder you in your search for the ultimate truth.'

'I feel that our paths have not crossed out of idle chance,' said the tramp, 'in fact, I will go so far as to say that destiny has pointed me to your door with a straight and unwavering digit.'

'Possibly this same destiny will point you in yet another direction tomorrow?'

'I doubt that,' said the tramp with a note of finality. 'Now, about this brandy?'

The Captain rose early the next morning. He had lain sleeplessly upon his bunk chewing at his knuckles and muttering nautical curses into the early hours. The ghastly truth that he was no longer alone beneath the Mission roof gnawed at his hermitical soul like a rat at a leper's foot. By dawn he had run himself dry of profanity and fallen into an uneasy sleep.

Now he stalked to and fro along the verandah emitting thick clouds of seaman's shag and grumbling to himself. Somehow he must rid himself of this unwelcome visitor, but if Brian Crowley was at the bottom of it he must be on his guard. He would just have to treat the hideous stranger with politeness while hinting with firm conviction that the traveller might fare better in distant and sunnier climes. He looked up at the sky and was appalled to see that it was likely to be another beautiful day.

Suddenly a voice at his elbow said, 'I see you like to make an early start to the day, Captain.'

Colour drained from the Captain's face and he dropped

his tobacco pouch, spilling its contents to the verandah floor. 'Must you always come damn well creeping up?' he coughed as he took a great gust of smoke up his nostrils.

'I must say that I slept very well,' said the tramp. 'What is on the menu for breakfast?'

The Captain folded his brow into a look of intense perplexity. 'You seem exceedingly spry for a man who demolished an entire bottle of brandy and better part of an ounce of shag in a single evening.'

'And very nice too,' said the tramp. 'Now as to breakfast?'

'I make it a rule never to over-eat at this time of the day,' the Captain explained. 'Makes a man sluggish, impairs the limbs, corrodes the arteries. A simple bowl of bran and a glass of salt water serve as my early morning repast.'

'I should kindly prefer double eggs, bacon, sausages, beans, mushrooms, tomato and a fried slice. Possibly, as I have no wish to lessen your resolve, you would prefer to eat alone,' said the tramp.

The Captain pulled upon his lower lip. 'Possibly that would be impolite of me, it is always wise to eat well before travel.' Here he looked at the tramp from the corner of his eye. 'Thus we shall have a hearty meal of it before your departure.'

The tramp smiled. 'Have no fear upon that account, I have no intention of moving on within the foreseeable future.'

The Captain frowned furiously and stalked away to the kitchen. The tramp scooped up the fallen pouch and proceeded to refill his pipe.

7

As founder and sole member of the Brentford and West London Hollow Earth Society Soap Distant thought it about time to put matters firmly into perspective. 'There have been many words spoken and much local controversy over the arrival of a certain extraordinary being upon our streets of late,' he announced to the Saturday lunchtime crowd in the Swan's saloon bar.

Neville nodded thoughtfully. The tramp had been pretty much the sole topic of conversation in the borough for nearly a month although his last sighting was more than a fortnight ago.

'I know that you all understand to whom I refer,' said Soap.

Those who did nodded. Those who did, but had no wish to listen to yet another of Soap's endless diatribes upon the denizens of the inner world took a sudden interest in the bottoms of their pint glasses.

'Speculation has been rife,' Soap continued, 'and up until now I have kept my counsel whilst the false prophets among you have battled one another to a standstill. Now and only now I am ready to impart to you the sole and unimpeachably cosmic truth.'

Omally groaned. 'I had an uncle once,' said he, hoping to change the subject, 'who swallowed a golf ball thinking it to be a plover's egg.'

'Really,' said old Pete, who hated Soap Distant and his 'bloody silly notions'. 'And what happened to your uncle, how was he?'

'A little under par,' said the Irishman.

'There are none so deaf as those who will not hear,' said Soap.

69

'Here, steady on,' said Norman.

'How many times have I propounded my theories regarding the lands beneath and their interterrestrial occupants, and how many times have I offered irrefutable proof as to their existence, only to be scoffed at and ridiculed by those pseudo-intellectuals who nestle in seats of authority having sprung up like mildewed fungi upon the rotting corpse of this present society?'

'Many times,' said Omally. 'A great many times.'

'Listen.' Soap rattled his pint glass upon the bar top in agitation. 'I know all about your views on the subject, you are a Philistine.'

'I resent that,' said John, 'I am from the South.'

'Beneath the surface of the globe,' said Soap in a reverent tone, 'is the vast and beautiful land of Agharta, and in that sunken realm at the very centre of the planet, Shamballah, capital city of Earth. Here in unimaginable splendour dwells Rigdenjyepo, King of the World, whose emissaries, the subterranean monks of black habit, weave their ways through the endless network of ink-dark corridors which link the capital cities of the ancient world.'

'Such is the popular Buddhist doctrine,' said Omally.

'Rigdenjyepo is in constant contact with the Dalai Lama,' said Soap.

'The Dalai rarely drinks in these parts,' said John.

Soap threw up his arms in dismay. 'When the great day comes and the portals are opened then the smile will flee your face like a rat from a sinking ship.'

Omally brought his smile into full prominence. 'I have always found it to be the case,' said he ingeniously, 'that most ships, especially those sailing under the colours of the Esoteric Line, generally sink due to a surfeit of rats weighing heavily upon the bows.'

'Holes in the Poles,' said Soap, thrusting the Irishman aside and stalking away to the gents.

'I think you may have offended him,' said Neville.

Omally shrugged. 'He'll be back. Give me another of the same please, Neville. And pray take one for yourself. And what is the explanation of that poster in your window?'

Neville, somewhat taken aback at the Irishman's generosity, reddened about the cheeks upon the mention of the poster. He pulled two pints in silence. 'Poster?' he said, finally. Omally accepted his pint.

'The poster displayed upon your window which reads, and I quote from memory, "Thursday Night is Cowboy Night at the Flying Swan, Yahoo, Barbeque Country Music Best-Dressed Cowboy Comp, Big Prizes, Fancy Dress Optional."'

Neville hung his head in shame. 'The brewery,' he said. 'After the Channel wading business the brewery seem to have been taking an indecent interest in the Swan's affairs.'

Omally drew deeply upon his pint. 'A sad business,' said he.

'I have been issued with an outfit,' said Neville in a hushed tone.

'Outfit?'

'Cowboy, chaps and all that.'

'Good God.'

'There are prizes for the best dressed cowboy, a bottle of scotch, two hundred cigarettes and a voucher which enables you to dine at one of the brewery's licensed eating-houses.'

Omally raised his bristling eyebrows. 'A bottle of scotch, eh?' His voice was one of casual unconcern. 'Has Pooley been in today?'

Neville shook his head. Omally gestured to Neville with a motion which counselled secrecy and discretion. 'It is better,' said he, 'that we do not cause any great rumpus over this cowboy thing. The regulars might become somewhat incensed, the Swan being an establishment renowned for its conservatism.' Omally pulled at his lower eye-lid suggestively.

Neville nodded thoughtfully. 'I can sympathize with your feelings, John,' said he, 'but you must understand that the brewery pull the strings as it were and I must comply with their wishes, no matter how unseemly they might appear.'

'Unseemly is hardly the word. And what's all this about a barbecue?'

'I've had one built on the patio of the beer garden.'

'Beer garden?' Omally leant forward across the bar and fixed Neville with a baleful stare. 'I have partaken of alcoholic beverage in this establishment man and boy these fifteen years. Possibly I suffer from some strange aberration of the optical apparatus which deprives my sight of beer gardens and patios thereupon, but if you might be referring to the tiny strip of back yard behind the Gents where you stack the empties then I might suggest that you reconsider your terminology.'

'The brewery have done a conversion,' said Neville.

'Oh, a conversion is it? Would this conversion by any chance have been carried out by those two master builders known locally as Jungle John and Hairy Dave?' The part-time barman nodded. 'And this patio has been built with the bricks and mortar we were led to believe were to be used in the restructuring of the bog roof?'

Neville hung his head in shame. He had led the deception, it was true. 'It was meant to be a nice surprise,' said he in a wounded tone.

'Might we view this nice surprise?' the Irishman asked.

'Not until Thursday,' said the barman, 'and Omally, I might beg you not to cause anything in the way of a scandal over this patio. A representative from the brewery will be present for the occasion and any controversy might reflect badly upon my position here.'

Omally sipped thoughtfully at his pint. 'How many are you expecting then?'

'About two hundred.'

Omally spluttered into his beer, sending a stream of froth up his nose. 'Two hundred?'

'The brewery say that such a turn-out is average, they have put some adverts in the local papers.'

'Regarding these two hundred cowboys who will shortly be descending upon the Flying Swan for a hoe-down in the ten-foot-square backyard,' said Omally. 'Can you expect to hear the crack of the mule whip, the roaring of Colt forty-fives, the rattle of wooden wheel and flap of canvas as the mighty covered wagons roll over the prairie bound for Brentford, the thunder of pony hoof upon tarmac and the lusty vocal renderings of "Mule Skinner Blues" and "Do Not Forsake Me, Oh My Darling"?'

'There will be cheap drinking and an extension until eleven-thirty,' said Neville

'"Do Not Forsake Me, Oh My Darling,"' sang John Omally, flinging an imaginary stetson into the air.

Soap Distant, who had finally returned from the gents, said, 'With a bottle of scotch as a prize, cut-price drink and an eleven-thirty extension we can expect to see at least one Irish John Wayne impersonator swaggering through the Saloon Bar door toting a six-gun and asking for two fingers of redeye.'

Omally smiled indulgently. 'Possibly, Soap,' said he, 'you will be taking the opportunity to invite up a few of your chums from the inner earth. Tell me now, does old Rigdenjyepo get the likes of Laramie on his underworld twenty-inch or is the reception a bit ropey down there?'

Soap rose purposefully to his feet and stood swaying to and fro, his hand upon the bartop for support. 'You, sir, are an ignorant Irish blaggard,' quoth he, raising a shaky fist to strike Omally.

'Soap was telling me that flying saucers are manifestations of the static souls of bygone civilizations,' said Neville, who was not only pleased that the subject of Cowboy Night had been forgotten but was also a great stirrer.

'I've heard that little gem on more than one occasion,' said John, 'but you and I know that there is a logical and straightforward explanation for that particular phenomenon.'

'There is?'

'Of course, flying saucers are in fact nothing more than the chromeplated helmets of five-mile high invisible fairy folk.'

The Irishman, having both sobriety and the eye for impending violence to his account, stepped swiftly out of the hollow-earther's range. Soap's fist whistled by harmlessly.

Neville was making some motion towards his knobkerry when the door swung open to reveal none other than Mr James Pooley. Jim stood framed in the opening, thumbs clasped into his belt and a licorish-paper roll-up in the corner of his mouth. 'Howdy pardners,' he drawled.

Omally groaned and hid his face in his hands.

'Howdy Soap,' Jim continued, 'you subterranean sidewinder, you look mighty like as if yore meaning to slap leather with this here Irish hombre.'

Soap was squaring up for another shot at Omally's chin; now his fist hovered motionless in mid-air as if freed from the powers of gravity. 'You what?' was all he could say.

Neville leant across the counter. 'Before you ask, Jim,' he said, 'I am fresh out of Buckskin bourbon, Mississippi Sippin' liquor, Kentucky rye, Redeye whiskey or any other brand of white man's firewater.'

'I shall just have a pint of the usual then Neville.' Jim seated himself between the two combatants and withdrew from his pocket the exact change. Neville drew off a pint of his very best.

Soap placed a drunken hand upon Jim's shoulder. 'I am glad you have arrived, Jim Pooley, for now you can witness the rapid demolition of this Irish lout here.'

Pooley whistled through his teeth. 'That indeed will be a sight worth watching.'

'It will be terrible but instructive,' said Soap.

'Soap,' said Jim, 'Soap, may I ask under which grand master of the oriental arts you study?'

Soap said, 'Eh?'

'Well, I take it that you are acquainted with Mr Omally's skills in this direction?'

Soap shook his head and peered suspiciously over Jim's shoulder at the Irishman.

'You are surely aware,' Jim continued, 'that Omally here is an exponent of Dimac, the deadliest form of martial art known to mankind, and that he could instantly disable you should he so wish, his hands and feet being deadly weapons.' Soap's face took on a look of bewilderment as Jim rambled on. 'That he was personally schooled by Count Dante, dubbed by friend and foe alike as none other than the Deadliest Man on Earth. That he is a master of Poison Hand, surely the most horrendous of all the vicious crippling skills, whose maiming, mutilating, disfiguring, tearing and rending techniques strike terror into the hearts of even the most highly danned and darkly belted Kung Fu, Karate and Ju-jitsu exponents. That with little more than a deft touch he can . . .'

'Enough, enough,' said Soap, 'it was merely a difference of opinion, nothing more. Here, John, let us speak no more of such things, join me in a pint.'

John waggled his fingers in a movement suggestive of immense dexterity. 'I shall be pleased to,' said he, 'and possibly as our friend Jim here has acted the role of arbitrator you would wish to show your appreciation with a similar gesture of goodwill.' He clicked his knuckles noisily.

'Three pints please, Neville,' said Soap, 'and have one yourself.' With many echoes of 'Cheers' and 'Down the hatchway', the three set in for an evening's drinking.

Thus did Omally form a deep and meaningful relation-ship with Soap Distant. That the two held each other generally in absolute and utter contempt was no longer important. Here, as Neville ejected the dear friends into the street and pushed the bolt home, Soap Distant, Jim Pooley and John Omally found themselves swaying along the highway, arms about each other's shoulders, engaged upon the vocal rendition of one of Pooley's own compositions, 'If there are no spots on a sugar cube then I've just put a dice in my tea.'

Omally halted to urinate into the doorway of Norman's papershop. 'That is for all waders to France,' he said.

'And for the exorbitant price of imported Fine Art Publications,' Pooley added, following suit.

'I have no axe to grind regarding the proprietor of this establishment,' said Soap, 'but I perform this function out of biological necessity and the spirit of pure badness!'

'Well said, Soap,' said Omally, 'I have surely misjudged you as an individual.'

'All for one and one for all,' said Jim Pooley, as three golden rapiers crossed in the moonlight. Amid much fly zipping, in which three separate shirt fronts were torn asunder, Soap said, 'I have maturing in my cellar several bottles of a home-produced claret which I think you gentlemen might find most pleasing.'

'If, in this newfound eloquence,' said Omally, 'you refer to that home-brewed lighter fuel which you call Chateau Distante, then we would be pleased to join you in a glass or three.'

8

Rumours abounded regarding the mysteries lurking behind the gaily painted front door of 15 Sprite Street. Strange noises had been heard in the nights coming as from the bowels of the earth, weird rumblings and vibrations. Cats gave Soap's back yard a wide berth and the milkman would venture no further than the front gate. How this ordinary little house had managed to gain such notoriety had always been beyond Omally's understanding. Believing as he did that Soap was little more than a buffoon, the way in which his neighbours avoided him and even crossed over the street before reaching his house had the Irishman baffled.

Pooley, to whom most doors swung open one way or another, had never yet managed to cross the portal, although he had employed many devious devices. He could probably have persuaded even Cerberus to leave his post and go off in search of a few dog biscuits. Soap had always been impervious. Thus it came as something of a shock to find himself and Omally now standing in the tiny front garden whilst Soap shushed them into silence and felt about in his pockets for the key.

'Now,' said Soap in a voice of deadly seriousness, 'before you enter I must ask that all you may see within must never be divulged to another living soul.'

Pooley, who had been in the Scouts for a day, raised two fingers to his forehead and said, 'Dib-Dib-Dib.' Omally, who was finding it hard to keep a straight face, licked his thumb and said, 'See this wet, see this dry, cut my throat if I tell a lie.'

Soap shrugged. 'I suppose I can expect no more. Now come, step carefully because the light will not function until the front door is closed and bolted from within.' He turned the key and pushed the door open into the stygian darkness within.

'You seem somewhat security-conscious, Soap,' said Omally.

Invisibly in the darkness Soap tapped his nose. 'One cannot be too careful when one is Keeper of the Great Mystery.'

Pooley whistled. 'The Great Mystery, eh?'

Soap threw the bolt, made several inexplicable clicking noises with what seemed to be switches and suddenly the room was ablaze with light.

'My God,' said Omally in a voice several octaves higher than usual. As the two stood blinking in the brightness Soap studied their faces with something approaching glee. These were the first mortals other than himself ever to see his masterwork and their awe and bewilderment were music to his eyes. 'What do you think then?'

Omally was speechless. Pooley just said, 'By the gods!'

The wall dividing the front room from the back parlour had been removed along with all the floorboards and joists on the ground floor. The section of flooring on which the three now stood was nothing more than the head of a staircase which led down and down into an enormous cavern of great depth which had been excavated obviously with elaborate care and over a long period of time. A ladder led up to the bedroom, the staircase having been long ago removed.

Omally stared down into the blackness of the mighty pit which yawned below him. 'Where does it go to?' he asked.

'Down,' said Soap. 'Always down but also around and about.'

'I must be going now,' said Pooley, 'must be up and making an early start, lots to do.'

'You've seen nothing yet,' said Soap, 'this is only the entrance.'

Omally was shaking his head in wonder. 'You dug this then?'

'No, not just me.' Soap laughed disturbingly. 'My great-grandfather began it shortly after the house was built, the lot fell then to my grandfather and down the line to me, last of the Distants, and guardian of the Great Mystery.'

78

'It's madness,' said Omally, 'the whole street will collapse.'

Soap laughed again. 'No, never, my family have the know as it were, they worked upon the Thames tunnel back in the days of Brunel.'

'But that collapsed.'

'Never, that's what the authorities said. The truth was that the navigators who dug that ill-fated pit stumbled upon an entrance to the worlds beneath and the tunnel had to be closed hurriedly and an excuse found to please the public.'

'You mean your old ones actually met up with these folk below?'

'Certainly. Shall we go down then?' said Soap.

Pooley said, 'I'll wait here.'

'I invited you in for a drink and a drink you are going to have.'

'I think that I am no longer thirsty,' said Jim, 'and after this, I think that I might take a vow of abstinence.'

'God,' said Omally, 'don't say such a thing even in jest.'

'Come on then,' said Soap, 'I will lead the way, it is not far to the first chamber.'

'First chamber?'

'Oh, yes, the caverns lead down into the bowels of the earth and subsidiary tunnels reach out in all directions, some for several miles at a stretch.' Soap flicked several more switches and led the way down the long flight of steps which reached downward into the darkness. As they descended the way before them sprung into light and the pathway behind fell to darkness.

'Clever that, eh?' said Soap. 'An invention of my great-grandfather's, don't ask me how it works because I don't know.'

'Must save some money on the electric bill,' said Jim.

'Electric bill?' Soap gave another of his hideous laughs which boomed along the corridors and down into the pit, returning in ghostly echoes back to them. 'I'm tapped directly into the grid. I've never paid for gas or electric as long as I've lived.'

Jim shook his head in dismay. 'This is unreal,' said he, 'how can all this exist and nobody know about it? And what did you and your forefathers do with all the earth from these diggings?'

'Aha,' said Soap having another tap at his nose, 'aha!'

At length they reached a vaulted chamber. Pooley later reckoned that it must have been about fifty yards in diameter but it was impossible to tell for certain as the lighting was only evident at whichever spot they stood.

'Now, about this wine,' Soap said. 'The temperature here is ideal for hocks, border rosés, Rhine wines, sweet sherry and growing mushrooms.'

From an enormous wine rack Soap withdrew a dusty-looking bottle and having no corkscrew readily at hand punched in the cork with his thumb. 'Bottoms up,' he said taking an enormous swig. He passed the bottle to Omally. 'Try it, it's a fifty-year-old vintage.'

Omally took a small indecisive sip, smacked his lips a few times, took a great swig and then one very very large swig. 'It is indeed good stuff,' said he, wiping his sleeve across his mouth and passing the bottle to Jim Pooley.

Jim, who had watched the Irishman's performance with interest, needed no telling twice. He put the bottle to his lips and drew off a long and satisfying draught.

'Very shortly now,' said Soap, accepting the bottle from Pooley and finishing it off, 'very shortly now contact will be made, I may be only inches away.'

Omally nodded, his eyes wandering over the wine rack. Soap pulled out another bottle and punched in the cork. 'Feel free,' he said.

Omally felt free.

'I have all the ancient maps you see, my forebears knew the locations and they knew it was the work of several generations, but now I am there, the moment is close at hand, mankind stands poised upon the brink of the greatest of all discoveries, the new Golden Age, the dawn of the new tomorrow . . .'

Soap's voice was rising in pitch. John Omally took another hasty pull upon the bottle and passed it hurriedly to Jim. 'We had best get out of here old pal, I have a feeling I know what's coming,' he whispered.

Soap was stalking about the cavern, arms raised, ranting at the top of his voice. Jim and John watched in stunned silence as the haunting light followed him from place to place, eerily illuminating his frantic motions. As he drew further from them his voice faded as if absorbed into the rock; his staccato movements and dramatic gestures lent to him the appearance of some bizarre mime artiste acting out an inexplicable saga beneath a travelling spotlight.

Soap lurched over to the wine rack and popped the cork from another bottle of wine. 'Here,' he said, 'here I'll show you, the legacy of the Distants, I'll show you.'

'We'll take your word for it,' said Omally.

'We really must be making a move now,' Jim added in a convincing tone which concealed the fact that he was having great difficulty in controlling his bladder.

'No, no! You are here, the only ones, you must be present when the Portals are unlocked, you cannot be allowed to leave!'

'That is what I thought was coming,' muttered Omally.

'This way, this way!' With the wine bottle bobbing in his hand and the eerie light shining about him Soap made his way rapidly down a side corridor leaving Pooley and Omally in the darkness.

'I cannot remember by which entrance we came into this place,' said John.

'I have no idea as to that myself,' Jim replied, 'and I am beginning to feel very poorly, vintage wine and Neville's Large making a poor cocktail.'

'I fear we must follow him or stand alone in the darkness,' said John, 'for the trick of light apparently works only to his account.' Jim wondered if magnetism might play some part in the situation. But now seemed a bad time for idle speculation, so he shrugged his shoulders in the darkness and the two set off to follow the glow-worm figure of Soap Distant as it moved away in front of them.

'I estimate, although it is impossible to be certain, that we must be somewhere beneath the London Road,' said John.

'I had the same feeling myself,' Jim replied. 'But I hope you realize and will record upon some tablet or graven plaque even though it be in my own memoriam that this whole thing is utterly fantastic and totally impossible.'

'Certainly these caverns appear to be the work of no earthly spade. I think that somewhere back along the bloodline of the Distants someone must have discovered this place by chance, although as to its original purpose and its manner of excavation, that is unimaginable.'

'Come quickly now!' screamed Soap, shining up ahead. 'We are nearly there!'

Of a sudden they came to a halt, the tunnel terminating unexpectedly in what appeared to be a pair of massive iron doors.

'You see!' screamed Soap. Omally noted that beads of perspiration were rolling down his forehead and that evil lines of white foam extended from the corners of his mouth and vanished beneath his chin. 'You see, you see, the holy Portal!'

Omally approached the gigantic doors. They were obviously of great age and looked capable of holding back the force of several armies. In the ghost light he could make out the heads of enormous rivets running in columns from top to bottom, and what appeared to be a large yet intricately constructed mechanism leading from two wheels that looked like the stopcocks on some titanic plumbing system. Central to each door was a brass plaque bearing upon it a heraldic device of uncertain origin.

It was the wheels that drew Omally's attention. There was something hauntingly familiar about them, and he tried to recall where he had seen them before. As he stepped forward Soap Distant barred his way. 'No, no!' he screamed. 'You may not touch, it is for me, I the last in the line, I who must fulfil the prophecies, I who must open the Portal.'

'Soap,' said John seriously, 'Soap, I do not feel that you should open these doors, something tells me that it would be a grave mistake.'

Pooley nodded wildly. 'Best leave them eh, Soap? Can't just go unlocking every door you come to.'

Soap turned and ran his hands over the pitted surface of the iron doors. 'I think,' said John who was fast realizing the gravity of this particular situation, 'I think Soap, that if you are adamant about this door opening business, then it would be better for you to be alone at the moment of opening. It would be wrong of us to stand around looking on. If the prophecies say that you are to open the Portal then open it you should. Alone!' Soap looked somewhat dubious but Omally continued unabashed, 'The honour must be yours, we have no right to share it, show us back to the foot of the staircase where we will await your glorious return.'

'Glorious return, yes.' Soap's voice was suddenly pensive. Pooley's head nodded enthusiastically while at the same time his legs crossed and recrossed themselves.

'So be it then!' Soap strode between the two men and as the light moved with him Omally took one last look at the gigantic doors, chewed upon his bottom lip a moment, then followed the receding Soap back along the death-black corridor.

Soap's will-o-the-wisp figure danced along ahead of

them like a marsh phantom, weaving through the labyrinth of tunnels and finally into the huge central chamber. Peering up Omally could make out the lights of 15 Sprite Street, a reassuring glow high above. Soap stood breathing heavily through his nose, his fists clenched and his face a wax mask of sweat. Pooley was clutching desperately at his groin. Omally shifted nervously from one foot to the other.

'You wait then!' said Soap suddenly. 'Tonight is the night towards which the entire course of mankind's history has inevitably run. Tonight the ultimate mysteries will be known! Tonight the Portal will be opened!'

'Yes, yes,' said Omally, 'we'll wait here then.'

Soap's eyes had glazed. It was clear that he no longer saw Pooley or Omally; he had become focused both mentally and physically upon some distant point. His voice boomed on, filling the caverns, washing over the black rocks like some evil sonic wave. 'Blessed be the Gods of Ancient Earth. The dark ones and dwellers of the deep places. Great Rigdenjyepo, King of the World, Lord of the Nether Regions, Guardian of the Inner Secrets!'

Omally cupped his hands about his ears and muttered the rosary beneath his breath. Pooley, whose bladder was on the point of giving up the unequal struggle, rolled his eyes desperately.

Without warning Soap suddenly jerked forward. The two friends watched his glittering form flickering away into the darkness, his voice bouncing to and fro about the vaulted corridors, until finally the light died away and the ghastly echoing cries became only a memory.

Omally and Pooley stood a moment faintly outlined by the light above. Slowly they turned to face one another, came to a joint decision which argued strongly for the authenticity of mental telepathy, and with one movement made for the stairs.

Minutes later on the corner of Sprite Street Omally

84

crouched, bent double, hands upon knees, gasping for breath. Pooley did little other than sigh deeply as he relieved himself through the railings into the Memorial Park. Between the gasps, gulps and Woodbine coughs, Omally uttered various curses, veiled blasphemies and vows of impending violence directed solely and unswervingly towards Soap Distant.

Pooley finished his ablutions to the accompaniment of one last all-embracing sigh. Having zipped himself into respectability he withdrew from his inner pocket a bottle of Soap's fifty-year-old wine. 'Shame to leave empty-handed,' he said. 'One for the road John?'

'One indeed,' the Irishman replied. He took a great pull and swallowed deeply.

Pooley said 'What should we do? Soap is clearly mad!'

Omally wiped his mouth and passed the bottle across. The full moon shone down upon them, in the distance cars rolled over the flyover and a late-night dog returning from some canine revelry loped across the road. All seemed so normal, so mundane, that their experience within the caverns was already taking on the nature of a bad dream. The clock on the Memorial Library struck two.

'If all that we saw was real and not some shared vision, I am truly at a loss to know what action we should take. Soap is not harming anybody, although I am certain that such an enormous maze of tunnels should be reported to the authorities, if only that they might be certified as safe. While I was down there I had the feeling that most of Brentford could have sunk easily into them, still leaving room for half of the Chiswick High Road.'

'But what about the doors?' said Jim. 'Surely one man could not open them alone, they looked pretty hefty. You don't really believe that they lead into the inner earth do you?'

Omally shook his head. 'I haven't a clue, although those crests, I've seen them before somewhere.'

All further conversation was however stifled by a low and ghastly rumble which came apparently from the lower end of Albany Road. Like a hideous subterranean clap of thunder it rolled forward. From far along the street, lights began to blink on in upstairs windows. Cats began to whine and dogs to bark.

Pooley said, 'It's an earthquake!'

Omally crossed himself.

Somewhere deep within the earth a monstrous force was stirring; great ripples ran up the paving stones of Sprite Street. A shock wave spread across the grass of the Memorial Park, stiffening the coarse blades into regimented rows. A great gasp which issued from no human throat shuddered up from the very bowels of the earth, building to an enormous crescendo.

Omally felt inclined to run but his knees had turned to jelly. Pooley had assumed the foetal position. By now Sprite Street was a blaze of light, windows had been thrown up, front doors flung open, people issued into the street clad in ludicrous pyjamas and absurd carpet slippers. Then as rapidly as it had begun, the ominous rumbling ceased, seemed to pass away beneath them and fade away. The denizens of Sprite Street suddenly found themselves standing foolishly about the road in the middle of the night. Shuffling their carpet slippers and feigning indifference to conceal their acute embarrassment they backed into their respective abodes and quietly closed their front doors.

The night was still again, the lights of Sprite Street dimmed away and Pooley rose to his feet patting dirt from his tweeds. 'John,' said he, 'if you will excuse me I am now going home to my bed where I intend to remain for an indefinite period. I fear that the doings of this evening have forever destroyed my vitality and that I am a broken man.'

'Certainly this has been an evening I should prefer to

forget,' said Omally. With that he put his arm about his companion's shoulder and the two friends wandered away into the night.

9

It was indeed a mystery. The pressmen thrust their way through the crowds of baffled onlookers and peered disbelievingly down from the bridge to the muddied track of twisted bicycle frames, old tin cans and discarded pram wheels which spread away into the distance. How an entire one-mile stretch of canal from the river lock to that of the windscreen-wiper factory could simply have vanished overnight seemed beyond anybody's conjecture.

'It couldn't have gone out through the river lock,' an old bargee explained, 'it is high water on the Thames and the river is six foot up the lock gates on that side.'

'And at the other end?'

The bargee gave his inquisitor a look of contempt. 'What, travel uphill into the next lock do you mean?' The interviewer coloured up and sought business elsewhere.

Archroy, who was a great follower of Charles Fort, explained what had happened. 'Teleportation,' said the lad. 'The water has been teleported away by those in sore need of it, possibly inhabitants of a nearby sphere, most likely the moon.'

The pressmen, although ever-anxious to accept any solution as long as it was logical, newsworthy or simply sensational, seemed strangely diffident towards his claims for the existence of telekinetic lunar beams.

It was certainly a most extraordinary event however, one which would no doubt catapult Brentford once more into the national headlines, and at least bring good trade to the Flying Swan. Neville was going great guns behind the bar. The cash register rang musically and the no-sale sign bobbed up and down like a demented jack-in-the-box.

'And don't forget,' said the part-time barman above the din, 'Thursday night is Cowboy Night.'

Jammed into an obscure corner and huddled over his pint, Jim Pooley watched with loathing the fat backside of an alien pressman which filled his favourite bar stool. Omally edged through the crush with two pints of Large. 'It was only after I got home that I remembered where I'd seen those crests before,' he explained as he wedged himself in beside Pooley. 'They were the coat of arms of the Grand Junction Water Works, those doors must have been part of the floodgate system from old Brentford dock.' Pooley sucked upon his pint, his face a sullen mask of displeasure. 'Then what of old Soap?'

A devilish smile crossed Omally's face. 'Gone, washed away.' His fingers made the appropriate motions. 'So much for old Rigdenjyepo and the burrowers beneath, eh?'

Pooley hunched closer to his pint. 'A pox on it all,' said he. 'The Swan packed full of these idiots, old Soap flushed away round the proverbial S-bend and Cowboy Night looming up before us with about as much promise as the coming of Ragnorok!'

Omally grinned anew. 'There are many pennies to be made from an event such as this; I myself have organized several tours of the vicinity for this afternoon at a pound a throw.'

Pooley shook his head in wonder. 'You don't waste a lot of time, do you?'

'Mustn't let the grass grow under the old size nines.'

'Tell me, John,' said Jim, 'how is it now that a man such as yourself who possesses such an amazing gift for the making of the well known "fast buck" has not set himself up in business long ago and since retired upon the proceeds?'

'I fear,' said John, 'that it is the regularity of "the work" which depresses me, the daily routine which saps the vital fluids and destroys a man's brain. I prefer greatly to live upon wits I have and should they ever desert me then, maybe then, I shall take to "the work" as a full-time occupation.' Omally took from his pocket a 'Book Here for Canal Tours' sign and began a 'roll up, roll up' routine.

Pooley rose from the table and excused himself. He had no wish to become involved in Omally's venture. He wished only to forget all about subterranean caverns and vanishing canal water, his only thoughts on that matter were as to what might happen should they attempt to refill the stretch of canal. Was Sprite Street lower geographically than the canal? If it was, would the attempt flood the entire neighbourhood? It really didn't bear thinking about. Pooley slouched over to the bar and ordered another pint.

'Looking forward to Thursday night I'll bet, Jim,' said Neville.

Pooley did not answer. Silently he sipped at his ale and let the snippets of barside conversation wash disjointedly about him. 'And my old grandad is sitting by the dartboard when he threw,' came a voice, 'and the dart went straight through the lobe of his right ear.' Pooley sipped at his ale. 'And as they went to pull it out,' the voice continued, 'the old man said "No don't, it's completely cured the rheumatism in my left knee."'

Pooley yawned. Along the bar from him huddled in their usual conspiratorial poses were Brentford's two resident jobbing builders, Hairy Dave and Jungle John, so named for their remarkably profuse outcroppings of cerebral hair. The twin brothers were discussing what seemed to be a most complex set of plans which they had laid out before them on the bar top.

'I don't think I can quite understand all this,' said Dave.

'It's a poser for certain,' his brother replied.

'I can't see why he wants the altar to be so large.'

'I can't see why there aren't to be any pews.'

'Nor an organ.'

'Seems a funny kind of a chapel to me.'

Pooley listened with interest; surely no-one in the neighbourhood could be insane enough to commission those two notorious cowboys to build a chapel?

Hairy Dave said, 'I can't see why the plans should be written in Latin.'

'Oh,' said his brother, 'it's Latin is it? I thought it was trigonometry.'

Pooley could contain his curiosity no longer, and turned to the two master builders. 'Hello lads, how's business?'

John snatched the plan from the bar top and crumpled it into his jacket. 'Ah, oh . . .' said his brother, 'good day Jim and how is yourself?'

'For truth,' Pooley replied, 'I am not a well man. Recently I have been party to events which have seriously damaged my health. But let us not talk of me, how is business? I hear that you are on the up and up, won a large contract I heard.'

The two brothers stared at each other and then at Pooley. 'Not us,' said one. 'Haven't had a bite in weeks,' said the other.

'My, my,' said Jim, 'my informant was certain that you had a big one up your sleeve, something of an ecclesiastical nature I think.'

John clutched the plan to his bosom. 'Haven't had a bite in weeks,' his brother reiterated. 'Been very quiet of late.' Hairy Dave shook his head, showering Pooley with dandruff. Jungle John did the same.

Neville stormed up the bar. 'Less of that you two,' said the part-time barman, 'I've warned you before about contaminating my cheese rolls.'

'Sorry Neville,' said the brothers in unison, and rising from their seats they left the bar, leaving their drinks untouched.

'Most strange,' said Pooley. 'Most astonishing.'

'Those two seem very thick together lately,' said Neville. 'It seems that almost everybody in this damn pub is plotting something.'

'Tell me Neville,' said Jim, 'did you ever see any more of our mystery tramp?'

'Thankfully no,' said the part-time barman, 'and with this canal business taking up everybody's attention, let's hope that no more will ever be said about him.'

Pooley shook his head. 'I wouldn't be too certain of that,' he said doubtfully.

Captain Carson stood upon the canal bridge staring down into the mud and idly casting his eyes along the bank to where an official-looking Mr Omally, dressed in a crested cap and jaunty blazer, led a group of Swedish students along the rutted track towards the woodyard. The Captain's loathing for tourists almost overshadowed that which he felt for the figure standing calmly at his side, hands in pockets and smoking seaman's shag in one of the Captain's favourite pipes. The figure was no longer distinguishable as the wretched and ill-clad monstrosity which had cast an evil shadow across his porch but two short weeks ago. Cleanly-shaven and smelling of Bryl-creem, the figure was dressed in a blue rollneck sweater and a pair of the Captain's best khaki trousers, a yachting cap and a pair of sailing shoes.

The tramp had become a kind of witches' familiar to the Captain, haunting his dreams and filling his waking hours with dread. Somehow, and the Captain was at a loss to explain how, the tramp had now permanently installed himself at the Mission. During meals he sat in the Captain's chair whilst the Captain was obliged to eat in the kitchen. No matter which way the Captain turned the tramp was always there, reclining upon the porch, smoking his cigarettes, lounging in the cosiest fireside chair, sipping rum. He had tricked the Captain, again by means that the Captain was at a loss to understand, out of his chair, his tobacco, his food, drink and finally out of his bed.

The tramp sucked deeply upon the Captain's briar and blew out a stream of multicoloured smoke. 'There would seem to be unusual forces at work in this neighbourhood,' he observed.

The Captain surveyed his unwelcome guest with ill-concealed hatred. 'There would indeed,' he replied. Somehow deep down in the lowest depths of his loathing for the tramp a strange and grudging respect was beginning to stir. The Captain could, again, not fully account for these feelings, but now, clean-shaven and well dressed as he was, the tramp seemed to exude a definite air of authority. Possibly of nobility. It was inexplicable. The aura of evil which surrounded him was almost palpable and the Captain seemed to sense his approach at all times; a kind of darkness travelled with the red-eyed man, a funereal coldness. The Captain shuddered.

'Cold?' said the tramp. 'We'd best be going back then, don't want you coming down with any summer colds now, do we?'

The Captain followed the tramp back towards the Mission with doglike obedience. As the tramp strode on ahead of him the Captain watched the broad shoulders swing to and fro in a perfect rhythm. Surely the tramp had grown, surely his bearing was prouder, finer than before.

No wonder, all the food he eats, thought the Captain. But who was he? His age was indeterminate; he could be anything between twenty and fifty. There was a vagueness about his features which eluded definition. The Captain had gone to great lengths to draw some information from him regarding his name, family and background, but the tramp was infuriatingly evasive. He had made only one statement upon these matters and this was, 'There are five

92

iere that know my name and when they speak it, all shall know.' As to who these five were, the Captain was unable to guess. Possibly the tramp alluded to five of the fictional names he had quoted from the Mission's yearly reports.

The tramp turned into the Mission, which he opened with his own key. The Captain followed meekly; the tramp was wearing down his resistance to a point that he no longer questioned any of his actions.

'I wish to speak to you upon a delicate matter,' said the tramp suddenly. 'It is a matter which affects both our futures and one which I know lies heavily upon your soul.' The Captain raised a bristling eyebrow. 'Possibly you will wish to open the reserve bottle of rum you keep in the locked cupboard beneath the stairs in order to fortify yourself for what I am about to say.'

The Captain humbly obeyed. The two seated themselves upon either side of the Captain's table and two large tots of rum were poured.

'It has come to my notice,' said the tramp, 'that there is one not far from here who would do us harm.'

The Captain's face showed no expression but his mind paid silent homage to anyone who would wish ill upon his guest.

'One Brian Crowley,' said the tramp. The Captain started up in astonishment. 'It has come to my notice,' the tramp continued, 'that this man harbours the desire to close down this Mission and to dismiss you, my honourable host, without thanks or pension. You who have done so much for the poor and needy, you who have dedicated your life to the unfortunate.' The Captain shifted uneasily in his seat. 'There is, I understand, a conspiracy between this Crowley,' again he spoke the hated name, 'and a certain Councillor Wormwood, to demolish this Mission in order to extend the Butts Car Park.'

The Captain bit upon his lip. So that was their intention

93

was it? How the tramp could have come by this intelligence was, of course, beyond any conjecture, but the Captain hung upon his every word. 'I have given the matter much thought,' he told the tramp. 'Night after night I have lain cursing the very name of Crowley and racking my brain for a solution, but none have I found.'

'I think that one might be relatively close at hand,' said the tramp, 'in fact, I feel its warm breath upon my neck even now.' The Captain poured two more large tots of rum. 'We shall invite these two individuals to dinner,' said the tramp.

The Captain bent double in a fit of frenzied coughing. 'Calm yourself,' said the tramp.

'I fear,' said the Captain, 'that the breath you feel upon your neck is one of severe halitosis.'

The tramp's face was without expression, he drank down his tot of rum and watched the Captain, his eyes unblinking, two drops of blood upon colourless orbs. 'Thursday night would be ideal,' said the tramp.

'But what if they won't come. After all, Crowley hates me and Wormwood will never want to expose himself in any way.'

'They will come,' said the tramp, 'and I think I can promise you a most entertaining evening.' His ghastly eyes glittered with a fierce luminosity and the Captain tossed back his rum with a quivering hand.

Brian Crowley held up the gilt-edged invitation card to the sunlight. It presented a most extraordinary appearance, almost transparent and clearly wrought of the finest vellum. Never for one moment would he have attributed such style, taste or elegance to the old sea captain. The edging of the card had more the look of being worked in gold leaf than sprayed in the gilded paint of the printer's shop. The typeface was of a design that Brian did not recognize, its finely drawn serifs and cunning arabesques

...eeming of almost Islamic origin. And the smell of it, something stirred within him, some recollection from his past. It was the smell of incense, church incense. He had smelt it many times before, as a choirboy at St Mary's, that was it, church incense.

While Brian's romantic imagination ran in luminous spirals about the card the callous side to his nature gloated, for the card which had flopped through his burnished letterbox to land with the many plain brown wrappers upon the purple shagpile bore an inscription which made his heart leap for joy.

YOU ARE FORMALLY INVITED
TO A RECEPTION & BANQUET
ON THURSDAY 15TH JUNE
AT THE SEAMAN'S MISSION, BRENTFORD
IN CELEBRATION OF THAT HONORABLE
ESTABLISHMENT'S CENTENARY YEAR
AND ALSO TO HONOUR
CAPTAIN HORATIO B. CARSON
UPON THE ANNOUNCEMENT OF HIS
RETIREMENT

Black Tie   R.S.V.P.
7.30 p.m. for 8.00 p.m.   Admission by this card only

Brian sighed deeply and pressed the scented card to his lips. Things could not have been better, the Captain to announce his retirement! He had not realized that it was the Mission's Centenary Year, but it was clear that for the sake of appearances he must attend. The rest of the Committee would be there and his absence would not go unnoticed.

He would R.S.V.P. this very morning. At last the wheels of fortune were beginning to turn to his advantage. He could almost smell the delicious odours of Mario's cooking.

10

As Monday turned into Tuesday and Tuesday did what was expected of it the patrons of the Flying Swan grew increasingly uneasy. Strange changes were taking place amid the timeless décor of the saloon bar. A grotesquely moth-eaten bison's head had materialized above the counter and traces of sawdust had begun to appear about the floor. A large painting of a rotund and pinkly powdered female, clad only in the scantiest of ostrich-feather boas and an enticing if tobacco-stained smile, had been hung lopsidedly over the dartboard. 'A temporary inconvenience,' Neville assured the irate dart-players. 'Hold on thar pardners.' But the casters of the feathered flight sought their amusements elsewhere at Jack Lane's or the New Inn.

'Son of a gun,' said Jim Pooley.

It was John Omally, a man who looked upon himself, no matter how ironically, as a guardian of the neighbourhood's morals, who was the first to notice the new selection which had found its way into the disabled jukebox. 'The Wheel of the Wagon is Broken?' he said suddenly, his coarse accent cutting through the part-time barman's thoughts like a surgeon's scalpel. 'A Four-Legged Friend?'

Neville hung his head in shame. 'It is regrettable,' said he, 'but the brewery feel it necessary to alter the selection on that thing to keep in pace with what they think to be the vogue.'

'Come on now,' said Omally, 'surely it is the brewery who are dictating this particular vogue with their horrendous plans for a Western Barbeque and all its attendant horrors.'

'Don't forget the extension and the cheap drink,' Neville reminded his Irish customer.

Omally cocked his head thoughtfully to one side. 'It is a poor consolation for the ghastly transfiguration currently taking place in this establishment, I am thinking.'

Jim agreed. 'To think I'd see the day when three of the Swan's finest arrowmen defect to Jack Lane's.'

Neville chewed upon his lip and went back to polishing the glasses.

'I see you are still sporting your official guide's cap,' said Pooley suddenly.

Omally smiled and reverently removed the thing, turning it between his fingers. 'You would not believe the business I am doing along that stretch of dried-up canal.'

Jim shook his head. 'Although to the average man the disappearance of a canal must seem an extraordinary thing, I frankly fail to see what pleasure can be derived from paying out good money to wander up and down the bank peering into the mud. By God, I was down that way myself earlier and the smell of it is no pleasant treat to the nostrils.'

'I have devised a most fascinating programme,' the Irishman said, 'wherein I inform the visitors as to the many varied and bizarre legends associated with that stretch of canal.'

'Oh yes?' said Jim.

'We visit the very spot where Caesar encamped prior to his march upon Chiswick.'

'Really?'

'The place where the ghost of Little Nellie Tattersall, who cast away her earthly shell into the murky depths one dark and wintry Victorian night, still calls her tragic cry.'

'Calls her tragic cry?'

'And to the site of the famous Ripper murder of 1889. It's a highly educational tour.'

'And they believe all this drivel?'

'Whether they believe it or not is unimportant. At the current rate of business I may well shortly be having to employ an assistant to deal with the parties that are forced to queue for several hours at a stretch. There are more of them every day. There are many pennies to be made in this game,' the Irishman said, flamboyantly ordering two pints.

Pooley peered round at the crowds which swelled the Swan. Certainly they were a strange breed, with uniformly blank expressions and a kind of colourless aura surrounding them. These were the faces which one saw jammed into a tight crowd surrounding an accident victim or one fallen in a fight. Ambulance men have to force past them and little short of outright violence will budge them an inch.

Old Pete entered the bar, his half terrier close upon his heel. 'There's a coachload of Japs out there asking for the guide,' he told Omally.

'Duty calls,' said John, leaping to his feet and thrusting his official cap on his head, 'I shall see you anon.'

Jim bid his companion farewell and with a satisfied smile settled down to tackle the two untouched pints.

'That will be ten and six please,' said Neville the part-time barman.

'Damn and blast,' said Jim Pooley.

Norman threw the door bolt and turned over the sign which informed customers that he was 'Closed Even for the Sale of Rubber Bondage Monthly'. Rubbing his hands together he strode across the shop and disappeared through the door behind the counter. The small kitchenette-cum-living-room at the rear had been allowed of late to run somewhat to seed. The sink was filled by a crazy mountain of food-besmirched crockery now in a state long beyond reclamation. Cigarette ends spotted the linoleum like the pock-marks of some tropical disease and great piles of newspapers, fine art publications and scientific journals were stacked into every available corner.

'Every cloud has a silver lining,' he said. Reaching to the back door he lifted down and donned a leather apron, welder's goggles and a pair of rubber gloves. 'And now, the end is near . . . And so, I face the final curtain.' With a grandiloquent gesture he crossed the room and flung aside a ragged strip of cloth which curtained a corner. There, lit by the kitchenette's naked light bulb and glowing like a rare pearl torn from its oyster shell, hung what must surely have been one of the most extraordinary suits of clothes ever viewed by mortal man. It was a stunning salmon-pink, and tailored from the best quality PVC. Its body and sleeves glittered with rhinestones and sequins worked into patterns roughly suggestive of Indian headwear and western horsemen. The trousers were similarly ornamented and ended in massive bell-bottoms edged with braid and long golden tassles. Emblazoned across the shoulders of the jacket in letters of gold, marked out with what were obviously at least a dozen sets of christmas-tree fairy lights, were the words: THE SPIRIT OF THE OLD WEST.

It was Norman's *pièce-de-résistance*, and it actually worked. In truth of course, no human hand, no matter how skilled, could have wrought the creation of such a costume in the short time given as notice by the Swan of the impending Cowboy Extravaganza. No, this was the work of several long years. Originally intended as THE SPIRIT OF THE JUBILEE, it had been far from completion at the time of that event and Norman had feared that its day would never dawn. It had taken him several long and sleepless nights to alter the coronation coach into a covered wagon and change the Prince of Wales feathers into the war-bonnet of an Indian chieftain. The effect, all in all, was one to bring a tear of pride into the eye of its creator.

The stetson had been a bit of a problem, as his source of PVC, a young woman customer who worked in the rubber factory, had been dismissed for unauthorized removal of the company's stock. He had persevered, however, and done what he could with an aged trilby and an improvised brim. This he had sprayed gold and sprinkled with glitter from the carnival shop.

The electrification of the fairy lights had been the biggest problem, and Norman's rudimentary knowledge of the workings of electricity had cost him many a scorched fingertip. He had toyed with the idea of simply running an extension lead to the nearest available wall socket but this was too limiting to his movements. Thus Norman, through his usual system of trial and error, had perfected an efficient though weighty set of precharged solid-cell batteries which were strapped about his waist very much in the nature of Batman's utility belt. A set of switches upon the buckle enabled him to alter the fluctuation and sequence of the lights in a manner both pleasing and artistic.

Happily the PVC of the suit acted as an excellent insulator and the whole contraption was earthed through leads which ran down the backs of his trouser legs to brass plates nailed to the heels of a pair of rented cowboy boots.

Norman tinkered happily about with screwdriver and soldering iron, here replacing a defunct bulb, here resoldering a faulty socket. Tomorrow all Brentford would salute his creative genius. No longer would they smile indulgently and allude to his previous failed ventures with unconcealed mirth. He'd show 'em.

Norman flicked a switch upon his belt buckle. Sadly he was not wearing the brass-heeled boots on this particular occasion and the crackle of electrical energy which snapped through his fingers crossed his eyes and rattled his upper set.

'Damn and blast,' said Norman.

Archroy sat in the doorway of his allotment shed, elbows

upon knees and chin cupped in the palms of his hands. At his feet a cup of cocoa was rapidly growing cold. His wife was up to something back at the marital home; there was a new roll of wire netting standing ominously in the hall and a large stack of red flettons in the back yard. She had muttered something about an aviary on the last occasion he had seen her. Also there was the affair of the beans weighing heavily upon his narrow shoulders.

Archroy sighed tragically. Why couldn't life be the straightforward affair it had once been?

As he sat in his misery Archroy's eyes wandered idly in the direction of Omally's allotment plot. There upon the rugged patch of earth stood the solitary stake which marked out the location of the planted bean. Archroy had diligently watered the spot night after night. Omally had not been down to the site once during the last couple of weeks, and Archroy felt he had lost interest in the whole affair. He rose from his orange box and slouched over to inspect the Irishman's dark strip of land. The stake appeared slightly crooked so he straightened it, stooping to smooth over the earth. There were no signs of life whatever, no pleasant green stripling or young plantoid raising its head to the sunlight. Nothing but the barren earth. Archroy bent his head near to the ground and squinted. This was, after all, his last bean and if this failed he would have nothing whatever to recompense him for the tragic loss of his Morris Minor.

Perhaps if he just dug it up for a moment to check that it was all right, it couldn't do any harm. Then if it showed any signs of life he could always replace it. No, it wouldn't hurt, one quick look. He needn't mention it to Omally.

The earth was soft and damp from its daily watering. Almost at once his fingers closed about a damp and clammy object which he hastily brought to the surface. Gently laying it upon his palm he smoothed away the dark earth which clung to it, exposing to his horror the familiar outlines of a common seed potato. Archroy's expression became one of grave concern. He hurled the potato aside and flung himself to his knees. Rooting to and fro across the plot like a demented hog in search of a truffle he delved into the earth. Oblivious to the muddy destruction of his tweeds, Archroy covered every inch of the plot to a depth of some ten inches.

There was nothing; the plot was as barren as a desert, although now it would be ready to yield many varieties of vegetable, having been so thoroughly turned. Archroy rose to his feet, mud clinging to the knees and elbows of his suit; his *toupet*, which the manufacturers had assured him would stand up to a channel swim, had become strangely detached from its moorings and swung above him like a spinnaker.

Archroy turned his eyes to the potato. So it was treachery, no wonder the Irishman had not troubled to come down and water the plot. Why should he wish to water a seed potato?

'Damn and blast,' said Archroy.

Captain Carson watched the vehicle approach the Mission. He had never seen anything quite like it before. The enormous lorry was absolutely, unutterably black. Not a trace of colour was there upon its deathly sides, but for a single red crest emblazoned in the likeness of a bull. The vehicle moved in total silence and seemed strangely lacking in form, like some half-remembered version of the way a lorry should be. It bore neither headlights nor radiator grille, and the windscreen, if such it were, was of the same night hue as the rest of the vehicle. The doors lacked any sign of handles nor even a crack or line to signify their location. It was a thing to inspire nightmare. Soundlessly it drew up before the Mission door, enveloping the Captain within its cold shadow. Shaking away his feeling of revulsion the Captain squared his shoulders and stalked up the short path to confront the dark vehicle.

Certainly it was a unique and striking thing. The Captain noted with interest that there was not a single sharp corner, edge or angle to it, the surfaces flowed away from one another in curve after curve.

The Captain stretched out an inquisitive finger to touch the lorry but withdrew it at a vastly accelerated rate. It was as if he had thrust it into a vat of liquid oxygen. 'By the gods,' he said, examining his frost-bitten digit.

As if in response to the Captain's oath there was a click near the front of the vehicle and the cab door swung slowly open. The Captain wandered towards it upon hesitant feet. No light showed from within, it was like peering into the black void of space.

Without warning a figure appeared from the darkness as one stepping from behind a velvet curtain. He was as black and featureless as his conveyance. Down from the cab he climbed, bearing in his gloved hand a clipboard to which was attached a sheaf of papers.

'Captain Horatio B. Carson?' he enquired in a voice of indeterminate accent. The Captain nodded slowly and without enthusiasm. 'Delivery.'

'I ordered nothing!'

'There is no cause for alarm,' said a soft voice behind and slightly above the Captain.

Turning, the Captain squinted up into the face of the tramp. 'What is all this?' he demanded.

'Kindly assist this gentleman with the removal of all the old furniture from the dining-room.'

'Old furniture? You can't do that, the furniture is the property of the Mission.'

'Kindly do as I request, all will be explained to you later.'

The Captain threw up his arms in a gesture of helplessness and led the dark figure into the Mission, where under the tramp's direction the two stripped the dining-room of its furnishings. When these had been heaped into an untidy pile in the yard, the tramp said, 'And now if you will be so kind, the new furniture is to be brought in. May I beg your caution when handling it as some pieces are of great worth and all irreplaceable.'

The Captain shook his head in bewilderment and mopped the perspiration from his brow with an over-sized red gingham handkerchief. For the next half an hour his life was nothing short of a nightmare. The truck's dark occupant swung open the rear doors of the mighty vehicle, exposing another fathomless void. Working without apparent effort and clearly oblivious to the great weight of some of the more ornate and heavily gilded pieces of furniture he and the Captain unloaded and installed in the Mission an entire suite, table, chairs, sideboard, cabinet, a pair of golden candelabra, velvet wall-hangings and a crested coat of arms. All these items would clearly have been well at home amid the splendours of Fontainebleau. Each was the work of exquisite and painstaking craftsmanship, and each bore etched into the polished woodwork or inlaid in precious metals the motif of the bull.

When all was installed the Captain numbly put his signature to the manifest, which was printed in a language he did not understand. The driver returned to his black cab, the door swinging closed behind him leaving no trace of its presence. The vast black vehicle departed as silently as it had arrived. The Captain leant upon the Mission porch exhausted, breathing heavily and clutching at his heart.

'There is one more thing to be done and you may return to your quarters,' said the tramp looming above him.

'I can do no more,' gasped the Captain, 'leave me here to die, I have seen enough of life, too much in fact.'

'Come now,' said the tramp, 'no need to be melodramatic, this is but a simple task.' He handed the Captain a gallon can of petrol. 'That rubbish in the garden, dispose of it.'

'What?'

'It is offensive, put it to the torch!'

The Captain took the can. Upon giddy legs he stumbled through the Mission and out into the yard to confront the mound of furniture which had served him these thirty long years.

'The torch,' ordered the tramp.

The Captain's fingers tightened around the petrol cap, he was powerless to resist. 'Damn you,' he mumbled beneath his breath. 'Damn and blast you to hell.'

11

It was Thursday. The sun shone enthusiastically down through Neville's window and twinkled upon the white cowboy suit which hung in its plastic covering upon the bedroom door. Neville raised a sleepy eyelid and yawned deeply. Today was going to be one to remember. He cast an eye towards the suit, pristine as a bridal gown. Beside it upon the chair hung the silver pistols in their studded holsters and the fringed white stetson. He put a hand beneath the pillow and withdrew the chromium sheriff's star. Squinting at it through his good eye he noted well how it caught the light and how the mirrored surfaces shone like rare jewels. Yes, he was going to look pretty dapper tonight, that was for sure.

He was still, however, harbouring some doubts regarding the coming festivities. It was always impossible to gauge exactly what the locals might do. He knew some would attend, if only for a chance at the scotch and to take advantage of the cheap drink and extended hours. But the dart players had already defected and the seasoned drinkers were hard upon their heels, tired of being jockeyed from their time-honoured places at the bar by the continual stream of tourists and sensation-seekers currently filling the Swan. But still, thought Neville, if only a small percentage of the morbid canal viewers turned up, the evening would be far from dull.

Neville climbed out of bed, placing his star reverently upon the side table. He stifled another yawn, straightened his shoulders and stepped to the window. From Neville's eyrie high in the upper eaves of the Swan he was afforded an excellent view of the surrounding district. With the aid of his spyglass he could see out between the flatblocks as far as the roundabout and the river. He could make out the gasometer and the piano museum and on further into the early haze where the cars were already moving dreamily across the flyover.

It was a vista which never ceased to inspire him. Neville's spirit was essentially that of the Brentonian. From this one window alone he could see five of Brentford's eighteen pubs, he could watch the larval inhabitants of the flatblocks stirring in their concrete cocoons, Andy Johnson's milkfloat rattling along the Kew Road and the paperboy standing in the shadow of the bus shelter smoking a stolen Woodbine and reading one of Norman's Fine Art Publications, destined for a discerning connoisseur in Sprite Street.

This morning, as he drew great draughts of oxygen through his nose, an ominous and hauntingly familiar perfume filled Neville's head. He had scented it vaguely upon the winds for many weeks, and had noted with growing apprehension that each day it was a little stronger, a little nearer, a little more clearly defined. What it was and what it meant he knew not, only that it was of evil portent. Neville pinched at his nostrils, shrugging away this disturbing sensation. Probably it was only nerves. He stepped into his carpet slippers and down two flights of stairs to the bar.

The paperboy, seeing the bar lights snap on, abandoned his study of the female form and crossed the Ealing Road to deliver Neville's newspaper.

Omally was stirring from his nest. Wiping the sleep away from his eyes with a soiled pyjama sleeve the man from the Emerald Isle rose, a reluctant phoenix, from the ashes of the night before. There was little fire evident in this rare bird, and had it not been for the urgency of the day which lay before him he would surely have returned to the arms of whatever incendiary morpheus rekindled his combustible plumage. He lit a pre-cornflake Woodbine and through the fits of terrible coughing paid his early morning respects to the statuette of Our Lady which stood noseless yet benign upon the mantelpiece.

The Irishman's suite of rooms was far from what one would describe as sumptuous. The chances of it appearing in *House and Garden*, except possibly as an example of the 'Before' school of design, were pretty remote. Upon this particular morning, however, the monotone décor was overwhelmed by an incongruous and highly coloured object which stood upon the Fablon table-top in Omally's dining-room. It was a large and gaudy carton bearing upon its decorative sides the logo of the carnival shop.

Within this unlikely container, which Omally had smuggled home in a potato sack, was nothing less than an accurate reproduction, correct to the smallest detail, even to the point of spurs and mask, of that well-known and much-loved mode of range-wear affected by the Lone Ranger. It was also identical in every way to the one which Jim Pooley had hired not an hour previous to the furtive Omally's entrance to the carnival shop.

For Mr Jeffreys, who ran the faltering business, it had been a day he would long remember. How he had come into the original possession of the ten identical costumes was a matter he preferred to forget. But upon this particular day that he should, within a few short hours, not only hire out these two costumes, but the other eight to boot, was quite beyond all expectation. Possibly the ancient series had returned to the small screen, bringing about a revival. Anyway, whatever the cause, he didn't care; the cash register had crashed away merrily and there would soon be enough in it to pay off the bill for the two dozen Superman costumes he had similarly ordered in error.

Neville picked up his newspaper from the welcome mat and gazed about the bar. He had been up until three in the morning arranging the finishing touches. Little remained of the Swan's original character; the entire bar now resembled to a Model T the interior of a western saloon. The sawdust which had for the last few days been getting into everybody's beer now completely smothered the floor. Wanted posters, buffalo horns, leather saddles and items of cowboy paraphernalia lined the walls.

The shorts glasses had been piled in pyramids behind the bar and the place was gaudy with advertisements promoting 'Old Snakebelly – The Drink That Made the South Rise Again'. This doubtful beverage was the sole cause of the Swan's bizarre transformation. It was the brainchild of the brewery owner's eldest son, who had spent two weeks on a package tour of the States and had returned with a mid-Atlantic accent and a penchant for Randolph Scott impersonations. It was not the finest blend of spirits ever to grace a bar optic, and would probably have been more at home removing tar from bargees' gumboots. The old brewer, however, was not only a man indulgent of his progeny's mercurial whims but a shrewd and devious entrepreneur who knew a tax dodge when he saw one.

Lunchtime trade at the Flying Swan was alarmingly slack. Two sullen professional drinkers sat doggedly at the bar, glowering into their pints and picking sawdust from their teeth. Old Pete entered the bar around twelve, took one look at the decorations and made a remark much favoured by gentlemen of his advanced years. Young Chips lifted his furry leg at the sawdust floor and the two departed grumbling to themselves.

When Neville cashed up at three, the till had taken less than two pounds. Neville counted the small change with nervous fingers; he was certain that the ominous smell he had detected that morning was beginning to penetrate the beer-soaked atmosphere of the saloon bar.

It all began in earnest when at three fifteen a van from the brewery catering division drew up outside the Swan in the charge of a young man with advanced acne and a cowboy hat. This diminutive figure strutted to and fro in a pair of boots which sported what the Americans humourously call 'elevator heels'. He announced himself to be Young Master Robert and said that he would be taking over personal control of the event. Neville was horrorstruck, he'd been looking forward to it for weeks, he'd got the sheriff's star and everything and now at the eleventh hour, this upstart . . .

To add insult to injury, the young man stepped straight behind the bar and drew himself a large scotch. Neville watched open-jawed as a parade of supplies sufficient to cater for half the British Army passed before his eyes in a steady and constant stream. There were packets of sausages, beefburgers, baconburgers, beans and baconburgers, sausage beef and baconburgers and something round and dubious called a steakette. There were enormous catering cans of beans which the porters rolled in like beer casks. There were sacks of french rolls, jars of pickled onions, radishes, beetroots, cocktail cucumbers and gherkins. There were hundredweight sacks of charcoal.

'I have been light on the cooking oil,' Young Master Robert announced as the slack-jawed Neville watched two porters manoeuvring an enormous drum in through the saloon bar door.

Young Master Robert drew himself another scotch and explained the situation. 'Now hear this,' he said, his voice a facetious parody of Aldo Ray in some incomprehensible submarine movie, 'what we have here is an on-going situation.'

'A what?'

'We have product, that is to say Old Snakebelly.' He held up a bottle of the devil brew. 'We have location' – he indicated the surroundings – 'and we have motivation.' Here he pointed to the banner which hung above the bar, draped over the moth-eaten bison's head. It read: GRAND COWBOY EXTRAVAGANZA PRIZES PRIZES PRIZES.

Neville nodded gravely.

'I have given this a lot of thought, brain-wise,' the youth continued. 'I ran a few ideas up the flagpole and they got saluted and I mean S-A-L-U-luted!'

Neville flexed his nostrils, he didn't like the smell of this. The young man was clearly a monomaniac of the first order. A porter in a soiled leather apron, hand-rolled cigarette dripping from his lower lip, appeared in the doorway. 'Where do you want this mouthwash then guv?' he asked, gesturing over his right shoulder.

'Ah, yes, the Product,' said Young Master Robert, thrusting his way past Neville and following the porter into the street. There were 108 crates of Old Snakebelly, and when stacked they covered exactly half the available space of the newly built patio.

'There is nowhere else we can put it,' Neville explained. 'There's no space in the cellar, and at least if they're here whoever is cooking at the barbeque can keep an eye on them.'

Young Master Robert was inspecting the barbeque. 'Who constructed this?' he queried.

'Two local builders.'

The youth strutted about the red brick construction. 'There is something not altogether A-O-K here design-wise.'

Neville shrugged his shoulders, he knew nothing about barbeques anyway and had never even troubled to look at the plans the brewery had sent. 'It is identical to the plan and has the Council's seal of approval, safety-wise!' Neville lied.

Young Master Robert, who also knew nothing of barbeques but was a master of gamesmanship, nodded thoughtfully and said, 'We will see.'

'What time will the extra bar staff be getting here?' Neville asked.

'18.30,' said the Young Master, 'a couple of right bits of crumpet.' He had obviously not yet totally mastered the subtler points of American terminology.

By half past six the Young Master had still failed to light the barbeque. The occasional fits of coughing and cries of anguish coming from the patio told the part-time bar-man that at least the young man was by no means a quitter.

At six forty-five by the Guinness clock there was still no sign of the extra bar staff. Neville sauntered across the bar and down the short passage to the patio door. Gingerly he edged it open. Nothing was visible of Young Master Robert; a thick black pall of smoke utterly engulfed the yard obscuring all vision. Neville held his nose and squinted into the murk, thinking to detect some move-ment amid the impenetrable fog. 'Everything going all right?' he called gaily.

111

'Yes, fine, fine,' came a strangled voice. 'Think I've got the measure of it technique-wise.'

'Good,' said Neville. Quietly closing the door, he collapsed into a convulsion of laughter. Wiping the tears from his eyes he returned to the saloon bar, where he found himself confronted by two young ladies of the Page Three variety, who stood looking disdainful and ill at ease. They were clad in only the scantiest of costumes and looked like escapees from some gay nineties Chicago brothel.

'You the guvnor?' said one of these lovelies, giving Neville the old fisheye. 'Only we've been 'anging about 'ere, ain't we?'

Neville pulled back his shoulders and thrust out his pigeon chest. 'Good evening,' said he in his finest Ronald Coleman. 'You are, I trust, the two young ladies sent by the brewery to assist in the proceedings?'

'You what?' said one.

'To help behind the bar?'

'Oh, yeah.'

'And may I ask your names?'

'I'm Sandra,' said Sandra.

'I'm Mandy,' said her companion.

'Neville,' said Neville, extending his hand.

Sandra tittered. Mandy said, 'It's a bit of a dump 'ere, ain't it?'

Neville returned his unshaken hand to its pocket. 'You didn't come through the streets in those costumes did you?'

'Nah,' said Mandy, 'we come in the car, didn't we?'

'And you are, I trust, acquainted with the running of a bar?'

Sandra yawned and began to polish her nails. Mandy said, 'We've worked in all the top clubs, we're 'ostesses, ain't we?'

Neville was fascinated to note that the two beauties

112

seemed unable to form a single sentence which did not terminate in a question mark. 'Well then, I'll leave you in charge while I go up and get changed.'

'We can manage, can't we?' said Mandy.

The cowboy suit hung behind the bedroom door in its plastic covering. With great care Neville lifted it down and laid it upon the bed. Carefully parting the plastic he pressed his nose to the fabric of the suit, savouring the bittersweet smell of the dry cleaner's craft.

Gently he put his thumbs to the pearl buttons and removed the jacket from the hanger. He sighed deeply, and with the reverence a priest accords to his ornamentum he slipped into the jacket. The material was crisp and pure, the sleeves crackled slightly as he eased his arms into them and the starched cuffs clamped about his wrists like loving manacles. Without further hesitation the part-time barman climbed into the trousers, clipped on the gun belt and tilted the hat on to his head at a rakish angle. Pinning the glittering badge of office carefully to his breast he stepped to the pitted glass of the wardrobe mirror to view the total effect.

It was, to say the least, stunning. The dazzling white of the suit made the naturally anaemic Neville appear almost suntanned. The stetson, covering his bald patch and accentuating his dark sideburns, made his face seem ruggedly handsome, the bulge of the gunbelt gave an added contour to his narrow hips and the cut of the trousers brought certain parts of his anatomy into an unexpected and quite astonishing prominence.

'Mighty fine,' said Neville, easing his thumbs beneath the belt buckle and adopting a stance not unknown to the late and legendary 'Duke' himself. But there was something missing, some final touch. He looked down, and caught sight of his carpet slippers, of course, the cowboy boots. A sudden sick feeling began to take hold of his

113

stomach, he did not remember having seen any boots when the suit arrived. In fact, there were none.

Neville let out a despairing groan and slumped on to his bed, a broken man. The image in the mirror crumpled away and with it Neville's dreams; a cowboy in carpet slippers? A tear entered Neville's good eye and crept down his cheek.

It was seven thirty. The bar was still deserted. The two hostesses were huddled at a corner of the counter, sipping shandy and discussing the sex lives of their contemporaries in hushed and confidential tones. The gaudily dressed bar had become a gloomy and haunted place. Once in a while a passer-by would cast a brief shadow upon the etched glass of the saloon bar door, conversation would cease and the two beauties would look up in wary expectation.

Neville descended the stairs upon tiptoe. The Page Three girls saw Neville's slippers before they saw Neville. They should have laughed, nudged one another, pointed and giggled and possibly on any other occasion they would have done just that, but as the part-time barman reached the foot of the stairs he had about him such an air of desperate tragedy that the two girls were moved beyond words.

Neville squinted around the empty bar. 'Hasn't anybody been in?' he asked.

Mandy shook her powdered head. Sandra said, 'Nah.'

'You look dead good,' said Mandy. 'Suits you.'

'Like that bloke in them films you look,' said Sandra.

Neville smiled weakly. 'Thanks,' he said. Just then the sound of a muffled explosion issued from the direction of the patio. The yard door burst open and down the short corridor staggered the blackened figure of Young Master Robert. He was accompanied by a gust of evil-smelling black smoke which made his entrance not unlike that of the Demon Prince in popular panto.

114

As he lurched towards the bar counter Neville stepped nimbly aside to avoid soiling his suit. The two Page Three beauties stood dumb with astonishment. Young Master Robert stumbled behind the bar. Tearing the whisky bottle from its optic he snatched up a half-pint mug and filled it to the brim.

'Two bloody hours,' he screeched in a tortured voice, 'two bloody hours puffing and blowing and fanning the bloody thing! Then I see it, then I bloody see it!'

'You do?' said Neville.

'The vents man, where are the bloody vents?'

Neville shrugged. He had no idea.

'I'll tell you where the bloody vents are, I'll bloody tell you!' The line of Neville's mouth was beginning to curl itself into an awful lopsided smirk. With great difficulty he controlled it. 'On the top, that's where the bloody vents are!'

Neville said, 'Surely that can't be right.'

'Can't be right? I'll say it can't be bloody right, some bastard has built the barbeque upside down!'

Neville clamped his hand over his mouth. Young Master Robert raised the half-pint pot in a charred fist and poured the whisky down his throat.

'What shall we do then?' asked Neville fighting a losing battle against hilarity. 'Call it off, eh?'

'Call it off? Not on your bloody life, no, I've fixed it, fixed it proper I bloody have, gave it what it bloody needed. Proper Molotov cocktail, got vents now it has, I'll tell you.'

'Oh good,' said Neville, 'no damage done then.'

Young Master Robert turned on the part-time barman a bitter glance. 'I warn you,' he stammered, 'I bloody warn you!' It was then that he realized the bar was empty. 'Here!' he said. 'Where is everybody?'

Neville moved uneasily in his chaps. The young master fixed him with a manic stare. Mandy watched his fingers tightening about the handle of the half-pint pot. She stepped between the two men. 'Come on Bobby,' she said, 'let's 'ave a look at them burns, can't 'ave you getting an infection can we?' With a comforting but firm hand she led the blackened barbequeist away to the ladies.

Neville could contain himself no longer. He clutched at his stomach, rolled his eyes and fell into fits of laughter. Sandra was giggling behind her hand but she leant over to the part-time barman and whispered hoarsely, 'You wanna watch that little bastard, he can put the poison in for you.'

'Thank you,' said Neville, and the two of them collapsed into further convulsions. Suddenly there was a sound at the bar door. The smiles froze on their lips for it was at this exact moment that the Lone Ranger chose to make his appearance.

He was quite a short Ranger as it happened, and somewhat stout. Neville immediately recognized the man in the mask to be none other than Wally Woods, Brentford's pre-eminent purveyor of wet fish. Wally stood a moment, magnificently framed in the doorway, considering the empty bar with a cold cod-eye of suspicion. For one terrible second Neville thought he was about to change his mind and make off into the sunset in the manner much practised in the Old West. 'What'll it be, stranger?' he said hurriedly.

Wally squared his rounded shoulders and swaggered to the bar, accompanied by the distinctive smell of halibut oil which never left his person come rain, hail or high water. 'Give me two fingers of Old Snakebelly,' he said manfully.

During the half hour that followed, the Flying Swan began slowly to fill. In dribs and drabs they came, some looking sheepish and muffled in heavy overcoats, despite the mildness of the season, others strutting through the doorway as if they had been cowboys all their lives. Three Mavericks had begun an illegal-looking game of poker at a corner table, and no less than six gunfights had already broken out.

Neville loaded another case of old Snakebelly on to the counter. Young Master Robert returned from the Ladies, a satisfied expression upon his face, which was a battle-ground of sticking plaster. Mandy was wearing her bustle on back to front. Two more Rangers arrived, swelling their ranks to eight. 'What is this, a bloody convention?' asked one. Old Pete arrived wearing a Superman costume. 'They were right out of Lone Rangers,' he explained.

A few stalwart professionals were sticking to their regular beverages, but most were taking advantage of the cut-price liquor and tossing back large measures of Old Snakebelly, which was proving to have the effect generally expected of white man's firewater.

The last of the Lone Rangers rounded the corners at either end of the Ealing Road and strode towards the Flying Swan. One was of Irish descent, the other a well-known local personality who had but several hours before come within one horse of winning £250,000. The two caught sight of one another when they were but twenty yards apiece from the saloon bar door. Both stopped. The Lone Pooley blinked in surprise. The Lone Omally's face took on a look of perplexity. Surely, he thought, this is some trick of the light, some temperature inversion or mirror image. Possibly by the merest of chances he had stepped through a warp in the time-space continuum and was confronting his own doppleganger. A similar thought had entered the Lone Pooley's mind.

They strode forward, each in perfect synchronization with his twin. The Lone Pooley made a motion towards his gunbelt, his double did likewise. But for these two lone figures, the street was deserted. The sun was setting behind the gasometers and the long and similar shadows of the two masked gunmen stretched out across the pave-ment and up the side walls of the tiny terraced houses.

It was a sight to make Zane Grey reach for his ballpoint, or Sergio Leone send out for another fifty foot of standard eight. Closer and closer stalked the Rangers, their jaws set into attitudes of determination and their thumbs wedged into the silver buckles of their respective gunbelts.

They stopped once more.

The street was silent but for the sounds of western jollity issuing from the saloon bar. A flock of pigeons rippled up from their perch atop one of the flatblocks and came to rest upon the roof of the church hall. A solitary dog loped across the street and vanished into an alleyway.

The Rangers stared at one another unblinking. 'This town ain't big enough for the both of us,' said the Lone Omally.

'Slap leather, hombre,' said the Lone Pooley, reaching for his sixguns. It would be a long reach, for they were back in his rooms upon the kitchen table where he had been polishing them. 'Oh bugger it,' said the Lone Pooley. Guffawing, the Ranger twins entered the Flying Swan.

'Cor look,' said Mandy, 'there's two more of 'em.'

'My god,' cried Pooley, 'ten Lone Rangers and not a Tonto between the lot of us.'

'Two shots of good Old Snakebelly please, Miss,' said Omally, ogling the extra barstaff. Mandy did the honours, and on accepting Omally's exact coinage pocketed it away in some impossible place in her scanty costume. 'A woman after my own heart,' smiled the man from the Emerald Isle.

Things were beginning to hot up at the Flying Swan. Old Pete was at the piano, rattling out 'I Wish I Was in Dixie' upon the moribund instrument. Young Chips was howling off-key as usual. A fight had broken out among the Mavericks and Neville was flourishing his knobkerry, yet seeming strangely reluctant to make a move from behind the bar.

Young Master Robert raised his hands to make an announcement. Being ill-acquainted with the manners and customs of Brentford he was ignored to a man.

'Ladies and gentlemen,' he bawled, the visible areas of his face turning purple, 'if I might have your attention.'

Neville brought the knobkerry down on to the polished bar counter with a resounding crash. There was a brief silence.

'Ladies and gentlemen,' roared the Young Master, his high voice echoing grotesquely about the silent bar, 'ladies and gentlemen I . . .' but it was no good, the temporary silence was over as swiftly as it had begun and the rumblings of half-drunken converse, the jingling chords of the complaining piano and the general rowdiness resumed with a vengeance.

'Time gentlemen PLEASE,' cried Neville, which silenced them once and for all.

Young Master Robert made his announcement. 'Ladies and gentlemen, as I was saying, as a representative of the brewery' – at this point young Chips made a rude noise which was received with general applause – 'as a representative of the brewery, may I say how impressed I am by this turnout, enthusiasm-wise.'

'Enthusiasm-wise?' queried Omally.

'As you may know, this evening has been arranged at the brewery's expense to launch a new concept in drinking pleasure.' He held up a bottle of Old Snakebelly. 'Which I am glad to see you are all enjoying. There will shortly be held a barbeque where delicacies of a western nature will be served, also at the brewery's expense. There will be a free raffle, prizes for the best dressed cowboy . . .' As he spoke, Young Master Robert became slowly aware that the assembled company of cowboys was no longer listening; heads were beginning to turn, whispers were breaking out, elbows were nudging. The Spirit of the Old West had entered the bar.

Norman stood in the Swan's portal, his suit glittering about him. The sequins and rhinestones gleamed and twinkled. He had added four more sets of fairy lights to

119

the arms and legs of the costume and these flashed on and off in a pulsating rhythm.

Norman came forward, his hands raised as in papal benediction. Spellbound, like the Red Sea to the wave of Moses's staff, the crowd parted before him. Turning slowly for maximum effect, Norman flicked a switch upon his belt buckle and sent the lights dancing in a frenzied whirl. To and fro about the golden motto the lights danced, weaving pattern upon pattern, altering the contours of the suit and highlighting hitherto unnoticed embellishments.

Here they brought into prominence the woven headdress of an indian chieftain, here the rhinestoned wheel of a covered wagon, here a sequined cowboy crouched in the posture of one ready to shoot it out. To say that it was wondrous would be to say that the universe is quite a big place. As the coloured lights danced and Norman turned upon his insulated brass conductor heels the assembled company began to applaud. In ones and twos they clapped their hands together, then as the sound grew, gaining rhythm and pace, Old Pete struck up a thunderous 'Oh Them Golden Slippers' upon the piano.

The cowboys cheered and flung their hats into the air, Lone Rangers of every colour linked arms like a chorus line and High-Ho-Silvered till they were all uniformly blue in the face. Pooley and Omally threw themselves into an improvised and high-stepping barn dance and the Spirit of the Old West capered about in the midst of it all like an animated lighthouse. Then a most extraordinary thing happened.

The sawdust began to rise from the floor towards Norman's suit. First it thickened about his feet, smothering his polished boots, then crept upwards like some evil parasitic fungus, gathering about his legs and then swathing his entire body.

'It's the static electricity,' gasped Omally, ceasing his

dance in mid kick. 'He's charged himself up like a capacitor.'

Norman was so overcome by his reception that it was not until he found himself unable to move, coughing and spluttering and wiping sawdust from his ears and eyes that an inkling dawned upon him that something was amiss. The crowd, who were convinced that this was nothing more than another phase in a unique and original performance, roared with laughter and fired their sixguns into the air.

Omally stepped forward. Norman's eyes were starting from their sockets and he was clutching at his throat. The sawdust was settling thickly about him, transforming him into a kind of woodchipped snowman. Omally reached out a hand to brush the sawdust from the struggling man's face and was rewarded by a charge of electrical energy which lifted him from his rented cowboy boots and flung him backwards over the bar counter.

Jim Pooley snatched up a soda siphon and without thought for the consequences discharged it fully into the face of the Spirit of the Old West. What followed was later likened by Old Pete to a firework display he had once witnessed at the Crystal Palace when a lad. Sparks flew from Norman's hands and feet, bulbs popped from their holders and criss-crossed the bar like tracer bullets. The crowd took shelter where they could, young Chips thrust his head into a spittoon, his elderly master lay crouched beneath the piano saying the rosary, the Page Three girls hurriedly ducked away behind the bar counter to where Omally lay unconscious, his face set into an idiot grin. Norman jerked about the room, smoke rising from his shoulders, his arms flailing in the air like the sails of a demented windmill. The final bulb upon his once proud suit gave out with an almighty crack and Norman sank to the floor, where he lay a smouldering ruin.

After a moment or two of painful silence the cowboys

rose sheepishly from their makeshift hideouts, patting the dirt from their rented suits and squinting through the cloud of sawdust which filled the room. Pooley came forward upon hesitant rubber-kneed legs and doused down the fallen hero with the remaining contents of the soda siphon. 'Are you all right, Norman?' he asked inanely.

'Oh bollocks!' moaned the Spirit of the Old West, spitting out a mouthful of sawdust. 'Oh *bollocks*!'

12

Captain Carson lay draped across an elaborately carved Spanish chair, peeping between his fingers at the preposterous display of exotic foodstuffs heaped upon the gilded tabletop. To think that any one of these rare viands might be purchased anywhere within a mile of the Mission would be to stretch the most elastic of imaginations to its very breaking point. Yet there they were. The Captain covered his eyes again and hoped desperately that they would go away. They did not.

Carrying the tramp's shopping-list, some of which was totally unpronounceable, he had traipsed from shop to shop. It had been almost as if the shopkeepers were lying in wait for him. He had wandered into Uncle Ted's greengrocery to enquire in a doomed voice as to the current availability of Bernese avocados. Uncle Ted had smiled broadly, torn a paper bag from the nail and asked if he would prefer reds or greens. At every shop it had been the same. When the Captain had demanded an explanation of how these gastronomic delicacies found their way on to the shelves, the shopkeepers had been extremely vague in their replies. Some spoke of consignments arriving by accident, others that it was a new line they were trying out.

After six such encounters in tiny corner shops which normally complained that they were out of sugar, that the cornflakes were late in again and that they couldn't get tomato sauce for love nor money, the Captain, his head reeling, had staggered into the High Street off-licence.

'Your usual?' said Tommy Finch, the manager. The Captain sighed gratefully. Could it be possible that here was sanctuary, that this one place had remained free from the tramp's contamination?

'Or,' said Tommy suddenly, 'could I interest you in a half a dozen bottles of a magnificent vintage claret which arrived here in error this very morning and which is most moderately priced?'

The Captain had cast a fatalistic eye down his list. 'That wouldn't by any chance be Château Lafite 1822?'

'That's the one,' Tommy had replied with no hint of surprise.

The Captain rose stiffly from his chair, picked up a can of pickled quails' eggs and gave the label some perusal. As with all the other items he had purchased, and as with everything else which surrounded the mystery tramp, there was something not quite right about it. The label appeared at first sight normal enough, an illustration of the contained foodstuffs, a brand name, a list of ingredients and a maker's mark; yet the more one looked at it the more indistinct its features became. The colours seemed to run into one another, the letters were not letters at all but merely rudimentary symbols suggestive of lettering.

The Captain returned the can to the table and shook his head as one in a dream. None of it made any sense. What could the tramp be planning? What had been his motive in inviting the hated Crowley to the Mission? Certainly on his past record alone it could be expected that his motives were nothing if not thoroughly evil. None of it made any sense.

'Is all correct?' said a voice, jarring the Captain from his thoughts. 'There must be no mistake.'

Turning, the Captain peered up at the red-eyed man towering above him. Never had he looked more imposing or more terrible, dressed in an evening suit of the deepest black, a dark cravat about his neck secured at the throat by a sapphire pin. His fingers weighed heavy with rings of gold and his face wore an unreadable expression.

'All is as you ordered,' said the Captain in a querulous voice, 'though as to how I do not know, nor do I wish to.'

'Good, our guests will arrive sharp at seven thirty. They must be received in a manner befitting.'

The Captain chewed ruefully upon his knuckles. 'What would you have me wear for this distinguished gathering?'

The tramp smiled, his mouth a cruel line. 'You may wear the Royal Navy dress uniform which hangs in your wardrobe, the hire company's label cut out from its lining. Pray remember to remove the camphor bags from its pockets.'

The Captain hunched his shoulders and slouched from the room.

When he returned an hour later, duly clad, the Captain discovered to his further bewilderment that the food had been laid out in the most exquisite and skilful manner, the claret twinkled in cut-glass decanters and the delicious smell of cooking filled the air. The Captain shook his befuddled head and consulted his half-hunter. There was just time for a little drop of short. He had lately taken to carrying a hipflask which he refilled with half bottles of rum purchased from the off licence. This seemed the only defence against the tramp, whose intuition of the location of hidden bottles seemed nothing short of telepathic. The two red eyes burned into his every thought, hovering in his consciousness and eating away at his brain like a ideous cancer. The Captain drew deeply upon his flask and drained it to its pewter bottom.

At seven thirty precisely a black cab drew up outside the Mission. The Captain heard the sound of footsteps crackling up the short path to the Mission door. There were two sharp raps. The Captain rose with difficulty, buttoned up his dress jacket and shuffled unwillingly towards the front door.

Upon the step stood Councillor Wormwood, wrapped in a threadbare black overcoat, a stained white silk scarf slung about his scrawny neck. He was tall, gaunt and angular, his skin the colour of a nicotine-stained finger and his eyes deeply sunk into cavernous black pits. Never had the Captain seen a man who wore the look of death more plainly upon his features. He withdrew a febrile and blue-veined hand from his worn coat pocket and offered the Captain a gilt-edged invitation card. 'Wormwood,' he said in a broken voice, 'I am expected.'

'Please come in,' the Captain replied making a courteous gesture. The jaundiced spectre allowed himself to be ushered down the corridor and into the dining-room.

The Captain took out the bottle of cheap sherry he kept in reserve for Jehovah's Witnesses.

'I see that I am the first,' said Wormwood, accepting the thimble-sized glass the Captain offered him. 'You have a cosy little nest for yourself here.'

The sound of taxi wheels upon the gravel drew the Captain's attention. 'If you will excuse me,' he said, 'I think I hear the arrival of another guest.' The Councillor inclined his turtle neck and the Captain left the room.

Before the Mission stood Brian Crowley. He was dressed in a deep-blue velvet suit, which caught the evening light to perfection. A hand-stitched silk dress-shirt with lace ruffles smothered him to the neck, where a large black bow-tie clung to his throat like a vampire bat. His shoes, also hand-made, were of the finest leather; he carried in his hands a pair of kid gloves and an ivory tipped malacca cane. He raised a limp and manicured hand to the Mission's knocker, which receded before his grasp as the Captain swung open the door.

'Mr Crowley,' said the Captain.

'Good evening, Carson,' said the young man, stepping forward. The Captain barred his way. 'Your card, sir?' said the Captain politely.

'Damn you Carson, you know who I am.'

'We must observe protocol.'

Muttering under his breath Crowley reached into his breast pocket and withdrew a monogrammed moroco wallet. From this he produced the invitation card which he held to the old man's face. 'All right?'

The Captain took the card and bowed graciously. 'Pray come in.' As he followed the effeminate young man down the corridor the Captain smiled to himself; he had quite enjoyed that little confrontation.

Crowley met Councillor Wormwood in the dining room. The Councillor took the pale white fingers in his yellow claw and shook them without enthusiasm. 'Wormwood,' he said.

Crowley's suspicions had been alerted. Surely this was a dinner exclusively for members of the Mission Trust to celebrate the centenary and the Captain's retirement? Why invite that withered cretin?

It was only now that Crowley became fully aware of the room in which he was standing. Lit only by the two magnificent candelabra upon the loaded table, the rich gildings and embossings upon the furniture glittered like treasure in the tomb of a Pharaoh. Crowley's gaze swept ravenously about the room. He became drawn towards an oil painting which hung in a frame of golden cherubim above a rococo commode. Surely this was a genuine Pinturicchio of his finest period? How could an elderly sea captain have come by it? Crowley had never credited the grizzled salt with any intelligence whatever, yet recalling his surprise upon receiving the invitation cards, he felt that he had truly misjudged this elder. The young man's eyes glittered with greed.

'Will you take sherry?' the Captain asked. Roused from his covetous reverie Crowley replied, 'Yes indeed, thank you.'

He accepted his sherry with a display of extraordinary politeness and wondered just how he might avail himself of the Captain's valuable possessions. 'I have been admiring this painting,' he said at length. 'Surely it is a Pinturicchio of the Romanesque school?'

The Captain fiddled nervously with the top of a cut-crystal decanter. 'I believe so,' he replied matter-of-factly.

'And the furniture.' Crowley made a sweeping gesture. 'Surely fifteenth-century Spanish Baroque. You have some most exquisite examples.'

'It serves,' said the Captain, studying his broken fingernails. 'Please be seated gentlemen, place cards have been set out.'

Crowley made a slow perambulation about the table, sherry glass held delicately in his pampered fingers. His eyes wandered over the display of food. 'Why, Captain,' he said in an insinuating voice, 'this is haute cuisine to numb the brain of a gourmet. I must confess complete astonishment, I had no idea, I mean, well, most worthy, most worthy.'

The Captain watched Crowley's every movement. While his expression remained bland and self-effacing, his brain boiled with hatred for the effeminate young man. Crowley dipped a hand forward and took up a sweetmeat, pecking it to his nose to savour its fragrance. With a foppish flurry he popped it into his mouth, his small pink tongue darting about his lips. Almost at once his face took on an expression both quizzical and perplexed.

'Extraordinary,' he said, smacking his lips, 'the taste, so

subtle, hardly distinguishable upon the palate. It is almost as if one had placed a cube of cold air into one's mouth, most curious.'

'It is an acquired taste,' sneered the Captain.

Wormwood had found his place at the bottom of the table and had seated himself without ceremony. Crowley shrugged his shoulders, licked the ends of his fingers and sought his seat. 'If you will pardon me, Captain,' he said, 'it would seem that but for our own, the other seven place cards are unlabelled.'

'Possibly an oversight on the part of the caterers,' grumbled the Captain, 'don't let it concern you.' He took his place between the two men and three sat in silence.

Crowley took out a cocktail cigarette from a gold case and tapped it upon the table. Wormwood wheezed asthmatically into his hand. Drawing a shabby handkerchief from his pocket he dabbed at his sinewy nose.

The Captain sat immobile, wondering what, if anything, was going to happen. Crowley lit his cigarette and looked down at his platinum wristwatch. 'It would seem that your other guests are a trifle late,' said he.

The Captain sniffed and said nothing. Wormwood turned his empty sherry glass between his fingers and shuffled his ill-polished shoes uneasily. Long minutes passed and no sound came to the Captain's ears but for the regular tock tock of the gilded mantelclock. There was no rumble of an approaching vehicle and no footstep upon the stairs that might herald the arrival of the red-eyed man. Surely it was not his intention to have the Captain sit here between these two hated individuals all evening? He had nothing to say to them.

Without warning, and silently upon its never-oiled hinge, the hall door swung open. White light streamed into the candlelit room, brighter and brighter it grew as if a searchlight had been turned upon the opening. The Captain blinked and shielded his eyes, Crowley squinted into the glare. 'Here,' he shouted, 'what's all this?'

In the midst of the now blinding light the silhouette of a tall and boldly proportioned man gradually became apparent. Well over six foot he stood, and finely muscled as an Olympic athlete. His garb was of the richest crimson, trousers cut impeccably yet without a crease, a waisted and collarless jacket, lavishly embellished with stitched brocade, a lace cravat about the neck. Upon his head the figure wore a small crimson skullcap.

The face might have been that of a Spanish grandee, tanned and imposing, the nose aquiline and the mouth a hard and bitter line. The chin was prominent and firmly set. Beneath thick dark eyebrows two blood-red eyes gleamed menacingly. The room became impossibly cold, the hairs rose upon the Captain's hands and his breath streamed from his mouth as clouds of steam which hovered in the frozen air.

Crowley found his voice. 'Dammit,' he spluttered, his teeth chattering and his face a grey mask of fear, 'what's going on, who the devil are you?'

Wormwood clutched at his heart with quivering hands and gasped for air.

The crimson figure stood in total silence, his eyes fixed upon the effeminate young man. The Captain had seen that look before and thanked his maritime gods that it was not directed towards him. 'So you would be Crowley?'

An icy hand clasped about the young man's heart. His head nodded up and down like that of an automaton and his lips mouthed the syllables of his own name although no sound came.

'And this is Councillor Wormwood?' The eyes turned upon the unhappy creature who cowered at the table-end.

'Horace Wormwood,' came the trembling reply. 'I was invited.'

'Good.' A broad if sinister smile broke out upon the tall

man's face. 'Then all is as it should be. Please be seated, gentlemen.'

The three men, who had risen unconsciously to their feet, reseated themselves, and the warmth of the summer's evening returned to the room. The tall man stepped forward and took his place at the head of the table. To the further horror of those already seated, the hall door swung silently shut and closed into its frame with a resounding crash.

'I hope you will enjoy this modest spread,' said the crimson figure. 'It is but local fare.'

Crowley finally found his voice. He was by nature a predator, and not one to be intimidated by such a theatrical display no matter how convincing it might appear. It would take more than a few bright lights and a bit of cold air to make him deviate from his calculated scheme. It was clear that the Captain had hired this man, possibly a local actor; there was definitely something familiar about him, and those eyes, certainly tinted contact lenses, no body could have eyes that colour surely?

'Local fare you say,' said Crowley merrily. 'It would seem that you have plundered the finest food halls of christendom and employed one of the world's master chefs to prepare this magnificent feast.'

The tall man in crimson smiled his thinnest of smiles and said, 'I fear that the other guests have declined their invitations and we shall be forced to dine alone, as it were. I also fear that by an unforgivable oversight the caterers have omitted to supply us with either cutlery or serving staff and you will be forced to serve yourselves. Captain, if you would be so kind as to bring in the fish.'

The Captain did as he was bid without hesitation. At the arrival of the fish Crowley clapped his hands together in glee and shouted, 'Magnificent! Magnificent!'

The four men sat about the enormous gilded dining table, the golden glow of candleflame eerily illuminating their faces whilst casting their shadows about the richly hung walls in a ragged, wavering *danse macabre*. Each man was occupied with his own thoughts. Crowley's brain was bursting with a thousand unanswered questions, everything here demanded explanation. His eyes cast about from face to face, and devious plots began to hatch inside his skull. Councillor Wormwood, although a man greatly in favour of connivance and double-dealing, was capable upon this occasion of no such premeditation. He was an old man and felt himself to be pretty well versed in the ways of the world, but here in this room he knew there was something 'different' going on. There was a dark aura of evil here, and it was evil of the most hideous and malignant variety.

Captain Carson glowered morosely about the table, he really didn't know much about anything any more. All he knew was that he was seated here in a room, which had been exclusively his for the past thirty years, with three men who out of the entire world's population he loathed and hated to a point well starboard of all sanity.

At a gesture from the red-eyed man the three set about the mouthwatering dishes. Crowley was amazed to find that the sweetmeat he had sampled minutes before had now taken on the most delicious and satisfying of tastes. He gurgled his delight and thrust large helpings into his mouth.

Councillor Wormwood pecked at his choosings like the ragged vulture he was, his claws fastened about the leg of some tropical fowl and his hideous yellow teeth tearing the soft white flesh away from the pinkly cooked bones. The Captain sampled this and that and found all equally to his liking.

As no cutlery had been supplied the three men dug into the finely dressed displays with their greasy fingers reducing each dish to a ruination suggestive of the march of soldier ants. The crimson figure at the head of the table left most of the dishes untouched. He dined upon bread, which he broke delicately between his muscular fingers, and drank occasionally from the decanter of claret set at his right elbow.

The hours passed and the gluttony of the three men was slowly satisfied. The Captain loosened the lower buttons of his jacket and broke wind in a loud and embarrassing manner. At length, when it seemed that the undignified destruction of the table was at an end, the crimson figure spoke. Sweeping his burning eyes over the three men he said, 'Is all to your liking, gentlemen?'

Crowley looked up, his mouth still bulging with food. 'It is all ambrosia,' he mumbled, wiping cream away with the cuff of his lace shirt.

'Mr Wormwood?'

The creature raised its yellow eyes. There was grease upon his cleft chin and he had spilt white sauce on his jacket lapel. 'Most palatable,' said he.

'And Captain?'

The Captain chewed ruefully upon a jellied lark's wing and grunted assent in a surly manner.

Crowley was growing bolder by the minute, and felt it high time that he put one or two of the questions he had stewing in his head. 'Dear sir,' said he, 'may I say how much I have enjoyed this dinner, never in my days have I tasted such claret.' He held up the short crystal glass to the candle-flame and contemplated the ruby-red liquid as it ran about the rim. 'To think that anything so exquisite could exist here in Brentford, that such a sanctuary dedicated to life's finer things could be here, it is a veritable joy to the soul.'

The red-eyed man nodded thoughtfully. 'Then you approve?'

'I do, I do, but I must also confess to some puzzlement.'

'Indeed?'

'Well,' and here Crowley paused that he might compose inquisitiveness into a form which might give no offence.

132

'Well, as to yourself for instance, you are clearly a man of extreme refinement, such is obvious from your carriage, bearing and manner of speech. If you will pardon my enquiry might I ask to which part of our sceptred isle you owe your born allegiance?'

'I am broadly travelled and may call no place truly my home.'

'Then as to your presence in these parts?'

'I am at present a guest of the good Captain.'

'I see.' Crowley turned his eyes briefly towards the elder. His glance was sufficient however to register the look of extreme distaste on the Captain's face.

'Then, sir, as you have the advantage of us might I enquire your name?'

The red-eyed man sat back in his chair. He took from a golden casket a long green cigar which he held to his ear and turned between thumb and forefinger. Taking up an onyx-handled cigar cutter he sliced away at one end. Satisfied with his handiwork he placed the cigar between his cruel lips and drew life into it from the candle-flame.

'Mr Crowley,' said he, blowing a perfect cube of smoke which hovered in the air a second or two before dissolving into nothingness. 'Mr Crowley, you would not wish to know my name.'

The young man sipped at his wine and smiled coyly. 'Come now,' he crooned, 'you have supplied us with a dinner fit for royalty, yet you decline to identify yourself. It is unfair that we are not permitted to know the name of our most generous and worthy host.'

The red-eyed man drew once more upon his cigar, while the index finger of his left hand traced a runic symbol upon the polished tabletop. 'It is to the Captain that you owe your gratitude,' said he. 'He is your host, I am but a guest as yourself.'

'Ha,' the young man crowed, 'I think not. You suit all

133

this a little too well. You sit at the table's head. I feel all this is your doing.'

'My doing?' the other replied. 'And what motive do you think I might have for inviting you to the Mission?'

'That is something I also wish to know. I suspect that no other guests were invited this evening and' – here Crowley leant forward in his seat – 'I demand an explanation.'

'Demand?'

'Yes, demand! Something funny is going on here and I mean to get to the bottom of it.'

'You do?'

'Who are you?' screamed Crowley, growing red in the face. 'Who are you and what are you doing here?'

'What are you doing here, Mr Crowley?'

'Me? I was invited, I came out of respect to the Captain, to celebrate the Mission's centenary. I have a responsible position on the board of trustees, in fact I am a man not without power. You would do well not to bandy words with me!'

'Mr Crowley,' said the crimson figure. 'You are a fool, you have no respect for the Captain, you have only contempt. It was greed that brought you here and it will be greed that will be your ruination.'

'Oh yes?' said Crowley. 'Oh yes?'

'I will tell you why you came here tonight and I will answer your questions. You came here because you knew that not to come would be to draw attention to yourself. It is your plan to have this Mission demolished at the first possible opportunity, and to make your shady and treacherous deals with this corpse here.' Wormwood cowered in his seat as the tall man continued. 'I will never allow a stone of this Mission to be touched without my consent!'

'Your consent?' screeched Crowley. 'Who in the hell do you think you are?'

'Enough!' The red-eyed man pushed back his chair and drew himself to his full height, his eyes blazing and his shoulders spreading to draw out his massive chest. His hands formed two enormous fists which he brought down on to the table with titanic force, scattering the food and shuddering the candelabra. 'Crowley,' he roared, his voice issuing from his mouth as a gale force of icy wind, 'Crowley, you would know who I am! I am the man to whom fate has led you. From your very birth it was ordained that our paths would finally cross, all things are preordained and no man can escape his fate. You would know who I am? Crowley, I am your nemesis!'

Crowley hurled his chair aside and rushed for the door, his desperate movements those of a wildly flapping bird. His hands grasped about the door-handle but found it as solid and unmoveable as if welded to the lock. 'Let me go,' he whimpered, 'I want nothing more of this, let me out.'

The giant in crimson turned his hellish eyes once more upon the young man. 'You have no escape, Crowley,' he said, his voice a low rumble of distant thunder. 'You have no escape, you are already dead, you were dead from the moment you entered this room, dead from the first moment you raised a glass to your mouth, you are dead, Crowley.'

'I'm not dead,' the young man cried, tears welling up in his eyes. 'I'll have the law on you for this, I'm not without influence, I'm . . .' Suddenly he stiffened as if a strong cord had been tightly drawn about his neck. His eyes started from their sockets and his tongue burst from his mouth. It was black and dry as the tongue of an old boot. 'You . . . you,' he gagged, tearing at his collar and falling back against the door. The tall figure loomed above him, a crimson angel of death. 'Dead, Crowley.'

The young man sank slowly to his knees, his eyes rolling horribly until the pupils were lost in his head. A line of green saliva flowed from the corner of his mouth and crept over his shirt. He jerked forward, his manicured nails tearing into the parquet flooring, crackling and snapping as convulsions of raw pain coursed through his body.

Above him, watching the young man's agony with inhuman detachment, stood the crimson giant. Crowley raised a shaking hand, blood flowed from his wounded fingertips, his face was contorted beyond recognition. He bore the look of a grotesque, a gargoyle, the skin grey and parched, the lips blue, bloodless. He raised himself once more to his knees and his mouth opened, the blue lips made a hopeless attempt to shape a final word. Another convulsion tore through his body and flung him doll-like to the floor where he lay, his limbs twisted hideously, his eyes staring at the face of his destroyer, glazed and sightless. Brian Crowley was dead.

The red-eyed man raised his right hand and made a gesture of benediction. With terrifying suddenness he turned upon the Captain, who sat open-mouthed, shaking with terror. 'You will dispose of this rubbish,' he said.

'Rubbish?' The Captain forced the word from his mouth.

The red-eyed man gestured at the twisted body which lay at his feet; then, raising his arm, he pointed across the table. The Captain followed his gaze to where Councillor Wormwood sat. His hands grasped the table top in a vice-like grip, his eyes were crossed and his head hung back upon his neck like that of a dead fowl in a butcher's window. The skin was no longer yellow, but grey-white and almost iridescent; his mouth lolled hugely open and his upper set had slipped down to give the impression that his teeth were clenched into a sickly grin.

The giant was speaking, issuing instructions: the bodies were to be stripped of all identification, this was to be destroyed by fire, the table was to be cleared, the decanters to be drained and thoroughly washed out. The bodies were to be placed in weighted sacks . . . the voice rolled over the Captain, a dark ocean of words engulfing and drowning him. He rose to his feet, his hands cupped about his ears that he might hear no more. The words swept into his brain, the black tide washed over him, dragging him down. The Captain fought to breathe, fought to raise his head above the black waters. This was the Mission, his life, the evil must be driven out while any strength remained in his old body. His hands sought to grasp these thoughts, cling to them for dear life.

But the hands were old and the tide strong. Presently the Captain could grip no more and the poison waters swept over him, covering him without trace.

13

The ambulance roared away from the Flying Swan, its bell ringing cheerfully. Most of the smoke had been fanned away through the Swan's doors and windows, but an insistent smell of electrical burning still hung heavily in the air. After the excitement was over and the ambulance had departed, the cowboys stood about, thumbs in gunbelts, wondering whether that was the night over and they should, out of respect to Norman, saddle up and make for the sunset.

Young Master Robert, however, had other ideas. He climbed on to a chair and addressed the crowd. As nobody felt much like talking at that particular moment he was able to make himself heard. 'Partners,' he began, 'partners, a sorry incident has occurred but let us be grateful that the party concerned has not been badly injured. I am assured by the ambulance man that he will be up and about within a couple of days.' There were some half-hearted attempts at a cheer. 'To show the brewery's appreciation of a brave attempt, we are awarding, sadly in his absence, the Best Dressed Cowboy award, which includes an evening out for two with one of our delightful young ladies here at one of the brewery's eating houses, a bottle of champagne and twenty small cigars, to our good friend Norman, the Spirit of the Old West!'

There was some slightly more enthusiastic cheering at this point, which rose in a deafening crescendo as Young Master Robert continued, 'The next three drinks are on the house!'

Suddenly Norman's unfortunate accident was forgotten, Old Pete set about the ancient piano once more and the Swan emerged again, a phoenix from the ashes of the Old West. Young Master Robert approached Neville behind the bar. 'I am going out to stoke up the barbeque now. I'll get the sausages on and then give you the nod to start leading them in.'

'Leave it to me,' said Neville, 'and I'll see to it that the free drinks are only singles.'

Omally, who had been revived by the aid of mouth-to-mouth resuscitation administered by each of the Page Three girls, overheard this remark and hastily ordered three doubles from Mandy before the part-time barman was able to communicate his instructions. 'Same for me,' said Jim Pooley.

Invigorated by their free drinks the cowboy patrons began to grow ever more rowdy. Old Snakebelly's qualities obviously combined those of Irish potheen, wool alcohol and methylated spirits. Old Pete had already attempted to blow out a lighted match only to find himself breathing fire and smoke. Small rings from glass bottoms had taken most of the polish from the bar top.

Omally leant across the bar and spoke to Neville. 'You have put on a fine show and no mistake,' said he. 'I had my misgivings about tonight but' – and here he took an enormous swig of Old Snakebelly, draining his glass – 'it promises to be a most memorable occasion.'

The part-time barman smiled lopsidedly and polished away at a dazzling pint pot. 'The night is far from over,' he said ominously, 'and are you feeling yourself again, John?'

'Never better,' said Dublin's finest, 'never better.'

''Ere,' said Mandy suddenly, 'that Lone Ranger what stinks of fish keeps pinching my bum.' Neville went over to have words with the unruly lawman. 'Omally,' the Page Three girl said when Neville was out of earshot.

'The same,' said himself.

'Listen.' Mandy made a secretive gesture and the man from the Emerald Isle leant further across the bar, just far enough in fact for a good view down the young lady's cleavage. 'You wanna buy a couple of dozen bottles of this Old Snake whatsit on the cheap?'

Omally grinned. He had not misjudged Mandy from the first moment he'd seen her pocket his pennies. 'What exactly is on the cheap?'

'How does a ten spot sound?'

'It sounds most reasonable, and where are these bottles at present?'

'In the boot of the white M.G. out the front.'

Omally delved into his money belt, and a ten-pound note and a set of car keys changed hands. Winking lewdly, Omally left the bar.

A strange smell of the kind one generally associates with crematorium chimneys had began to weave its way about the bar. Some thought it was the last relics of the taint left by the Spirit of the Old West, others sensed its subtle difference and began to fan their drinks and cough into their stetsons. Suddenly there was a mighty crash as Neville brought his knobkerry down on the bar top. 'The barbeque is served,' said the part-time barman.

Knowing the rush that would ensue at the announcement of free food, and still wishing to shield his carpet slippers from critical onlookers, Neville remained behind the bar to watch with some interest the way that one hundred or so cowboys might fit into a six-foot-square patio. Young Master Robert, clad in lurid vinyl apron and tall chef's hat, was going great guns behind the barbeque. Mountains of sizzling sausages, and steakettes and bubbling cauldrons of beans simmered away on the grill and Sandra stood near at hand proffering paper plates and serviettes printed with the legend, 'A Souvenir of Cowboy Night.'

The first half-dozen lucky would-be-diners squeezed their way through the Swan's rear door and found themselves jammed up against the blazing barbeque. 'One at a bloody time,' bawled a scorched Ranger, patting at the knees of his trousers. 'Don't push there,' screamed another as his elbow dipped into a vat of boiling beans.

Order was finally maintained by the skilful wielding of a red-hot toasting fork in the hands of the young master. A human chain was eventually set up and paper plates bearing dollops of beans, a steakette, a sausage and a roll were passed back along the queue of drunken cowboys.

'More charcoal,' the Young Master cried as a helpful Jim Pooley heaped stack after stack on the flames of the blazing barbeque. 'More sausages, more beans.' Jim dutifully set about the top of a five-gallon drum with a handy garden fork.

Rammed into the corner of the patio and watching the barbeque with expressions of dire suspicion were two Rangers whose abundance of cranial covering identified them to be none other than Hairy Dave and Jungle John, well known if largely (and wisely) distrusted members of the local building profession.

Jim had watched these two surly individuals from the corner of his eye for the better part of the last half hour and had wondered at their doubtful expressions and occasional bouts of elbow nudging. A sudden sharp report from the base of the brick-built barbeque which slightly preceded their hasty departure from the patio caused Pooley to halt in his can-opening and take stock of the situation.

The barbeque was roaring away like a furnace and the grill had grown red hot and was slightly sagging in the middle. Young Master Robert was perspiring freely and calling for more charcoal. Jim noticed that his vinyl apron was beginning to run and that the paint on the Swan's rear door was blistering alarmingly. The heat had grown to such an extent that the remaining cowboys were pressed back against the wall and were shielding their faces and privy parts with paper plates.

'More charcoal,' screamed Young Master Robert.

Pooley's eyes suddenly alighted upon a half empty bag of cement which lay among a few unused red flettons in the corner of the patio. He recalled a time when, taking a few days' work in order to appease a sadistic official at the Labour Exchange, he had installed a fireplace at a lady's house on the Butts Estate. Knowing little about what happens when bricks and mortar grow hot, and having never heard of fireproof bricks and heat resistant cement, he had used these very same red flettons and a bag of similarly standard cement. The fire-engine bells still rang clearly in Jim's memory.

There was another loud report from the base of the barbeque and Pooley reached out to make a grab at Young Master Robert's shoulder. 'Come on, come on,' he shouted, trying to make himself heard above the roaring of the fire. 'Get inside.'

'Leave off, will you?' the young master shouted back. 'Open those beans.'

Jim was a man who would do most things to protect his fellow man, but he was not one to scoff at self-preservation. 'Run for your life,' bawled Jim, thrusting his way into the suddenly stampeding herd of cowboys who had by now similarly realized that all was not well with the barbeque, and that the all that was not well was of that kind which greatly endangers life and limb.

The mad rush burst in through the Swan's rear door,

carrying it from its hinges and depositing it on the cross-legged form of 'Vindaloo Vic', the manager of the Curry Garden, who had been busily employed in the heaping of sausages and steakettes into a stack of foil containers to be later resold in his establishment as Bombay Duck. He vanished beneath the rented soles of forty-eight trampling cowboy boots.

The merrymakers in the saloon bar were not long in discerning that something was going very wrong on the patio. As one, they rose to their feet and took flight. Neville found himself suddenly alone in the saloon bar. 'Now what can this mean?' he asked himself. 'The bar suddenly empty, drinks left untouched upon tables, cigarettes burning in ashtrays, had the Flying Swan become some form of land-locked *Marie Celeste*? Is it the steakettes, perhaps? Is it the Old Snakebelly, stampeding them off to the Thames like lemmings?' Neville's ears became drawn to the sound which was issuing from the direction of the patio and which appeared to be growing second upon second. Something was building up to a deafening crescendo on the back patio and Neville had a pretty good idea what it was. It was Old Moloch itself, the ill-constructed brick barbeque, about to burst asunder.

Before Neville instinctively took the old 'dive for cover' beneath the Swan's counter he had the impression that a being from another world had entered the bar from the rear passage. This vision, although fleeting and seen only through the part-time barman's good eye, appeared to be clad in a steaming skin-tight vinyl space-suit and wearing the remnants of a chef's hat.

The first explosion was not altogether a large one; it was by no means on the scale of Krakatoa's outburst, and it is doubtful whether it even raised a squiggle upon the seismographs at Greenwich. It was the second one that was definitely the most memorable. Possibly a scientist schooled in such matters could have estimated the exact megatonnage of the thirty cases of Old Snakebelly. However, we must accept, in the untechnical jargon of John Omally who was returning at that moment from the allotment where he had been burying twenty-four bottles of the volatile liquid, that it was one 'bloody big bang'.

The blast ripped through the Swan, overturning the piano, lifting the polished beer-pulls from the counter and propelling them through the front windows like so many silver-tipped torpedoes. The Swiss cheese roof of the gents' toilet was raised from its worm-eaten mountings and liberally distributed over half-a-dozen back gardens. The crowd of cowboys who had taken cover behind the parked cars in the Ealing Road ducked their heads and covered their ears and faces as shards of smoke-stained glass rained down upon them.

Neville was comparatively unscathed. When he felt it safe he raised his noble head above the counter to peer through shaking fingers at the desolation that had been his pride and joy.

The Swan was wreathed in smoke, but what Neville could see of the basic structure appeared to be intact. As for the cowboy trapping and the pub furniture, little remained that could by any stretch of the imagination be called serviceable. The tables and chairs had joined the patrons in making a rapid move towards the front door, but unlike those lucky personnel their desperate bid for escape had been halted by the front wall, where they lay heaped like the barricades of revolutionary Paris. Sawdust filled the air like a woody snowstorm, and in the middle of the floor, lacking most of his clothes but still bearing upon his head the charred remnants of a chef's hat, lay Young Master Robert. Neville patted away the sawdust from his shoulders and found to his amazement one lone optic full of whisky. This indeed had become a night he would long remember.

The now emboldened cowboys had risen from their

shelters and were beating upon the Swan's door. Faces appeared at the glassless windows and inane cries of 'Are you all right?' and 'Is anybody there?' filled the smoky air.

Neville downed his scotch and climbed over the bar to inspect the fallen figure of the Young Master, who was showing some signs of life. The patrons finally broke into the bar and came to a crowded and silent standstill about the prone figure.

'He's all right, ain't he?' said Mandy. 'I mean he's still breathing, ain't he?' Neville nodded. 'Sandra's phoned for an ambulance and the fire brigade.'

A great dark mushroom cloud hung over the Flying Swan. The first brigade, who arrived in record time, on hearing that it was a pub on fire, contented themselves with half-heartedly squirting an extinguisher over the blackened yard and salvaging what unbroken bottles of drink remained for immediate consumption. The ambulance driver asked sarcastically whether Neville wanted his home number in case of further calamities that evening.

When the appliances had finally departed, dramatically ringing their bells in the hope of waking any local residents who had slept through the blast, a grim and sorry silence descended upon the Flying Swan. The cowboys drifted away like western ghosts and the onlookers who had been awakened by the excitement switched out their lights and returned to their beds.

Neville, Pooley and John Omally were all who remained behind. Neville had brought down a couple of bottles of scotch from the private stock in his wardrobe. The three sat where they could in the ruined bar sipping at their drinks and contemplating the destruction.

'Heads will roll for this,' sighed Neville, 'mine in particular.'

Omally nodded thoughtfully. 'Still,' he said, 'at least we'll get that new bog roof now.'

'Thanks a lot,' said Neville.

'It was a good old do though, wasn't it,' said Jim. 'I don't suppose the brewery would be thinking of following it up at all, I mean maybe Hawaiian Night or a Merrie England festival or something?'

Neville grinned painfully. 'Somehow I doubt it.'

'You must sue that Hairy Dave,' John suggested. 'Him and his hirsute brother are a danger to life and limb.'

Neville opened the second bottle of scotch. 'Come to think of it,' he said, 'I don't recall any specifications for materials coming with that plan from the brewery.'

'Aha!' said John. 'Then all may not be lost.'

'The poor old Swan,' said Pooley, 'what a tragedy.'

'We've had fine times here,' said Omally.

'They'll ruin it you know,' said Neville, 'the brewery, probably turn it into a discotheque or a steak house or something. There's nothing they like better than getting their hands on a piece of England's heritage and thoroughly crucifying it. It'll be fizzy beer and chicken in a basket, you wait and see.'

'We'll get up a petition,' said Jim. 'Brentonians won't stand for any of that.'

'Won't they though?' Neville nodded towards the broken front windows. 'Look there and what do you see?'

'Nothing, the lights of the flatblocks that's all.'

'Yes, the flatblocks. Fifteen years ago there was a whole community there, small pubs, corner shops, the pottery, streets full of families that all knew each other.'

Jim nodded sadly. 'All gone now,' said he. The three men sipped silently at their drinks as the air grew heavy with nostalgic reminiscence.

Omally, always the realist, said, 'There's little use in sobbing about the good old days. When my family came over from the old country we moved in to one of them little dens where the flats now stand. I can remember them sure enough. No hot water, no bath, outside toilet that froze in the winter, rats, bedbugs, the children coughing with diptheria, great old times they were. I'll tell you I cheered when the bulldozer pushed our old house down. Bloody good riddance I said.'

Jim smiled slightly. 'And if I remember rightly the bailiffs were still chasing your lot six months after for five years' back rent.'

Omally laughed heartily. 'Tis true,' said he, 'tis true enough, the daddy took the lot of them back home then, sure he did. "Back to the land John," said he, "there's a fortune to be made in the land." Mad as a hatter the daddy.'

'Is he still alive your da?' said Neville.

'Oh yes, he's that all right. I read not so long ago in the Dublin press of an old fella at eighty-six being named in a paternity suit by a sixteen-year-old convent girl, that would be the daddy right enough.'

'The Omallys are notable womanizers, that is for certain,' said Jim. 'There is many a well-pleased widow woman hereabouts who will testify to that.'

Omally smiled his winning smile. 'I would thank you to keep your indiscreet remarks to yourself, Jim Pooley,' said he. 'I am a man of the highest principles.'

'Ha,' said Jim as he recalled the spectacle of Omally's moonlit bum going about its hydraulic motions in Archroy's marriage bed. 'You are an unprincipled bounder, but I am proud to call you friend.'

'You are both good men,' said Neville, a tear unexpectedly forming in his good eye. 'Friendship is a wonderful thing. Whatever the future holds for the Swan, I want you to know that it has always been my pleasure to serve you.'

'Come now,' said Jim, patting the part-time barman on the shoulder. 'There are great days ahead, of this I am certain.'

'Forgive me this sentiment,' said Neville, 'I am drunk.'

'Me also,' said John.

'I am still able to stand and must thus confess my

sobriety,' said Jim, refilling his glass with the last of the whisky.

Some time later two thoroughly drunken Lone Rangers, now somewhat shabby and lacking in hats and masks, were to be found wandering in the direction of the St Mary's allotment. 'I have a little crop upon my pastures which you will find most satisfying,' the Irish Ranger told his staggering compadre. Jim was desperately hoping that the Irishman was not alluding to some supposed narcotic sproutings from the purloined bean.

The two arrived at the iron gate and stood before that rusting edifice leaning upon one another for support. 'I've done a little deal,' grinned Omally, pulling at his lower eyelid in an obscene manner and staggering forward into the silent allotment. It was another fine moonlit night and the old selenic disc sailed above in a cloudless sky. Long jagged shadows cast by bean poles, abandoned wheelbarrows and heavily padlocked allotment sheds etched stark patterns across the strangely whitened ground.

Omally's ambling silhouette lurched on ahead and vanished down into the dip before his plot. Jim, who had fallen to the ground upon his companion's sudden departure, climbed shakily to his feet, tightened his bandana against the crisp night air and stumbled after him.

When he reached Omally he found the Irishman upon all fours grubbing about in the dirt. Happily he was some way from the spot where the magic bean had originally been buried.

'Aha,' said Omally suddenly, lifting a dusty bottle of Old Snakebelly into the moonlight. 'Ripe as ninepence.'

'Good show,' said Jim collapsing on to his behind with a dull thud. The bottle was speedily uncorked and the two sat drawing upon it turn by turn, at peace with the world and sharing Jim's last Woodbine. 'It's a great life though,

147

isn't it?' said Jim wiping the neck of the bottle upon his rented sleeve.

'It's that to be sure.'

Pooley leant back upon his elbows and stared up wistfully towards the moon. 'Sometimes I wonder,' said he.

'I know,' Omally broke in, 'sometimes you wonder if there are folk like us up there wondering if there are folk like them down here.'

'Exactly,' said Jim.

Suddenly, away into the darkness and coming apparently from the direction of the Mission's rear garden wall, the two wonderers heard a heavy if muffled thump.

'Now what do you wonder that might be?' asked John.

'Truly I have no idea, give me a drag of that Woody.' Omally passed Jim the cigarette and taking the bottle drained away a large portion of its contents. 'Probably a pussycat,' said he.

'Big one though.'

'Archroy told me he once saw a giant feral tom roaming the allotment by night, the size of a tiger he said.'

'Archroy as you well know is greatly subject to flights of fancy.'

'He seemed very sincere at the time, came rushing into the Swan and ordered a large brandy.'

Pooley shifted uncomfortably on his earthy seat. 'I should not wish to end my days as a pussycat's dinner,' said he. Without warning there was a second and slightly louder thump, which was followed almost immediately by the sound of scrambling feet. 'The monster moggy!' said Jim.

Omally threw himself down commando-fashion and crawled to the rim of the dip. Pooley snatched up a fallen farrowing fork and, draining the last of the bottle, stealthily followed him. Sounds of grunting and panting now drifted in their direction and were followed by a distant 'squeak-squeak'.

'A giant mouse perhaps,' whispered Jim hoarsely.

'Don't be a damn fool,' Omally replied, 'there's only one thing around here makes a noise like that, my bloody wheelbarrow.'

'Sssh!' said Jim. 'It's coming nearer.' The two lay in silence squinting lopsidedly into the gloom.

The indistinct form of a man appeared from the shadows. As it drew nearer both Pooley and Omally recognized the dark figure as that of the grizzle-chinned seafarer Captain Carson. He was dressed in a Royal Navy uniform and was pushing with some difficulty Omally's wheelbarrow, which was weighed down heavily by two large and strangely swollen potato sacks.

He was now but ten yards away and the two hidden Rangers caught sight of the Captain's face. It was a thing to inspire horror, the skin deathly white and glowing hideously in the moon's septic light, the mouth turned down into an attitude of intense hatred and the eyes glazed and lifeless.

Pooley shuddered and drew his Irish chum down as the wheelbarrow and its zombiesque operator passed them at close quarters. 'Something's not right here,' said John, straightening up upon creaking knee-joints, 'let's follow him.'

Jim was doubtful. 'It's home for me,' he said.

Omally cuffed his cowardly companion. 'That's my damn wheelbarrow,' he said. Ducking low and scurrying from one hiding place to another the two thoroughly besmutted Rangers followed the ghastly figure with the squeaking wheelbarrow across the allotment.

'He's heading for the river,' said Jim breathlessly, still grasping the farrowing fork. From a little way ahead of them came the sounds of more straining followed by two loud splashes. 'I'd say he was there,' said John.

There was a squeak or two, then another loud splash. 'He's dumped my barrow, the bastard!' wailed Omally.

Jim said, 'If you'll pardon me, John, I'll be off about my business.' He turned and blundered into a forest of bean poles.

'Duck, you fool,' whispered John, tripping over the struggling Pooley, 'he's coming back.'

The Captain appeared suddenly from the shadows of the riverside oaks. He surely must have seen the two fallen Rangers, yet his eyes showed no sign of recognition. Forward he came upon wooden legs, moving like a somnambulist, past the Rangers and back off in the direction of the Mission.

'There's a bean pole stuck up my right trouser,' groaned Jim, 'help, help, fallen man here!'

'Shut up you bally fool,' said John, flapping his arms and attempting to rise, 'look there.' Pooley raised himself as best he could and stared after John's pointing finger.

Away across the allotment a bright light shone from the Mission. Like a beacon it swept over their heads. For a fleeting moment they saw him, the silhouette of a huge man standing upon the Mission wall, his arms folded and his legs apart. Although the two saw him for only a brief second, the feeling of incontestable grandeur and of malevolent evil was totally overwhelming.

Omally crossed himself with a trembling hand.

Pooley said, 'I think I am going to be sick.'

14

The Flying Swan was closed for three weeks. The sun blazed down day after day, and there were all the makings of a Long Hot Summer. There was never a cloud in the sky, the boating pond in Gunnersbury Park was down a full six inches and the bed of the dried-up canal cracked and hardened into a sun-scorched jigsaw puzzle. As each evening came the air, rather than growing blessedly cool, seemed to boil, making sleep impossible. Windows were permanently open, butter melted upon grocers' shelves and every kind of cooling apparatus gave up the ghost and ground to a standstill. The residents who nightly tilled their allotment patches watched sadly as their crops shrivelled and died. No amount of daily watering could save them, and the press had announced that water rationing was likely.

When the Swan reopened it was with little ceremony. Nothing much seemed to have changed, some portions of the bar had been half-heartedly repainted and the gents' toilet had been rebuilt. Neville stood in his usual position polishing the glasses and occasionally dabbing at his moist brow. It was as if Cowboy Night had never taken place.

The beer pulls had been returned to their places upon the bar, but only three of them were fully functional. 'I put it down to vindictiveness upon the part of the brewery,' he told Omally.

'Good to see you back though,' said the Irishman, pushing the exact money across the counter and indicating his usual.

'That one's still off,' said Neville. 'And the beer's up a penny a pint.'

Omally sighed dismally. 'These are tragic times we live in,' said he. 'A half of light ale then.'

Archroy sat alone upon the sun-scorched allotment, his head gleaming like the dome of an Islamic mosque. His discarded wig hung upon the handle of a rake in the fashion of a trophy before the lodge of a great chief. Evil thoughts were brewing in Archroy's polished cranium. It had not been his year at all: first the loss of his cherished automobile and then the disappearance of his magic beans, the decimation of his tomato crop and now the aviary. The aviary! Archroy twisted broodingly at the dried stalk of what had been a promising tomato plant and hunched his shoulders in utter despair.

Things could not continue as they were. One of them would have to go, and the accursed aviary looked a pretty permanent affair. Three weeks in the construction and built after the design of Lord Snowdon's famous bird house, the thing towered in his back garden, overshadowing the kitchen and darkening his bedroom. Its presence had of course inspired the usual jocularity from his workmates, who had dubbed him 'the bird man of Brentford'.

So far the monstrous cage had remained empty, but Archroy grew ever more apprehensive when he contemplated the kind of feathered occupants his wife was planning to house within its lofty environs. He lived in perpetual dread of that knock upon the door which would herald the delivery of a vanload of winged parasites. 'I'll do away with myself,' said Archroy. 'That will show them all I mean business.' He twisted the last crackling fibres from the ruined tomato stalk and threw them into the dust. 'Something dramatic, something spectacular that all the world will take notice of, I'll show them.'

Captain Carson sat huddled under a heavy blanket in the old steamer chair on the Mission's verandah. His eyes stared into the shimmering heat, but saw nothing. At intervals his head bobbed rhythmically as if in time to some half-forgotten sea shanty. From inside the Mission poured the sounds of industry. For on this afternoon, and in the all-conquering heat which none could escape, great changes were taking place. Timber was being sawn, hammers wielded and chisels manfully employed. The metallic reports of cold chisel upon masonry rang into the superheated air, the splintering of wormy laths and the creaking of uplifted floorboards. Major reconstruction

152

work was in progress and was being performed apparently with robotic tirelessness.

Hairy Dave swung the five-pound club hammer wildly in the direction of the Victorian marble fireplace. The polished steel of the hammer's head glanced across the polished mantel, raising a shower of sparks and burying itself in the plaster of the wall. Normally such an event would have signalled the summary 'down tools and repair to the alehouse lads', but Dave merely spat upon his palm and withdrew the half-submerged instrument of labour for another attempt. His thickly bearded brother stood upon a trestle, worrying at a length of picture rail with a crowbar. Neither man spoke as he went about his desperate business; here was none of the endless banter, cigarette swopping and merry whistling one associated with these two work-shy reprobates, here was only hard graft, manual labour taken to an extreme and terrifying degree.

The long hot summer's day wore on, drawing itself into a red raw evening which turned to nightfall with a sunset that would have made the most cynical of men raise his eyes in wonder. Jim Pooley stirred from his hypnotic slumbers upon the Memorial Library bench and rose to his feet, scratching at his stomach and belching loudly. The gnawing within his torso told him that he was in need of sustenance and the evening sky told the ever-alert Jim that day had drawn to a close.

He found his cigarette packet lodged in the lining of his aged tweed jacket. One lone Woody revealed itself. 'Times be hard,' said Jim to no-one in particular. He lit his final cigarette and peered up at the sprinkling of stars. 'I wonder,' said he. 'I wonder what Professor Slocombe is up to.'

With the coming of the tropical summer naught had been seen of the learned ancient upon the streets of

Brentford. His daily perambulation about the little community's boundaries had ceased. Pooley tried to think when he had last seen the elderly Professor and realized that it was more than a month ago, on the night of his valiant deed.

'The old fellow is probably suffering something wicked with the heat,' he told himself, 'and would be grateful for an evening caller to relieve the tedium of the sultry hours.'

Pleased with the persuasiveness of this reasoning Pooley drew deeply upon his cigarette, blew a great gust of milk-white smoke into the air and crossed the carless road towards the Professor's house.

The Butts estate hovered timelessly in its splendour. The tall Georgian house-fronts gleamed whitely in the moonlight, and the streetlamps threw stark shadows into the walled courtyards and guarded alley entrances.

Hesperus, the first star of evening, winked down as Pooley, hands in pockets, rounded the corner by the Professor's house. The garden gate was ajar and Pooley slipped silently between the ivy-hung walls. A light glowed ahead, coming from the open French window, and Jim gravitated towards it, thoughts of the Professor's sherry spurring him on.

It was as he reached the open windows that the sounds first reached him. Pooley halted, straining his ears, suddenly alert to a subtle unidentifiable strangeness, a curious rustling from within, a scratching clawing sound, agitated and frantic.

Pooley reached out a cautious hand towards the net curtain, and as he did so heard the scrabbling sounds increase in urgency and agitation.

There was a sudden movement, firm fingers fastened about his wrist and he was hauled forward with one deft jerk which lifted him from his feet and sent him bowling across the carpet in an untidy tangle of tweed. With a

154

resounding thud the tumbling Pooley came to rest beneath one of the Professor's ponderous bookcases.

'Mercy,' screamed Jim, covering his head, 'James Pooley here, pacifist and friend to all.'

'Jim, my dear fellow, my apologies.'

Jim peered up warily through his fingers. 'Professor?' said he.

'I am so sorry, I was expecting someone else.'

'Some welcome,' said Jim.

The ancient helped the fallen Pooley to his feet and escorted him to one of the cosy fireside chairs. He poured a glass of scotch which Pooley took in willing hands.

'That was a nifty blow you dealt me there,' said Jim.

'Dimac,' said the elder, 'a crash course via the mail-order tuition of the notorious Count Dante.'

'I have heard of him,' said Jim, 'deadliest man on earth they say.'

The Professor chewed at his lip. 'Would it were so,' said he in an ominous tone.

Pooley downed his scotch and cast his eyes about the Professor's study. 'A noise,' he said, 'as I stood at the windows, I heard a noise.'

'Indeed?'

'A scratching sound.' Pooley lifted himself upon his elbows and peered about. All seemed as ever, the clutter of thaumaturgical books, bizarre relics and brass-cogged machinery. But there in the very centre of the room, set upon a low dais which stood within a chalk-drawn pentagram, was a glass case covered with what appeared to be an altar-cloth. 'Hamsters?' said Jim. 'Or gerbils is it, nasty smelly wee things.'

Pooley rose to investigate but the Professor restrained him with a firm and unyielding hand. Jim marvelled at the ancient's newly acquired strength. 'Do not look, Jim,' the Professor said dramatically, 'you would not care for what you saw.'

'Hamsters hold little fear for the Pooleys,' said Jim.

'Tell me,' said the Professor. 'What unlikely adventures have befallen you since our last encounter?'

'Now you are asking,' said Jim and between frequent refillings of scotch he told the chuckling Professor of the excitements and diversions of Cowboy Night at the Flying Swan.

The Professor wiped at his eyes. 'I heard the explosion of course.' Here the old man became suddenly sober. 'There were other things abroad that night, things which are better not recalled or even hinted at.'

Pooley scratched at his ear. 'Omally and I saw something that night, or thought we did, for we had both consumed a preposterous amount of good old Snakebelly.'

The Professor leant forward in his chair and fixed Jim with a glittering stare. 'What did you see?' he asked in a voice of dire urgency which quite upset the sensitive Pooley.

'Well.' Pooley paused that his glass might be refilled. 'It was a strange one, this I know.' Jim told his tale as best he could remember, recalling with gothic intensity the squeaking wheelbarrow and its mysterious cargo and the awesome figure upon the mission wall.

'And the bright light, had you ever seen anything like it before?'

'Never, nor wish to again.'

The Professor smiled.

'Omally crossed himself,' said Jim. 'And I was taken quite poorly.'

'Ah,' said the Professor. 'It is all becoming clearer by the hour. Now I have a more vivid idea of what we are dealing with.'

'I am glad somebody does,' said Jim, rattling his empty glass upon the arm of the chair. 'It's the wheelbarrow I feel sorry for.'

'Jim,' said the Professor rising from his seat and crossing slowly to the French windows where he stood gazing into the darkness. 'Jim, if I were to confide in you my findings, could I rely on your complete discretion?'

'Of course.'

'That is easily said, but this would be a serious vow, no idle chinwagging.' The Professor's tone was of such leaden seriousness that Jim hesitated a moment, wondering whether he would be better not knowing whatever it was. But as usual his natural curiosity got the upper hand and with the simple words 'I swear' he irrevocably sealed his fate.

'Come then, I will show you!' The Professor strode to the covered glass case and as he did so the frantic scrabbling arose anew. Jim refilled his glass and rose unsteadily to join his host.

'I should have destroyed them, I know,' said the Professor, a trace of fear entering his voice. 'But I am a man of science, and to feel that one might be standing upon the brink of discovery . . .' With a sudden flourish he tore the embroidered altar cloth from the glass case, revealing to Jim's horrified eyes a sight that would haunt his sleeping hours for years to come.

Within the case, pawing at the glazed walls, were frantically moving creatures, five hideous manlike beings, six to eight inches in height. They were twisted as the gnarled roots of an ancient oak, yet in the 'heads' of them rudimentary mouths opened and closed. Slime trickled from their ever-moving orifices and down over their shimmering knobbly forms.

Jim drew back in outraged horror and gagged into his hands. The Professor uttered a phrase of Latin and replaced the cloth. The frantic scratchings ceased as rapidly as they had begun.

Pooley staggered back to his chair where he sat, head in hands, sweat running free from his forehead. 'What are they?' he said, his voice almost a sob. 'Why do you have them here?'

'You brought them here. They are Phaseolus Satanicus, and they await their master.'

'I will have nothing of this.' Pooley dragged himself from his seat and staggered to the window. He had come here for a bite to eat, not to be assailed with graveyard nastiness. He would leave the Professor to his horrors. Jim halted in his flight. A strange sensation entered his being, as if voices called to him from the dim past, strange voices speaking in archaic accents hardly recognizable yet urgent, urgent with the fears of unthinkable horrors lurking on the very edges of darkling oblivion.

Pooley stumbled, his hands gripping at the curtain, tearing it from its hooks. Behind him the scrabbling and scratching rose anew to fever pitch, small mewings and whisperings interspersed with the awful sounds. As Pooley fell he saw before him standing in the gloom of the night garden a massive, brooding figure. It was clad in crimson and glowing with a peculiar light. The head was lost in shadows but beneath the heavy brows two bright red eyes glowed wolfishly.

When Pooley awoke he was lying sprawled across the Professor's *chaise longue*, an icepack upon his head and the hellish reek of ammonia strong in his nostrils.

'Jim.' A voice came to him out of the darkness. 'Jim.' Pooley brought his eyes into focus and made out the willowy form of the elderly Professor, screwing the cap on a bottle of smelling salts. He offered the half-conscious Jim yet another glass of scotch, which the invalid downed with a practised flick of the wrist. Now fully alert, Pooley jerked his head in the direction of the window. 'Where is he,' he said, tearing the icepack from his forehead. 'I saw him out there.'

The Professor sank into a high-backed Windsor chair. 'Then he did come, I knew he would.'

The first rays of sunlight were falling through the still-open, though now curtainless, French windows. 'Here,' said Pooley. 'What time is it?' As if in answer the ormolu mantelclock struck five times. 'I've been out for hours,' said Jim, holding his head, 'and I do not feel at all well.'

'You had best go home to your bed,' said the Professor. 'Come again tonight and we will speak of these things.'

'No,' said Pooley taking a Turkish cigarette from the polished humidor. Through force of habit he furtively thrust several more into his top pocket. 'I must know of these things now.'

'As you will.' The Professor smiled darkly and drew a deep breath. 'You will recall the evening when you first came to me with that single bean. You saw my reaction when I first observed it, and when later that night you brought me the other four I knew that my suspicions were justified.'

'Suspicions?'

'That the Dark One was already among us.'

Pooley lit his cigarette and collapsed into an immediate fit of coughing. 'The Dark One?' he spluttered between convulsions. 'Who in the name of the holies is the Dark One?'

The Professor shrugged. 'If I knew exactly who he was Jim, our task would be simpler. The Dark One has existed since the dawn of time, he may take many forms and live many lives. We are lucky in one respect only, that we have observed his arrival. It is our duty to precipitate his end.'

'I know of no Dark Ones,' said Jim. 'Although I do remember that several months ago the arrival of a mouldy-looking tramp caused a good degree of speculation within the saloon bar of the Flying Swan, although in truth I never saw this dismal wanderer myself.'

The Professor nodded. 'You have seen him twice, once upon the allotments and again this very night within my own garden.'

'Nah,' said Pooley. 'That was no tramp I saw.'

'I am certain there is a connection,' said the Professor. 'All the signs are here. I have watched them for months, gathering like a storm about to break. The time, I fear, is close at hand.'

Jim sniffed suspiciously at his Turkish cigarette. 'Are these lads all right?' said he. 'Only they smell somewhat doubtful.'

'You are still a young man, Jim,' said the Professor. 'I cannot expect you to take altogether seriously all that I say, but I swear to you that we are dealing with forces which will not be defeated by simply being ignored.'

Jim glanced distastefully towards the covered glass case. 'You can hardly ignore those,' said he.

'By fire and water only may they be destroyed,' said the Professor. 'By fire and water and the holy word.'

Pooley pulled at his sideburns. 'I'll put a match to the blighters,' he said valiantly.

'It is not as simple as that, it never is. These beans are the symptom, not the cause. To destroy them now would be to throw away the only hope we have of locating the evil force which brought them here.'

'I don't like the sound of this "we" you keep referring to,' said Jim.

'I want you to tell me, Jim, everything you have heard about this tramp. Every rumour, every story, anything that might give us a clue as to his motives, his power and his weaknesses.'

Pooley's stomach made an unmentionable sound. 'Professor,' said he, 'I would be exceedingly grateful for some breakfast, I have not eaten for twenty-four hours. I am feeling a trifle peckish.'

'Of course.' The Professor rang the bell which summoned his musty servant. Presently a fine breakfast of heated rolls, eggs, bacon, tomatoes, coffee and toast appeared and Pooley set about it with ravenous zeal.

For the next hour thereafter Jim spoke of all he had

heard regarding the mystery tramp, from Neville's first encounter to Norman's terrifying experiences in the Plume Café, and of the welter of theories, conjectures and speculations which had been rife in the Swan. He spoke of Soap Distant's talk of the Hollow Earth, omitting his own experiences within the mysterious subterranean world, and of Omally's faerie ramblings and of those folk who held the belief that the tramp was the Wandering Jew.

The old Professor listened intently, occasionally raising his snowy eyebrow or shaking his head until finally Jim's tale had run its course. 'Fascinating,' he said at length, 'quite fascinating. And you say that all those who had any personal dealings with this tramp felt an uncanny need to cross themselves?'

'As far as I can make out, but you must understand that a lot of what I have told you was heard second-hand as it were, nobody around here gives away much if they can possibly help it.'

'So much I know.'

'And so, what is to be done?'

'I think at present there is little we can do. We must be constantly on watch. Report to me with any intelligence, no matter how vague, which comes to hand. I will prepare myself as best I can, both mentally and physically. Our man is close, that is certain. You have seen him. I can sense his nearness and it is likewise with the creatures in the case. Soon he will come for them and when he does so, we must be ready.' Pooley reached out a hand towards the humidor. 'Why don't you have one of the ones in your top pocket?' asked the old Professor, smiling broadly.

15

Pooley sat that lunchtime alone in a corner seat at the Flying Swan, a half of pale ale growing warm before him. He sighed deeply. All that the Professor had said weighed heavily on his soul, and he wondered what should be done for the best. He thought he should go around to the Mission and confront Captain Carson regarding what Holmes would have referred to as 'the singular affair of the purloined wheelbarrow', which was something he and Omally should really have done the very next day. But the Captain's animosity towards visitors was well known to all thereabouts, especially to Jim who had once been round there to scrounge a bed for the night and had been run off with a gaff hook. Anyway, it was Omally's wheelbarrow and if he chose to forget the matter then that was up to him.

Maybe, he thought, it would be better for the Professor simply to hand over the bean things to this Dark One, whoever he might be, in the hope that he would depart with them, never to return. But that was no good, Pooley had felt the evil and he knew that the Professor was right. It would not go away by being ignored. Pooley sighed anew. A bead of perspiration rolled down the end of his nose and dropped into his ale.

Archroy entered the Flying Swan. Pooley had not seen him for some weeks; he had been strangely absent from the Cowboy Night fiasco. Jim wondered in which direction his suspicions pointed in the matter of the stolen beans. 'He doesn't know how lucky he is,' he thought.

Archroy, however, looked far from lucky upon this particular occasion. His shoulders drooped and his lopsided hairpiece clung perilously to his shining pate. Pooley watched him from the corner of his eye. He could not recall ever having seen anybody looking so depressed, and wondered whether the sorry specimen might appreciate a few kind words. For the life of him Jim couldn't think of any. Archroy looked up from the pouring of his ale and sighted Pooley, nodded in half-hearted greeting and sank back into his misery.

Pooley looked up through the pub windows. The flat-blocks quivered mirage-like in the heat and a bedraggled pigeon or two fluttered away into the shimmering haze. The heat strangled the bar-room air, everything moved in slow motion except Father Móity, resident priest to St Joan's, Brentford, who unexpectedly entered the bar at this moment. He strode towards the bar, oblivious to the battering heat, and ordered a small sherry. Neville poured this and noted that the priest made no motions towards his pocket upon accepting same. 'You are far from your cool confessional upon such a hot day,' said Neville cynically.

'Now, now, Neville,' said the priest, raising his blessing finger in admonishment. 'I have come to seek out two members of my flock who seem to have fallen upon stony ground.' Pooley much enjoyed listening to the young priest, whose endless supply of inaccurate quotation was a joy to the ear. 'Two prodigal sons who have sold their birthrights for a mess of porridge.' Pooley chuckled. 'You know them as Hairy Dave and Jungle John.'

'They're barred!' said Neville with a voice like thunder.

'Barred is it, and what pestilence have they visited upon you on this occasion?'

'They blew my bloody pub up.'

'Anarchists is it?'

'Bloody maniacs!' said Neville bitterly.

'Raise not thine hand in anger,' said the priest, bringing his blessing finger once more into play. 'How many times

163

shall I forgive my brother, seven isn't it? I say unto you seven hundred times seven, or some such figure.'

'Well, they are barred and they stay barred!'

'Tsk, tsk!' said the priest. 'It is because of bars that I find myself here, a lamb amongst wolves.'

'And how is the bar of your Catholic Club?' asked Neville sarcastically. 'Still doing a roaring trade with its cut-price drinks and taking the bread of life from the mouths of hardworking publicans?'

'Judge not, lest thyself be judged,' said the priest. 'The bars I refer to are of the gymnastical variety.'

Keeping fit was an obsession with Father Moity which verged at times upon the manic. He was forever jogging to and fro about the parish; as Pooley watched the young priest he noted the giveaway track-suit bottoms and striped running shoes peeping from beneath his robes of office. He did chin-ups in the vestry, calisthenics in the pulpit and had developed a system of Tai-Chi exercises to correspond with the ritual movements of the mass. Even as Pooley observed him at the bar, the young priest was flexing his biceps and doing the occasional kneesbend.

None of these things went unnoticed, and the handsome, tanned and manly figure of the priest raised extraordinary feelings within the breasts of both matronly females and young housewives alike. He had become a focus for their erotic desires. Confession became a nightmare. Even women of well-known and obvious virginity confided to the handsome young priest their nights of passion in the satyric embraces of demonic succubi. Father Moity marvelled at their invention, but more often he covered his ears and allowed his mind to wander. Consequently his penances were likely to be 'three Hail Marys and a hundred press-ups' or 'an our father and a work out on the heavy bag.'

'Gymnasium bars,' the young priest continued, 'for the church hall. I was promised that they would be

164

constructed before the Olympic trials came on the television. I wish to take a few pointers.'

'Well I haven't seen them,' sneered Neville, 'and I have no wish to.'

Father Moity said nothing but peered into his empty sherry glass and then about the bar. 'Jim Pooley,' he said, his eyes alighting upon that very man.

'Father?'

'Jim, my lad.' The priest bounced across the bar and joined Pooley at his table. 'Would you by any chance have seen those two local builders upon your travels?'

'I have not,' said Jim, 'but Father, I would have a few words with you if I may.'

'Certainly.' The priest seated himself, placing the empty sherry glass noisily upon the table. It vastly amused Pooley that even a priest of such olympian leanings was not averse to a couple of free sherries. Pooley obliged and the young priest thanked him graciously.

'Firstly,' said Jim in a confidential tone, 'I have been given to understand that Hairy Dave and Jungle John were doing a great deal more construction work for you than a set of gymnasium bars. I heard mention of an entire chapel or the like being built.'

'Did you now?' The young priest seemed genuinely baffled. 'Well I know nothing of that, chapel is it?'

'I took it to be R.C., because the plans were in Latin.'

The priest laughed heartily. 'Sure you are taking the rise out of me Jim Pooley, although the joke is well appreciated. The Church has not drawn up its plans in Latin since the fifteenth century.'

Jim shrugged and sniffed at his steaming beer. 'Stranger and stranger,' said he.

'Strange, is it?' said the priest. 'It is indeed strange that those lads downed tools last Thursday night and never returned to be paid for what they had so far accomplished, for those fellows that I would call strange.'

Jim sighed once more. Something was going on in Brentford and it seemed not only he was involved. 'Father,' said Jim with a terrible suddenness, 'what do you know of evil?'

The priest raised his fine dark eyebrows and stared at Pooley in wonder. 'That my son, is a most unexpected question.'

'I mean real evil,' said Pooley, 'not petty getting off the bus without paying evil, or the sin of pride or anger or minor trivial forms of evil, I mean real pure dark evil, the creeping sinister evil which lurks at the corners of men's minds, the low horrible . . .'

The priest broke in upon him. 'Come now,' said he, 'these are not fine things to talk of on a hot summer's day, all things bright and beautiful as they are.'

Pooley studied the honest face of the young priest. What could he know of real evil? Nothing whatever Jim concluded.

'My son,' said Father Moity, noting well Pooley's disturbed expression, 'what is troubling you?'

Pooley smiled unconvincingly. 'Nothing,' he said, 'just musing I suppose. Of Dave and John, I have seen nothing. Possibly they drink now at the New Inn or Jack Lane's, I should try there if I were you.'

The priest thanked Jim, wished him all of God's blessing for the balance of the day and jogged from the bar.

Pooley returned to his melancholic reverie. When Neville called time at three he left the bar, his half of light ale still steaming in its glass, and shambled out into the glare. He wandered off down Sprite Street and crossed beside his beloved memorial bench to enter the sweeping tree-lined drive which curved in a graceful arc towards the Butts Estate. He passed within a few yards of the Professor's front door and crunched over the gravel footway before the Seamen's Mission to emerge through the tiny passageway into the lower end of the High Street near the canal bridge.

As he leant upon the parapet, squinting along the dried-up stretch of ex-waterway into the shimmering distance, Pooley's thoughts were as parched and lifeless as the blistered canal bed. He wondered what had become of Soap Distant. Had he been blasted to dark and timeless oblivion by the floor tide which engulfed him, or had the rank waters carried him deep into the inner earth where even now he swapped drinking stories with old Rigdenjyepo and the denizens of that sunless domain? He wondered at Archroy's misery and at what urgent business might have lured Hairy Dave and his hirsute twin from their Friday payment at St Joan's.

Pooley tried to marshal his thoughts into some plan of campaign, but the sun thrashed down relentlessly upon his curly head and made him feel all the more dizzy and desperate. He would repair to the Plume Café for a cup of char, that would invigorate and refresh, that was the thing, the old cup that cheers. Pooley dragged his leathern elbows from the red-hot parapet and plodded off up the High Street.

The door of the Plume was wedged back and a ghastly multi-coloured slash curtain hung across the opening. Pooley thrust the gaudy plastic strips apart and entered the café. The sudden transition from dazzling sunlight to shadowy gloom left him momentarily blind and he clung to a cheap vinyl chair for support.

Lily Marlene lurked within, fanning her abundant mammaries with a menu card and cooling her feet in a washbowl of iced water. She noted Pooley's entrance without enthusiasm. 'We still give no credit, Jim Pooley.'

Pooley's eyes adjusted themselves, and he replied cheerfully, if unconvincingly, 'I return from foreign parts, my pockets abulge with golden largesse of great value.'

'It's still sixpence a cup,' the dulcet voice returned, 'or eight pence for a coffee.'

'Tea will be fine,' said Pooley producing two three-penny bits from his waistcoat pocket.

The grey liquid flowed from the ever-bubbling urn into the chipped white cup and Pooley bore his steaming prize to a window table. Other than Jim the café contained but a single customer. His back was turned and his shoulders hunched low over his chosen beverage, but the outline of the closely cropped head was familiar. Jim realized that he was in close proximity to the semi-mythical entity known as the Other Sam.

Strange rumours abounded regarding this bizarre personage, who was reputed to live the life of a recluse somewhere within an uncharted region of the Royal Botanical Garden at Kew. Exactly who he was or where he came from was uncertain. It was said that he rowed nightly across the Thames in a coracle of ancient design to consort with Vile Tony Watkins, who ran the yellow street-cleaning cart, a grim conveyance which moved mysteriously through the lamplit byways.

Vile Tony was an uncommunicative vindictive, with an ingrained distrust of all humanity and a dispassionate hatred for anything that walked upon two legs and held its head aloft during the hours of sunlight. Being a deaf-mute he kept his own counsel no matter what should occur.

Pooley had never spoken with the Other Sam, but felt a certain strange comfort in the knowledge of his being. The stories which surrounded him were uniformly weird and fantastical. He was the last of a forgotten race, some said; daylight would kill him, some said, for his eyes had never seen it. Others said that during her pregnancy his mother had observed something which had gravely affected her and that the midwife upon seeing the child had dropped it in horror, whereupon the tiny creature had scampered from the room and disappeared into the night.

Pooley the realist pooh-poohed such notions, but Pooley the mystic, dreamer and romantic sensed the aura of pagan mystery which surrounded the crop-headed man.

'Will you not join me at table, James Pooley,' said a voice which weakened Jim's bladder in a manner that formerly only large libations of ale had been able to do. 'I would have words with you.'

Pooley rose from his chair and slowly crossed the mottled linoleum floor of the Plume, wondering whether a leg-job might be preferable to a confrontation that most of Brentford's population would have taken great lengths to avoid.

'Be seated, James.' The face which met Jim's guarded glance was hardly one to inspire horror; it was pale, such was to be expected of one who dwelt in darkness, but it was a face which held an indefinable grandeur, an ancient nobility. 'Your thoughts press heavily upon me, James Pooley,' said the Other Sam.

'I do not know which way to turn,' said Jim, 'such responsibilities are beyond my scope.'

The Other Sam nodded sagely and Jim knew that he had nothing to fear from the pale blue eyes and the haunting thoughts which dwelt behind them. 'The evil is among us,' said the Other Sam. 'I will help you as best I may, but my powers are limited and I am no match for such an adversary.'

'Tell me what I should do.'

'The Professor is a man who may be trusted,' said the Other Sam. 'Act upon his instructions to the letter, accept no other advice, although much will be offered, follow your own feelings. The Dark One is vulnerable, he lives a life of fear, even Satan himself can never rest, truth will be for ever the final victor.'

'But who is he?' said Jim. 'I have been plunged into all this. Outside the sun shines, in offices clerks toil away at their mundane duties, buses rumble towards Ealing Broadway and I am expected to do battle with the powers of darkness. It all seems a little unfair.'

'You are not alone, James.'

'I feel rather alone.'

The Other Sam smiled wanly; wisdom shone in his ageless blue eyes. Professor Slocombe was a wise and learned man, but here was knowledge not distilled from musty tomes, but born of natural lore. Pooley felt at peace, he was no longer alone, he would cope with whatever lay ahead.

'I have stayed too long already,' said the Other Sam, 'and I must take my leave. I will not be far when you need me again. Take heart, James Pooley, you have more allies than you might imagine.'

With this he rose, a pale ghost who did not belong to the hours of daylight, and drifted out into the sunlit street where he was presently lost from view behind the gasometers.

Pooley took his teacup to his mouth, but the insipid grey liquid had grown cold. 'Cold tea and warm beer,' said Jim, 'and they say an army marches on its stomach.'

16

As August turned into September the residents of Brentford stared from their open windows and marvelled at the endless sunshine. Norman tapped at his thermometer and noted to his despair that it was up another two degrees. 'It's the end of the world for certain,' he said for the umpteenth time. 'I am working at present on an escape ship,' he told Omally, 'I am not going to be caught napping when the continents begin to break up.'

'I wish you luck,' replied Omally. 'I notice that there are no new Fine Arts Publications in your racks.'

'Business has fallen off of late.'

'Oh,' said John, 'must be the heat.'

'I hear,' said Norman, 'that the rising temperatures have started something of a religious revival hereabouts.'

'Oh?' said Omally, thumbing through a dog-eared copy of *Latex Babes*.

'The Church of the Second Coming, or suchlike, seems to be taking the ladies' fancy, although' – and here Norman's thoughts drifted back to his own bitter experiences as a married man – 'one can never expect much common sense from women.'

John's eyes rested upon the full-colour photograph of a voluptuous young female in leather corsets and thigh boots wielding a riding crop. 'They have their uses,' he said lecherously. 'Can I borrow this magazine?'

'No,' said Norman.

'And where is this Church of the Second Coming then?'

'I've no idea,' said Norman, 'news of it apparently travels by word of mouth. The ladies I have questioned have been loud in their praises for the place but reticent about its location.'

'Oh?' said John. 'I'll bring this back in half an hour.'

'No,' said Norman, 'it is well known that you photostat them at the library and sell the copies in the Swan.'

'Merely satisfying a need,' said John. 'Your prices are too high.'

'Get out of my shop!' said Norman, brandishing a lemonade bottle. Omally made a rapid and undignified departure.

As he tramped up the Ealing Road towards the Flying Swan, John's thoughts turned back towards the Church of the Second Coming. Hard times always brought out the religion in people, and this long hot summer with its rationed water and rising temperatures was enough to set the nervous and susceptible legging it towards the nearest church. There was a good deal of money to be had in that game, and after all one was serving the community by fulfilling a need. Any rewards could be said to be of a just nature. It was a thought, and not a bad one. By the time he reached the Flying Swan his mind was made up. He would seek out the Church of the Second Coming and insinuate himself into a position of responsibility. He would gain respect and prestige, might even become a pillar of the community.

Yes, Omally could feel the call of the mother church, he was by now completely certain that he had a true vocation. He pushed wide the saloon bar door and entered the Flying Swan.

'God save all here,' he said, 'and mine's a pint of Large please, Neville.'

The part-time barman did the business and counted Omally's coinage into his hand. 'It's gone up another penny,' he told the Irishman.

Omally smiled pleasantly and produced the coin. 'How are things with your good self, bar lord?' he said. 'It is another beautiful day is it not?'

'It is not.'

'Makes one feel good to be alive.'

'It does not.'

'God is in his heaven and all is right . . .'

'Turn it in, Omally.'

'Just remarking upon the splendours of creation.'

'Well, do it elsewhere.'

Omally removed himself to a side table where old Pete sat leaning upon his stick, his dog, Chips, belly up before him.

'Good day to you Pete,' said John seating himself. 'It is another beautiful day is it not? I thank God to be alive.'

Old Pete spat in the direction of the cuspidor, which was the last relic of Cowboy Night, having been retained owing to its overwhelming popularity. 'You should take to the wearing of a hat, Omally,' said he. 'The harsh sun has befuddled your brain. I have an old homburg I might sell you.'

172

'God is in his heaven,' said Omally.

Pete was lining up for another shot at the cuspidor. 'A pox on God,' said the surly old bastard.

It was clear, thought Omally, that the joys of the Church of the Second Coming had not yet made themselves manifest to the barstaff and patrons of the Flying Swan. A more direct approach was in order.

'Don't you ever go to church, Pete?' he enquired.

'Never,' said the ancient. 'I have a straw boater if you don't fancy the homburg.'

'Listen,' said Omally, who was rapidly losing his patience. 'Just because I feel the need to extol the glories of God for once it doesn't follow that I'm heading for a padded cell in St Bernard's.'

'Glories of God?' said Pete in a sarcastic tone. 'You are an ungodly womanizer, Omally, with about as much religious inclination as young Chips here.'

'Ah,' said Omally. 'That may have once been true but I have seen the light. I am mending my ways.'

'I have a very inexpensive cloth cap I might let you have.'

'I don't want a bloody cloth cap.'

'Go down to Father Moity's then.'

'No,' said Omally, 'I need to find a church of a new denomination, one which would offer an honest godfearing man a chance to be at peace with himself and his maker.' Young Chips made one of those unholy noises he was noted for and his elderly master chuckled maliciously.

'I can see I am wasting my time here,' said John. 'A seeker after truth is not welcome hereabouts, a prophet is without honour in his own land so he is.'

'Listen,' said Old Pete. 'If you really feel the need for something a bit different in the religious line why don't you go down to the Church of the Second Coming, I hear they have rare old times down there.'

Omally pricked up his ears. All this waste of breath and

he might just as well have asked the old fellow straight out. 'Church of the Second Coming?' said he. 'I don't think I've heard of that one.'

'Well, all I know is that two old dears were talking about the place in the supermarket. Seems that there's some sort of New Messiah fellow started up in business, very popular with the ladies he is.'

'And where is this church to be found?'

'Search me,' said Old Pete. 'I didn't overhear that.'

What Omally said next was a phrase in Gaelic which his father had taught him when still a lad for use against the Black and Tans.

'And you,' said Old Pete as Chips set about the Irishman's trouser bottoms. He might not have much religious inclination, that dog, but he did speak fluent Gaelic.

Omally shook the mutt free from his ankles and finished his drink at the bar. He began to understand how saints came to get martyred. It wasn't all tea and crumpets with the vicar this getting into the church. And then a pleasant thought struck him; amongst the many ladies of his acquaintance there must surely be one who had taken up within the new church, and even if there wasn't it would be a pleasure finding out.

Omally took out his little black book and thumbed at the pages. Where to start? A for Archroy's missus. He would pay her a visit that very night.

'Another pint please, Neville,' said the Irishman jovially, 'and to hell with the extra penny.'

Archroy stood in his back garden gazing up at the colossal mesh-covered construction which all but engulfed the entire yard. The deafening chatter of a thousand gaily coloured birds filled his ears.

Archroy's worst fears had been realized that very morning when the dreaded lorry had arrived, bearing the exotic cargo which now flapped and twittered before him.

He had never seen birds quite like them before, nor had he seen such a lorry, black as death and seemingly without windows. And the driver – Archroy shuddered, where did his wife meet these people?

There must be a thousand of them in there, thought Archroy peering into the cage. The din was appalling, the neighbours weren't going to like this one. Mrs Murdock appeared at the garden fence, a bundle of limp washing in her arms and a clothespeg in her mouth. 'Lovely aren't they?' she mumbled. 'Just what this neighbourhood needs to brighten it up.'

'You *like* them?' Archroy shouted.

Mrs M. nodded enthusiastically. 'Them's lovely.'

Archroy shook his head in wonder, the whole neighbourhood was going mad. It must be the heat.

'I'll bring them out some breadcrumbs,' said Mrs Murdock, oblivious to the row. 'They'll like them.'

'Better tell the bakery to staff up its night shift then,' muttered Archroy. What *did* they eat? He leant forward upon the mesh and squinted at the mass of fluttering feathers. As if in answer to his question a single bird detached itself from the ever-circling throng and swooped down upon him, removing with one deft peck a goodly lump of flesh from his right thumb.

'Damn you,' shrieked Archroy, drawing back in anguish. Blood flowed from the wound and through it he could glimpse the ivory whiteness of exposed bone. 'Oh my God,' wailed Archroy, coming over faint. 'Oh my God.'

He staggered back into the kitchen and bound the gory thumb with a length of dishcloth. The thumb throbbed like a good 'un, it was definitely a casualty department job. Archroy's mind, alert to the slings and arrows of outrageous fortune which constantly assailed him, could see it all in advance: BRENTONIAN SAVAGED BY BUDGIE. The lads at the wiper works would have a field day. Archroy groaned in a manner that he had come to perfect of late. Blood began to ooze through the makeshift bandage. Archroy tottered off in the direction of the cottage hospital.

He had no sooner turned the corner into Sprite Street, leaving behind him the kind of trail that bloodhounds love so dearly, when John Omally appeared pedalling slowly from the direction of the Ealing Road. He dismounted from his iron stallion and leant Marchant against Archroy's fence. With a beaming smile upon his face he strode up the short garden path and rapped upon Archroy's gaily coloured front door. 'Helloee,' he called through the letter box.

All was silent within but for a brief rattling flutter, suggestive of a venetian blind being noisily and rapidly drawn up. 'Helloee,' called Omally again. 'Anybody home?' Clearly there was not. 'I'll just have a look around the back,' said John loudly to the deserted street. 'He may be asleep in his deckchair.'

Omally stealthily edged his way along the side of the house and tested the garden door. It swung soundlessly upon its oiled hinge to reveal the mighty mesh-covered structure. 'By the light of the burning martyrs,' said John.

The cage was partly lost in the shadow of the house and appeared to be empty. Omally prodded at the wire mesh. It was solidly constructed, surely no flock of budgies merited such security. The door was solidly framed in angle-iron and triple-bolted. Omally slid the first bolt back. It wouldn't hurt to have a swift shufty within. The second bolt shot back with a metallic clang. Omally looked furtively about the gardens. Mrs Murdock's washing hung in a sullen line, dripping into the dust, but there was no sign of any human onlookers.

The third bolt went the way of its fellows and Omally swung the cage door slowly open. There was not a sound but for the tiny muted explosions of the drips. John stepped nimbly into the cage and peered up into the shadows. All was silent.

Without a second's warning a vast multicoloured mass of squawking violence descended upon him. He was engulfed by a screaming, tearing oblivion of claws and beaks. Sharp horny bills tore at his tweeds and sank greedily into his flesh. Omally howled in pain and battered away at the wildly flapping horde which bore down upon him. He tore his jacket up over his head and blindly fought his way back to the door of the cage, the demonic creatures ripping at his shirt-tails and sinking their razor-sharp beaks remorselessly into him.

With a superhuman effort born from his infinite reserve of self-preservative energy Omally threw himself through the door, driving it closed behind him and flinging one of the bolts to. He sank to his knees before the cage door, blood flowing from countless wounds. His treasured tweed suit was in ribbons and he clutched between his fingers tufts of his own hair. Bitterly he looked back towards his tormentors, but the feathered fiends had withdrawn once more to their lofty perches high in the shadows. Nothing remained to signify their presence but a few prettily coloured feathers upon the cage floor.

Omally set a painful course for his rooms. His suit was in such exquisite ruin that there was no hope of restoration. His face had the appearance of one recently engaged in a pitched battle with a rampaging lawnmower. 'Foul feathered bastards,' said John through clenched teeth. He ran a tender hand over his scalp and felt to his horror several large bald patches. 'Feathering their bloody nests with my barnet.' He looked down at his hands as he steered Marchant somewhat erratically towards its destination. They were a mass of tiny v-shaped wounds. 'Carnivorous canaries, what a carve-up!' Archroy would pay dearly for this.

An hour later Omally lay soaking in his bathtub, the water

a nasty pink colour. He had affixed small strips of toilet paper to the cuts on his face, and made some attempt to comb his hair forward and up into an extraordinary quiff to cover his bald patches. He drank frequently from a bottle of Old Snakebelly and swore between sips. 'I will set traps upon the allotment,' he said, 'and catch the monster moggy – let's see how those flying piranhas like that up their perches.'

When the bottle was finished Omally felt a little better, but there was still the matter of his suit. What a tragic circumstance. The remnants of his favourite tweed hung upon the bathroom door, he had never seen anything so absolutely destroyed. Fifteen years of constant wear had hardly impinged upon the hardy fabric, but five or so short seconds in that cage of fluttering death had reduced it to ribbons.

'God,' said Omally, 'I bet those lads could strip down an elephant in under a minute, nothing left but four umbrella stands!'

An hour later Omally was out of his tinted bathwater and dressed. Actually he looked pretty natty but for the speckled face and bizarre hairstyle. He had found a pair of cricketer's white flannels, a Fair Isle jumper and a clean cotton shirt. This had evidently been a Christmas present, as it was wrapped in green paper decorated with holly and foolish fat santas. As to footwear (the winged attackers having even played havoc with his hobnails) he chose a rather dapper pair of black patent dancing pumps he had borrowed from Pooley for some unremembered social function. He slung an old silk cravat about his neck and fastened it with a flourish.

Presently the clock struck seven and Omally wondered whether it might be worth chancing his arm for a swift pedal around to Archroy's. If the bewigged one was there he could always think up some excuse for his visit. But if Archroy's insatiable better half was home then he should

178

at least be able to charm his way into a bit of compensation for the afternoon's tragic events.

Archroy, as it happened, was not on the night shift. He had suffered the horrors of a tetanus injection, administered at the sneaky end by a sadistic nurse, and had received fourteen stitches in his thumb. The thumb was now liberally swathed in bandages and hidden within the overlarge folds of an impressive-looking sling. This sling now rested upon the bar of the Flying Swan.

'Caught it in the lathe,' he told Neville, but the part-time barman suspected otherwise. 'Honest,' insisted Archroy, 'nearly took my arm off.'

'Looks pretty bad,' said Jim Pooley. 'You'll be in for compensation.'

'Could be hundreds,' said Old Pete.

'Thousands,' said Neville. 'You'll be rich.'

'Mine's a pint then,' said Pooley.

'And mine,' said Old Pete.

Archroy bought another round, there being little else he could do.

'Cut yourself shaving, John?' said Archroy's wife as she answered the unexpected knock.

'In my eagerness to look my best for you my dear.'

'I like the strides.'

'They are all the rage in Carnaby Street.'

Omally was ushered hastily into the front room, where Archroy's wife pulled the curtains.

'And who might this be?' Omally's eyes had been drawn to a fine oil painting which hung above the fireplace in an ornate gilded frame, looking strangely out of place amid the pink dralon and mock veneer. It was the portrait of a stern, yet imposing figure of indeterminate years clad in crimson robes and sporting what appeared to be a skull-cap. 'Looks very valuable.'

'It is. Will you take tea?'

'I'd prefer something a little stronger if I may.'

'Gin then?'

'Absolutely.'

Archroy's wife poured two large gins and joined Omally upon the quilted pink sofa facing the portrait. Omally found it hard to draw away his eyes as he received his drink. 'There is something familiar about that painting,' he said. 'But I can't quite put my finger on it.'

'It was a present,' said Archroy's wife pleasantly. 'Drink up John, here's a toast to the future: *Auspicium melioris gevi.*'

Omally raised his glass and from the corner of his eye noticed that Archroy's wife held hers towards the portrait as if in salute. 'Surely that is Latin, is it not?'

'It is?' said Archroy's wife innocently. 'I think it's just a toast or something, don't know where I heard it.'

'It's not important,' said John, sipping his gin. In *vino veritas*, thought he. 'Shall we have one more?' he said, springing to his feet. As Omally decanted two large gins into the dainty glasses, he had a definite feeling that he was being watched – not by Archroy's wife who sat demurely drawing her skirt up above her knees, but by some alien presence which lurked unseen. It was a most uncomfortable feeling and one which Omally threw off only with difficulty. He returned to the sofa bearing the drinks, his a single and hers a triple.

'To us,' he said.

'*Ab aeterno, Ab ante, Ab antiquo,*' said Archroy's missus.

'Down the hatch,' said John.

After three more ill-proportioned tipples Archroy's wife began to warm to her unexpected guest in the passionate manner Omally had come to appreciate.

'Shall we go upstairs?' he asked as the lady of the house began to nibble at his ear and fumble with his Fair Isle.

'Let's do it here,' she purred.

'What, on your new three-piece?'

'Why not?'

Omally kicked off his black patents with practised ease and divested himself of his cricket whites.

'Been shaving your legs as well?' said Archroy's wife, noticing the bloody scars about Omally's ankles.

'Caught myself in the briar patch.'

The pink sofa was solidly constructed and well padded with the finest foam rubber. It stood the assault upon it uncomplainingly, but something was wrong. Omally felt himself unable to perform with his usual style and finesse, the spark just wasn't there.

Archroy's wife noticed it almost at once. 'Come on man,' she cried, 'up and at it!'

Omally sat upright. 'Someone's watching us,' he said. 'I can feel eyes burning into me.'

'Nonsense, there's nobody here but us.'

Omally made another attempt but it was useless. 'It's that picture,' he said in sudden realization. 'Can't you feel it?'

'I can't feel anything, that's the trouble.'

'Turn its face to the wall, it's putting me off my stroke.'

'No!' Archroy's wife flung herself from the sofa and stood with her back to the portrait, her arms outspread. She appeared ready to take on an army if necessary.

'Steady on,' said Omally. 'I am sorry if I have offended you, hang a dishcloth over it then, I won't touch it.'

'Hang a dishcloth over *him*? Don't be a fool!'

Omally was hurriedly donning his trousers. There was something very wrong here. Archroy's wife looked completely out of her head, and it wasn't just the gin. The woman's possessed, he told himself. Oh damn, he had both feet down the same trouser leg. He toppled to the floor in a struggling heap. The woman came forward and stood over him laughing hysterically.

'You are useless,' she taunted, 'you limp fish, you can't do it!'

'I have a prior appointment,' spluttered John trying to extricate his tangled feet. 'I must be off about my business.'

'You're not a man,' the mad woman continued. '"He" is the only man in Brentford, the only man in the world.'

'Who is?' Omally ceased his vain struggling a moment, all this had a quality of mysterious intrigue. Even though he was at an obvious disadvantage at the feet of a raving lunatic he would never forgive himself if he missed the opportunity to find out what was going on.

'Who is "He"?'

'He? He is the born again, the second born, He . . .' The woman turned away from Omally and fell to her knees before the portrait. Omally hastily adjusted his legwear and rose shakily to his feet. Clutching his patent shoes, he made for the door. He no longer craved an explanation, all he craved was a large double and the comparative sanity of the Flying Swan. Phrases of broken Latin poured from the mouth of the kneeling woman and Omally fled. He flung open the front door, knocking Archroy who stood, his key raised towards the lock, backwards into the rose bushes. He snatched up the peacefully dozing Marchant and rode off at speed.

As he burst into the saloon bar Omally's dramatic appearance did not go unnoticed. His cricket whites were now somewhat oily about the ankle regions and his nose had started to bleed.

'Good evening, John,' said Neville. 'Cut yourself shaving?'

'The match finished then?' asked Jim Pooley. 'Run out, were you?'

'Want to change your mind about that hat?' sniggered Old Pete, who apparently had not shifted his position since lunchtime.

'A very large scotch,' said John, ignoring the ribaldry.

'John,' Pooley said in a voice of concern. 'John, what has happened, are we at war?'

Omally shook his head vigorously. 'Oh no,' said he, 'not war.' He shot the large scotch down in one go.

'What then, have you sighted the vanguard of the extraterrestrial strike force?'

'Not those lads.'

'What then? Out with it.'

'Look at me,' said Omally. 'What do you see?'

Jim Pooley stood back. Fingering his chin thoughtfully, he scrutinized the trembling Irishman.

'I give up,' said Jim at length. 'Tell me.'

Omally drew his breath and said, 'I am a man most sorely put upon.'

'So it would appear, but why the fancy dress? It is not cricketers' night at Jack Lane's by any chance?'

'Ha ha,' said John in a voice oddly lacking in humour. He ordered another large scotch and Pooley, who was by now in truth genuinely concerned at his close friend's grave demeanour, actually paid for it. He led the shaken Irishman away from the chuckling throng and the two seated themselves in a shadowy corner.

'I have seen death today,' said Omally in a low and deadly tone. 'And like a fool I went back for a second helping.'

'That would seem an ill-considered move upon your part.'

John peered into his double and then turned his eyes towards his old friend. 'I will tell you all, but this must go no further.'

Inside Pooley groaned dismally, he had become a man of late for whom the shared confidence spelt nothing but doom and desolation. 'Go ahead, then,' he said in a toneless voice.

Omally told his tale, omitting nothing, even his

intention towards Archroy's wife. At first Pooley was simply stunned to hear such a candid confession of his colleague's guilty deeds, but as the tale wore on and Omally spoke of the Church of the Second Coming and of the sinister portrait and the Latin babblings his blood ran cold.

'Drink up,' said Jim finally. 'For there is something I must tell you, and I don't think you are going to like it very much.' Slowly and with much hesitation Pooley made his confession. He told the Irishman everything, from his first theft of the magic bean to his midnight observation of Omally, and on to all that the Professor had told him regarding the coming of the Dark One and his later meeting with the Other Sam.

Omally sat throughout it all, his mouth hanging open and his glass never quite reaching his lips. When finally he found his voice it was hollow and choked. 'Old friend,' said he. 'We are in big trouble.'

Pooley nodded. 'The biggest,' he said. 'We had better go to the Professor.'

'I agree,' said Omally. 'But we had better have one or two more of these before we go.'

17

When Neville called time at ten thirty the two men stumbled forth into the street in their accustomed manner. They had spoken greatly during that evening and there had been much speculation and much putting together of two and two. If the Messiah to the Church of the Second Coming was the man in the portrait and the man in the portrait was none other than the dreaded Dark One himself, then he was obviously gaining a very firm foothold hereabouts.

As Omally pushed Marchant forward and Pooley slouched at his side, hands in pockets, the two men began to feel wretchedly vulnerable beneath the moon's unholy light.

'You can almost come to terms with it during the day,' said Pooley. 'But at night, that is another matter.'

'I can feel it,' said John. 'The streets seem no longer familiar, all is now foreign.'

'I know.'

If Marchant knew, he was not letting on, but out of sheer badness he developed an irritating squeak which put the two men in mind of the now sea-going wheelbarrow, and added to their gloom and despondency.

'This lad is heading for the breaker's yard,' said Omally suddenly. Marchant ceased his rear-wheel loquaciousness.

A welcoming glow showed from the Professor's open French windows when presently they arrived. From within came the sound of crackling pages being turned upon the laden desk.

'Professor,' called Jim, tapping upon the pane.

'Come in Jim,' came the cheery reply. 'And bring Omally with you.'

The two men looked at one another, shrugged and entered the room. Pooley's eyes travelled past the old Professor and settled upon the spot where the bean creatures had been housed. 'Where are they?'

'They have grown somewhat, Jim,' said the Professor. 'I have been forced to lodge them in larger and more secure quarters.' He rang his bell and Gammon appeared as if by magic, bearing a bottle of scotch upon a silver salver.

'Now then,' the Professor said, after what he felt to be a respectable pause, adequate for the settling into armchairs and the tasting of scotch, 'I take it you have something to tell me. I take it further that you have confided all in Mr

Omally?' Pooley hung his head. 'It is all for the best, I suppose, it was inevitable that you should. So, now that you know, what are your thoughts on the matter, Omally?'

Omally, caught somewhat off guard, was hard pressed for a reply, so he combined a shrug, a twitch and a brief but scholarly grin to signify that he had not yet drawn upon his considerable funds of intellect in order to deal fully with the situation.

The Professor, however, read it otherwise. 'You are at a loss,' said he.

'I am,' said John.

'So,' the Professor continued, 'what brings you here?'

Omally looked towards Jim Pooley for support. Jim shrugged. 'You'd better tell him the lot,' said he.

Omally set about the retelling of his day's experiences. When the Irishman had finished the Professor rose to his feet. Crossing to one of the gargantuan bookcases he drew forth an old red-bound volume which he laid upon the desk.

'Tell me John,' he said. 'You would recognize the figure in the portrait were you to see his likeness again?'

'I could hardly forget it.'

'I have the theory,' said Professor Slocombe, 'that we are dealing here with some kind of recurring five-hundred-year cycle. I would like you to go through this book and tell me if a facsimile of the portrait you saw exists within.'

Omally sat down in the Professor's chair and began to thumb through the pages. 'It is a very valuable book,' the Professor cautioned, as John's calloused thumb bent back the corner of yet another exquisite page.

'Sorry.'

'Tell me, Professor,' said Jim, 'if we can identify him and even if we can beat on his front door and confront him face to face, what can we do? Omally and I have both seen him, he's getting on for seven feet tall and big with it. I wouldn't fancy taking a swing at him and anyway as far as we can swear to, he hasn't committed any crime. What do we do?'

'You might try making a citizen's arrest,' said Omally, looking up from his page-turning.

'Back to the books, John,' said the Professor sternly.

'My wrists are beginning to ache,' Omally complained, 'and my eyes are going out of focus looking at all these pictures.'

'Were they sharp, the beaks of those birds?' asked the Professor. John's wrists received a sudden miraculous cure.

'Well,' said Jim to the Professor, 'how do we stop him?'

'If we are dealing with some form of negative theology, then the tried and trusted methods of the positive theology will serve as ever they did.'

'Fire and water and the holy word.'

'The same, I am convinced of it.'

'Got him!' shouted John Omally suddenly, leaping up and banging his finger on the open book. 'It's him, I'm certain, you couldn't mistake him.'

Pooley and the Professor were at Omally's side in an instant, craning over his broad shoulders. The Professor leant forward and ran a trembling hand over the inscription below the etched reproduction of the portrait. 'Are you certain?' he asked, turning upon Omally. 'There must be no mistake, it would be a grave matter indeed if you have identified the wrong man.'

Pooley bent towards the etching. 'No,' said he, 'there is no mistake.'

The Professor turned slowly away from the two men at the desk. 'Gentlemen,' he said solemnly, 'that is a portrait of Rodrigo Borgia, born in Valencia January 1st, 1431, died in Rome August 18th, 1503. Rodrigo Borgia – Pope Alexander VI!'

'That is correct,' said a booming voice. 'I am Rodrigo Lenzuoli Borgia and I have come for my children!'

The French windows flew back to the sound of shattering glass and splintering woodwork and an enormous figure entered the portal. He was easily seven feet in height and he inclined his massive head as he stepped through the casement. He was clad in the rich crimson robes of the Papacy and was surrounded by a weirdly shimmering aura which glittered and glowed about him.

The Professor crossed himself and spoke a phrase of Latin.

'Silence!' The giant raised his hand and the old Professor slumped into his chair as if cataleptic. Pooley and Omally shrank back against the wall and sought the lamaic secrets of invisibility. The mighty figure turned his blood-red glare upon them. Pooley's knees were jelly, Omally's teeth rattled together like castanets.

'I should destroy you now,' said the giant, 'you are but worms that I might crush beneath my heel.'

'Worms,' said Omally, 'that's us, hardly worth the trouble.' He laughed nervously and made a foolish face.

'Ha!' The giant turned away his horrible eyes. 'I have pressing business, you may count yourselves lucky.'

The two men nodded so vigorously that it seemed that their heads would detach themselves at any minute from their trembling bodies and topple to the floor.

'Come unto me my children,' boomed the awful voice, 'come now, there is much work to be done.'

There was a terrible silence. Nothing moved. The two men were transfixed in terror, and the giant in the crimson garb stood motionless, his hands stretched forth towards the study door. Then it came, at first faintly, a distant rattling and thumping upon some hidden door, then a loud report as if the obstruction had been suddenly demolished. Scratching, dragging sounds of ghastly origin drew nearer and nearer. They stopped the other side of the study door and all became again silent.

The two men stood in quivering anticipation. A mere inch of wood stood between them and the nameless, the unspeakable.

The silence broke as a rain of blows descended upon the

study door, the huge brass lock straining against the onslaught. Suddenly the panels of the elegant Georgian door burst asunder. As gaping holes appeared, the two men caught sight of the malevolent force which battered relentlessly upon them.

The beings were dwarf-like and thickly set, composed of knobby root-like growths, a tangle of twisted limbs matted into a sickening parody of human form, dendritic fingers clutching and clawing at the door. Forward the creatures shambled, five in all. They stood clustered in the centre of the room, their gnarled and ghastly limbs aquiver and their foul mouths opening and closing and uttering muffled blasphemies.

The giant raised his hand and gestured towards the French windows. The fetid beings shuffled towards the opening, one raising its vile arm defiantly at the two men.

Omally gripped his chum's jacket, his face white and bloodless. Pooley shook uncontrollably, his eyes crossed, and he sank to the floor in a dead faint.

The last of the creatures had left the room and the giant in crimson turned his eyes once more to Omally. 'Irishman,' he said, 'are you a good Catholic?'

Omally nodded.

'Then kneel.'

Omally threw himself to his knees. The giant stepped forward and extended his hand. 'Kiss the Papal ring!' Omally's eyes fell upon the large and beautiful ring upon the giant's right hand. 'Kiss the ring!' said Pope Alexander VI.

Omally's head swayed to and fro, the ring came and went as he tried to focus upon it. Although he would have done anything to be free of the evil crimson giant, this was too much. He was not a good Catholic, he knew, but this was supreme blasphemy, one might do a million years in purgatory for this.

'No,' screamed Omally, 'I will not do it,' and with that

189

he too lost consciousness and fell to the floor at the feet of the giant.

A shaft of early sunlight passed through the broken framework of the French windows and fell upon the prone figure of Jim Pooley. Pooley stirred stiffly and uncomfortably in his unnatural sleep, groaned feebly and flung out his arms. His eyes snapped open, nervously turning on their orbits to the right and left. He flexed his numbed fingers and struggled to his knees. Omally lay a few feet from him, apparently dead.

Pooley pulled himself to his feet and struggled to his chum. 'John,' he shouted, gripping the Irishman by his Fair Isle jumper and shaking him violently, 'John, can you hear me?'

'Away with you, Mrs Granger,' mumbled Omally, 'your husband will be back from his shift.'

'John,' shouted Pooley anew, 'wake up damn you.'

Omally's eyes opened and he peered up at his friend. 'Bugger you, Pooley,' said he, 'out of my boudwah!'

'Pull yourself together, man.'

Omally's eyes shot to and fro about the room in sudden realization. 'The Professor!' The old man lay draped across his chair, his mouth hung open and his breath came in desperate pants. 'Bring some water, or better still scotch.' Pooley fetched the bottle. Omally dipped in his finger and wiped it about Professor Slocombe's parched lips.

The old man's head slumped forward and his hands came alive, gripping the arms of the chair. His mouth moved and his aged eyes flickered back and forth between the two men. 'W-where is he?' he stuttered. 'Has he gone?' He tried to rise but the effort was too much and he sank back limply into the chair. 'Give me a drink.'

'What price Dimac,' said Pooley to himself. Omally poured the Professor an enormous scotch and the ancient tossed it back with a single movement. He flung his glass aside and buried his face in his hands. 'My God,' said he, 'I knew he was powerful, but I never realized, his force is beyond comprehension. I set up a mental block but he simply swept it aside. I was helpless!'

Pooley knelt beside the Professor's chair. 'Are you all right, sir?' he asked, placing a hand upon the old man's arm.

'The creatures!' said the Professor, jerking himself upright. 'Has he taken them?'

Pooley gestured towards the broken study door. 'With apparent ease.'

Professor Slocombe climbed to his feet and leant against the fireplace for support. Omally was pouring himself a scotch. 'He will have to be stopped!'

'Oh fine,' said Omally. 'We'll get right to it.'

'I know little of the Catholic faith,' said Pooley, 'who was Pope Alexander VI?'

'He was not what one would describe as a good egg,' said Omally. 'He was father to Lucretia Borgia, a lady of dubious renown, and of five or so other byblows along the way. He achieved his Papal Throne through simony and died, so the fable goes, through mistakenly taking poison intended for Cardinal Adriano de Cornetto, with whom he was dining. He is not well remembered, you could say.'

'A bit of a stinker indeed,' said Pooley, 'but a man of his time.'

The Professor had been silent, but now he raised himself upon his elbows and looked deep into the Irishman's eyes. 'I believe now that my previous proposition was incorrect. The Dark One does not have form, he assumes the form of others by recalling their ambitions and increasing their powers to his own ends. This alien force is capable of acting upon a powerful ego, adding to it and enlarging it until it becomes a power of diabolic magnitude. Alexander VI died before his time, and I suggest that he has returned to carry on where he left off.

Only now he is more powerful, he is no longer a mere human, now he can fully realize his ambitions unburdened by the fear of retribution. He thinks himself to be invulnerable. Let us pray that he is not.'

Omally shrugged. 'So what chance do we stand?'

'This is earth and we are alive. Anything that encroaches upon us must by definition be alien. It may appear to have the upper hand, but its unnaturalness puts it at a disadvantage.'

'He didn't look much at a disadvantage.'

'What puzzles me,' said the Professor, 'is why he did not kill us. He knows us to be a threat to him, yet he allowed us to live.'

'Good old him.'

'It is possible,' the old man continued, 'that his powers are limited and that he can only expend a certain amount of energy at one time. Certainly the destruction of the cellar door must have required enormous force, the creatures alone could never have accomplished that. It was reinforced with steel.'

'What about the light which surrounded him?' queried Omally. 'It was blazing when he entered but it had quite dimmed away when last I set eyes upon his accursed form.'

'What happened after I blacked out?' Pooley asked.

Omally turned away. 'Nothing,' said he in a bland voice, but the violent shaking of his hands did not go unnoticed by Jim or the Professor.

'It looks like another sunny day,' said Jim, changing the subject.

'Will you gentlemen take breakfast with me?' asked the Professor.

There is little need to record the answer to that particular question.

192

18

As September neared its blazing end, the heat showed no sign of lessening. Now the nights were made terrible by constant electrical storms. Omally had penned Marchant up in his allotment shed, having read of a cyclist struck down one night by the proverbial bolt from the blue.

There could now be no doubt of the location of the Church of the Second Coming. Nightly its grey-faced flock stalked through the tree-lined streets of the Butts Estate en route for its unhallowed portals. Father Moity was going through agonies of self-doubt as his congregation deserted him in droves.

The Professor stood at his window watching them pass. He shook his head in sorrow and pulled down the blind. Many had seen the five red monks moving mysteriously through the midnight streets. It was rumoured that they attended at the rites of the new church. The Professor felt the hairs on the nape of his neck rise when he thought of the alien monstrosities which inhabited those saintly crimson robes. He had seen them again only the night before, clustered in a swaying group outside his very garden gate, murmuring amongst themselves.

A streak of lightning had illuminated them for a moment and the Professor had seen the ghastly mottled faces, muddy lustreless masks of horror. He had slammed shut his doors and drawn down the iron screen he had fitted for security. His house was almost in a state of siege now, and he was certain that his every move was closely observed.

Omally had been acting as messenger and delivery boy, freighting quantities of thaumaturgical books which arrived daily in wax-paper packages at Norman's corner shop. The old man rarely slept now, and his hours were spent committing to memory vast passages of obscure Latin.

'Every day draws us nearer,' he told the struggling Irishman as Omally manhandled another half dozen weighty tomes into the study.

'You must surely have half the stock of the British Museum here by now,' said the perspiring John.

'I have almost all I need,' the Professor explained, 'but I have another letter for you to post.'

'Talking of books,' said Omally, 'I have loaned your Dimac training manual to Archroy.'

The Professor smiled briefly. 'And what became of yours?'

'I never owned one,' said Omally, 'it was a rumour put about by Pooley. It kept us out of fights.'

'Well, good luck to Archroy, he has suffered more than most over this affair. I hear that as well as losing his car, his magic beans and the use of his thumb, he was also unlucky enough to have had his arm broken and his head damaged by a lunatic in a Fair Isle jumper.'

Omally, who now no longer adopted that particular mode of dress, nodded painfully. 'I am grateful that my companions at the Swan have been discreet over that particular matter and I must thank my good friend Jim for the permanent loan of his second suit.'

The Professor whistled through his teeth. 'Two suits Pooley, a man of means indeed.'

Omally sipped at his drink thoughtfully and knotted his brow. 'Will all this soon be over?' he asked. 'Is there any end in sight?'

The Professor stood at the open French windows, the setting sun casting his elongated shadow back across the room. 'Great forces are at work,' he said in a distant voice, 'and as it is said, "The wheels of God grind slowly but they grind exceedingly small".'

If that was intended as an answer to Omally's question the Irishman failed to understand it, but as the old man's back was turned he took advantage of the fact and poured himself another very large scotch.

'*Woosah*!' An enormous scream and a startling figure clad in silk kimono, black trousers fastened tightly at the ankles and grimy plimsolls leapt from the allotment shed, clearing the five-foot bean poles in a single bound to descend with a sickening crash amongst a pile of upturned bell cloches.

'Damn it!' The figure stepped from the wreckage and straightened its wig, then, '*Banzai*!' The figure strutted forward, performed an amazing *Kata* and drove the fingers of his right hand back through the corrugated wall of his shed.

The figure was Archroy, and he was well on the way to mastering the secrets of the legendary Count Dante. The area around his shed was a mass of tangled wreckage, the wheelbarrow was in splinters and the watering can was an unrecognizable tangle of zinc.

Archroy strode forward upon elastic limbs and sought things to destroy. The Dimac manual lay open at a marked page labelled 'The Art of the Iron Hand'.

'*Aaaroo*!' Archroy lept into the air and kicked the weathervane from the top of Omally's shed, returning to the ground upon bouncing feet. He laughed loudly and the sound echoed over the empty dust bowl, bouncing from the Mission wall and disappearing over his head in the direction of the river. 'Iron Hand,' he said, 'I'll show them.'

He had read the Dimac manual from cover to cover and learned it by heart. 'The deadliest form of martial arts known to mankind,' it said, 'whose brutal tearing, rending, maiming and mutilating techniques have for many years been known only to the high Lamas of Tibet, where in the snowy wastes of the Himalayas they have perfected the hidden art of Dimac.' Count Dante had scorned his sacred vow of silence, taken in the lofty halls of the Potala, never to reveal the secret science, and had brought his knowledge and skill back to the West where for a mere one dollar ninety-eight these maiming, disfiguring and crippling techniques could be made available to the simple layman. Archroy felt an undying gratitude to the black-masked Count, the Deadliest Man on Earth, who must surely be living a life of fear lest the secret emissaries from Lhasa catch him up.

Archroy cupped his hand into the Dark Eagle's Claw posture and sent it hurtling through the padlocked door of Omally's shed. The structure burst asunder, toppling to the ground in a mass of twisted wreckage and exposing the iron frame and sit-up-and-beg handlebars of Marchant.

'Luck indeed,' said Archroy, sniggering mercilessly. He lifted the old black bicycle from the ruins of the allotment hut and stood it against a heap of seed boxes which had escaped his violent attentions.

'You've had it coming for years,' he told Marchant. The bicycle regarded him with silent contempt. 'It's the river for you, my lad.' Marchant's saddle squeaked nervously. 'But first I am going to punish you.'

Archroy gripped the handlebars and wrenched them viciously to one side. 'Remember the time you tripped me up outside the Swan?' Archroy raised his left foot to a point level with his own head, spun around on his right heel and drove it through Marchant's back wheel, bursting out a dozen spokes which spiralled into the air to fall some twenty feet away.

Marchant now realized his dire predicament and began to ring his bell frantically. 'Oh no you don't.' Archroy fastened his iron grip about the offending chime and tore it free from its mountings. Crushing its thumb toggle, he flung it high over his shoulder.

The bell cruised upwards into the air and fell in a looping arc directly on to the head of John Omally, who was taking a short cut across the allotment en route to the post box on the corner of the Ealing Road.

'Ow! Oh! Ouch! Damn!' screamed Omally, clutching at his dented skull and hopping about it pain. He levelled his boot at what he thought must surely be a meteorite and his eyes fell upon the instantly recognizable if somewhat battered form of his own bicycle bell. Omally ceased his desperate hopping and cast his eyes about the allotment. It took hardly two seconds before his distended orbs fixed upon Archroy. The lad was carrying Marchant high and moving in the direction of the river.

Omally leapt upon his toes and legged it towards the would-be destroyer of his two-wheeled companion. 'Hold up there!' he cried, and 'Enough of that! Let loose that velocipede!'

Archroy heard the Irishman's frenzied cries and released his grip. Marchant toppled to the dust in a tangle of flailing spokes. Omally bore down upon Archroy, his face set in grim determination, his fists clenched, and his tweed trouser-bottoms flapping about his ankles like the sails of a two-masted man-o-war. 'What villainy is this?' he screamed as he drew near.

Archroy turned upon him. His hands performed a set of lightning moves which were accompanied by sounds not unlike a fleet of jumbo jets taking off. 'Defend yourself as best you can,' said he.

Omally snatched up the broken shaft of a garden fork, and as the pupil of the legendary Count advanced upon him, a blur of whirling fists, he struck the scoundrel a thunderous blow across the top of the head.

Archroy sank to his knees, covering his head and moaning piteously. Omally raised his cudgel to finish the job. 'No, no,' whimpered Archroy, 'enough!'

Omally left him huddled in the foetal position and went

197

over to survey the damage done to his trusty iron steed. 'You'll pay for this,' he said bitterly. 'It'll mean a new back wheel, chain set, bell and a respray.'

Archroy groaned dismally. 'How did you manage to fell me with that damned stick?' he asked. 'I've read the manual from cover to cover.'

Omally grinned. 'I had a feeling that you were not being a hundred per cent honest with me when I lent it to you, so I only gave you volume one. Volume two is dedicated to the art of defence.'

'You bastard.'

Omally raised his stick aloft. 'What did you say?'

'Nothing, nothing.'

'And you'll pay for the restoration of my bicycle?'

'Yes, yes.'

Omally caught sight of the heap of splintered wood and warped iron that had once been his second home. 'And my shed?'

'Yes, anything you say.'

'From the ground up, new timbers, and I've always fancied a bit of a porch to sit in at the end of a summer's day.'

'You bas . . .'

'What?' Omally wielded his cudgel menacingly.

'Nothing, nothing, leave it to me.'

'Good, then farewell. All my best to you and please convey my regards to your dear wife.'

Omally strode off in the direction of the post box, leaving the master of the iron fist on the dusty ground thrashing his arms and legs and cursing between tightly clenched teeth.

The Professor's letter duly despatched, Omally set his foot towards the Flying Swan. He looked up at the empty sky, blue as the eyes of a Dublin lass. He would really have enjoyed this unusual summer had it not been for the sinister affair he had become involved in. As he approached the Swan he ran into Norman. It was early closing day and like Omally he was thirsting for a pint of cooling Large and the pleasures of the pot room. The two men entered the saloon bar and were met by a most extraordinary spectacle.

Captain Carson, on whom none had laid eyes for several months, stood at the counter evidently in a state of advanced drunkenness and looking somewhat the worse for wear. He was clad in pyjamas and dressing-gown and surrounded by what appeared to be his life's possessions in bundles and bags spread about the floor. 'Thirty bloody years,' he swore, 'thirty bloody years serving the troubled and down-at-heel, doing the work that should have won me a Nobel Prize, never a complaint, never a word said against me, and here I am, out on my ear, penniless, banjoed and broken.'

Omally followed Norman to the polished counter and the lad ordered a brace of Largi. 'What's all this then?' Omally whispered to the part-time barman.

Neville pulled upon the pump handle. 'He's got his marching orders from the Mission. It's been converted into a church now and he's no longer required.'

Omally, who felt somewhat emboldened after his recent encounter with Archroy, wondered if now might be the time to broach the subject of his wheelbarrow, but the sheer wretchedness the Captain displayed drove any such thoughts from his mind. 'Who kicked him out then, the Mission Trust?'

'No, the new vicar there, some high Muck-a-Muck it seems.'

High Muck-a-Muck, thought Omally, if only they knew the truth. But the fates must surely be with him, for the Captain must know a good deal about the cuckoo he had harboured within his nest. 'Get him a large rum on me,' said Omally, 'he looks as if he needs it.'

The Captain took the rum in both hands and tossed it back down his open throat. 'God bless you, John Omally,' said he, wiping his mouth on his dressing-gown sleeve. 'You are a good man.'

'I take it that the times are at present against you,' said John.

'Against me? What do you think I'm doing here in my bloody jim-jams, going to a fancy-dress party?'

'It has been known.'

'Listen.' Captain Carson banged his empty glass upon the bar. 'That bastard has driven me from my home, evicted me, me with thirty years serving the troubled and down at heel, me who should have won a Nobel bloody Prize for my labours, me who—'

'Yes, yes,' said Omally, 'I can see you are a man sorely put upon, but who has put you in this dire predicament?'

'That bloody Pope geezer, that's who. Came into my Mission as a stinking old tramp and look what he turned out to be.'

Neville pricked up his ears. 'Tramp?' said the part-time barman. 'When was this?'

'About three months ago, called at my door and I extended him the hospitality that was expected of me, should have kicked him out on his bloody ear that's what I should have done.'

Neville leant closer to the drunken Sea Captain. 'What did he look like?' he asked.

''Oribble, filthy, disreputable, evil creature, ragged as a Cairo cabbie.'

'And is he there now?' Neville continued.

'Well.' The Captain hesitated, swaying somewhat on his slippered feet, and held the bar counter for support. 'You could say he is, but then again he isn't. He was little when he came,' he made a levelling gesture at about chest height, 'small he was, but now, huge, bloody big bastard, bad cess upon him.' His hand soared into the air high over his head and the eyes of the assembled company travelled with it.

'Aw, get out of here,' said Neville, returning to his glass polishing, 'no-one can grow that big in a few months.'

'I should bloody know,' screamed the Captain, shattering his glass upon the bar counter, 'I should bloody know, I've fed him, cleaned and swept for him, treated him like some Holy God all these months. He had me like a ship's rat in a trap, no-one can stand against him, but now I'm out, he's kicked me out of my Mission, but I'll finish him, I'll tell all I know, things he's done, things he made me do . . .' Here his voice trailed off and his eyes became glazed.

'Yes?' said Omally. 'What have you done?'

Captain Carson spoke not a word. Neville, who had taken shelter beneath the counter, rose again, wielding his knobkerry. 'Get out!' he shouted. 'You're barred.'

The old man stood unblinking. His mouth was open as if in the formation of a word, but it was a word which never came.

'What's happened to him?' said Neville. 'He's not dead is he?'

Omally walked slowly about the paralysed figure in the dressing-gown. He snapped his fingers and waved his hands in front of the staring eyes. But the Captain would not move, he was frozen to the spot. Those drinkers who had made vague attempts at private conversation or the perusal of the sporting press during all this, now came slowly forward to view the strange tableau. Suggestions were forthcoming.

'Flick your lighter, that brings them out of it.'

'Bucket of water, that's your man.'

'Ice cube down his neck.'

'Make a grab at his wallet, that will bring him round.'

Omally held an empty wine-glass to the Captain's lips. He turned it between his fingers then held it up to the light. 'He's stopped breathing,' he said, 'this man is dead.'

'Get him out of here,' screamed Neville, climbing over the counter, 'I won't have a stiff in my bar.'

'Quick then,' said Omally, 'give me a hand to carry him out into the sun, maybe we can resuscitate him.'

Omally grasped the Captain under the armpits and Neville made to lift up the slippered feet. What followed was even more bizarre than what had gone before. The old man would not move; it was as if he had been welded to the Saloon bar floor. Omally could not shift the old and crooked shoulders an inch, and Neville let out a sudden 'Oh!' and straightened up, holding his back.

Several men stepped forward and attempted to shake and pull at the Captain, but he would not be moved, not one foot, one inch, one iota.

'Do something,' said Neville in a voice of terror, 'I can't have him standing there forever looking at me, he'll go off in this heat, he'll ruin my trade, it's bad luck to have a stiff in the saloon bar.'

Omally prodded at the Captain's dressing-gown. 'He appears to be freezing up,' he said, 'the material of his gown here is stiff as a board, you can't even sway it.'

'I don't care!' Neville was beginning to panic. 'He can't stay here, get him out. Get him out!'

Omally returned to the bar and took up his glass, while the crowd closed in about the Captain. 'That is certainly the strangest thing I have ever seen,' he said. 'This might make you famous.' Omally's brain suddenly switched on. There was money in this, that was for sure. He swept back his glass of Large and made for the door, but the part-time barman had anticipated him and stood, knobkerry in hand, blocking the Irishman's exit. 'Oh no you don't,' said he.

Omally began to wheedle. 'Come on Nev,' he said, 'we can't do anything for him now and we certainly can't ignore him. You can't just stick a bar cloth over his head and pretend he's a pile of cheese sandwiches.'

'No publicity,' said Neville, fluttering his hands, 'make me famous? This could ruin me. "Frozen Corpse in Saloon Bar Scandal", I can see it all.' (So could Omally, but he had phrased the headline a little better.) 'They'll say it was the beer, or that I poisoned him or God knows what else. The brewery will be down on me like a ton of red flettons, this is just the excuse they need.'

Omally shrugged. 'All right,' he said, 'I'll say nothing, but that lot,' he gestured over his shoulder, 'I can't vouch for them.'

'Well don't let them out, do something, stop them, get them away from him.'

'Which would you like doing first?'

'The last one.'

'All right.' Omally held his chin between thumb and forefinger, thought for a moment. 'Just back me up on whatever I say.' He took a deep breath and strode into the midst of the throng. 'Nobody touch him,' he shouted, 'for God's sake don't touch him.' The fingers which were inquisitively prodding the Captain withdrew in a hurried rush. 'Who's touched him?' said Omally in alarm. 'Which one of you?'

There was a lot of shuffling and murmuring. 'We've all touched him,' said someone in a guilty voice.

'Oh no!' Omally put his hand to his forehead in a gesture of vast despair.

'What's he got?' someone said. 'Out with it, Omally.'

Omally supported himself on the counter and said gravely, 'It's Reekie's Syndrome . . . the Frozen Death!'

Neville nodded soberly. 'I've heard of it,' he said. 'When I was serving in Burma a fellow caught it, horrible end.'

Someone in the crowd, for there is always one, said, 'That's right, a mate of mine had it.'

Omally struck the counter with his fist. 'What a fool!' he said. 'What a fool, if only I had recognized it sooner.'

'It's contagious then?' somebody asked.

'Contagious?' Omally gave a stage laugh. 'Contagious . . . worse than the Black Death. We'll have to go into quarantine. Bar the door Neville.'

Neville strode to the door and threw the brass bolts.

'But how long?' asked a patron whose wife had the dinner on.

Omally looked at Neville. 'Two days?' he asked.

'Twenty-four hours,' said Neville. 'Twelve if the weather keeps up.'

'Still,' Omally grinned, 'you've got to look on the bright side. He's certainly keeping the bar cool, like having the fridge door open.'

'Oh good,' said Neville unenthusiastically, 'better put up a sign in the window, "The Flying Swan Welcomes You, Relax in the Corpse-Cool Atmosphere of the Saloon Bar".'

Omally examined the tip of his prodding finger. It had a nasty blister on it which the Irishman recognized as frostbite. 'If he gets much colder, we should be able to smash him up with a hammer and sweep the pieces into the street.'

The Swan's patrons, some ten in all, who with the addition of Omally, Norman, who had hardly spoken a word since he entered the bar, and Neville, made up a most undesirable figure, were beginning to press themselves against the walls and into obscure corners. Most were examining their fingers and blowing upon them, some had already begun to shiver. Omally knew how easily mass hysteria can begin and he wondered now whether he had been wise in his yarn-spinning. But what had happened to the Captain? Clearly this was no natural ailment, it had to be the work of the villain calling himself Pope Alexander VI. Obviously his power could extend itself over a considerable distance.

Neville had fetched a white tablecloth and covered the Captain with it. There he stood in the very middle of the bar like some dummy in a store window awaiting a change of clothes. 'If you'd let me throw him out none of us would be in this mess,' said Neville.

Omally rattled his glass on the bar. 'I shall have to apply myself to this matter, I am sure that in some way we can save the situation, it is a thirsty business but.'

Neville snatched away the empty glass and refilled it. 'If you can get me out of this,' he said, 'I might be amenable to extending some credit to you in the future.'

Omally raised his swarthy eyebrows. 'I will give this matter my undivided attention,' said he, retiring to a side table.

Time passed. The corpse, for all his unwelcome presence, did add a pleasantly soothing coolness to the atmosphere within the bar, not that anyone appreciated it. By closing time at three the bar had become perilously silent. At intervals one or two of the quarantined patrons would come to the bar, taking great care to avoid the Captain, and order the drinks which they felt were their basic human right. Neville, though a man greatly averse to after-hours drinking, could do little but accede to their demands.

There were a few vain attempts to get a bit of community singing going but Neville nipped that in the bud for fear of beat-wandering policemen. Two stalwarts began a game of darts. There had been a few movements towards the pub telephone, but Neville had vetoed the use of that instrument on the grounds that careless talk costs lives. 'Have you come up with anything yet, John?' he asked, bringing the Irishman another pint.

'I am wondering whether we might saw out the section of floor on which he is standing and despatch him into the cellar, at least then if we can't get rid of him he will be out of the way, and if he remains preserved indefinitely in his icy cocoon he will do wonders for your reserve stock.'

Neville shook his head. 'Absolutely not, I have no wish

to confront him every time I go down to change a barrel.'

'All right, it was just a suggestion.'

By nine o'clock the mob, by now extremely drunk and ravenously hungry, began to grow a little surly. There were murmurings that the whole business was a put-up job and that Omally and Neville were in cahoots to con the punters out of their hard-earned pennies. In the corner, a couple of ex-Colditz types were forming an escape committee.

Then, a little after ten, one of the prisoners went over the wall. He had been out in the gents for more than his allotted two minutes, and when Neville went to investigate, there was no sign of him. 'Legged it across the bog roof,' the part-time barman said breathlessly as he returned to the saloon, 'dropped down into the alley and away.'

'Who was it?' asked Omally.

'Reg Wattis from the Co-op.'

'Don't worry, then.'

'Don't worry? You must be joking.'

'Listen,' said Omally, 'I know his wife and if he tries to give her any excuses about frozen corpses in the Flying Swan he will get very short shrift from that good woman. It occurs to me that we might let them escape. If they talk nobody will believe them anyway.'

'They can always come back here to prove it.'

'Not much chance of that, is there?'

'So what do we do?'

'I suggest that you and I withdraw to your rooms and gave them an opportunity to make their getaways.'

'I hope you know what you are doing.' Neville struck the bar counter with his knobkerry. 'Omally and I have some pressing business upstairs,' he announced. 'We will not be long and I am putting you all on your honour not to leave.' Conversation ceased and the eyes of the patrons flickered from Omally to Neville and on to the bolted door and back to Neville again. 'We swear,' they said amid a flurry of heartcrossing and scoutish saluting.

Omally beckoned to Norman. 'You might as well come too, you overheard everything.' The three men left the bar and trudged up the stairs to Neville's bedroom.

'So what now?' asked the part-time barman.

'We sit it out. Do you still keep that supply of scotch in your wardrobe?'

Neville nodded wearily. 'You don't let much get by you, do you, John?'

Below in the saloon bar there came the sudden sound of bolts being thrown, followed by a rush of scurrying footsteps. Neville, who had brought out his bottle, replaced the cap. 'Well, we won't be needing this now, will we?'

Omally raised his eyebrows. 'And why not?'

'Well, they've gone, haven't they?'

'Yes, so?'

'So, we go down and dispose of the Captain.'

'Oh, and how do we do that?'

Neville, who had been sitting on the edge of his bed, rose brandishing the whisky bottle. 'So it's treachery is it, Omally?' he roared. 'You had no intention of getting rid of him.'

'Me? No.' Omally wore a quizzical expression, mingled with outraged innocence. 'There is nothing we can do, he is welded to the floor in a most unmovable manner. If I was a man with a leaning towards science fiction I would say that an alien force field surrounded him.'

Neville waggled his bottle at Omally. 'Don't give me any of that rubbish, I demand that you act now, do something.'

'If you will give me a minute or two to explain matters I would greatly appreciate it.'

Neville took out his hunter. 'Two minutes,' said he, 'then I waste this bottle over your head.'

'I deplore such wastage,' said John, 'so I will endeavour to speak quickly.'

'One minute fifty-three seconds,' said Neville.

John composed himself and said, 'As we both observed what happened to the Captain I do not propose to lecture you upon the sheer inexplicable anomaly of it. It was clearly the work of no mortal man, nor was it any natural catastrophe, or at least none that I have ever heard of.'

'It's Reekie's Syndrome,' said Norman.

'Shut up Norman,' said Neville.

'It was caused,' said Omally, 'I believe, to shut the Captain up. He was about to spill the beans over what was going on at the Mission and so he was silenced.'

Neville scratched his Brylcreemed scalp. 'All right,' said he, 'but what do we do about him, we can't let him stay there indefinitely.'

'No, and nor can they. Now, I have listened to certain propositions put forward by Professor Slocombe.'

Neville nodded. 'A good and honourable man.'

'Exactly, and he believes that there has come amongst us of late an individual who can affect the laws of chance and probability to gain his own ends. This individual is presently ensconced in the Seamen's Mission and calls himself Pope Alexander VI. I believe that he is to blame for what happened to the Captain, and I also believe that he cannot afford to be tied into it and will therefore arrange for the disposal of same.'

'You went over your two minutes,' said Neville, 'but if all is as you say, it would go a long way towards explaining certain matters which have been puzzling me for some months now. Have I ever spoken to you of the sixth sense?'

'Many times,' said Omally, 'many, many times, but if you wish to retell me then may I suggest that you do it over a glass or two of scotch?'

'Certainly.'

'And may I also suggest that we keep a watch on the road at all times?'

208

'I will do it,' said Norman, 'for I have had little to say or do during this entire chapter.'

Night fell. Almost at once the sky became a backcloth for a spectacular pyrotechnic exhibition of lightning. The lights of the saloon bar were extinguished and the frozen Captain stood ghostly and statuesque, covered by his linen cloth. Norman stood at Neville's window staring off down the Ealing Road, and Omally drained the last of the scotch into his glass. Neville held his watch up to what light there was. A bright flash of lightning illuminated the dial. 'It's nearly midnight,' he said. 'How much longer?'

Omally shrugged in the darkness.

The Guinness clock struck a silent twelve below in the bar and in Neville's room Norman said suddenly, 'Look at that, what is it?'

John and Neville joined him at the window.

'What is it?' said Neville. 'I can't make it out.'

'Down by Jack Lane's,' said Norman, 'you can see it coming towards us.'

From the direction of the river, moving silently upon its eight wheels, came an enormous jet-black lorry. It resembled no vehicle that the three men had ever seen, for it bore no lights, nor did its lustreless bodywork reflect the street lamps which shone to either side of it. There was no hint of a windscreen nor cracks that might indicate doors or vents. It looked like a giant mould as it came to a standstill outside the Flying Swan.

Omally craned his neck to look down upon it but the overhang of the gabled roof hid the mysterious vehicle from view. The familiar creak of the saloon bar door, however, informed the three men that someone had entered the bar. 'Here,' said Neville suddenly, 'what are we doing? Whoever it is down there could be rifling the cash register.'

'Go down then,' said Omally, 'you tell them.'

The part-time barman took a step towards the door then halted. 'Best leave it, eh?'

'I think it would be for the best,' said Omally.

The saloon bar door creaked again and after a brief pause Norman said from the window, 'It's moving off.' The three men watched as the hellish black lorry crept out once more into the road and disappeared over the railway bridge past the football ground.

Together the three men descended the stairs. The bar was empty, lit only by the wan light from the street. The lightning had ceased its frenzied dance on the great truck's arrival and the night had become once more clear and silent. In the centre of the floor lay the white linen table cloth. Neville flicked on the saloon bar lights. Norman picked up the table cloth. Holding it out before him he suddenly gave a cry of horror and dropped it to the floor. Omally stooped to retrieve it and held it to the light. Impressed upon the cloth was what appeared to be some kind of negative photographic image. It was clear and brown as a sepia print and it was the face of Captain Carson.

'There,' said Omally to the part-time barman, 'now you've something to hang behind your bar. The Brentford Shroud . . .'

19

Omally lost little time in conveying news of the previous night's events to Professor Slocombe. The old man sat behind his desk surrounded by a veritable Hadrian's Wall of ancient books. 'Fascinating,' he said at length. 'Fascinating although tragic. You brought with you the table-cloth, I trust?'

'I thought it would be of interest.'

'Very much so.' The Professor accepted the bundle of white linen and spread it over his desk. In the glare of the brass desk lamp the Captain's features stood out stark and haunting. 'I would never have believed it had I not seen it with my own eyes.'

'It takes a bit of getting used to.'

The old Professor rolled up the tablecloth and returned it to Omally. 'I would like to investigate this at a future date when I have more time upon my hands, but matters at present press urgently upon us.'

'There have been further developments?'

'Yes, many. News has reached me that our adversary is planning some kind of papal coronation in the near future, when I believe he will reach the very zenith of his powers. We must seek to destroy him before this moment comes. Afterwards I fear there will be little we can do to stop him.'

'So how long do we have?'

'A week, perhaps a little more.'

Omally turned his face towards the French windows. 'So,' said he, 'after all this waiting, the confrontation will be suddenly upon us. I do not relish it, I must admit. I hope you know what you are doing, Professor.'

'I believe that I do John, never fear.'

The door to the Seaman's Mission was securely bolted. Great iron hasps had been affixed to its inner side and through these ran a metal rod the thickness of a broom handle, secured to the concrete floor by an enormous padlock. Within the confines of the Mission the air was still and icy cold. Although long shafts of sunlight penetrated the elaborate stained glass of the windows and fell in coloured lozenges upon the mosaic floor, they brought no warmth from the outer world. For no warmth whatever could penetrate these icy depths. Here was a tomb of utter darkness and utter cold. Something hovered in the frozen air, something to raise the small hairs upon the neck, something to chill the heart and numb the senses.

And here a face moved from the impenetrable darkness into the light. It was rigid and pale as a corpse, a face cut from timeless marble. The nose aquiline, the nostrils flared, the mouth a cruel slit, and the eyes, set into that face, two hellish blood-red orbs of fire. The face traversed the stream of frozen sunlight and was gone once more into the gloom.

Slow yet certain footsteps crossed the marbled floor and firm hands gripped a monstrous throne which rose at the end of the pilastered hall. The brooding figure seated himself. Whatever thoughts dwelt within his skull were beyond human comprehension. His being was at one with the sombre surroundings, the gloom, the terrible cold.

And then from hidden recesses of the darkling hall, there came other figures, walking erect upon two legs yet moving in a way so unlike that of humankind as to touch the very soul with their ghastliness. Forward they came upon dragging feet, to stand swaying, five in all, before their master. Then low they bowed, touching the chill floor with their faces. They murmured softly, imploringly.

The being upon the throne raised a languid hand to silence them. Beneath the hems and cuffs of their embroidered garments, touched upon briefly by the cold sunlight, there showed glimpses of their vile extremities. Here the twisted fibrous claw of a hand, here a gnarled and rootlike leg or ankle, for here were no human worshippers, here were the spawn of the bottomless pit itself. Foul and unspeakable creations, sickening vomit of regions beyond thought.

The red-eyed man gazed down upon them. A strange light began to grow around him, increasing in power and clarity. His very being throbbed with a pulsating energy.

He raised his mighty hand above his head and brought it down on to the arm of his throne. A voice rose up in his throat, a voice like no other that had ever spoken through earth's long aeons.

'I will have it,' he said, 'soon all shall be mine.' The creatures below him squirmed at his feet in an ecstasy of adoration. 'There will be a place for you my children, my five grand Cardinals of the Holy See, you will know a place in my favour. But now there is much to be done; those who would plot my destruction must be brought to their destiny; the Professor, he must be dragged before me, and the Irishman. Tonight you must go for them. I will tolerate no mistake or you shall know my displeasure. Tonight it must be, and now be gone.'

The writhing creatures drew themselves erect, their heads still bowed in supplication. One by one they shuffled from the great hall leaving the red-eyed man alone with his unspeakable thoughts.

Atop the Mission roof and hanging sloth-like by his heels, a lone figure had watched this gothic fantasy through a chink in the Mission's ventilator. The lone figure was none other than Jim Pooley, Brentford's well-known man of the turf and spy for the forces of mankind, truth and justice, and he had overheard all of the ghastly speech before he lost his footing and descended to the Mission's row of dustbins in a most undignified and noisy manner.

'Balls,' moaned mankind's saviour, wiping clotted fish scales from his tweeds and making a timely if somewhat shop-soiled departure from the Mission's grounds and off across the Butts Estate.

Archroy was working out on Father Moity's horizontal bars. Since the arrival through the post of book two and later book three of Count Dante's course in the deadly arts of Dimac the lad had known a renewed vigour, a vibrant rejuvenation of his vital forces. The young priest watched him exercise, marvelling at the fluency of his movements, the ease with which he cleared the vaulting horse at a single bound. All he could do was to clap enthusiastically and applaud the astonishing exhibition of super-human control and discipline.

'You are to be congratulated, Archroy,' said Father Moity. 'I have never seen the like of this.'

'I am only beginning, Father,' Archroy replied, 'watch this.' He gave out with an enormous scream, threw his hands forward into the posture the Count described as 'the third poised thrust of penetrating death' and leapt from the floor on to a high stanchion atop the gymnasium clock.

'Astonishing.' The young priest clapped his hands again. 'Amazing.'

'It is the mastery of the ancient oriental skills,' Archroy informed him, returning to the deck from his twenty-foot eyrie.

'Bravo, bravo, but tell me my son, to what purpose do you intend that such outstanding gymnastics be put to? It is too late now for the Olympics.'

Archroy skipped before him, blasting holes in the empty air with lightning fists. 'I am a man sorely put upon, Father,' said he.

The priest bowed his head in an attitude of prayer. 'These are sorry times for all of us. Surely if you have problems you might turn to me, to God, to the Church?'

'God isn't doing much for your Church at present.'

The priest drew back in dismay. 'Come now,' said he, 'these are harsh and cruel words, what mean you by them?'

Archroy ceased his exercises and fell into a perfect splits, touched his forehead to his right toe and rose to his feet. 'You have no congregation left, Father, hadn't you noticed?'

The young priest dropped to his knees. 'I have fallen from grace.'

'You have done nothing of the sort, your flock has been lured away by a callous and evil man. I have taken a lot of stick over the past few months and I have gone to some lengths to find out what is going on hereabouts. My ear has, of late, been pressed against many a partition door and I know what I'm talking about.'

Father Moity rose clumsily to his feet. 'I would know more of this my son, let us repair to my quarters for a small sherry.'

'Well, just a small one, Father, I am in training.'

The breathless Pooley staggered in through the Professor's open French windows and flung himself into a fireside chair.

'I take it from your unkempt and dishevelled appearance, Jim, that you bring news of a most urgent nature,' said Professor Slocombe, looking up from his books.

Pooley took a heavy breath. 'You might say that,' he gasped.

'Steady yourself, Jim, you know where the scotch is.'

Pooley decanted himself a large one. 'Not to put too fine a point on the matter, Professor,' said he, 'you and Omally are in big trouble, in fact, the biggest.'

'So, our man is going to make his move then?'

'Tonight he is sending those nasty looking creatures after you.'

'Well now.' Professor Slocombe crossed to the windows, pulled them shut and lowered the heavy iron screen. 'We must not be caught napping then, must we?'

'Where is John?' Pooley cast his eyes about the room. 'I thought he was here.'

Professor Slocombe consulted his watch. 'I should imagine that by now the good Omally is propped up against the bar counter of the Flying Swan raising a pint glass to his lips.'

'I'd better go round and warn him.' The Professor nodded. 'Bring him back as soon as you can.'

Omally was indeed to be found at the Swan, a pint glass in his hand and a large waxpaper package at his elbow. 'The Professor,' he would say by way of explanation to the curious who passed him by at close quarters, 'very valuable, very old.'

Pooley entered the saloon bar. Neville greeted him with a hearty 'Morning Jim, pint of the usual?' and Omally merely nodded a greeting and indicated his parcel. 'The Professor,' he said, 'very valuable, very old.'

Pooley accepted his pint and pushed the exact change across the counter in payment. Neville rang it up in the till. 'No Sale,' it said. 'The brewery have been offering me one of these new computerized micro-chip cash register arrangements,' the part-time barman told Pooley. 'They do seem to have some obsession about cash registers actually registering the money that is put into them. I can't see it myself.'

'Possibly they would take it kindly if you were to keep accounts,' Pooley suggested, 'it's a common practice among publicans.'

'We always run at a profit,' Neville said in a wounded voice, 'no-one could accuse me of dishonesty.'

'Of course not, but breweries are notorious for that sort of thing. Why don't you just accept the new cash register and let Omally give it the same treatment he gave to the juke box?'

The Irishman grinned wolfishly. A brewer's dray drew up before the Swan and Neville disappeared down the cellar steps to open the pavement doors. Pooley took Omally aside.

'You had better get around to the Professor's right

216

away,' he said urgently. 'There is a bit of trouble coming your way from the direction of the Mission, our man Pope Alex is out for your blood.'

'Always the bearer of glad tidings eh, Jim,' said Omally. 'I have to go down there anyway, the Professor's last book has arrived.' Omally gestured to the parcel upon the bar.

'More magic of the ancients?' said Pooley. 'I wonder what this one is all about.'

'More unreadable Latin texts I should expect. That old fellow absorbs knowledge like a sponge, I do not understand where he puts it all, for certain his head is no larger than my own.'

Pooley lifted the package from the counter and shook it gently. 'It is extremely heavy for its size. You are sure that it is a book?'

'I have no reason to doubt it, all the others have been.'

Pooley ran a finger over the glossy surface. 'It's almost like metal, but look here, how is it sealed? There are no flaps and no joint, the book appears to be encased in it rather than packed in it.'

'Indeed, now try and get it open.'

'Better not to, the Professor would not appreciate it.'

'Try anyway, I already have.'

Jim dug his thumb nail into a likely corner of the package and applied a little pressure. The package remained intact. Pooley pressed harder, working his thumbnail to and fro across the edge. 'Nothing,' he said in dismay, 'not even a scratch.'

'Use your pocket knife then, don't let it defeat you.'

Pooley took out his fifteen-function scout knife and selected the most murderous blade. Holding the parcel firmly upon the bar counter he took a vicious stab at it. The blade bent slightly, skidded cleanly off the package and embedded itself in the counter top.

'You bloody vandal,' screamed Neville, who was entering the saloon bar door. 'I saw that!'

'I am trying to open this parcel,' Pooley explained, withdrawing his knife and rubbing a bespittaled fingertip over the counter's wound.

'Give it to me,' said the part-time barman gruffly, 'I'll open it for you.' He took up the can opener which hung on a chain from his belt. 'Nothing to parcels if you have the know.'

He scratched the opener roughly down the length of the package. There was not a mark. 'What's this then?' said the part-time barman. 'Trick is it, or some new kind of paper?' He began scratching and scraping with renewed vigour. He laboured at the parcel as one possessed, but succeeded in doing nothing whatever, save taking the nail from his left thumb and totally destroying his opener. 'Bugger,' yelled the part-time barman, 'that was my favourite. Wait here!' He strode from the bar leaving a fine trail of blood behind him.

'Did he mean that the opener was his favourite or the thumbnail?' wondered Omally.

Neville reappeared behind the bar with a fourteen-inch meat cleaver clutched in a bandaged hand. 'Put it here,' he demanded.

'Now steady on,' said Pooley, 'after all it isn't even our package. You will clearly destroy it with that thing.'

'One good swing,' said Neville, 'just one. I'll merely snip the end, I won't damage the contents, I swear!'

'He's a good man with a cleaver,' said someone. 'He'll open the bugger, never fear.'

Pooley looked to Omally. 'What do you think?'

'Can't hurt. If he damages it we can always say that the Post Office did it in transit.'

'OK,' said Pooley, 'one swing then, but for God's sake, be careful.'

The parcel was placed upon the bar counter and the spectators withdrew to what they considered to be a safe distance. Neville squared up to the parcel, placed his feet firmly apart and wiggled his behind in a manner much practised by top pro golfers before applying their wedges to a bunker-bound ball. Spitting on to his palms he raised the cleaver high above his head and brought it down with a reckless force which would truly have done credit to the Wolf of Kabul wielding the legendary Clicki-Ba.

The patrons let out a collective gasp as the cleaver struck the parcel amidships and rebounded from the part-time barman's grip to go hurtling over their ducking heads like a crossbow bolt and lodge itself up to the hilt in the dart board.

'Double top,' said Old Pete, 'give that man a pint.'

Neville stood pale-faced and trembling, regarding the package with horrified eyes. 'Not even bloody dented,' he said in a quivering voice, 'not even bloody scratched.'

Leo Felix, who was making one of his rare appearances at the Swan, thrust his way through the crowd. 'I an' I got me an oxyacetylene cutter back at me work,' said the newly converted Rastafarian.

'Come on now,' said Pooley, 'this has all got out of hand. Omally, take that package around to the Professor at once!'

The crowd would have none of it. 'Fetch your blow-torch, Leo,' said somebody. Leo left the bar.

Omally picked up the package from the bar counter and made to move in the direction of the door. The mob surrounded him. 'Put that down, mister,' said someone. 'Leave it be till Leo gets back.'

'Come now lads,' said Omally, 'this is madness, mob law in Brentford? Come now.'

'This is going too far,' said Jim, stepping into the fray.

'You do what you want mate,' said a burly navvy, 'but the parcel stays here.'

'This man knows Dimac,' said Pooley, indicating his Irish companion, 'deadliest form of martial art known to mankind, and can . . .'

219

'Instantly disable, mutilate and kill, his hands and feet being deadly weapons,' chimed the crowd in unison. 'We've heard it.'

'Strike them down, John,' said Pooley, 'give them iron hand.'

'My iron hands are a little rusty at present,' said Omally. 'Archroy is your man for that sort of thing.'

'Did somebody call me?' The voice came from the saloon bar door, and the crowd, turning as one man, were stunned into absolute silence by what they saw. Framed dramatically by the Swan's doorway, which had always been so excellent for that sort of thing, stood an imposing figure which the startled throng recognized with some difficulty as none other than Archroy.

He had discarded his usual ill-fitting wig for an ornate dark coiffure of oriental inspiration which was secured by elaborately carved ivory pins tipped with jet. He wore a full-length black kimono emblazoned with Chinese characters embroidered richly in gold thread, and walked upon the high wooden shoes much favoured by Samurai warlords of the fourteenth Dynasty.

'Blimey,' said Old Pete, 'it's bloody Hirohito.'

Archroy strode forward, scattering the crowd before him. 'Show me the package,' he demanded.

Pooley was amazed to note that Archroy had even adopted a pseudo-Japanese accent. And there was something indefinably different about him, not just the eastern trappings. He had physically changed, that much was certain, broader about the shoulders and narrower at the hip. Through the folds of his silken sleeves muscles seemed to bulge powerfully.

Omally handed him the parcel with an extraordinary display of politeness. 'If you please,' said he, smiling sweetly.

'And it cannot be opened?' The crowd took to shaking its collective head. 'Impregnable,' said somebody.

'Huh!' said Archroy without moving his lips, 'two men hold it up, one either side.'

Omally shrugged. 'What can happen? Might as well do what he says.' He and Pooley stood several feet apart in the centre of the bar, holding the parcel between them in outstretched hands.

'Better get some assistance,' said Archroy, taking up a stance before the parcel. Several he men stepped forward and assisted with the gripping and supporting. They made quite an impressive-looking little group really, not unlike one of William Blake's visionary tableaux of struggling heroic figures pressing on one upon another in endless titanic conflict. The subtler points of that particular similarity were however lost to most of those present, who merely cleared a path for the lunatic in the kimono.

'When I cry out, hold on as tight as you can,' commanded Archroy.

The grippers, holders and supporters nodded assent. Archroy took a step back and performed a series of ludicrous sweeping motions with his arms. He took a deep breath and closed his eyes; slowly he drew back his right arm, knotting the fingers of his hand into a fist with a sickening crackle of bones and gristle.

'Woosah!' he screamed.

Those who watched him throw the punch say to this day that they never saw his hand move; one moment it was suspended motionless at shoulder height behind him, the next it was similarly motionless but outstretched, fist clenched, at the spot where the parcel had just been.

The two clusters of grippers, holders and supporters collapsed in opposite directions like two tug-of-war teams suddenly bereft of their rope. There was an almost instantaneous crash, followed by two more. The awe-struck spectators swung in the direction of the crashes. The parcel had travelled across the bar and straight through the outside wall, leaving a perfectly shaped rectangular hole to mark the point of its departure.

Through this the sun threw a crisp shaft of sunlight which fell in a pleasant golden diamond on to a section of the carpet which had never previously known the joys of solar illumination. Neville looked at the hole, then at Archroy, back to the hole and back once more to the destroyer of his wall. 'You're barred!' he screamed, searching for his knobkerry. 'You're bloody barred! Vandal! Vandal!'

Archroy was examining his knuckles. 'What's in that parcel?' was all that he could say.

The crowd was making moves towards the door, eager to see what the other two crashes might have been. 'Maybe he's demolished the flatblocks,' said somebody.

Pooley and Omally, intent only upon retrieving the Professor's book, elbowed their way through the push and found themselves the first to emerge into the very daylight which was now beaming so nicely through the neat hole in the Swan's front wall.

'My oh my,' said Omally

Before them was a vehicle parked at the kerb, a pickup truck of a type much favoured by used-car dealers. It was one of this doubtful breed of men who sat in the front seat, white-faced and staring. That he should be white-faced was reasonable enough, for sliced through each side of the truck's bodywork was a sharp-edged hole corresponding exactly in shape and size to that of the Professor's parcel. Regarding further this whiteness of face, its sole unusual quality was that the driver of the see-through pickup was none other than that well-known local Rastaman Leo Felix. The hurtling missile had escaped striking, only by the briefest of inches, the oxygen canister strapped inside his vehicle. Had it struck home there is not much doubt that very little would have remained of Haile Selassie's latest follower.

Pooley and Omally peered through the holes in the hope

222

of lining up on the Professor's parcel. 'It's over there,' said Jim, 'in Mrs Fazackerley's front garden.'

The two men skipped across the carriageway, dodging the traffic which had mercifully escaped the bazooka attack a moment before, and retrieved the parcel.

'Not even a scratch,' said Pooley, examining it. 'Nothing.'

The crowd was now in the street thronged about Leo's ventilated pickup pointing and speculating. Someone was waving a handkerchief before Leo's wildly staring eyes. Neville danced in the doorway of the Swan, ranting and raving, and Archroy stood calmly regarding his demolition work and wearing a satisfied expression upon his face.

Omally nudged Pooley in the rib area. 'Best make a break for it, eh?'

'Best so.'

The two fled away down the Ealing Road.

20

As they stood puffing and panting in the heat of the Professor's back garden Pooley asked his companion why he thought it was that neither of them ever seemed to be able to visit the old gentleman without arriving in either a harrassed or a drunken condition.

'I have no idea whatever,' Omally wheezed. 'It's all go nowadays isn't it?'

'Lunchtime drinking at the Swan is not the peaceful affair it once was.'

The metal shutters were drawn down upon the French windows, and only prolonged knockings, shoutings and rattlings finally succeeded in eliciting a reply from within. The shutters rose, exposing first carpet-slippered feet, then an expanse of tweed trousering, then a red velvet smoking jacket and quilted waistcoat and finally the old white head of Professor Slocombe.

He beamed upon them. He spotted the parcel Omally clutched in his perspiring hand. 'Good lad, John,' he said. 'The last book I require, excellent.' Closing and bolting the heavy iron shutters, he took the parcel from Omally's outstretched hand and turned away to his desk. There was a brief rustle of waxen paper and he held the exposed book proudly aloft. 'Excellent, and I see it has withstood the rigours of Post Office despatch unscathed.'

'Don't ask,' said Pooley as he noticed Omally's mouth opening, 'it is probably better not to know.'

'You look somewhat dishevelled,' said the Professor, noticing for the first time the state of his guests. 'Why is it, do you think, that neither of you ever seems able to visit me without arriving in either a harrassed or in a drunken condition?'

'We have wondered that ourselves,' said Jim.

'And now,' said the aged host as the two men slumped before him sipping scotch and sighing deeply, 'to business, as they say. There are very few hours left for me to school you in all you must know regarding our prospective attackers. I do not expect that their master will take an active part in the proposed assault upon us. That would not be fitting to his dignity. He will despatch his five minions to us, and at least on this score we should be grateful.'

'Extremely,' said Pooley.

'Here's to you, Alex boy,' said Omally, raising his glass.

'I admire your bravado,' the Professor said gravely, 'for my own part I find the situation somewhat alarming. I would have hoped that we could have had a try at him before he has a try at us, if you get my meaning.'

'You are pretty secure here,' said Jim, 'as long as you keep well bolted up.'

'I have considered several manoeuvres,' said Professor Slocombe. 'Abandoning the house and taking refuge at some undisclosed location, for instance, but this I could not do, for it would mean leaving the books. I considered calling on some help, your friend Archroy I understand has recently mastered certain techniques which I struggled with to a lesser degree.'

'He has?' queried Pooley.

'Most interesting,' said Omally.

'But I do not wish to draw more folk than are strictly necessary into this unfortunate business, so I was left with only one option.'

'Which is?'

'That the three of us should remain on the premises to battle it out.'

Omally said, 'Surely there are other options? Let us put some to a vote.'

'I would gladly stay, but have a pressing engagement elsewhere,' said Jim.

'You should have mentioned it earlier,' the Professor said, a wicked twinkle appearing for a moment in his eye, 'and I would not have closed the shutter; you see I have set automatic time locks on all the doors and they will not open for another fifteen hours.'

Pooley's face fell. 'You can use the telephone if you wish,' said the Professor brightly.

'I might call a locksmith then?' Jim asked.

'I think not.'

Omally put his hands behind his head and smiled broadly. 'When I was in the army,' said he, 'I was a happy man, never had to make a decision; it is a pleasure to know those times once more.'

'Oh good old you,' said Jim, 'I have never known the joys of army life and can find little to recommend in that of the trapped rat. I greatly prefer freedom.'

'I am sorry,' said Professor Slocombe, 'to have brought you to this, but it must be the old musketeer philosophy I am afraid, all for one, one for all.'

'This one would have liked a choice in the matter,' said Jim sourly. 'After all, the character at the Mission did not mention me by name.'

'Do you think he would destroy us and let you off scot free then?'

'I do not believe he thinks me as much of a threat.'

'Never fear.' The Professor tapped his nose.

'Never fear?' Pooley threw up his hands in a helpless gesture. 'After you with that decanter, John.'

Long hours passed. In the Professor's study the temperature rose alarmingly, and the air became torpid and unbreathable. Jackets were removed and shirt-tails flapped aplenty. The Professor laboured away at his books as best he could and when Pooley found the energy he paced the floor like a caged animal. To add to his disgust Omally had the perfect effrontery to curl up in one of the Professor's armchairs and fall asleep.

The mantelclock struck nine and Pooley tapped at the Victorian barometer which hung beside the marble fireplace. 'Stormy' it read, but the temperature was still in the mid-80s.

The Professor looked up from his reading. 'Try to relax, Jim,' he said, wiping the perspiration from his deeply lined forehead.

'Relax? I can hardly draw breath. We will suffocate in here for sure, we are all doomed.'

'Come now, control yourself.' The Professor closed the heavy damask curtains across the iron-shuttered French windows.

'Control myself? Three rats in a trap we are, you've brought us to this. I have no wish to control myself, I prefer to panic.' Pooley began delving amid the curtains and rattling at the iron shutters of the window. 'Let me out,' he shouted, kicking at the lock with his steely toecaps, 'I choose not to end my days here.'

Omally awoke with a start. 'Do turn it in, Jim,' he yawned.

'I'm not turning anything in,' Jim said morosely, 'I'm for panic, what say you?'

'I say that we stand by the Professor. After all we are as much to blame for his plight as he for ours.'

'I have no desire to die,' said Jim. 'I am yet a young man, and a potential millionaire to boot.'

'Pooley, your sixth horse will never come up.'

'Not if I stay here, it won't,' said Pooley petulantly.

The Professor raised his eyes once more from his books. 'I think the time has come for us to discuss this matter fully,' he said. 'We are in a state of siege; panic is a useless and negative commodity which we cannot afford.'

'It's always served me well enough in the past,' Pooley grumbled.

'If we do not stand together,' the Professor continued, 'we shall surely be doomed. Our adversary is a ruthless, cunning individual. In his former incarnation he had the power of life or death over thousands, millions, he was a dictator, a brilliant strategist, he held sway over kingdoms. We are not dealing with some street-corner villain. It is clearly his plan to usurp the Papacy, to reclaim his lands and duchies. He sees himself carried aloft through Vatican City. Ensconced upon the Papal throne. Lord High Ruler of the Holy See. This is only the beginning for him.'

'We had best give up,' said Jim, 'all is lost.'

'Bottle job,' said Omally to the Professor, indicating Pooley and making an obscene gesture below the waist. 'His bottle's gone.'

'We can't fight him,' Pooley whined. 'You know how powerful he is.'

'If the Prof says we can, then we can, that's all there is to it. Listen, I'm a Catholic, not a good one, but a Catholic.' Omally opened his shirt and pulled out the army dogtag he still wore about his neck. '8310255 Private J. V. Omally, Catholic, I'm not letting that gobshite at the Mission get one over on the Church, I hate him!'

Pooley turned upon his companion. 'What *did* happen after I blacked out that night, what did he say to you?'

Omally replaced his dogtag and rebuttoned his shirt. 'Nothing,' he said, draining his glass.

'All right,' said Pooley, 'as panic is clearly ill-received hereabouts, what do we do?'

The Professor rose from his desk, a book tucked beneath his arm. 'We will fight. I am an old man but I have no intention of dying yet awhiles. We can expect a concentrated attack upon these premises, midnight being the traditional hour for such events. Things might not be as bad as they first appear; although we know that the Dark One can extend his power over a considerable distance, I do not feel that he will wish to do so tonight. His minions greatly fear the wrath of his displeasure, as well they might; they will use every power they possess to succeed in their quest.'

'We are outnumbered,' said Jim.

'But not without power. I consider these beings to be the product of conjuration, therefore they are vulnerable. I intend to use the rites of Holy Exorcism, and if these fail I have recourse to several other possible methods for their destruction. These beings are not immortal.'

'That is a big weight off my mind,' sneered Jim, 'but listen, the rites of Holy Exorcism take a while to perform. I do not believe that such time will be made available.'

'Well, with the aid of this volume that Omally has brought to me I believe that I have isolated the key words and phrases which give the rite of exorcism its power. Much of that spoken by the priest is merely padding, theological jargon; if I am correct the exorcism can be broken down to nothing more than a few lines of ancient Latin and still retain its basic power.'

'Let us hope you are correct.'

'Well,' said the Professor smiling darkly, 'if I am not then the matter will be purely academic.'

'That's it Professor, cheer us up.' Jim Pooley returned to his contemplation of the wallpaper.

The Memorial Library clock struck midnight. The Butts Estate was in darkness, the century-old horse chestnut trees rising like clenched fists against the sky. Beneath them, bowered in the void, the Mission showed no lights. All was silent. Faintly then came sounds, the dragging of feet and the rustling of ancient cloth. A great iron bolt was suddenly drawn up and the aged door creaked ajar. An icy white shaft of light pierced the darkness, silhouetting the trees and casting their elongated shadows forward through the night. The door swung inwards upon its hinge and now dark forms swayed into the dazzling radiance. Misshapen forms, heavily robed and indefinite of shape, one by one they issued from the Mission, until five in all they stood before it. Then that heavy panelled door swung closed again, the blinding light was snapped away and the Butts slept once more in darkness.

But it was no easy sleep, for here moved creatures of nightmare. Slow of foot they laboured across the gravel drive, the ghastly dragging of their feet echoing over the empty estate. Low murmurings accompanied their progress, hoarse whispers and lamenting sobs. For they belonged not here, these spawn of ancient evil, and yet their tasks they must perform.

The slow ungodly procession trailed onward, keeping ever to the shadows beneath the ivy-hung walls. Now they neared the gate to the Professor's garden and stood together swaying and murmuring.

Within the Professor's study the three men waited tensely. They too had heard the midnight chimes. Pooley stood with his back to the wall, wielding a poker. The

Professor himself was on the edge of his chair, book in hand. Omally supported himself upon the fireplace; the decanter was empty and he was dangerously drunk.

Long minutes ticked away upon the mantelclock, its pendulum swung its gilded arc and the three men held their breath.

Suddenly there came a rattling upon the window, a repeated and urgent tapping. Pooley shifted the poker from his sweating palm and wiped his hand upon his trousers.

The Professor said, 'Who is there?'

'Is that you, Professor?' came a voice. 'Omally with you? I've brought a crate of beer over. Open up.'

'It's Neville,' said Pooley, breathing a monumental sigh of relief and flinging his poker to the carpeted floor. 'What's he doing here?' Jim crossed the room to throw back the curtains.

The Professor leapt to his feet and barred his way. 'Stop, Jim,' said he in a desperate voice, 'do not open the curtains.'

'But it's Neville, he can pass the drink in through the iron screens, be reasonable.'

The Professor held up his hand and shook his head. 'Neville?' said he loudly. 'What is the name of your father?'

Pooley turned helplessly to John Omally. 'What sort of question is that, I ask you?'

There was no sound. 'Neville?' called the Professor again, but there was no reply.

'He's gone,' said Jim. 'What I would have given for a cold beer.'

Suddenly the knocking and rattling began again with renewed vigour, a voice rang out. 'Help, help, let me in will you, I've got to use the phone.' It was the voice of Old Pete. 'Please open up, you must help me.'

'Something's wrong there,' said Jim, 'open those curtains.'

'My dog,' wailed the voice, 'a bloody lorry's run down Chips, let me in, I must phone for help.'

'For pity's sake,' said Pooley, 'open the curtains.'

The Professor would have none of it. 'Stand your ground, Jim,' he said sternly. 'Put your hands over your ears if you do not wish to hear it, but make no move towards the curtains.'

'But you've got to do something, let him in.'

The Professor turned to Omally. 'If he makes one step towards those curtains strike him down.'

Jim threw up his arms in defeat. 'Wise up, Pooley,' said Omally. 'Don't you see, old Pete isn't out there, it's a trick.'

The Professor nodded his old head. 'First temptation through Neville, then an appeal for pity, what next? Threats, I should imagine.'

Pooley had little time to mull over the Professor's words before a deafening voice roared from the garden, 'Open up these windows or I'll smash the bastards down.' This time it was the voice of Count Dante's most accomplished adept in the deadly arts of Dimac. 'Open up in there, I say, or it will be the worse for you!'

Pooley threw himself into a chair. 'If it is all right with you chaps I should prefer to simply panic now and have done with it,' he said.

Archroy's voice slowly faded, still uttering threats, and the three men were left alone once more.

'Do you think that's it then?' Omally asked, tottering to the nearest chair.

The Professor's face was grave. 'I should hardly think so, I suspect that their next attempt to gain entry will be a little less subtle.' In that supposition the Professor was entirely correct.

Omally twitched his nostrils. 'What's that smell?'

The Professor's eyes darted about the room. 'It's smoke, something is burning.'

Pooley pointed helplessly. 'It's coming under the study door, we are ablaze.'

'Ignore it,' said the Professor. 'There is no fire, the doors are shuttered and bolted, nothing could have entered the house unheard.'

'I can see it with my own eyes,' said Pooley. 'Smoke is something I *can* recognize, we'll all be burned alive.'

'I don't see any flames,' said the Professor, 'but if the smoke bothers you so much.' He stepped forward and raised his hands; of the syllables he spoke little can be said and certainly nothing written. The smoke that was gathering thickly now about the room seemed suddenly to suspend itself in space and time and then, as if a strip of cinema film had been reversed, it regathered and removed itself back through the crack beneath the door, leaving the air clear, although still strangling in the tropical heat.

'That I have seen,' said Pooley, 'but please do not ask me to believe it.'

'A mere parlour trick,' said the Professor matter-of-factly. 'If our adversaries are no more skilful than this, we shall have little to fear; it is all very elementary stuff.'

'It is all sheer fantasy,' said Jim, pinching himself. 'Shortly I shall awake in my bed remembering nothing of this.'

'The clock has stopped,' said Omally pointing to the silent timepiece upon the mantelshelf.

The Professor took out his pocket watch and held it to his ear. 'Bother,' he said, giving it a shake, 'I must have mispronounced several of the minor convolutions. Give the pendulum a swing, will you John?'

Omally rose unsteadily from his chair and reached towards the mantelshelf. The alcohol, however, caused him to misjudge his distance and he toppled forward head first into the fireplace. Turning on to his back in an effort to remove himself from the ashes Omally suddenly let out a terrified scream which echoed about the room rattling the ornaments and restarting the mantelclock.

Not three feet above, and apparently wedged into the chimney, a hideous, inhuman face snarled down at him. It was twisted and contorted into an expression of diabolical hatred. A toothless mouth like that of some vastly magnified insect opened and closed, dripping foul green saliva upon him; eyes, two flickering pinpoints of white light; and the entire horrific visage framed in a confusion of crimson cloth. The sobering effect upon Omally was instantaneous. Tearing himself from his ashy repose he leapt to his feet and fell backwards against the Professor's desk, spilling books and screaming, 'Up the chimney, up the chimney.'

'I don't think it's Santa,' said Pooley.

Omally was pointing desperately and yelling, 'Light a fire, light a fire!'

Pooley cast about for tinder. 'Where are the logs, Professor? You always have logs.'

The Professor chewed upon his knuckle. 'The shed,' he whispered in a trembling voice.

'We'll have to burn the books then.' Omally turned to the desk and snatched up an armful.

'No, no, not the books.' Professor Slocombe flung himself upon Omally, clawing at his precious tomes. The broadshouldered Irishman thrust him aside, and Pooley pleaded with the old man. 'There's nothing we can do, we have to stop them.'

Professor Slocombe fell back into his chair and watched in horror as the two men loaded the priceless volumes into the grate and struck fire to them. The ancient books blazed in a crackle of blue flame and from above them in the chimney there came a frantic scratching and clawing. Strangled cries rent the air and thick black smoke began to fill the room. Now the French windows burst assunder with a splintering of glass and the great curtains billowed in to a blast of icy air. The burning creature's hooded companions beat upon the shuttered metal screen, screeching vile blasphemies in their rasping inhuman voices. There was a crash and the creature descended into the flames, clawing and writhing in a frenzy of searing agony.

Pooley snatched up his poker and lashed out at it viciously. Omally heaped more books on to the fire. The Professor stepped forward, knowing what had to be done.

Slowly raising his hand in benediction he spoke the magical words of the Holy Exorcism. The creature groaned and twisted in the flames, its arms flailing at its tormentors. Pooley held it at bay and as the Professor spoke and Omally applied more fuel to the fire, its movements began to slow and presently it crumpled in upon itself to be cremated by the all-consuming flames.

The curtains ceased their billowing and from the garden there came a great wailing and moaning. Pooley cupped his hands over his ears and the Professor stood, book in hand, frozen and corpse-like. Omally was beating away at the burning books which had fallen from the fireplace on to the carpet. His face was set into a manic grin and he prodded at the remains of the fallen creature with undisguised venom.

The wailing from the garden became fainter and as it passed into silence the Professor breathed a great sigh and said, 'All the ashes must be gathered and tomorrow cast into the Thames; by fire and by water and the holy writ shall they be destroyed.'

Omally plucked a half-charred volume from the grate. 'I am sorry about the books,' he said, 'but what else could we do?'

'It is no matter, you acted wisely and no doubt saved our lives.' The Professor fingered the ruined binding of the ancient book. 'A pity though, irreplaceable.'

Pooley had unfastened his hands from about his head. 'Are they gone?' he asked inanely.

'Unless they are regrouping for another assault.'

The Professor shook his head. 'I think not, they will be none too eager to return now, but what will happen when they report the loss of their comrade I shudder to think.'

Omally whistled. 'Our man is not going to be very pleased.'

'We are doomed,' said Pooley once more, 'all doomed.'

'Jim,' said Omally wearily, 'if you say "we are doomed" one more time I am going to set aside the long years of our noble friendship and remodel your beak with the business end of my knuckles.'

'Come now gentlemen,' said the Professor, 'I have a bottle of port which I suggest we now consume before taking a well-earned rest.'

Omally rubbed his hands together. 'That would be excellent.'

Pooley shrugged his shoulders. 'What else can happen?' he asked.

A pink dawn came to Brentford, gilding the roof tops with its sickly hue. Birds that should have by now flown south to winter it in tropical climes sat in silent rows musing upon the oddness of the season. As the old sun dragged itself into the sky there was all the promise of another fine and cloudless day ahead.

Pooley was the first to awake. He heard the milk float clattering over the cobblestones of the Butts, and, rising stiffly, he stumbled to the French windows and drew back the heavy curtains. The sunlight beamed down through the metal screen, laying golden diamonds upon the Professor's carpet and causing Jim to blink wildly whilst performing the ritualistic movements of finding the first fag of the day.

Like all first fags it was a killer. Jim did his best to draw some breath from the fragrant garden between coughs while he surveyed the damage the night had brought. The French windows had been torn from their hinges once more and their splintered remains littered the small lawn and surrounding flowerbeds. Shards of glass twinkled bright in the morning sunlight.

Pooley's vile coughing awoke Omally who, scratching his nether regions, shambled over to join him. 'A rare mess,' said the Irishman, 'the glaziers will think the Professor a fine man for the wild parties and no mistake.'

Pooley gripped the metal framework of the screen. 'What time does this open?' he asked.

'Nine o'clock, wasn't it?'

The Memorial Library clock struck eight.

'An hour yet then.'

Omally shook the Professor gently awake. The old man stretched his slender limbs to the accompaniment of ghastly bone-cracking sounds. He yawned deeply. 'So we are still alive then, that is a blessing.'

'Not much left of your windows,' said Jim. 'Might be more economical to wall up the opening.'

The Professor looked at his watch and checked it with the mantelclock. 'Time for breakfast I think.' He rang the Indian brass bell upon his desk and presently there came a knocking upon the study door, followed by the sound of a key turning in the lock. The door swung open and the decrepit figure of Gammon appeared. 'Breakfast for three, sir,' he said, hefting an oversized butler's tray into view.

'I gave him the night off,' the Professor explained as the three men sat about the Moorish coffee table ravenously devouring the mountainous piles of toast, sausages, eggs and bacon loaded upon the tray. 'I told him to return at seven and if he found the house intact, to arrange breakfast for three.'

'And what if the house had not been intact?' Omally asked between mouthfuls.

236

'If the doors were broken in and it was obvious that an entry had been made I ordered him to set the house ablaze and leave immediately, never to return.'

'And he would have done that?'

'Unquestioningly.'

Omally whistled. 'He is a loyal servant indeed. It would have been my first thought to remove several of the more choice objects in order to spare them from the blaze, as it were.'

'Gammon has no need for that, I have seen to it that his long years of service will not go unrewarded.'

'You are a strange man, Professor.'

The Professor shook his head. 'On the contrary, my motives are most simple, to advance science and to combat evil.'

'You make it *sound* simple.'

The Professor munched upon a piece of toast. 'I believe in destiny,' he said, 'I believe in the existence of the cosmic masterplan. No man is without a purpose, but few if any find theirs before it is too late. Perhaps I am lucky to believe that I have found mine, possibly not. Possibly ignorance as they say is bliss. It is written that "a little knowledge is a dangerous thing, but a great deal of knowledge is a disaster".'

'Probably written by Norman,' said Pooley, pushing another sausage into his mouth.

'A man without talent or ambition is a man most easily pleased. He lives his life with no delusions, other men set his purpose and he is content.'

'That is a depressing thought,' said Omally, 'as that particular definition covers most individuals in this present society.'

'The balance must always be maintained. All have a purpose, be he pauper or king, such it has always been. There could be no giants if there were no dwarves.'

Pooley thought that there probably could be, but he

held his counsel as he had no wish to be drawn into an arduous discussion at this time of the day. 'Here,' he said suddenly, 'how did Gammon get in if all the doors were on time-locks?'

Omally raised his eyes suspiciously towards the Professor, but the old man merely chuckled and continued with his breakfasting. Black coffees were drunk and at length Gammon returned to dispose of the tray. At nine o'clock the time-lock upon the metal shuttering snapped open and the Professor raised it. Gammon had swept every ash from the fireplace into a sack and this the Professor handed to Omally with explicit instructions.

'You must sprinkle it over at least half a mile,' he explained, 'there must be no chance of the particles regrouping. And now I must say farewell to you gentlemen. It is no longer safe for me to remain here. I have other apartments not far from here and I will lodge there. When the moment comes that I need you I will be in contact. Go now and await my call, speak of these matters to no-one and be constantly on your guard. You should be safe during the hours of daylight, but at night go nowhere alone, do not allow yourselves to become separated.'

The two men stepped through the French windows, over the mess of shattered glass, and out towards the Professor's gate. They turned to wave him a cheery farewell but the old man had gone.

21

The people of Brentford had taken to calling them the Siamese Twins. From the moment they had despatched the sinister contents of the sack along the river John Vincent Omally and James Arbuthnot Pooley were never to be seen apart. The days passed wearily with no call from the Professor. Pooley wondered if the old man might possibly have lost his nerve and decided to do a runner, but Omally, whose faith in the Professor bordered upon the absolute, would have none of that. 'He has seen too much,' he assured Pooley, 'he will not rest till that Pope Alex is driven back into the dark oblivion from whence he came.'

'There is a definite sword of Damocles air to all this,' said Jim. 'I feel that around every corner something is lurking, every time a telephone rings or a postman appears I have to make a dash for the gents.'

'My own bladder has not been altogether reliable of late,' said John dismally.

'Talking of bladders, it would appear to be opening time.'

John nodded. He owned no timepiece but his biological clock told him to the minute the licensing hours of the county. 'A pint of Large would be favourable.'

Outside the Swan a builder's lorry was parked and two swarthy individuals of tropical extraction laboured away at the damaged brickwork with mortar and trowel. Neville, his hand still bandaged from his recent encounter with the Professor's unopenable parcel, put down the glass he was polishing and addressed them with a surly 'What'll it be?'

Omally raised an eyebrow. 'Not still sulking over the hole in the wall, surely, Neville?' he said.

'I am a patient man,' said the part-time barman, 'but I have stood for a lot this year, what with the perils of Cowboy Night and the like. Every time I sit down and catalogue the disasters which have befallen this establishment over recent months, Omally, your name keeps cropping up, regular as the proverbial clockwork.'

'He is a man more sinned against than sinning,' Pooley interjected helpfully.

'Your name comes a close second, Pooley.'

'They're doing a nice job on the front wall,' said Pooley, smiling painfully. 'What did the brewery say?'

'As it happens,' said Neville, 'things didn't work out too badly there, I told them that it was a thunderbolt.'

'A thunderbolt? And they believed it?'

'Yes, indeed, and not only that, they said that due to the evident danger they would give me an increase in salary, but did not think it wise to install the new computerized cash register in case its electronic workings attracted further cosmic assault upon the premises.'

'Bravo,' said Jim, 'so all is well that ends well.' He rubbed his hands together and made a motion towards the beer pulls as if to say 'Merits a couple of free ones then.'

'All is not well,' said Neville coldly, waggling his still bandaged thumb at them. 'Someone could have been killed, I will have no more of it. This is a public house, not a bloody missile proving station.'

Neville counted the exact number of pennies and halfpennies into the till and rang up 'No Sale'. The Siamese Twins took themselves and their pints off to a side table. They had little to offer each other by the way of conversation; they had exhausted most subjects and their enforced closeness had of late caused them generally to witness and experience the same events. Thus they sat, for the most part speechless, oppressed by fears of unexpected telegrams or fluttering pigeon post.

The bar was far from crowded. Old Pete sat in his regular seat, Chips spread out before him shamming indifference to the unwelcome attention being paid to his hind quarters by a blue-bottle. Norman sat at the bar, wearing an extraordinary water-cooled hat of his own design, and a couple of stalwarts braved the heat for a half-hearted game of darts. An electronic Punkah-fan installed by the brewery turned upon the ceiling at a dozen revolutions an hour gently stirring the superheated air. Brentford had fallen once more into apathy. The sun

240

streamed in through the upper windows and flies buzzed in eccentric spirals above the bar.

Pooley gulped his pint. 'Look at them,' he said. 'The town has come to a standstill, we spend the night matching wits with the forces of darkness while Brentford sleeps on. Seems daft, doesn't it?'

Omally sighed. 'But perhaps this is what we are doing it for, just so we can sit about in the Swan while the world goes on outside.'

'Possibly,' said Pooley finishing his pint. 'Another of similar?'

'Ideal.'

Pooley carried the empty glasses to the bar and as Neville refilled them he did his best to strike up some kind of conversation with the part-time barman. 'So what is new, Neville?' he asked. 'How spins the world in general?'

'Once every twenty-four hours,' came the reply.

'But surely something must be happening?'

'The boating lake at Gunnersbury is dry,' said the part-time barman.

'Fascinating,' said Pooley.

'The temperature is up by another two degrees.'

'Oh good, I am pleased to hear that we can expect some fine weather.'

'They pulled two corpses out of the river at Chiswick, stuck in the mud they were when the water went down.'

'Really?' said Jim. 'Anybody we know?'

'I expect not. Only person to go missing from Brentford in the last six months is Soap Distant, but there was only one of him.'

Pooley's face twitched involuntarily, it was certain that sooner or later someone would miss old Soap. 'No-one ever did find out what happened to him then?' he asked casually.

'The word goes that he emigrated to Australia to be nearer to his holes in the poles.'

'And nobody has identified the corpses at Chiswick?'

'No,' said Neville pushing the two pints across the bar top. 'The fish had done a pretty good job on them but they reckon they must have been a pair of drunken gardeners, they found a wheelbarrow stuck in the mud with them.'

Pooley, who had raised his pint to his lips, spluttered wildly, sending beer up his nose.

'Something wrong, Jim?'

'Just went down the wrong way, that's all.'

'Well, before you choke to death, perhaps you wouldn't mind paying for the drinks?'

'Oh yes,' said Jim, wiping a shirtsleeve across his face, 'sorry about that.'

Omally had overheard every word of the conversation and when the pale-faced Pooley returned with the pints he put a finger to his lips and shook his head. 'Who do you think they were?' Jim whispered.

'I haven't a clue, and there's no way that the Captain is going to tell us. But it's the wheelbarrow I worry about, what if somebody identifies it?' Omally chewed upon his fingers. 'I should have reported it stolen,' he said. 'It's a bit late now.'

'Even if they identify it as yours, there is nothing to tie you into the corpses. We don't know who they were; it is unlikely that you would have killed two complete strangers and then disposed of them in your own wheelbarrow.'

'The English Garda have no love for me,' said John, 'they would at least enjoy the interrogation.'

'Anyway,' said Jim, 'whoever the victims were, they must have been killed sometime before being wheeled across the allotment by the Captain and dumped in the river, and we have perfect alibis, we were here at Cowboy Night, everybody saw us.'

'I slipped out to bury a crate of Old Snakebelly,' moaned Omally, 'on the allotment.'

Pooley scratched his head. 'Looks like you'd better give

yourself up then. We might go down to the Chiswick nick and steal back your wheelbarrow, or set fire to it or something.'

Omally shook his head. 'Police stations are bad places to break into, this is well known.'

'I have no other suggestions,' said Jim. 'I can only counsel caution and the maintaining of the now legendary low profile.'

'We might simply make a clean breast of it,' said John.

'We?' said Pooley. 'Where do you get this "we" from? It was your wheelbarrow.'

'I mean we might tell the police about what we saw; it might start an investigation into what is going on in the Mission.'

'I don't think the Professor would appreciate that, it might interfere with his plans. Also the police might claim conspiracy because we didn't come forward earlier.'

Up at the bar Norman, who had quietly been reading a copy of the *Brentford Mercury*, said suddenly, 'Now there's a thing.'

'What's that,' asked Neville.

Norman prodded at his paper. 'Wheelbarrow clue in double slaying.'

'I was just talking about that to Pooley,' said Neville, gesturing towards Jim's table.

But naught, however, remained to signal that either Jim Pooley or John Omally had ever been there, naught but for two half-consumed pints of Large going warm upon the table and a saloon-bar door which swung quietly to and fro upon its hinge.

Norman's shop was closed for the half day and a few copies of the midweek *Mercury* still remained in the wire rack to the front door. Jim took one of these and rattled the letterbox in a perfect impression of a man dropping pennies into it. He and Omally thumbed through the pages.

'Here it is,' said Jim, '"Wheelbarrow Clue in Double Slaying. Chiswick Police leading an investigation into the matter of the two bodies found on the foreshore upon the fall of the Thames last week believe that they now have a lead regarding the owner of the wheelbarrow discovered at the scene of the crime. Detective Inspector Cyril Barker said in an exclusive interview with the *Brentford Mercury* that he expected to make an early arrest".'

'Is that it?' Omally asked.

'Yes, I can't see the *Mercury*'s ace reporter getting the journalist of the year award for it.'

'But there isn't a photograph of the wheelbarrow?'

'No, either the reporter had no film in his Brownie or the police didn't think it necessary.'

'But "early arrest", what do you think that means?'

The words were drowned by the scream of a police-car siren. Driven at high speed, the car came through the red lights at the bottom of Ealing Road, roared past them and screeched to a standstill a hundred yards further on, outside the Flying Swan. A plainclothes detective and three burly constables leapt from the vehicle and swept into the saloon bar.

The two men did not wait to see what might happen. They looked at each other, dropped the newspaper and fled.

There are many pleasures to be had in camping out. The old nights under canvas, the wind in your hair and fresh air in your lungs. An opportunity to get away from it all and commune with nature. Days in sylvan glades watching the sunshine dancing between the leaves and dazzling the eyes. Birdsong swelling at dawn to fill the ears. In harmony with the Arcadian Spirits of olden Earth. At night a time for reverie about the crackling campfire, the sweet smell of mossy peat and pine needles. Ah yes, that is the life.

Omally awoke with a start, something was pressing firmly into his throat and stopping his breath. 'Ow, ooh, get off, get off.' These imprecations were directed towards Jim Pooley, whose oversized boot had come snugly to rest beneath Omally's chin. 'Will you get off I say?'

Pooley jerked himself awake. 'Where am I?' he groaned.

'Where you have been for the last two days, in my bloody allotment shed.'

Pooley groaned anew. 'I was having such a beautiful dream. I can't go on here,' he moaned, 'I can't live out my days a fugitive in an allotment shed, I wish Archroy had never rebuilt it. You must give yourself up, John, claim diminished responsibility, I will gladly back you up on that.'

Omally was not listening, he was peeling a potato. Before him a monstrous heap of such peelings spoke most fluently of the restricted diet upon which the two were at present subsisting. 'It is spud for breakfast,' said he.

Pooley made an obscene noise and clutched at his rumbling stomach. 'We will die from spud poisoning,' he whimpered. 'It is all right for you blokes from across the water, but we Brits need more than just plain spud to survive on.'

'Spud is full of vitamins,' said Omally.

'Full of maggots more like.'

'The spud is the friend of man.'

'I should much prefer an egg.'

'Eggs too have their strong points, but naught can in any way equal for vitamins, carbohydrates or pure nutritional value God's chosen food, the spud.'

Pooley made a nasty face. 'Even a sprout I would prefer.'

'Careful there,' said Omally, 'I will have none of that language here.'

'Sorry,' said Pooley, 'it just slipped out.' He patted at his pockets in the hope that a cigarette he had overlooked

245

throughout all of his previous bouts of pocket-patting might have made a miraculous appearance. 'I have no fags again,' he said.

'You've got your pipe,' said Omally, 'and you know where the peelings are, there are some particularly choice ones near the bottom.'

Pooley made another tragic sound. 'We eat them, we smoke them, we sleep on them, about the only thing we don't do is talk to them.'

Omally chuckled. 'I do,' he said, 'these lads are not as dumb as they may look.' He manoeuvred the grimy frying-pan on to the little brick stove he had constructed. 'Bar-b-que Spud,' he announced, lighting the fire. 'Today, fritters lightly fried in their own juices, turned but once and seasoned with . . .'

'Seasoned with?'

'Tiny golden flakes . . . of spud!'

'I can't go on,' said Pooley, raising his voice to a new pitch of misery. 'Two days here wondering who will get us first, the police or that maniac in the Mission. I can't go on, it is all too much.'

'Your fritters are almost done,' said Omally, 'and this morning I have a little treat to go with them.'

'Spudburgers?' queried Pooley. 'Or is it Kentucky fried spud, or spud chop suey?'

'You are warm,' said Omally, 'it is spud gin.' He hefted a dusty bottle into the light. 'I thought I had a few bottles of the stuff left, they were in the bottom of one of the potato sacks. Good place to hide them eh?'

Pooley ran a thoughtful hand over his stubbly chin. 'Spud gin, is it good stuff?'

'The best, but seeing as you have this thing against spuds, I shall not offend you by offering you any.'

'It is no offence, I assure you. In fact,' Pooley scooped up a spud fritter and flipped it into his mouth, 'I am growing quite fond of the dear fellows. Ooh, ouch!' He spat out the fritter and fanned his tongue desperately.

'They are better left to cool awhile,' Omally informed him. 'Here, have a swig.' He uncorked the bottle and passed it to Pooley.

Pooley had a swig. 'Not bad,' said he. Omally watched him with interest. Pooley noticed that he was counting under his breath. 'Nine, ten,' said Omally.

'Ye Gods!' croaked Pooley in a strangled voice, clutching at his throat. Sweat was appearing upon his forehead and his eyes were starting to pop.

'Creeps up on you doesn't it?' Omally asked, grinning wickedly and taking a lesser swig from the bottle Pooley had dropped into his wisely outstretched hands.

Pooley's nose had turned a most unpleasant shade of red and his eyes were streaming. 'That definitely has the edge on Old Snakebelly,' he said when finally he found his voice, 'but I feel I have the measure of it now, give me another swig.'

The two men sat awhile in the morning sunlight sharing the bottle and chewing upon Omally's potato fritters. At length Jim said seriously, 'You know, John, we really cannot keep this up much longer, we are dangerously close to the Mission and if that character does not get his Papal paws upon us then someone else is bound to observe the smoke from our fire and report our presence to the police.'

Omally nodded sombrely. 'All these things have of course crossed my mind, our imposed isolation here has given us both time for reflection. For myself I am prepared to sit it out and await the Professor's word, what of you?'

Pooley shrugged helplessly. 'What can I say, I am up to my neck in it, I suppose we have little choice.'

Omally passed him the bottle once more and leant back amongst the potato sacks. 'We shall not starve,' said he, 'although I am afraid there is a limit to the things even I can do with a potato.'

Pooley had risen to his feet, his right hand shielding his eyes from the sunlight, and he appeared to be gazing off into the distance. 'Now what do you make of that?' he asked in a puzzled voice.

Omally rose to join him. 'Where?' he asked. 'What are you looking at?'

Pooley pointed. 'It's like a swirl of smoke, or a little black cloud.'

Omally shielded his eyes and squinted off into the haze. There was a dark shape twisting and turning in the sky, and as he watched it grew larger and blacker.

'It's locusts,' said Jim, 'a bloody plague of locusts.'

'It's not locusts,' Omally squealed in a terrified voice, 'it's birds, the birds from Archroy's garden. Run for your life.'

Pooley's feet were welded to the ground. 'I can't run,' he whimpered, 'I fear that the potato gin has gone to my legs.'

'Into the shed then.' Omally grabbed his companion by the shoulders and yanked him backwards, slamming the door shut behind them. He was not a moment too soon as the screeching mass of birds covered the allotment in a whirling feathery cloud, obliterating the sun. The sound was deafening, horny bills scratched and scraped at the corrugated iron of the small hut, a thousand tiny hooked claws tore at it. Pooley's hands found themselves once more clapped over his ears while Omally beat away at the snapping beaks which forced their way in through the cracks of the door.

'Do something, Jim,' he shouted, his voice swelling above the din. 'If they get in here, there won't be enough of you left to send home in a tobacco tin.'

Pooley took to turning about in circles, flapping his hands wildly and shouting at the top of his voice. It was a technique he had perfected as a lad and it had always served him well, when it came to getting his own way.

The birds, however, seemed unconcerned by Pooley's behaviour and if anything their assault upon the hut became even more frenzied and violent. There was the sound of splintering wood and Omally saw to his horror that scores of tiny dents were beginning to appear on the corrugated walls. Then suddenly the attacks ceased. Pooley found himself spinning, flapping and shouting in absolute silence. The birds had gone.

'The birds have gone,' said Jim, ceasing his foolish gyrations.

'They have not,' Omally replied, 'I fell for a similar trick on my first encounter with them.'

Pooley pressed his eye to a crack in the door. 'I can't see them.'

'They'll be around, on the roof or around the back.'

'Then should we make a break for it?'

'That I would not advise.'

The two men slumped on the potato sack in the semi-darkness. It was cramped and with the sun beating down upon the roof it was also extremely hot.

'We'll die in here for certain,' said Pooley, 'suffocate we will, like rats in a trap.'

'Don't start all that again,' said Omally, raising his fist in the darkness.

Long minutes passed; in the distance the Memorial Library clock struck ten. Several yards away from the shed Omally's bicycle Marchant lay in its twisted wreckage, musing upon man's inhumanity to bike and bird's inhumanity to man. Jim struggled out of his jacket and rolled up his sleeves. 'Have you any more of that potato gin?' he asked. 'Only if I am going to die, I should prefer to die as I have lived, drunkenly.'

'Nobody is going to die,' Omally assured him (although to Pooley his voice had a somewhat hollow quality), 'but I would appreciate it if you could be persuaded to channel your enormous intellect towards some means by which we might facilitate our escape.' He pulled another bottle from the potato sack and handed it to his companion.

'You have a lovely turn of phrase, John,' said Jim, drawing the cork from the bottle and taking a large swig. He passed it back to Omally, who took a sip and returned the bottle. 'How does one drive off birds, such a thing is surely not impossible?'

'A shotgun is the thing,' said Pooley, 'both barrels, small shot.'

'I fear that we will have a long time to wait for a passing gamekeeper,' said John.

'We might tunnel our way out then, possibly dig down, we might even break into one of Soap's underground workings.'

Omally tapped the concrete floor with his hobnails. 'We can forget that I am thinking.'

'A scarecrow then.'

Omally stroked his chin, 'I can't really imagine a scarecrow putting the fear of God into these lads, but if you will give me a few moments I think I have an idea.'

The Memorial Library clock struck the half hour and within the small hut upon the allotment Jim Pooley stood wearing nothing but his vest and underpants. 'Don't you ever change your socks?' Omally asked, holding his nose.

Jim regarded him bitterly in the half darkness. 'Are you sure this is going to work?' he asked.

'Trust me,' said Omally, 'the plan is simplicity itself.'

Pooley chewed upon his lip. 'It doesn't look very much like me,' he said, 'I am hardly that fat.' His remarks were addressed to the life-sized dummy Omally was fashioning from Pooley's garments. He had knotted the sleeves and trouser bottoms and stuffed the thing with potatoes.

'We've got to give it a little weight,' said John. 'How is the head coming?'

'Splendidly, as it happens,' said Jim. 'I like to pride

myself that given a turnip, which I am disgusted to find that you had secreted from me for your own personal consumption, and a penknife, I am able to model a head of such magnificence as to put the legendary Auguste Rodin to shame.' Pooley passed across his sculptured masterpiece and Omally wedged it firmly between the dummy's shoulders. 'Very nice,' he said.

'Very nice if it fools the birds.'

'It will,' said Omally. 'Have some faith in me will you?'

'But what of me?' Pooley complained. 'I shall be forced to run through the streets in my underwear.'

'I have thought of all that, leave it to me. Are the bottles ready?'

Pooley held up two bottles of the potato gin. They had been uncorked and gin-dampened strips of cloth torn from Jim's shirt-tail thrust into the necks, Molotov cocktail-style.

'Better douse our good friend here,' said Omally, 'we want this to work to maximum effect.' Pooley took up the last bottle and poured it over the dummy. 'Right.' Omally held the dummy with one arm and made the sign of the cross with the other.

'That is very comforting,' said Jim.

'We only get one chance at this, Pooley, don't mess it up, will you?'

Pooley shook his head. 'Not I, but it seems a tragic end to a good suit.'

'I will buy you another,' said Omally.

'What with? You have no money, you are wearing my other suit.'

'You may have my Fair Isle jumper and cricket whites.'

'Bless you,' said Jim Pooley.

Omally edged open the hut door. All was still upon the allotment, the relentless sun beat down upon the parched earth and in the distance, a train rolled over the viaduct. 'Now as ever,' said Omally firmly; gripping the dummy he flung it forward with as much strength as he could muster.

There was a great ripple in the sky above the hut and down upon the dummy in a squawking, screaming cascade the birds fell in full feathered fury. Pooley struck his lighter and set flame to the strips of shirt tail.

'Throw them,' screamed Omally.

Pooley threw them.

There was a double crash, a flash and a great flaring sheet of flame engulfed the feathered hoard. Without looking back Pooley and Omally took once more to their heels and fled.

22

Brentford's Olympic hope and his Irish trainer jogged around the corner into Mafeking Avenue, up the street a short way, down a back alley and through the gate into the rear yard of Jim Pooley's house. Mrs King next door peered over the washing line at them. 'People been round here asking for you Jim Pooley,' she said. 'Why are you running about in your underpants?'

'He's in training,' said Omally. 'Who's been round here asking then?'

'You mind your own business, I was talking to Mr Pooley.'

Omally smiled his winning smile. She was a fine-looking woman, he thought, how had he previously failed to make her acquaintance?

'Who has been calling,' asked Jim, 'friends or what?'

'The police were here,' said Mrs King smugly, 'D. I. Barker, he left his card.' She delved about in her apron pocket and pulled out a damp and crumpled card which had obviously been doing the local rounds.

'What did he want?' Jim asked innocently, accepting the card.

'Didn't say, just said you were to notify them of your return as soon as what you did, if you see what I mean. Mind you, I'm not surprised, you've had this coming for years, Jim Pooley. In and out at all hours, rolling home drunk, making all that noise.'

Pooley ignored her ramblings. 'Anybody else call?'

'An old man with white hair and a black coat.'

'The Professor,' said Omally.

'I wasn't talking to you. Here, what do you think you're looking at?'

Omally's eyes had been wandering up and down Mrs King's tightly fitting apron. 'I was undressing you with my eyes.'

'Oh yes?'

'Yes, and that safety pin which is holding up your knickers is getting a bit rusty.'

Mrs King snarled furiously at Omally, flung down her washing and stalked off into her house, slamming the back door behind her.

'Was that wise?' Jim asked. 'She'll probably phone the police now.'

'I don't think so,' said John, grinning lewdly, 'I think she quite fancies me.'

Pooley shrugged and rolled his eyes. 'Your technique is to say the least original,' said he.

The two men mounted the back staircase and disappeared in through Pooley's kitchen door. There was little left to wear in Pooley's wardrobe and so he was forced to don the shirt, Fair Isle sweater and cricketer's whites left by Omally. He passed over the patent leather pumps, however, preferring to remain in his hobnails.

'A regular dude,' said Omally. Pooley remained unconvinced. 'So what do we do now?' he asked.

'We might begin by a decent, if late, breakfast. What supplies have you in your larder?'

Pooley found two tins of beans, which he and Omally

253

consumed with relish. 'And now what?' he asked.

'We will just have to wait for the Professor to return.'

'Or the police.'

Omally nodded grimly. 'Or the police.'

The day passed; there was little to do. Omally fiddled with the knobs on Pooley's archaic wireless set, but raised little but static and what appeared to be a wartime broadcast. By five thirty the two men were pacing the floor like caged tigers and tempers were becoming dangerously short.

Finally Pooley could stand it no longer. 'I think I will just step out to Jack Lane's for a couple of bottles of light ale.'

Omally looked doubtful. 'We had better not separate,' he said, 'I will come with you.'

'Good man.'

If the atmosphere of the Flying Swan's saloon bar was timeless, then that of Jack Lane's was even more so. There was a positive sense of the museum about the place. No-one could recall a single change being made in the decor since 1928 when Brentford won the FA Cup and Jack Lane retired from the game to take over as landlord. 'The Four Horsemen', as the establishment was more correctly known, although none had used the name within living memory, had become a shrine to Brentford's glorious one and a half hours upon the sacred turf of Wembley.

True, when Jack departed the game to take up the licensed trade his team lost its finest dribbler and dropped through the various divisions like a two-bob bit in a Woodbine machine. Jack himself became a kind of living monument. The faded photographs of the team he captained showed him standing erect in his broad-striped shirt, his shorts reaching nearly to his ankles and the leather ball between his feet. A close examination of these blurry mementoes revealed that Jack had changed hardly at all during the preceding fifty-odd years. Proudly he stood, his toothless face smiling and his bald head nobly reflecting the Wembley sunlight.

Now well over eighty and taking advantage of the fact, Jack held court over his cobwebbed castle, gnomelike and droll and caring nothing for the outside world and the so-called 'changing times'. He had only noticed the Second World War because the noise had woken him up and he had wondered about why so many of his younger patrons had taken to the wearing of uniforms.

When Pooley and Omally sheepishly entered the saloon bar, the old gnome was perched upon his stool beside the cash drawer and eyed them with but a passing interest. 'Close that door,' he mumbled, 'you're letting the weather in.'

Pooley looked at Omally, who shrugged. 'He probably still thinks it's winter.'

Pooley was going to say two bottles of pale ale please, but the words would not come. 'Two pints of Large,' he said presently. Omally patted his companion on the back. The sporting ancient climbed down with difficulty from his stool and shuffled over to the pumps. Pooley recalled that it was always advisable to buy two rounds at a time in the Horsemen, as one's thirst could not always survive the wait while Jack methodically pulled his pints.

'Better make that four pints,' said Omally, who harboured similar recollections.

Jack muttered an obscenity beneath his breath and sought two more pint glasses.

'So what's the news then, Jack?' Omally asked cheerfully.

Jack Lane smiled and ran a ragged pullover sleeve across his nose, 'News?' he said. 'I haven't heard of any news, what news should there be?'

Omally shrugged. 'Just wondered, not much of interest ever gets by you.'

'You been barred from the Swan then, Omally?'

'Hardly that, just thought we'd pop in as we were passing, trade seems a little slack.' He indicated the empty bar.

'It's early yet.' It was well known to all that Jack's licensing hours were flexible; few entered his establishment until the hostelries they previously frequented were closing up their doors.

'We had a Lascar in last week,' said Jack struggling over with the first of the four pints. 'Big buck he was, I told him, out of here I said.'

'Fascinating,' said John, 'but nothing else out of the ordinary happened recently then.'

Jack was by now halfway back towards the pumps and as Omally was on his deaf side he did not reply.

'I think we'll be safe enough in here then,' Pooley whispered.

'Might as well settle in then,' said Omally. 'It will take us a goodly number of pints to catch up upon our last few days of abstinence.'

'I will drink to that.'

By around seven, both Pooley and Omally were in an advanced state of drunkenness. They leant upon one another's shoulders, each extolling the other's virtues and expressing his undying friendship. It was a touching thing to behold.

'Buffoons,' muttered Jack Lane.

'I fear that nature is calling me,' said Pooley, 'and in a voice of no uncertain tone.'

'I myself must confess to having overheard her urgent cries,' Omally replied.

The two men lurched up from their chairs and staggered towards the door. Jack Lane's establishment boasted no 'accommodations' and it was therefore necessary to do one's business in the public lavvies next door. The two men stumbled out into the early evening; it seemed unwontedly dark considering the weather, and there was a definite chill in the air. Omally stared up towards the sky, there was something not quite right about it, but he was unable to make out exactly what it was.

Jim swayed in through the ever-open door of the gents and sought out the first available cubicle. He relieved himself amid much sighing and heavy breathing. 'A job well done,' he said pulling the chain.

Suddenly a soft voice spoke his name. 'Who's that?' Pooley said, looking around in surprise. 'John, is that you?'

Evidently it was not, because Pooley could make out the sounds of a similar bout of sighing and gasping from the next cubicle.

'James,' said the voice again; it was coming from a mesh grille beneath the water cistern.

'Good God,' said Pooley, 'I have lost myself and stumbled into a confessional. Father forgive me, for I know not what I do.'

'James, listen to me.' Jim pressed his ear to the grille. 'There is not much time,' whispered the voice. It was the Other Sam!

'Much time, much time for what?'

'Tonight is to be the night, the two of you must go at once to Professor Slocombe's.'

Pooley groaned dismally. 'I hardly feel up to it,' he complained, 'couldn't we put it off until tomorrow?'

The Other Sam's voice was both harsh and urgent. 'You must go at once, waste not a moment, go now and keep together.'

Pooley was about to voice further complaint but the Other Sam had gone and Omally was rattling at the door. 'John,' said Jim, 'John, you are not going to like what I have just heard.'

The Irishman stood swaying in the doorway supporting himself upon the doorpost. 'Do not bother to relate your conversation,' he said simply, 'for I have overheard every syllable.'

Pooley dragged himself up to his feet and patted his companion upon the shoulders. 'The fates are against us,' he said, 'we had better go.'

The two men staggered off down Mafeking Avenue, en route for the Butts Estate and Professor Slocombe's house. At intervals Omally stopped to stare again at the night sky. 'Something is definitely amiss in the heavens,' he said.

Pooley stumbled on. 'I would gladly offer you my opinion,' he said, 'but I fear that any increased elevation of the head might result in a catalepsy, possibly terminating in death.'

Outside the Memorial Library Pooley stopped and held up his hands. 'Enough,' said he, 'I can go no further.' He collapsed on to his favourite bench, breathing heavily and clutching at his heart.

Omally pulled at his shirtsleeve. 'Come now, it's only around the corner and I am sure that there will be time for a glass or three of the Professor's whisky.'

Pooley rose unsteadily. 'We must aid our noble colleague, a fine and learned old gentleman. Come Omally, let us not delay here.'

The Professor's house was shuttered and absolutely silent. As Pooley and Omally stared at the front door the old man's hand appeared, frantically beckoning them to enter.

The Professor bolted the door firmly behind them. The house was in darkness, lit only by the silver candelabra which the old man carried. By the flickering light Pooley could see that his face looked pale, drawn and deeply lined. He seemed to have aged terribly since they had seen him last. 'Are you all right, Professor?' Pooley asked in concern.

Professor Slocombe nodded impatiently. 'I will be all right. What of you two, how have things been for you since last we met?'

'Oh, fine,' said Omally, 'we are wanted by the police, we came within inches of being eaten alive, other than that, fine.'

The Professor led them through the ink dark corridors towards his study. 'The police,' he said, 'how are they involved?'

'They have found my wheelbarrow stuck in the mud at Chiswick accompanied by two corpses. They raided the Swan and were also at Pooley's asking questions.'

By now the three men had entered the Professor's study and the old man lit from his candelabra an assortment of candles around the room. 'Fear not, John,' he said, seating himself at his desk, 'I have recorded upon paper all that I know regarding this business. It has been witnessed and it is lodged in a safety-deposit box. Should I not survive this night then at least you will be safe upon that account.'

'That is pleasing to my ears,' said John, 'but come now, survive this night, what can you mean by that?'

As Omally filled glasses Professor Slocombe seated himself at his desk. 'Tonight,' he said, 'the followers of the being who calls himself Pope Alexander VI will gather at the Seamen's Mission to glorify their new Messiah. Tonight he will instal himself upon his Papal throne and "sanctify" his "Holy See". The Mission is to be his new Vatican. Tonight will be our last opportunity to stop him. Should we fail then I can see little future for any of us.'

Pooley gulped back his scotch. 'But do you think we alone can stop him?'

'We must try.'

'And at what time will this mockery of the true Church take place?' Omally asked.

'A little after nine. We must lose ourselves amongst the crowd, and once we get inside you must do exactly as I say.'

Pooley refilled the glasses and looked up at the great mantelclock. It chimed eight-thirty. 'We have half an hour.' He smiled, dropping back into one of the Professor's high-backed fireside chairs.

Omally fingered the neck of the crystal decanter. 'Plenty of time,' said he.

The minutes ticked slowly away. Pooley and Omally fortified themselves until the decanter was spent, and the Professor sat at his desk scribbling away with a goose-feather quill upon a length of parchment.

Omally watched the old man working. Could he really stand up to this Pope Alex? Omally felt somewhat doubtful. Certainly the Professor was full of good intentions and his knowledge of the esoteric and the occult was profound. But who knows what might be lurking within the Mission? It seemed reasonable to suppose that Pope Alex would not be unguarded. Better a more positive approach then. Something more physical than mere babblings of ancient words. Something more concrete. More concrete?

A smile crossed Omally's face and broadened into a grin of Cheshire cat proportions. Concrete, that was the thing. Or better still, the good old half brick, always a friend in time of need.

23

The Professor's clock struck nine and the old man rose unsteadily to his feet. 'We had better go,' he said, 'slip these about your shoulders.' He indicated two mud-brown cloaks draped across a side table. 'They should help you merge into the crowd.'

Omally raised himself to his feet and swayed over to the table. 'Very pleasing,' he said, casting the cloak about his broad shoulders, 'very ecclesiastical.'

Pooley climbed from his chair and donned his cloak. 'You would make a fine monk, Jim Pooley,' said Omally, chuckling irreverently.

With that the two caped crusaders helped the Professor to extinguish the candles and followed the old man through the darkened house to the front door. Professor Slocombe eased it open a crack and the three men stared out into the mysterious night.

All across the Butts Estate grim-faced crowds were moving. They moved with a strange, stiff-legged gait like tailors' dummies removed from their shop windows and grotesquely animated. The eyes of these dummies seemed glazed and sightless, yet stared ever ahead in the direction of the Mission.

Professor Slocombe turned up the astrakhan collar of his elderly coat. 'Come,' he whispered. He ushered Pooley and Omally out through the front door, which he locked with a heavy iron key. Whilst he was thus engaged his two inebriated colleagues exchanged knowing glances, furtively stooped and swept up two likely-looking house bricks which each secreted within the folds of his robes.

Lovingly patting their respective bulges they followed the old Professor down the short path and out into the Butts Estate. The three men slipped in amongst the sombre crowds, doing their best to adopt the stiff-legged gait and lacklustre stare. Pooley's impersonation was astonishingly convincing, but that was because he was paralytic. Omally stumbled along at his side, occasionally peering up at the sky and muttering to himself.

As the crowd, which was now several hundred strong, neared the Mission it soberly formed into a single file. The three men could see that the heavily braced door had been thrown open and that a soft light glowed from within. Pooley fell into line behind the Professor, with the muttering Omally bringing up the rear. As each of the zombiesque walkers crossed the threshold of the Seamen's

Mission he or she genuflected and mouthed a short phrase of archaic Latin.

Pooley was pleased to note that the phrase spoken by the Professor as he entered the portal differed substantially from that of the rest. Jim was no scholar of language so he merely mumbled incoherently and hoped that none would notice. Omally was the next to bow his knee, an action which he achieved more through luck than judgement. His knowledge of Latin was extensive, but it was two words of the Gaelic that he chose. 'Pog Mahoun,' said the man from the Emerald Isle, raising two fingers.

There was already a considerable number of people assembled within the Mission, and the three would-be party-poopers could see little above the multitude of heads.

Omally felt the Professor's sinewy hand closing about his arm as the old man drew the Irishman away towards a shadowy corner. Pooley followed them. Here and there he saw a face he recognized, but doll-like, vacant of expression and seeming to lack some essential ingredient of humanity.

The three men squeezed themselves into a darkened niche at the rear of a large column. The Professor pressed a slender finger to his lips. 'Watch and wait,' he counselled.

Pooley bobbed up and down in the hope of observing what was going on. Tiring of this futile occupation he whispered to Omally, 'Give us a shin up this pillar and I'll have a look around.' Amid a fair amount of puffing and cursing, all performed in muted tones, Pooley was borne aloft.

What he saw sent his brain reeling at the fantastic transformation which had been wrought within the ivy-hung walls of Brentford's Seamen's Mission. The entire building had been gutted, partition walls, doors, the upper floor, all were gone. Pooley found himself staring into what must surely be a cathedral. Rows of elaborately carved doric columns soared upwards towards the roof which, once the haunt of nesting wasps and sleeping bats, was now a glistening dome painted and frescoed in the style of Michaelangelo, depicting mighty biblical scenes.

There was Adam, wide-eyed and innocent, staring into the godly face of his bearded creator. Eve's temptation, with the hideous black serpent entwined about the tree of knowledge. The flood, ferociously portrayed with roaring skies and smashing waters, Noah's ark pitching and the Man of God raising his hands towards Heaven. There was the fall of the Tower of Babel, the destruction of Sodom and Gomorrah and countless other scenes depicted so cunningly that the eye might wander for ever amongst them.

The great hall was lit by rows of tall wrought-iron torchères of ponderous proportions, and their steady light illuminated the astonishing adornments which lined the walls: the gilded icons and embossed tableaux, the bronze statues of the saints, the silver madonnas, and the rows of heraldic crests, each of which bore the emblazoned figure of a great bull. There was a king's ransom here, that of many kings in fact, in this unlikely setting.

And then Pooley's eyes fell upon the altar. He had seen pictures in library books of the altarpieces of the world's most notable cathedrals, but they paled into insignificance before this. It was magnificence beyond magnificence, opulence and grandeur taken to a point where it surpassed all beauty and became a thing to fear.

A profusion of fatly bummed cherubim fluttering and fussing in their golden nakedness; row upon row upon row of candles blazing amid the rising gem-covered columns; the traceried woodwork and carved adornments; the proliferation of wondrous beings, half human half animal, set in attitudes of supplication, gazing ever upwards towards the titanic figure which crested the altarpiece and held in his outstretched arms a hanging tapestry woven in cloth of gold and depicting once again the motif of a great black bull. The banner of the bull. The banner of the Borgias.

Pooley could have spent long hours in reverent contemplation of these wonders had not Omally chosen this particular moment to topple backwards into the darkness, bringing Jim down from his perch and tumbling him to the floor.

'Sorry,' said John. 'Anything to see?'

Pooley shook his befuddled cranium, unable to find words to describe what he had seen. 'You have a look,' he said finally. 'I'll give you a leg up.'

Omally's head rose unsteadily above the crowd, which still flowed unabated through the Mission door. He saw what Pooley had seen. Certainly the glories were undeniable in their magnificence, but there was something more. Omally cocked his head upon one side. The geometry of the entire hall was slightly amiss; it was not immediately noticeable, but the more he looked at it then the more obvious it became.

He squinted up at the great pillars supporting the marvellous domed ceiling. Surely they were slightly out of true? Several seemed more closely spaced than the others and the one at the end was not quite perpendicular. And the dome itself, it was not absolutely round, more ovoid, or more accurately it was egg-shaped.

The great golden altar, for all its unworldly spectacle, was definitely crooked, top heavy. The statuary was similarly lopsided, some leaning at dangerous angles. The icons seemed to have been nailed into place and the raised dais which filled an enclosed space before the altar was far from level.

Some attempts had obviously been made here to correct the deficiency and Omally noted that a number of red flettons had been wedged under one corner of it. Red flettons!

Omally stifled a great guffaw. So that was it! Old Pope Alex was certainly far from omnipotent if he dwelt under the misconception that present day jobbing builders could repeat the masterworks wrought by their fifteenth-century counterparts. The thought that the crimson giant at the Mission was actually capable of error set Omally in fine spirits. These fine spirits, however, were soon dispelled by what next occurred.

The door of the Seamen's Mission swung shut with a death cell finality and a cry rose up from the throats of the assembled multitude. It was not so much a cry as a howl. Omally hastily returned to floor level and endeavoured to lose himself once and for all amongst the shadows. The howl went up from all corners of the room, animal in nature, atavistic, echoing down centuries, primeval and cruel.

The howl rose up, filling the great hall, reverberating about the dome and rebounding from the pillars. It rose and rose in pitch, forming into a scream. The hierophants threw back their heads; hands crossed on their chests like a thousand dead Pharaohs, they swayed upon their heels and howled. Pooley tightened the grip upon his ears, Omally rolled his eyes, and the Professor gripped the silver cross he wore about his neck and mumbled his phrases of Latin. All at once the howl changed, dropped down in tone and formed itself into a low chant.

The Professor pricked up his ears. 'It is a mantra,' he said, although none heard him.

Slowly the syllables formed upon one another, the chant went up time after time, driving itself almost physically at the three men crouched in the darkness behind the column. Omally was staring goggle-eyed and the Professor forced the Irishman's hands up over his ears. 'You must not hear this,' he whispered. 'You must not hear.'

Omally hummed to himself one of his favourite Republican songs, the much-loved standard, 'Kevin Barry'. He was halfway through the now legendary line about the British soldiers torturing the dear lad in order that he might reveal the names of his brave comrades when he suddenly realized that he was humming alone. Omally unclasped his ears. There was no sound, the awful chanting had stopped, nothing moved, the air was still. Or was it?

It was a low incessant hissing sound, soft yet persistent. Omally raised his eyes once more towards the astonishing ceiling; it was coming from above. He chewed upon his lower lip, this was a sound he recognized, a reassuring natural sound, not a part of the ghastly unnatural cacophony, this was something real.

And then he knew why the sky had seemed so strange to him that evening. The stars were missing, the moon had gone; while he and Pooley had been sitting in Jack Lane's the sky had clouded over. John turned to his companion, who still had his hands desperately clamped about his ears. 'Listen Jim,' he whispered, prising Pooley's hands from his head. 'It is beginning to rain.'

Outside the Mission and all across Brentford great drops were starting to fall. They struck the dust of the streets with muted explosions, spattered upon the roof tops and sizzled in the trees.

At the Flying Swan Neville the part-time barman set aside his polishing cloth and gazed at the front windows in awe as long teardrops of water began to smear the dusty panes. It was gathering in strength now and any thoughts Brentford's dehydrated populace may have had of dancing in the streets were rapidly smothered as the thunder began to roll ominously across the heavens and the lightning tore the sky apart. It was as if at some God-given signal the very floodgates of Heaven had been opened, the rain fell in torrents, a solid sheet of water. The parched ground sucked and gurgled, the allotment lands drew in the life-giving liquid and the stretch of dried-up canal bed devoured the downfall greedily. It was a storm such as none living could remember. Old Pete ordered himself another large rum and peered out through the Swan's open doorway with much shaking of his ancient head. Norman leant upon the bar counter. 'Annus Mirabilis,' he said to the part-time barman. 'The year of wonders.'

At the Seamen's Mission Pope Alexander VI's congregation paid no heed to the downpour. As the lightning flashed about Brentford, bursting like a million flashbulbs behind the gigantic stained-glass windows above the altarpiece, they stood resolute, unmoving. Pooley and Omally ducked their heads as the thunder crashed deafeningly above. Professor Slocombe stared upwards, an unreadable expression in his pale blue eyes.

Suddenly the Mission seemed to draw backwards, sideways, forward, simply away, to suck itself into a vacuum beyond the reach of the maelstrom which roared without. It was as if the building had been snatched away into a limbo, a separate dimension insulated totally from all that was real and touchable. The lightning was still visible, flashing behind the stained glass, but now it seemed unable to pierce the panes, stopping short of them as if held at bay by some invisible barrier. The roaring of the storm could still be heard, but it was muffled as if somebody had closed a padded door.

A great light began to fill the hall. It grew and grew in brightness until every standing figure, every icon, statue and column became nothing more than a cardboard cutout, lit dazzlingly from one side and lost in a void of absolute blackness to the other.

Omally shielded his eyes and squinted into the glare. Pooley dragged his cloak over his head, dropping his cherished half brick to the floor. Professor Slocombe stood transfixed. From the side of the hall, amid the blinding glare, figures were beginning to appear, moving from the realm of dream, or nightmare.

The congregation were shuffling backwards, forming themselves into a great arc stretching from the side enclosure to the raised dais of the golden altarpiece. The figures were moving forward in a slow methodic rhythm. Omally could make out their silhouettes, sunspots upon the solar disc. There were four shapeless stubby creatures bearing upon their shoulders something enormous upon a kind of chair. Before this procession a lone being moved unsteadily, gaunt and bowed, a golden censer swinging from his clasped hands.

Omally widened his eyes; the figure was that of Captain Carson. He nudged the Professor but the old man put his finger to his lips and whispered, 'I know.'

The Captain was dressed in rough sacking robes, a golden sash knotted about his waist. His head was shaven and his feet were bare. His face was as vacant as those of the congregation.

Behind him trod the four red-clothed and dwarfish figures, the identity of which was well enough known to the three watchers. Upon the shoulders of these creatures they supported a gilded travesty of the Papal throne, carved from a rich red timber of exotic origin, inset with many precious stones. The arms of this throne terminated in large gilded bulls' heads, as did the very crest upon the chair's high back.

The eyes of these bovine spectres were great red rubies, glittering flawlessly in the pulsating light which flowed from the being who lounged on the velvet cushioning of the fabulous chair. He was enormous, a titan; his great hands rested upon the bulls' heads and one could have passed a copper penny through any one of the rings he wore. He was clad in the richest of crimsons, his gown smothered in jewels. These were woven into cunning arabesques, symbols of cuneiforms, diamonds, spirals and trapezoids, each complete of itself yet playing an integral part in the overall design. The gown swam in the throbbing light which surrounded the giant and appeared to pass through several dimensions, shrinking, growing and moving forwards and backwards as if alive. It was belted at the waist by a broad golden cummerbund and heavily quilted at the sleeves. Over his massive shoulders the giant wore the holy mantle and upon his head the papal mitre, cloth of gold and set again with priceless gems.

The three men shrank back into the shadows that they might not meet the gaze of the giant as he passed. Never had they seen such a face, surely the very face of death. It was terrible, but it was also magnificent in its perfect control, absolute power and supreme arrogance. The great hawk of a nose, the prominent chin, the high cheekbones, the broad forehead, and the eyes two flaming red fires of hell.

The throne halted at the dais of the altar. The being who called himself Pope Alexander VI stepped from it on to the platform. The four creatures lowered the great throne chair to the floor and prostrated themselves before their master. Captain Carson stood ghostlike; the censer swinging from his gnarled and tattooed fingers suddenly ceased its movement in mid swing and hung in the air in defiance of all the laws of gravity.

Outside, great peals of thunder burst overhead, the lightning flashed and fought with the heavens and the rain smashed deafeningly upon the Mission roof. Within was silence: the flames of the candles upon the torchères stood absolutely still and offered little light.

The giant slowly folded his herculean arms and gazed down upon his congregation, who stood immobile, heads bowed, before him. He spoke, and his voice echoed cavernously about the great pillars and filled the dome.

'My people,' he said, 'my own people, to you is granted the supreme honour, to you my first chosen; this night you will bear witness to the consecration of the new Holy See. You are my disciples, and I, the born again, the logos, the

269

master, I grant you this honour. You will spread word of my coming across the world, that all might know my power and marvel at my return.'

The words rolled on and on, a litany of terror. In the shadows of the pillar Professor Slocombe closed his hand about his silver crucifix. Omally bared his teeth and fingered his half brick. Pooley wondered whether there might be a back door open somewhere near at hand.

'For centuries mankind has awaited my return, and now I am here to fulfil the prophecies and to reclaim my throne. You who stand before me are my vessels, into you shall I pour my powers. You will be masters of men, none shall stand before you, through you shall I regain what is rightfully mine.'

Professor Slocombe held his breath; so this was it, there were easily four hundred people in this hall and if each received only a portion of the giant's powers they would be virtually unstoppable.

'Kneel before me,' roared the giant, 'prostrate yourselves before me.' The congregation threw themselves to the floor, pressing their faces down into the cold mosaic. Omally turned his head away.

'Kneel, I say!'

Omally's eyes flashed back to the figure upon the dais, the face was contorted, twisted into a snarl, and the eyes were blazing.

'You will kneel!'

Across the hall, some ten or so yards from the three hidden figures, two men were standing defiantly amid the sea of fallen bodies. Omally had little difficulty in recognizing one of them. This individual was clad in a dark silk kimono, his head covered by an elaborate Japanese wig. His oversized eyebrows had been dyed the very jettest of blacks and were twisted at their extremities into short spikes.

It was Archroy. As Omally watched, the samurai's

companion coolly divested himself of his dufflecoat to reveal a clerical collar and the vestments of a priest. It was Father Moity.

Omally turned to the Professor, who shrugged helplessly. Pooley whispered, 'This is going to be good, what odds the Chinee then, John?'

'You will kneel before your Master.' The giant knotted his fists and drew himself up to even greater heights.

Archroy curled his lip and Father Moity drew from his raiment a shining crucifix. The congregation were still, their faces pressed to the cold mosaic floor. They would not have dared to rise even if they could. Before the dais the four creatures were shambling to their unearthly feet.

The Professor drew his two cohorts further back into the shadows. 'If the opportunity should arise,' he whispered, 'I trust that you will employ those two poorly concealed bricks to good advantage.'

Omally winked, Pooley said, 'In for a penny.'

The rain lashed down upon Brentford and Pope Alexander VI raised his massive arm and pointed towards Archroy and the young priest. 'You, I will make an example of,' he roared. 'You will know the exquisite agonies of lingering death.'

Archroy thumbed his nose. 'Balls,' said he.

The giant gestured to his four hooded cardinals. 'Bring them to me, spare only their lives.'

The grotesque creatures turned upon the two men, forward they came upon their twisted legs, murmuring and whispering. They had lost their fifth brother to a son of mankind and yearned only for vengeance upon the entire race. Their beaked mouths opened and closed, dripping vile slime. Closer they came, steering their way amongst the prone figures; slowly they approached the man of the cloth and the student of Count Dante. Archroy watched them come. 'My bloody beans,' he said, nudging the young priest.

Suddenly they were upon him, their clawlike hands reaching out, knobby, crooked appendages displaying wicked barbs. Father Moity held up his cross and said the words of the rosary. Archroy pivoted upon his heel and swung about, his foot curling through the air in a blurry arc. He struck one of the creatures a devastating blow, sweeping it from its feet and propelling it through the air. It tumbled to the floor several yards away and came to rest beneath one of the great pillars, silent and unmoving. Its unholy brothers slashed at him but Archroy leapt high into the air above their heads, dropping to the floor behind them.

As they turned, the master of Dimac let out a mighty yell and drove forward an iron fist. He struck one of the creatures firmly at neck height. There was a sickening report as the thing's head departed its body, a brief swish as it whirled through the air and a dull thud as it landed amongst the shadows to the rear of the hall. The decapitated body remained upright a moment, the arms flailing about and clawing at the space its head had occupied, then it toppled backwards, a crumpled heap of red cloth.

The giant upon the dais raised his hands towards the great dome. 'Destroy him,' he screamed, 'destroy him.'

Archroy stood undaunted, perfect testimony to the confidence-boosting powers of Count Dante's art. As the two demented godless beings fell on him he drew back both his arms and flung them forward in perfect unison. His fists passed clear through the chests of the creatures, emerging from their spines amid a tangle of rootlike fibres and a great tearing of cloth. Archroy shook the now limp forms away from him and turned upon Alexander VI. 'You're next pal,' he said.

Omally stared in awe. This was the Archroy he had struck down upon the allotment? Pooley said, 'That particular blow seems uniformly effective.'

Archroy stood thumbing his nose and flexing his muscles. Clearly it was impossible for him to feel any fear, no matter how appalling his adversary. Father Moity knelt at his side, hands clasped in prayer. Omally's heart went out towards the young priest who, possessing none of Archroy's ripping, tearing, maiming and mutilating techniques had come armed only with his faith to face the diabolical power of the crimson giant.

Upon the dais Pope Alexander VI stood, his entire body trembling, throbbing with unimaginable anger. Behind him, through the stained-glass window, the lightning flashed, casting his massive shadow across the great hall. The light about him grew and grew and became a blazing white inferno, forming itself into a blinding corona. His contours blurred, and naught could be seen of him but for the two red blood-bowls of his eyes.

A strange vibration ran through the air of the Mission. Omally felt the skin of his face being forced back as if by the pressure of increased g-forces. His cheeks seemed to stretch and draw themselves towards his ears, tears flew from his eyes and he found it impossible to close them. Pooley clung desperately to the great pillar and the frail Professor staggered back against the side wall. It was as if a hurricane of icy wind had been directed at them. The congregation were beginning to rise, shaking their heads like awakened sleepwalkers and shielding their faces from the glare.

Archroy stood firmly anchored to the floor, his kimono flapping about him. His exotic wig was torn from his head, exposing his alopecia to full effect. Father Moity raised his hand in benediction and uttered the first words of the holy exorcism, but the force struck him, buffetting him backwards and silencing his voice. Folk were tumbling over one another like rag dolls, bowling over the floor and fluttering against the walls. The door of the Mission burst outwards and crashed into the rain-lashed night, cartwheeling over and over across the Butts Estate. The figure upon the dais came and went amid the corona of light, his arms outstretched and his head thrown back.

And then, amid the icy unstoppable blast, a low rumble penetrated the Mission, issuing up from the very bowels of the Earth. Its reverberations rolled across the floor, quivering the mighty torchères and spilling out the candles. Omally felt the vibrations growing beneath his feet and knew where he had felt them before: that night in Sprite Street when Soap Distant had performed his ill-fated act of inner portal opening. The deluge had raised the level of the Thames, spilling the waters over the lockgates and down into the dried-up canal. The water was flooding from there into Soap's subterranean labyrinth, which must surely run directly beneath the Mission.

The great ill-constructed columns trembled and the figure upon the dais looked up, an expression of horror covering his hideous face. For a moment his power faltered, and that moment was all which was required. The congregation, freed of the binding force, began a mad exodus, cramming through the doorway and out across the Butts Estate. Sections of the frescoed ceiling began to fall away. A great crack appeared in the floor near the doorway and shot across the marble mosaic to the foot of the dais. Pope Alexander stepped back and prepared to marshal his power against the ruination of his Vatican.

Father Moity climbed uncertainly to his feet. The floor was shifting beneath him and portions of it were breaking away and tumbling into the foaming waters which roared beneath. Archroy clutched his clerical companion and the two stood staring towards the figure on the dais.

Pooley and Omally were endeavouring to raise the fallen Professor, who looked near death. 'Don't worry about me,' the old man gasped, 'his defences are down, strike now before it is too late.'

Pooley scrambled off in search of his half brick, which

had been torn away along with his cloak. Omally, who had clutched his throughout as the drowning man clutches at the proverbial straw, bore it into the light.

Sadly Omally was no accurate hurler of half bricks; had he been sober it is possible that his aim would have been greatly improved. As it was his ill-flung projectile looped through the air, missing the crimson figure by several feet and striking one of the torchères, cleaving out a row of the candles. These fell upon one of the woven tapestries, setting it ablaze.

The crimson figure whirled as the flames licked up behind him. Archroy was advancing across the hall, his bald head flashing like a neon sign in the lightning flares. The rain lashed in through the doorway and the waters beneath roared deafeningly.

The last of the congregation had long since departed. Pope Alexander VI was alone with his tormentors. They would all die for their blasphemy, each in turn. The old man scrambling across the crumbling floor, the young priest kneeling, those two skulking in the shadows and the maniac in the kimono. He would be the first.

Archroy leapt on to the dais and confronted the glowing giant. 'Come and get your medicine,' he sneered, 'come and get your—' The words froze in his throat as the giant raised his hand. Archroy became welded to the spot. His face took on an expression of dire perplexity as he strained against the force which surrounded him.

Professor Slocombe had reached Father Moity, and held out his old black book to the priest. 'Read with me,' he said. Pope Alexander turned in satisfaction from the oriental statue upon the dais. He raised his hands aloft and the light reached out from his fingertips and blazed across the hall, striking the two men. But nothing happened. The Professor and the young priest continued to mouth the ancient formula, and although their words were lost in the storm the effect was manifest. Their mouths moved in unison, intoning the spell, syllable upon syllable. Pope Alexander folded his brow and increased his power, the light radiating from his hands flooding the hall. His eyes burned and his body shuddered and trembled.

Pooley's hands closed about his half brick.

The giant stiffened, concentrating every last ounce of his energy upon the two men. The corners of the old black book began to smoulder, sweat ran down the face of Father Moity, the Professor's fingernails scorched and crackled. Jim Pooley threw his half brick.

The missile struck the giant firmly between his flaming eyes. He had channelled his entire energy into attack and had kept little in reserve for his own defence. He stumbled back, his arms flailing, the beams of light criss-crossing the Mission like twin searchlights. And now another figure was moving across the dais. It was Captain Carson, and he clutched two blazing candles.

The giant saw him approaching but it was too late; Captain Carson thrust the candles at the crimson robes, which caught in a gush of fire, enveloping the struggling figure. As he tottered to and fro, striking at himself, his power relaxed and Archroy, free of the paralysing trance, leapt forward. His foot struck the giant squarely in the chest, buffeting him back into the blazing tapestry which collapsed upon him.

'By fire!' shouted Professor Slocombe, looking up from his book.

Pope Alexander staggered about the dais, an inhuman torch. Above the flames the unnatural light still glowed brightly about him, pulsating and changing colour through the spectrum. Captain Carson was clapping his hands and jumping up and down on his old legs in a delirium of pleasure.

The Professor and the priest continued to read. Pooley emerged from the shadows and Omally patted him upon the shoulder. 'Nice one,' he said.

Archroy's vindictiveness, however, knew no bounds. He was being given, at long last, a chance to get it all out of his system: his car, his beans, the birdcage, his mad wife and this staggering inferno before him who embodied everything he loathed and detested and who was indeed the cause of all the indignities he had suffered during the last year.

With a cry of something which sounded like number 32 on the menu of Chan's Chinese Chippy, Archroy leapt at the blazing giant. He struck him another devastating blow; the giant staggered back to the edge of the dais, wildly flapping his arms beneath the blazing tapestry in a vain attempt to remain upright, then fell with a hideous scream down through the gaping crack in the Mission's floor to the torrents beneath.

'By water!'

Archroy slapped his hands together. 'Gotcha!' he chortled. The Professor and the young priest crossed the floor towards the chasm and stood at the brink. 'He will not die,' yelled the old man above the maelstrom, 'we have not yet finished the exorcism.'

Pooley joined the Professor and peered down into the depths. 'He is going down the main drain,' he said, 'we can follow him.'

The flames had by now reached the tracery work of the great altar and were taking hold. Smoke billowed through the Mission and several of the great columns looked dangerously near collapse. 'Out then,' shouted the Professor. 'Lead the way, Jim.'

Pooley looked up towards Captain Carson, who was still dancing a kind of hornpipe upon the dais, the altar flaring about him. 'You'll have to bring him,' cried Jim, 'we can't leave him here.'

The Professor despatched Omally to tackle the task, while he, Jim Pooley, Father Moity and Archroy tore out into the rain-lashed night. Pooley aided the Professor, although the old man seemed to have summoned up considerable stores of inner strength.

It was almost impossible to see a thing through the driving rain, but as the four ran across the Estate Pooley suddenly called out, 'There, that grille at the roadside.'

Up through the grating a fierce light burned. As they reached it the old Professor and the young priest shouted down the words of the Exorcism. The lightning lit the pages of the old black book to good effect and as the glow beneath the grating faded and passed on, the four men rushed after it.

Up near Sprite Street Omally caught them up. 'I got him outside,' he panted, 'but he wouldn't leave, said he wanted to see every last inch of the place burn to the ground.'

'There, there,' shouted Pooley as a glow appeared briefly from a drain covering up ahead. Professor Slocombe handed his book to Father Moity. 'You must finish it,' he gasped, 'my breath is gone.'

They passed up Sprite Street and turned into Mafeking Avenue, Omally aiding the wheezing ancient as best he could while Pooley, Archroy and the young priest bounded on ahead stopping at various drains and reciting the Exorcism. As they neared Albany Road, several great red fire engines screamed around the corner on their way to the blazing Mission.

At the Ealing Road Archroy, Pooley and Father Moity stopped. Omally and the Professor caught up with them and the five stood in the downpour. 'We've lost him,' panted Jim. 'The drains all split up along here, he could have gone in any direction, down most probably.'

'Did you finish the exorcism?' the Professor asked, coughing hideously.

The young priest nodded. 'Just before we lost him.'

'Then let us pray that we have been successful.'

Omally looked about him. Before them gleamed the

lights of the Four Horsemen, for the five bedraggled saviours of society were now standing outside Jack Lane's. 'Well then,' said Omally, 'if that's that, then I think we still have time for a round or two.'

Professor Slocombe smiled broadly. 'It will be a pleasure for me to enjoy a drink at your expense, John,' he said.

'A small sherry,' said Father Moity, 'or perhaps upon this occasion, a large one.'

As they entered the establishment Pooley felt Archroy's hand upon his shoulders. 'Just a minute, Jim,' said he, 'I would have words with you.'

Jim turned to the waterlogged samurai. The rain had washed the dye from his eyebrows, and they hung doglike over his eyes. 'That pair of cricketer's whites you are wearing,' Archroy continued, 'and the unique pattern upon the Fair Isle jumper, surely I have seen these before?'

Jim backed away through the rain. 'Now, now, Archroy,' he said, 'you are making a mistake, I can explain everything.' With these words Jim Pooley took to his heels and fled.

24

By two thirty the following morning, the storm was over. Along near the Brentford docks all lay silent. The yellow streetlamps reflected in the broad puddles and a damp pigeon or two cooed in the warehouse eaves. After such a storm the silence had an uneasy quality about it, there was something haunting about the glistening streets, a certain whiteness about the harshly clouded sky.

Above the soft pattering of the leaking gutters and the

gurgling of the drains another sound echoed hollowly along the deserted streets. A heavy iron manhole cover was slowly gyrating on one of the shining pavements. The cover lifted an inch or two and then crashed back into place. Slowly it eased up again and then with a resounding clang fell aside.

A hand appeared from the blackness of the hole beneath. Dreadfully charred and lacking its nails, it scrabbled at the wet pavement, then took hold. An elbow edged from the murky depths, swathed in what had obviously once been the sleeve of a lavish garment but was now torn and filthy.

After a long moment the owner of both elbow and hand, a hideous tramp of dreadful aspect and sorry footwear, drew himself up into the street. He dragged the manhole cover back into place and sat upon it breathing heavily. His head was a mass of burns, while here and there a lank strand of hair clung to the scar tissue of his skull. Below two hairless eyebrows, a pair of blood-red eyes glittered evilly. He made a feeble attempt to rise but slumped back on to the manhole cover with a dull echoing thud. A faint light glowed about him as he swayed to and fro, steaming slightly.

A faint sound reached his ears, a low hissing. He raised his bloody eyes and cocked his head upon one side. Around the corner of the street came a canary-coloured vehicle. Upon the top of this an orange beacon turned, its light flashing about the deserted roadways. It was the council street-cleaning cart and in the front seat, hidden by the black-tinted windows, sat Vile Tony Watkins.

He saw the tramp squatting upon the manhole cover clad in what appeared to be the remnants of some fancy-dress costume. He saw the faint glow about him, probably a trick of the light, and his hand moved towards the power button of the water jets. The ghastly tramp raised his hand as the cart approached. He stared up into the windscreen and a low cry rose in his throat, a look of horror crossed his hideous face. But the cart was upon him, its occupant laughing silently within his dumb throat. The jets of water bore down upon the tramp and the yellow vehicle passed on into the night.

Vile Tony squinted into the wing mirror to view his handiwork but the street was deserted. Nothing remained but a pool of blood-coloured water which glowed faintly for a moment or two then faded into the blackness.

From the shadows of a nearby shop doorway, a crop-headed man stared out at the street, a smile upon his lips. He watched the yellow cart disappear around the corner, emerged from the shadows and stood looking down into the blood-coloured puddle. The toe of his right foot described a runic symbol upon the damp pavement. This too presently faded and the crop-headed man drew his robes about him, turned upon his heel and melted away into the night.

Epilogue

Spring has come once more to Brentford. Neville the part-time barman draws the brass bolts upon the Swan's doors and stares out into the Ealing Road. Happily, of ill-favoured tramps the street is bare. Old Pete appears from Norman's papershop, his dog Chips at his heels. Pooley is upon his bench studying the racing papers and Omally is stirring from his nest, clutching at his hangover and muttering something in Gaelic.

Archroy has left Brentford. The patrons of the Swan got up a whip-round for him and he has gone off to America to challenge Count Dante to life-or-death combat. Sadly, when he reaches New York he will be thwarted, since the legendary Count is nearing eighty and crippled with arthritis.

Professor Slocombe still performs his daily perambulation of the village boundaries, Father Moity rarely has less than a full house come Sunday mornings and Norman is currently engaged upon a new project involving the Einstein's unified field theory.

For all Brentford's other citizens, life goes on very much as before. Captain Carson has retired to a cottage beside the sea, the Trust awarding him a small pension. The Mission still stands, partially rebuilt; it is ironic to note that it could never have been demolished, for Crowley's defunct uncle had seen to it that a preservation order had been put on the place.

All in all, nothing has really changed. The events of last year have absorbed themselves into local folklore, and current conversation revolves around the newly planted crops upon the allotment.

As to what the future may hold, few can say. Those who can are keeping it pretty close to their chests.

THE END

THE BRENTFORD TRIANGLE
by Robert Rankin

'A born writer . . . Robert Rankin is to Brentford what William Faulkner was to Yoknapatawpha County'
Time Out

'Omally groaned. "It is the end of mankind as we know it. I should never have got up so early today" and all over Brentford electrical appliances were beginning to fail . . .'

Could it be that Pooley and Omally, whilst engaged on a round of allotment golf, mistook laser-operated gravitational landing beams for the malignant work of Brentford Council?

Does the Captain Laser Alien Attack machine in the bar of the Swan possess more sinister force than its magnetic appeal for youths with green hair?

Is Brentford the first base in an alien onslaught on planet Earth?

The second novel in the now legendary *Brentford Trilogy*

0 552 13842 8

EAST OF EALING
by Robert Rankin

'Robert Rankin is a deep-down humorist, one of the rare guys who can always make me laugh'
Terry Pratchett

'Ahead, where once had been only bombsite land, the Lateinos & Romiith building rose above Brentford. Within its cruel and jagged shadow, magnolias wilted in their window boxes and synthetic Gold top became doorstep cheese . . .'

Something is happening east of Ealing. Lateinos & Romiith, an important organisation, has changed all the rules. A personal account enumeration scheme using laser-readable implantations on the right hand of every living punter instead of old-fashioned money. A scheme to end civilisation as we know it, even to change the drinking habits of regulars in the Swan . . .

Can Armageddon, Apocalypse and other symptoms of progress be stopped by the humble likes of Pooley and Omally, even with the help of Professor and a time-warped incarnation of Sherlock Holmes of Baker Street . . .?

The third novel in the now legendary *Brentford Trilogy*

0 552 13843 6

THE SPROUTS OF WRATH
by Robert Rankin

Amazing, but true: Brentford Town Council, in an act of supreme public-spiritedness (and a great big wodge of folding stuff from a mysterious benefactor) has agreed to host the next Olympic Games. The plans have been drawn up, contracts, money and promises are changing hands. Norman's designed some stunning kit for the home team, and even the Flying Swan's been threatened with a major refit (gasp!). But something is very wrong . . . primeval forces are stirring in ancient places . . . dark magic is afoot in Brentford and someone must save the world from overpowering evil . . .

. . . Jim Pooley and John Omally, come on down!

This must be the daring duo's toughest assignment yet. No longer can they weigh up the situation over a pint of lager at random moments during the day. No, this time, to save the world as we know it, the lads must contemplate – nay, undertake – the most horrible, the most terrifying, the heretofore untried – REGULAR EMPLOYMENT !!!

'A very funny book . . . a brilliant and exceedingly well written series' Colin Munro, *Interzone*

The fourth novel in the now legendary *Brentford Trilogy*

0 552 13844 4

A SELECTED LIST OF FANTASY TITLES AVAILABLE FROM CORGI AND BLACK SWAN